The Plateau

dedication

To Dave
for believing and so much more

and

in memory of Kilty

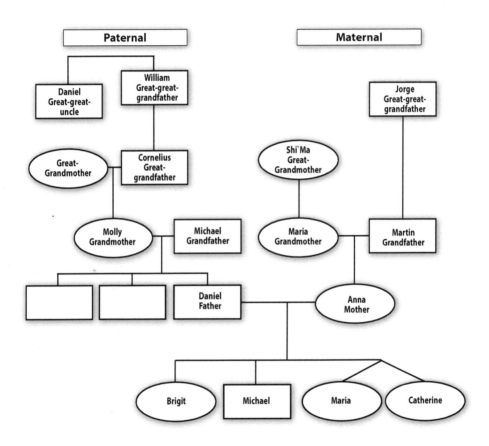

Acknowledgments

I would like to thank the teachers I have had in my life.

I have been privileged to have had some remarkable people stand in front of me in a classroom. Each of them generously shared their knowledge, without hesitation, asking only that their students listen and learn, ask questions, and search for the answers. I am especially grateful to my seventh grade science teacher, Sister Lois; my freshman high school English teacher, Miss Haag; and my Environmental Engineering professor and friend, Rod James.

Not all teachers are found in a classroom. There is always something more to learn. Thanks to Toni Holm, Publisher of Word Keepers, Inc., who for the last several years has imparted a great deal of her knowledge to me.

Not all teachers are obvious. I have had too many to list here but I appreciate all that I have learned and will endeavor to continue listening, questioning, and searching.

I would also like to thank the Reader Reviewers that took the time and effort to read the manuscript and provide feedback. I appreciated the considered critiques. Thank you: Christine Andrew, George Edward, Kristen Fairgrieve, Teresa Espaniola, Barbra Espey, Esther M. Good, Melissa Lincoln, Danny Long, Kim Luyckx, Joshua McDaniel, Patricia Mutch, Kathleen O'Toole, Bob Schneider, and Teresa Untiedt.

Modern people interpret spirals in a lot of different ways, but in ancient Ireland it is believed that the spiral represented the Sun. One interpretation of the clockwise spiral is the Sun and harmony with the Earth.

"Those who contemplate the beauty of the earth find reserves of strength that will endure as long as life lasts. There is something infinitely healing in the repeated refrains of nature—the assurance that dawn comes after night, and spring after winter."

—Rachael Carson, Silent Spring

CHAPTER 1

C atherine looked out at the vast expanse of prairie and the highway that stretched before her, which severed the land in two. Above the fluttering, wheat-colored grass, the sky was a gleaming, unbroken blue. A quick movement caught Catherine's attention, and she was just able to catch a glimpse of an antelope as it sprung behind a small ridge. Catherine smiled.

"What a gorgeous day," she said, before she heard the deep breathing coming from the passenger seat.

Catherine peered over at Henry, just for confirmation, and saw that his eyes were closed and his mouth slightly ajar. She stifled a laugh and tilted the rearview mirror to check on the backseat passenger. Connor had stretched himself out across the entire length of the backseat, obscuring his head and tail from her view, but she could see the dog's brindle chest rising and falling in the steady rhythm of sleep.

Catherine focused her attention back on the road and was startled to see that the sky was teeming with ominous storm clouds. In the rearview mirror, she could no longer see Connor. Catherine craned her neck around; the backseat was empty. She turned back around and reached for Henry, but there was no one in the passenger seat, and outside, the day had turned into night.

Catherine jerked awake. She'd been dreaming. It took her a minute to realize she had fallen asleep in her living room reading a pile of documents about global warming that she had not been able to get to at work, including the one on her chest about the melting Arctic sea ice. She glanced at the date—March 5, 2004—and shook her head; she was over a month behind and the volume of information was increasing. She sat up. Her neck was stiff, and when she reached back to rub it, she felt the tieback she had used to pull her hair into a ponytail. She tugged it out, leaned forward, and massaged her neck and head. The phone, located on the divider between the kitchen and the dining room, started ringing. She jumped up off the couch, threw her long black hair back from her face, and caught the edge of the coffee table with her little toe.

"Son-of-a!" she yelled, biting her lower lip as the phone continued to ring. It had to be Henry. He was the only one who would let the phone ring so long without getting frustrated that there was no voice-messaging system and hanging up. She grimaced and hobbled over and snatched up the receiver as she looked at the clock in the kitchen. Two-thirty in the afternoon.

"Hello," she said through clenched teeth.

"Catherine?" a female voice asked.

"Brigit," Catherine recognized her sister's voice immediately. "What's wrong?"

"Oh my God, Catherine!" Henry exclaimed, just as shocked as Catherine was by the news about her father.

"Brigit said he just collapsed. After everything he's been through, how can it be his heart?"

The anguish in her voice made Henry feel helpless. "I'll be on the first plane back," he croaked.

"Henry," she shook her head as though he could see her, "listen to me, it would take you too long to get here. Brigit said it's pretty dicey. I need to leave now."

The last thing he wanted was for her to be alone, but he also knew that the odds of getting a flight out before the morning was not good. "What flight are you taking?" he asked.

When she hesitated, he barked, "You're not driving! Not on your own." He waited, and when she still did not answer him, he exploded in alarm. "You *can't* be serious! You can't drive by yourself, not in your current frame of mind. It's too far. You'll be driving at night. You could fall asleep. Please," he implored, "get a flight in the morning."

"Best-case scenario," Catherine responded in a controlled but soft tone, "a flight won't get me there until five in the afternoon. Best-case, Henry. If I drive, worst-case, I'll get there late morning."

"That isn't the worst-case, Catherine. The last thing your dad needs is you in a ditch somewhere."

"That is not helpful."

"I'm not trying to be helpful. I'm trying to be rational."

"My father is in the Intensive Care Unit; he's had a massive heart attack. There is nothing rational about this."

Henry sighed. "I know, Catherine, I know, but he needs you to get there safe and sound. I need you to get there safe and sound." When she didn't respond, he added, "Besides, you know how much you hate that road at night."

"I don't need *you* to remind me of that," Catherine snapped, thinking of the strange dream.

"The animals can be right next to the road and they're almost impossible to see until you're practically on top of them. And what about the other things that have cropped up out there at night?"

"*Things*, Henry?" she asked ominously.

"How would you like me to describe it, Catherine?"

"I don't want you to describe it at all, Henry."

"I'm just trying to get you to look at this reasonably, Catherine, please. There are a lot of long, lonely stretches, and there have been times when you've woken me up to say that you thought you saw . . . something."

"Well, you know it can be a lot of nothing out there and a person's imagination can get the better of them when there is no one to talk to," Catherine stated.

"Exactly, I won't be there to talk to you if you drive up to Montana by yourself." Henry wanted to add that she was not the type of person that let her imagination run amok, but he knew Catherine would not find that helpful.

"Henry, you haven't been there to talk to me in the past; you've been asleep."

"Hey, a prone body is better than none at all."

"True."

"So you'll think about waiting?" he asked hopefully.

A long silence.

"Catherine?"

She was thinking about the dream. She couldn't tell Henry about it; that would just make him worry more. After all, it was just one of her weird dreams. So? Connor was in the back seat. Connor had been in other dreams in the years since he died. It didn't mean anything except that she missed him. And so what if it ended with her driving alone at night, in Wyoming? Her skin started to tingle.

"Catherine?"

His voice startled her. "What, Henry?"

"Will you wait?" he repeated.

"I'm sorry, Henry, I need to do this," she said with resolve. "If I don't—," her voice broke.

Henry could hear her sobbing softly, so he reluctantly finished for her. "You might not get there in time."

Catherine sniffed and wiped her eyes with her sleeve. "Yes."

Henry absentmindedly scratched his beard as he tried to think of something he could say that would change her mind, but he knew it was a lost cause. "At least promise me you will stop if you get sleepy," he insisted.

"I promise."

"Take the thermos and make sure you have plenty of coffee."

"I will."

"Call me when you stop. No, call me even if you don't stop. No, call me at—.

"Henry, how old am I?"

"What?"

"How old am I?"

Henry's bushy red eyebrows almost touched as he furrowed his brow in bewilderment. "Thirty-nine. What does that have to do with anything?"

"I think I've done this a time or two."

"Yeah, well," he replied, undeterred, "just make sure you call me."

Catherine drove on autopilot, noting the traffic on the highway heading north out of Denver but barely noticing any of the familiar landmarks along her route. As she approached the state line between northern Colorado and southern Wyoming, she saw a highway patrol car flash its lights to pull over another vehicle. She reflexively eased up on the gas pedal, looked at the clock on the dash, and couldn't believe how much time had passed without her being aware of her surroundings. She turned the radio up and forced herself to keep her mind on the road and not on her father.

She stopped to gas up before hitting the first long stretch of highway. As she filled the gas tank, she looked at the warning sign: "Do not use cell phones around gas pumps." Static. Something must have happened, somewhere. Warnings usually cropped up after an incident, no matter what the likelihood of it happening again. Catherine had called Henry before pulling into the gas station, but when she glanced at the car opposite hers, she noticed that the man in the passenger seat was having a heated exchange—on his cell phone. No one paid attention to signs. The pump handle clicked, she took her receipt and exited the station quickly.

She merged back onto the highway and found a radio station with a mix of more or less familiar music so she could sing along and keep her brain engaged. So what if she made up some of the words? Who would she bother? Catherine felt a twinge of unease and glanced to her left, where the sun was sinking ever lower in the sky. She pulled the visor up and over to her side window to help shield the glare on her flank and was thankful that she was still travelling north so that the sun was not going down directly in front of her. From years of experience, she knew that the visor would do nothing to shield a direct onslaught of the brilliant, blinding light. As the car crested a slight incline, she heard a voice on the radio say that overnight thunderstorms were likely in the northern part of the state. Crap. In April, she would be lucky if they only held rain. The image of the ominous clouds from her dream popped into her head, and she pushed it away. She needed to keep going. When the radio station began to break-up, she reached down to grab a CD out of the side pocket next to her, but all she could feel was the plastic well. She reached up, flicking on the overhead light, and glanced down. Empty. She stretched her neck and quickly glanced over at the passenger door. It looked empty too. "Damn it!" Catherine yelled, hitting the steering wheel with the heel of her hand. She had no choice but to turn her attention back to the radio, painstakingly advancing through each position on the FM and AM bands. She listened intently to the beep, beep, beep and was rewarded each time with nothing but static.

"It should be easier to find a station at night," she protested. A drop of rain hit the windshield and danced across the glass. "Oh give me a break!" Driving through the dark, she had spaced out the threatening storm. She had grown up travelling on highways where the dark closed in around her as the lights from human habitation disappeared entirely and the lights from other vehicles were spotty or non-existent for many miles. Yet the darkness she now found herself in felt merciless because the clouds had so completely blanketed the night sky that the comforting shine from the moon and stars could not penetrate them.

Catherine suddenly felt entirely alone, cut off from everything and everyone. She shuddered just as the rain began to pick up. She turned on the wipers and the heat.

The rain danced in the beam of her headlights, mesmerizing her. The downpour grew more and more frenzied; the tympani on the car roof, louder and louder. Catherine squirmed uneasily as the tires fought through standing water on the road. She reduced her speed, imagining the car hydroplaning right off the glistening blacktop.

"Please, please let up," she whispered, "please."

It had to, otherwise she would have to pull over and wait out the storm on the shoulder of the highway. The skin on her arms tingled. No! She would not sit alone on the side of the highway in the middle of a deluge in the middle of the night. If another car came along, the driver might not see her in time, and no matter what, she was not about to sit gazing off into the vast emptiness that really wasn't quite so empty. The prickling sensation spread down her spine. She stomped on the gas pedal, but the resistance of the water against the tires made her slow down again. Suddenly, headlights flooded the rear view mirror, almost blinding her. In a feeble attempt to stay out in front of the approaching car, she increased her speed. As the other car tore past, creating a tidal wave of water in its wake, she frantically pulled on the windshield wiper lever to make the blades move faster, just as the water smashed onto her windshield, completely blinding her view of the road.

"Son of a bitch!" she screamed, reflexively lifting her foot off the gas pedal.

Every nerve in her body was on high alert as the car slowed. As she tried to reorient herself, she frantically checked the rear view mirror to make sure no other jerk was speeding up behind her. She pulled over to the side of the road, killing the engine in the process.

"Son of a bitch!" Catherine screamed again, gripping the steering wheel with a determination to quell her rattled nerves. A flash of motion to her right caught her attention, just as she was able to release the steering wheel. She froze.

"Please, please, please be an animal," Catherine whispered, her eyes locked on her trembling hands. She closed her eyes but flashed on all the things she did not want approaching her in the dead of the night on a deserted stretch of highway. Her eyes shot open, and she stared into the darkness. Nothing was there. She laughed uneasily as she reached for the ignition and turned the key; the instrument lights came on, but the engine did not turn over. She gaped at the panel, fighting off the resurging panic.

"Damn it," she said through clenched teeth before realizing the car was in gear instead of in neutral. She tried again and the engine caught. As she put in the clutch and shifted the car into first gear, she checked the rearview mirror: no approaching headlights, so she could carefully accelerate back onto the highway. She glanced into her side mirror—no sign of another car. Instinctively she turned her head to glance out the passenger side mirror, and the air in her lungs expelled in one huge gasp as she stared into gleaming eyes looking at her through the window. What should have been a bloodcurdling scream came out as a tiny squeak as Catherine forced the gas pedal down in a desperate attempt to get away from the side of the road. The tires spit up wet gravel until the front driver's-side tire hit the asphalt, jerking the car to the left, causing the front passenger-side tire to jump onto the road. She almost lost control as the rear end whipped, but she let up on the gas, and hit the highway at an oblique angle. When all four tires finally connected with the pavement, she straightened the car and pressed the gas pedal to the floor.

Catherine propelled the car down the highway, struggling to keep her emotions from overwhelming her. She looked at the clock on the dash, but her mind was so jumbled, the glowing numbers meant nothing to her. She concentrated all of her energy on the white stripe in the middle of the road, not even registering that the rain had eased to a steady drizzle. As she came over a small crest she could see the twinkle of lights in the distance, or at least she thought she did. She really wasn't sure if she could trust her own eyes . . . but wait, there, there, a road sign. She sat up very straight, feeling the strain in her muscles, as she approached the first exit. The pain almost made her cry out, but she refused to let herself succumb. She needed to make it to a motel. Only then could she release the tight control she was maintaining on herself. As she pulled into the parking area of the first motel she found, she felt a wave of relief, but she still had to make it to a room before she could allow the tension in her body to ease.

Catherine gripped the motel room key with both of her trembling hands to steady her aim. After several failed attempts, she finally succeeded in unlocking the door. In a numb stupor, she dropped her bag on the floor, locked the deadbolt, and set the security bolt in place. She stood in the middle of the room staring blankly until her knees buckled and she collapsed. She struggled over to the foot of the bed, propping herself up against it, and began to cry without uttering a sound.

She didn't know how long she stayed that way before she forced herself up off the floor and into the bathroom. When she saw her reflection in the mirror, she recoiled. The whites of her eyes were gone, her blue irises consumed by rings of fiery red, the dark circles beneath them drooping toward her unnaturally pale cheeks. No wonder the night clerk wouldn't look at her directly. She looked haunted. She splashed cold water onto her face repeatedly until her hands began to ache from the chill. She stared into the mirror so long that the eyes staring back became the very same eyes that had stared at her through the car window. She spun away from the mirror. The eyes weren't real, of course. Her rattled nerves had just caused her imagination to go completely wild.

But why, then, had the anguish in those eyes seemed so palpable?

Suddenly, she heard ringing. "Get a grip," she instructed herself, thinking it was in her head, until she realized it was coming from the other room . . . from her cell phone . . . from Henry.

CHAPTER 2

Keitha bolted upright, the ringing still echoing in her ears. She looked at Murphy, hoping that she had not woken him up this time. But no, even in the restricted light that crept into the room, she could see his beautiful chestnut eyes watching her, waiting to see what she would do next. As her eyes adjusted, she could distinguish the rest of his body from the rock wall he was leaning against. He had such a gentle, loving face, but it currently held the worried look she had seen so many times before, when something from the other woman's life had jarred her awake.

She leaned over and in a soothing voice said, "It's okay, Murphy," and for added reassurance, "Everything is all right." At the sound of her steady, calm voice, the dog's ears, which had been standing straight up, relaxed.

Keitha swung her legs over the edge of the cot, which immediately caused the dog to get up and come over to her side. She patted Murphy's neck as she rose and stretched her long, muscular legs. After she worked a few kinks out of her neck, she stepped over to the wall opposite her cot where several shirts were hanging on a steel peg protruding from the rock. She threw one over her head, extracted a pair of pants from a short stack on the floor, and pulled them on. She felt Murphy tense and whipped around; a shadowy form stood in the entry, but before she could say or do anything, the figure spoke.

"It's just me." There was no mistaking the low, steady timbre.

"How long have you been standing there, Terran?" Keitha confronted the man.

"About half a second," he replied.

Keitha raised an eyebrow. "You should have announced yourself."

"I did," he asserted, taking a step into the room, abruptly halting as Murphy moved to block him. Terran moved his gaze from the dog to Keitha. "Could you please ask him to let me come in?"

Keitha looked at Terran impassively. He was five-foot-ten, a couple of inches taller than she was, and, even though his neck and shoulders were indicative of a stockier frame, his clothes hung loosely on him. The gray hair on top of his head, according to some people, gave him an older, distinguished appearance, which was completely ridiculous as far as Keitha was concerned, since he was thirty-five, only six years older than she was.

"Why don't you ask him yourself?"

Terran sighed heavily.

"What do you want, Terran?" Keitha asked impatiently.

"I'd like to come in."

Keitha nodded at Murphy and the dog stepped aside. Terran walked into the room and took a seat on a piece of old wood that Keitha had found years ago and fashioned into a small bench.

"Make yourself comfortable."

"I was just coming to let you know that Clara would like to have a word with you," Terran stated, ignoring her sarcasm and standing back up.

"And she sent you as her messenger. I'm honored," Keitha said through clenched teeth. "What could she possibly want to see me about?"

"Seriously, Keitha," he said in a tone that conveyed his displeasure at her feigned ignorance.

"I don't have anything new to report," she said, dismissively.

"Nothing," he said in disbelief. "You haven't heard or seen anything?"

"I didn't say that," she replied, "I said there was nothing *new*."

"You need to talk to Clara if you've seen or heard anything, anything at all," he said firmly.

Keitha straightened her back. "Run on back and tell Clara that if anything critical happens, she'll be one of the first to know."

"You might not recognize something as critical."

"I think it's time for you to go," Keitha said sharply.

Murphy moved over and stood directly in front of Terran.

"Could you ask him not to stand so close?" Terran requested as calmly as he could. Although Terran knew the dog would not harm him, the proximity of the dog's teeth to his crotch made him instinctively shift his hands in a protective move.

Keitha grinned.

"It isn't funny," Terran said.

"Just leave, Terran," Keitha said, stepping forward to touch Murphy on the shoulder. The dog backed away so Terran could depart.

She made sure Terran was nowhere near the entrance and then looked at Murphy. "Who the hell does Clara think she is sending him down here like that? So the woman is traveling, so what? She's traveled before. I know, I know, she's on her own. That is a little unusual, and something did unnerve her." Murphy tilted his head as he listened. "The problem is, I couldn't see what it was. It could have been anything. You know how jumpy she can be." Murphy tilted his head in the other direction.

"Well she can," Keitha stated definitively, running her hand over her close-cropped, dark brown hair. Most of the adults in the colony, those that weren't naturally or in some cases unnaturally bald, kept their hair cut very short. "So, like I said, nothing critical," she continued, brightening her tone. "Do you want to see if there is enough time to go visit the kids?"

Murphy's tail started wagging in delight. Keitha grabbed a pair of goggles off another peg as they exited the room, side-by-side, and made their way down the side tunnels to the only clock in the colony.

Most of the side tunnels allowed three people, or two people and one dog, to walk abreast of each other without any problem. During a shift change, or after a meal, if people came upon other people walking in the opposite direction, they would immediately form single file lines in order to pass without stopping. Keitha and Murphy's room was at the farthest end of the longest side tunnel, which narrowed to the point where two people could not walk abreast of each other comfortably, but they rarely ran into anyone this deep in. She had specifically asked the council for approval to move to the secluded location, which had never been used as a sleeping area, because she wanted—needed—the isolation. She found it interesting that even though the colony was established generations ago, a lot of people still hesitated at the idea of being too deep within the tunnels or too deep underground. Keitha, however, was unfazed by either.

The tunnel began to widen as they passed a smattering of other rooms, but it wasn't until they came to an intersection with another side tunnel and took a right turn that they hit one of the more densely occupied area of rooms. Keitha and Murphy moved forward quietly so that they would not disturb anyone who was sleeping. Finally, the side tunnel converged with one of the main tunnels, which were large enough to allow groups and machinery to move unhindered in both directions.

The walls of the side tunnels had a gray concrete covering over the raw earth, a throwback to the time when their habitat had been a working mine. But the main tunnels were ablaze with colorful murals. The artwork, unlike the clock, was not something that the founders of their colony planned. Although the founders knew that people would need a sense of the passage of time underground, they had erroneously believed that short periods on the surface would be enough to stave off the oppressive bleakness. Just as an increasing number of the people began to show signs of mental fatigue, a girl began creating the exquisite images on the rock. The paintings gave people a sense of being in the art itself, and while others tried to replicate what the girl was able to achieve, none possessed the ability to make their art pulse with life. When the girl died at the age of fifteen, the people of the colony chose to leave the remaining walls gray, as a sign of respect and gratitude.

The main tunnel opened into a large circular space where several other tunnels converged. The clock floated above the room, suspended from the ceiling with Teflon cabling that also allowed someone to lower the clock every month to be hand wound.

Keitha and Murphy exited into one of the other main tunnels and from there into another side tunnel until they made their way to a shaft. Other people were already congregating in front of a metal gate. After everyone exchanged greetings, the person closest to the gate opened it revealing the conveyance within. Four people stepped onto a platform comprised of steel mesh grids, the same as the four-man cages from the mining era. One of the people still waiting hit a button on a panel outside the cage, and the bottom platform sank below the floor level, revealing the top platform. When Keitha was little her father told her that cages were similar to conveyances called elevators, used to move people vertically within structures. Except elevators did not have multiple tiers and were enclosed, where cages did not have walls, only a steel exoskeleton.

Keitha picked up a mat that was propped against the wall and placed it over the exposed metal to provide Murphy with a comfortable place to stand. She and the remaining two people stepped onto the top platform after the dog. A button on the inside of the cage was pushed several times, to signal the hoist operator that they were ready for the cage to begin the ascent.

Keitha and Murphy entered the cage on the twenty-five-hundred-foot level, each level designated according to how many feet it was below the surface entrance to the mine. Everyone else exited the cage at the two thousand foot level, and before Keitha could press the button to continue the ascent, a hand appeared on the gate and an older woman glared in at her.

"I understand you saw or heard something," the woman demanded without the prelude of a greeting.

Keitha's eyes narrowed. "Who told you that?"

"I don't have time for your normal evasions, Keitha."

"Really, Clara? Well I don't have time for this. We're heading to the classroom." Keitha pressed the button three times.

"I'm not done talking to you, Keitha." Clara's voice was sharp.

Keitha made no comment as the cage began to rise. She and Murphy exited on the fifteen hundred foot level and made their way down to the classroom, which was located immediately off the main tunnel.

One of the youngest children spotted Keitha and Murphy at the entry to the room and squealed with delight, alerting everyone else to their presence. The children ran to Murphy and surrounded him, touching his sleek gray-black coat as he gently waved his bushy tail in the delighted faces of the smaller children standing by his rear end.

"We thought we would stop by before I started my shift," Keitha said to the two adults in the room.

"The children have missed you both," Eddy noted.

"I know it's been a while."

"It's been over a month."

"Eddy, really, don't admonish Keitha like that; she comes when she can," Brina, the other teacher, said. "We were just about to take the children up. Can you join us?"

"We have some time," Keitha replied.

"Excellent," Eddy said. As he moved towards the cubbyholes that contained protective outerwear of various sizes, plus goggles and hats.

Keitha followed him and began helping the younger children to get dressed.

"And perhaps you can tell the children a story?" Brina asked graciously as she handed the older children their goggles.

"Perhaps," Keitha responded, but she knew she would.

The children lined up at the entrance to the room when they were completely outfitted and then paraded out into the main tunnel and over to the largest cage in the colony. When the cage reached the top of the shaft, everyone exited and walked out into a domed area submerged in darkness.

The dome, designed by the founders, was made up of hundreds of thermoplastic panels that were lightweight yet strong and resistant to both hot and cold temperature changes. The panels interlocked without the use of adhesives, nails, screws, or other hardware.

The original purpose of the dome was to protect a large outdoor area from ultraviolet radiation and allow visible light penetration for agronomic production. Vegetative plots were also established outside of the dome to track the effects of ultraviolet intensity on various plants species; however, those plants no longer existed. Only a handful of plant species inside the dome had survived as a viable food source. The rest had either died out or mutated. The founders anticipated the need for a second source of sustainable food for the colony. While the surface plants were still healthy, development and testing of the 'next generation' of red and blue grow lights, to support the plants in the underground agronomic environment, proceeded. The founders also knew that they had to negate what would in essence be a continuous situation of the "winter blues" and developed a viable "visible light" source at the same time.

The one thing the scientists could not negate was the sensation of being confined underground. Although the creation of the living art proved invaluable in counteracting the reaction, people still craved being on the actual surface. As surface conditions deteriorated, even under the dome with protective gear, the amount of time people could safely spend above ground decreased until finally people were only allowed to surface for short periods at sunrise or at sunset.

Brina and Eddy led the children to a location where the land sloped slightly downhill, allowing the best view to the east. The area was a mix of rock, dirt, and surviving vegetative remnants, which had spread unchecked by human hands. The children took up their favorite perches on the rocks, worn smooth in places by the continuous use, while the adults, and Murphy, sat upon the ground.

"Keitha, a story please," Eddy said.

She stared at Eddy for a moment but knew she couldn't say no.

"What story do you want to hear?" Keitha asked the children.

"Tell us about how the archivists started," one child asked.

"Yes, please." All of the younger children immediately joined in.

"But the older children have heard that story many times," Keitha noted, not at all in the mood to tell that particular tale. "Pick another one, Skyler," she said to the child.

"We don't mind if you tell it again, Keitha," an older boy assured her.

Keitha tried to keep the irritation out of her voice. "That's nice of you, Phelan, but why don't I tell everyone . . ." The cry of 'please' by the children drowned out the rest of what she was trying to say.

Keitha held up her hand, her facial muscles hardening. Just as she was about to yell over the din, Murphy's big paw landed in her lap. She looked into the dog's eyes and let her hand drop. "Fine," she acquiesced, "I'll tell you how the archivists began." The children applauded wildly, and when everyone calmed down, Keitha began the story.

"The founders of our colony believed that societies collapsed, in part, because people never seemed to learn from history. The same pattern would repeat in different times, in somewhat different manifestations, but the same obsessions tended to drive people, power, and greed. When the founders established our colony, they brought thousands upon thousands of documents with them that recorded what had happened to their country and to other countries throughout the world, throughout time. They wanted their descendants to understand human history and to understand what caused them, some said forced them, to establish this place."

Keitha paused for effect. "A place that many people of their time said was an experiment in futility destined to fail."

"Keitha?" Brina asked in a concerned voice.

"Sorry," Keitha apologized. "That is a different story."

Brina nodded and Keitha continued.

"Unfortunately it didn't take long before all of the combined efforts of the people had to be spent developing and honing skills and expertise necessary to ensure the colony's continued existence. Documents contained in the computer memory systems that dealt with crops, water, power, sanitation, and the prevention and treatment of illnesses for both the people and the animals, as well as many more issues, became the focus of document research. As a result, over the course of many decades, the historical records were left largely untouched, but in honor of the founders, they were preserved and maintained on one of the protein-based memory storage devices. Most of the historical documents would probably still be lying idle, with the original intent of the founders unfulfilled, except for one particular girl who dreamt amazing dreams.

"The girl had vivid dreams that she would try to tell her parents about when she woke, but she didn't always remember everything or understand what she saw. Many times her stories sounded jumbled. One day she overheard her parents talking about what a strange imagination she had, so she stopped telling them about her dreams. It wasn't until she dreamt about the founders, conducting one of their early experiments, that she first began to wonder if there was something more to her dreams. Yet she had to admit that it could just as easily have been the lesson they had in class about the experiment that fueled her imagination. Then, right before she turned thirteen, she dreamt about a teeming mass of people roaming around each other in the open air. The girl could look up, as if she were really standing amongst them, and see the sky. It was so breathtaking she started to cry, waking herself up. The same dream kept recurring, and each time she saw more and more. Because there were so many things in her dream that she couldn't identify or understand, she knew her parents were wrong; her dreams were not coming from her imagination, and they were more than just dreams. She decided to find out if there was any evidence in the old historical records that the event she had been witnessing actually occurred.

"The girl submitted an off-task request to the council to allow her access to a data retrieval computer so she could review the historical records of the mid-twentieth century. At that time, a retrieval computer could only be used if it had not been assigned to a primary data retrieval effort, and only if it was not during the daily conservation cycle. Because of the restrictions, very few off-task requests were ever made, which caused some members of the council to ask the young girl for the reason for her request, and she told them she wanted to access an obscure plant research project that she thought might assist in the gardens."

The younger children, who had never heard the story before, gasped.

"She lied?" Skyler asked.

"She was afraid that the adults would just dismiss her request as the imaginings of a child, and then she would never be able to find out the truth for herself," Keitha replied.

Skyler and many of the other children nodded.

Keitha continued.

"The girl's research proved very arduous. The retrieval computer was capable of searching through large volumes of information with great efficiency, but she only had a general idea, based on announcements that she glimpsed, when the event in her dream occurred. An inordinate amount of data met her broad search parameters, and because only the history of the colony was taught in the classroom, she had no sense of what might distinguish one decade from another so that she could narrow the queries.

"After months of reading, she finally happened across a document that appeared to match elements of the dream, which helped her fix the exact time period. From there she was able to retrieve a great deal that documented the event. The more she found the more frustrated she became. She found publications and news stories that varied slightly, leaving out, skewing, or completely contradicting parts of what she had observed in the dream. She became obsessed with determining what had really happened. When she finally exhausted every lead and found every bit of information available to her, she knew she had to talk to someone.

"She decided to confide in a young man. He was seventeen and the only person that had ever been allowed to forgo the final years of classroom training to apprentice in the gardens. Even though he worked with adults, he was not an adult in her eyes, and she was sure he would believe her.

"The young man had come to speak to her class about the horticultural work a couple of months before she began her investigation into her dream. His talk had been very precise, scientific, emotionless. It was obvious that he was uncomfortable in the classroom. When he was hurriedly leaving, he abruptly stopped and picked up a small kitten. She watched as his eyes changed, widening in delight as he gently stroked the kitten's fur and spoke to it in a melodic, soothing tone. She silently inched forward, hoping to hear a little of what he was saying, when he turned suddenly and almost fell over her. He quickly recovered, handed her the kitten, ordered her teacher to change the feeding schedule and the formula, stated that the kitten was male, and left. He was correct about everything, and the kitten thrived.

"The girl didn't see the young man again until after she had begun her research and she asked him how he knew about the kitten. He shrugged but didn't answer. She pressed, telling him that she saw him talking to the kitten. He narrowed his eyes and told her she was mistaken. She asked him why he would want to lie about being able to understand animals the way he could. She wished she could do something so special. The young man stared at her for a long time before simply saying that he had no idea what she was talking about and walked away.

"The girl made her way down to the gardens and found the young man sitting at a bench littered with pots of fledgling vegetation. She asked if she could talk to him about something urgent, and he turned an appraising eye on her, motioning for her to sit on a stool.

"She began slowly, suddenly afraid that she had been wrong about his communication with the kitten. What if he would think she was just being silly about her dreams. But she couldn't keep it all to herself any longer and her words started to come out faster and faster, until they spilled out of her in a torrent. He listened to every word without showing any emotion and without interrupting her or telling her to slow down. After the girl finished, she took a deep breath and waited anxiously. The young man remained silent, lost in thought until he finally said, 'You need to go to the council and ask them for continued access to the historic records, and you have to tell them the real reason this time.'

"The girl protested vehemently, stating that the adults on the council would never believe her. He offered to go with her, to speak for her, but she refused and started to leave.

"'You have a unique ability,' the young man stated.

"The girl turned to him, her eyes wide, terrified globes. He immediately regretted being so direct, especially when her fear turned into anger.

"'Ability? You don't know what you're talking about.'

"'I have some idea,' the young man replied evenly.

"'If you're talking about what you can do with animals, that's different. That's special. My dreams are just annoying.'

"'They're more than that.'

"The young man continued to talk to her and was able to convince her that there was a reason that she was seeing the past, just as there was a reason why the founders brought the historical records with them and insisted that the colonists learn about what happened.

"'That's something I don't understand,' the girl said. 'Why would the founders bring erroneous records with them?'

"'Maybe they wanted to teach us how easy it can be to skew facts. The observer always sees things unfold through their own eyes, and that means they introduce a bias, even if they don't mean to.'

"'Are you saying that my version is no more valid than any of the ones I read?' the girl asked him angrily.

"The young man smiled, and she felt mesmerized. She had never seen him smile before and almost didn't hear him when he replied. 'No,' he said, 'I think you have the advantage of being an impartial witness.'"

Keitha paused. A pearly light, which foretold the coming of dawn, was beginning to break the shadowy blackness. She quickly finished the story.

"The young man persuaded the girl to go to the council, where he spoke for her. He was extremely persuasive when he told them about her dreams and requested that they allow the girl continued access to the records that the founders had taken such care to bring with them. Several of the council stated that there was no reason to waste time and energy on historical records that meant nothing to them based solely on the dreams of a child.

The young man persisted, pointing out that the colony had failed to uphold one of the edicts of the founders: to learn from the past. He argued that there had to be a reason that the founders had been so adamant and that, without the girl's dreams, they would no longer know what records were accurate. The majority of the council agreed that it wouldn't do any harm if the girl continued her research, and if nothing came from it, they could always have her stop. When the rest of the colony was told what the girl was doing, two other young people came forward and said that they too had been having dreams. The council unanimously decided to appoint an adult to assist the children, and that is how the archivists were established."

Keitha ended the story and looked over at two people who were standing by the portal to the mine, listening discretely. She first saw the smile on the man's face, warm and reassuring; then she looked into the sharp, penetrating eyes of the woman.

"Well," Keitha inquired, "was that a satisfactory rendition?"

Clara looked at her and said, "I was not that emotional, and I was not mesmerized by his smile."

"Nonsense, I definitely mesmerized you," the man interjected, still smiling.

"That's what you always say, Greer," Clara noted as Greer broke into laughter, the children joining in, applauding wildly. Eddy and Brina smiled but looked ill at ease.

"I need to speak to Keitha," Clara stated brusquely. "We'll wait for you down on fifteen." It was a command.

Keitha shifted her gaze back to the students who were all watching in anticipation. "The sun is rising," she said. And as everyone else turned their attention to the shimmering sky, Keitha and Murphy made their way over to the shaft. When the cage returned, they quietly got on.

When the cage stopped on level fifteen hundred, Keitha flung the metal gate open and snarled, "Don't ever order me like that again, Clara."

"I wouldn't have to if you were forthcoming with information," Clara countered.

"I don't have any new information," Keitha snapped as she got off the cage and glared at Clara, who was a good four inches shorter than Keitha and had large brown eyes, which, even at fifty, made her look remarkably cute. Not that anyone was insane enough to call her cute, at least not to her face.

"I think you do," Clara stated unemotionally.

"Why? Did you see something?" Keitha asked sardonically.

"Keitha, don't disrespect your mother like that," Greer admonished.

Keitha turned to him. "Don't scold me like I'm a child, Father."

"Don't act like one."

Keitha looked into Greer's eyes, hazel with flashing golden flecks, and she backed off, because even though her father looked imposing, he was really a very gentle man and rarely let his anger get the better of him. "I swear, Greer, there isn't anything new."

"Just tell us what you did see."

"All I saw was the woman traveling on one of those highways . . . at night . . . by herself."

Greer raised a hand when he saw Clara's face contort. "Do you know why she was on the highway? Where she was going?"

"No. She was really anxious, so it was difficult to—"

"She was anxious? You don't think that's important?" Clara snapped.

"So the woman was anxious. *That isn't anything new!*"

"You make it sound as if Catherine is perpetually anxious, which she is not." Clara threw her hands up in the air and stared at Greer. "She's never going to be able to get through to Catherine."

"Well, that will mean that I'm just following in your footsteps, Mother," Keitha said icily and walked away with Murphy at her side. Clara started to follow, but Greer held her back.

"She needs to understand how important this is," Clara said.

"How do you expect her to know when you haven't told her everything?"

Clara looked at his hand on her arm and then brought her head up and stared at him rigidly. "Leave go of me, Greer."

"Promise me you will tell her," he said, releasing his grip.

"No, and you promised me you wouldn't." Clara turned and began walking away from him.

"Some promises shouldn't be kept," he said resolutely, causing her to hesitate for a moment before continuing to walk away from him.

CHAPTER 3

Catherine strode through the main entrance to the hospital. Exhaustion had caused her to fall into an uneasy sleep at the motel, and now it was nearly noon. The person at the information desk kept trying to get Catherine's attention, but she didn't have time to stop or even acknowledge the exasperated woman, as she eyed an open elevator door and sprinted forward just as it began to close.

Catherine exited on a floor with the all-too-familiar sign and arrow pointing toward the Intensive Care Unit. She made her way down the corridor and glanced into the waiting area. The plastic chairs looked exactly the same as the ones that had been there years before, and so did the couch—well, sort of a couch. It was constructed out of laminated ply board and weird industrial-strength fabric cushions stuffed with a stiff material that could withstand hundreds, maybe thousands of butts, without giving an inch. Rounding out the room there was a matching coffee and end table set made from the same laminated ply board as the couch, and a television hung from suspended cabling in the corner. The one thing that *wasn't* there was her sister, so Catherine proceeded directly to the electric doors that led to the inner sanctum of the unit where she found Brigit standing outside one of the rooms.

Catherine and her older sister looked like polar opposites. Catherine with her straight black hair and blue eyes, which her mother always said were azure, and Brigit with her wavy warm red hair and dark brown eyes. The one thing they had in common was their height; even though Brigit teased Catherine about being taller, Catherine always responded that five foot three-and-*a-half* could hardly be called tall.

When Brigit saw her little sister she wrapped Catherine in her arms and hugged her so hard Catherine's heart started to beat in trepidation.

"How is he?" Catherine asked, stepping back from her sister.

"It's not good," Brigit replied. "His heart has been badly damaged."

"Mike?" Her older brother's name was all Catherine could manage to say before her voice broke.

"He'll get in at about four o'clock. He took the flight that you should have taken."

Catherine ignored her sister's reproach. "Can I go in and see Dad?"

"He was sleeping, but I'll go check with the nurses while you go to the restroom."

"How did you know I needed—"

"Besides the obvious," Brigit cut in, "you might want to, you know, tidy yourself a little."

"Tidy myself?" Catherine looked down at her clothes. They looked like she had slept in them—wait a minute, she had slept in them. She smoothed the front of her shirt, which did nothing to alleviate the wrinkles, and shrugged.

"Just, you know," Brigit repeated, sweeping her hand around in a circle as she walked over to the electric doors that separated the waiting area from the actual Intensive Care Unit.

When Catherine exited the stall in the women's restroom and finally looked at herself in the mirror, she broke out laughing. At least her reflection explained the look on the woman's face at the information desk. She did the best she could with the generic hospital soap and her hair pick, and by the time she returned to the Intensive Care Unit Brigit had cleared the way for both of them to see their dad.

The room could have been any hospital room, except for the plethora of medical monitoring equipment and the large glass window that faced the nurse's station, strategically situated in the middle of the horseshoe ring of identical intensive care rooms. Their father was lying on the mechanized hospital bed, his head slightly elevated, oxygen tubing around his ears with two small prongs positioned in his nostrils. He gave them a thumbs up with his right hand as he started to remove the tubing from his face with his left.

Brigit, who had entered the room ahead of Catherine, immediately made her way over to the bed. "You can't do that, Dad; you have to leave it on."

Catherine went over to the other side and took her father's hand. "Don't worry about trying to talk to us now, Dad. You need to leave that on."

"You two like bossing me around, don't you?" He smiled faintly and Catherine managed to smile back even though the muted, raspy sound of his voice made her heart catch.

"Henry with you?"

"Dad," Catherine said sternly.

"Why don't you give him a rundown on what's been going on with you and Henry?" Brigit said catching her eye.

"That sounds like a good idea. How about I talk and you listen," Catherine said brightly as she sat on the edge of his bed so she could keep holding his hand.

"I need to go do a couple of things, Dad, but I'll be back in a minute," Brigit said.

After she exited the room, Catherine felt her father's hand move. "She's going to talk to my doctor again," he said with certainty and squeezed her hand. His grip was surprisingly strong. Catherine stared into her father's eyes that so often twinkled with laughter but were now intense and penetrating.

Catherine nodded but had to look away from him so he would not see her eyes fill with tears. She shifted slightly, not realizing how precarious her perch on the bed was, and fell off.

"Shit!" she exclaimed as she hit the floor.

A nurse, who saw Catherine drop from sight, came running into the room. "Are you okay?" she asked as Catherine was getting to her knees.

"I'm fine."

"There is a chair right there." The nurse pointed at a hard plastic chair in the corner of the room before snapping the guardrail for the bed into place. Catherine was on her feet when the nurse turned and tersely said, "You have ten more minutes. He needs his rest."

Catherine turned back to her father after the nurse left the room and saw that he was grinning. "I'm going to bruise you know," she said, rubbing her butt.

Her father looked over at the plastic chair and whispered, "Maybe that is more your speed."

"You're very funny." She moved the chair close to the bed and gingerly sat down.

"Henry?" he asked with a one-word question.

"Henry. Well obviously he wanted to fly back immediately when I got hold of him." Her father gave a small wave of his hand. "You might not think he needed to, but Henry did. I had to convince him to stay for the meeting today. You know the one I told you about last week." Her father nodded. "It just took so long to get the people in the same room at the same time." She had unconsciously draped one of her hands over the railing, and her father patted it reassuringly.

She smiled. "Henry will be here as soon as he can."

Her father nodded and his eyes began to droop. Catherine sat and watched him sleep until the nurse came to the door and motioned for Catherine to come out.

As Catherine got to the automatic door that led out to the waiting area, she felt a hand on her shoulder and turned around. Brigit was staring at her intently.

"What did the doctor say," Catherine asked anxiously.

"Let's talk out there." Brigit motioned with her head and they walked out of the Intensive Care Unit and sat down on the couch, side by side. As Brigit relayed the latest information from the doctor, Catherine absently registered the odd fact that there was no one else in sight.

Catherine held her face in her hands and could feel the moisture from her tears smearing her face. Brigit was rubbing Catherine's back as her own tears ran freely. Catherine inhaled raggedly as she straightened up and fought to stop crying. She got up, went over to the entrance to the ICU and peered through the glass that bordered either side of the electric doors.

"When do you think we can we go back in?" Catherine asked, turning to her sister. But before Brigit could answer, there was a sudden flurry of activity inside. Catherine and Brigit rushed in, but a nurse spotted them and cut them off before they could go any further.

"You have to stay outside," the woman ordered.

"That's our father's room," Catherine yelled, fear taking hold of her.

Brigit grabbed Catherine and propelled her towards the electronic door. Catherine tried to spin out of her grasp, but Brigit had a strong grip on her shoulders.

"We need to let them do their job," Brigit insisted.

Catherine managed to pull away from her sister and glared at her in defiance.

"There isn't anything you can do," Brigit snapped, then adding quietly, "There isn't anything either of us can do."

Catherine slumped against the wall and remained there, as time slid past, until a woman and man finally emerged through the electronic doors.

Brigit stepped toward them and said, "Doctors?" in a strange mix of formal greeting and questioning.

Catherine stayed by the wall, and as she heard the words "I'm afraid that your father," blood rushed to her head. The intense pressure caused a painful throbbing and her ears plugged so that she could barely hear the litany of words that followed. But the solemn looks, and the hand on Brigit's shoulder, told her all she needed to know.

After the doctors walked away, Catherine forced herself away from the wall; a piercing pain griped her chest. She let out a wretched, guttural noise and started to sob.

KEITHA GASPED AND GRABBED THE TABLE in front of her to keep from falling off her stool. She held on tightly and lowered her head as the surge of emotion slowly ebbed from her body. She looked up into concerned eyes and realized that someone had a strong grip on her arms.

"Keitha, Keitha, can you hear me?"

There was something incongruous about the voice, causing Keitha to look around the room, where there were two rows of deep tables that held a collection of what appeared to be random pieces of computer equipment. In fact, the conglomeration was the deliberate result of cannibalizing, retooling, and redesigning the colony's finite resources. Stools positioned at various locations along the length of the tables provided the archivists a place to sit while they retrieved data.

"Is something wrong?" she rasped.

Terran stared at her in disbelief before bellowing into her ear, "Is something wrong? Is something wrong!"

"Stop repeating what I just said, damn it, and answer my question."

"You want me to answer, fine," he paused and lowered his voice. "First you were absolutely motionless, then you started to tremble, and I haven't been able to get you to say anything for the last couple of minutes."

He was so tense that she sat up straight and began pulling her arms from side to side in an attempt to shake off his grasp.

"Let go of me, Terran," she demanded.

He held her tight for a moment until he saw the look in her eyes. "I was just trying to help."

"I always find being yelled at helpful."

"I didn't . . . you surprised me, that's all," he said self-consciously. "I didn't realize you were . . ."

She held up a hand to stop his explanation and began to rise off the stool, until she felt light headed and sat back down. "Give me just a second."

Terran waited, knowing that any comment or attempt to assist was not welcomed.

"What time is it?" Keitha asked, once the pounding in her head subsided.

Terran blinked. "Time? You want to know the time?"

"I need to know," she stated, getting to her feet again.

"Just, wait, will you," Terran protested, motioning to a red-haired boy who had just entered the room, who panted as though he had been running. "Go and see what time the clock says," Terran instructed. The young man nodded and rushed back out of the room.

Terran turned his attention back to Keitha. She was wiping her forehead with one of her hands, and he detected a slight tremor. When Keitha saw the direction of his gaze, she quickly dropped the hand to her side.

"I need to know the time," she reiterated.

Terran nodded and they waited in silence until the young man returned to report that the clock said half past one.

"Her father is dead," Keitha announced.

Everyone else in the room, who had managed to remain silent and inconspicuous, collectively gasped. Terran, hearing the sadness in Keitha's voice, was momentarily taken aback because she always kept an emotional distance from Catherine.

"Are you sure?" he asked.

Keitha peered at him. Images and bits of conversation flashed through her mind as though she were witnessing the incident all over again, and although Keitha could still sense the woman's pain, she no longer felt the intense grief as if it was her own.

"Yes, I'm sure her father is dead," Keitha snapped.

"I wasn't doubting you."

"Sure you weren't," she said snidely, before she heard the sound of someone crying and, for the first time, turned her focus to the other people in the room.

A few just stood in apparent disbelief, while several others had tears in their eyes. The boy who had checked on the time and a young woman wept openly. It was as though they had heard the news of the death of someone in the colony, instead of the death of someone long ago, before any of them had been born—such was the power of Keitha's words. She was a storyteller, and the stories she told the colony about Catherine, her life, and those in her life were so vibrant that the people of the colony felt like they knew all of them. Terran often wondered how Keitha's narratives could be so affective while she remained so impassive.

"The council needs to be informed," Terran asserted, "but everyone will want to hear the telling."

Keitha nodded her head and started looking around the room. "Where's Murphy?"

No one responded.

"Where is he?" she demanded, looking directly at Terran.

"Phelan came by to take him for a walk, remember?" he replied calmly but motioned to the boy who again left the room.

Keitha narrowed her eyes. She remembered Phelan coming by to take Murphy on a walk. The boy had acumen when it came to animals, but he needed to develop his skill, and Murphy was a fine teacher.

"Where is he now?" she said menacingly, knowing that Murphy would have been aware of her agitation and made his way back to her long before now.

Suddenly the dog burst into the room on a dead run. He splayed his feet to stop the forward momentum before running into Keitha. She smiled with relief and knelt down as he sniffed her all over to make sure no harm, physical or emotional, had come to her in his absence. Murphy took a step back, flattened his ears against his head, and turned and glowered at Terran.

"I'm all right," she said, stroking his neck to lessen his anxiety, but the dog refused to break off his glare.

Keitha looked up at Terran. "What did you do to him?" she hissed.

"You know I wouldn't do anything to him," Terran replied but then admitted, "When you started . . . all I did was ask Thomas to head Phelan off and have him take Murphy to the classroom."

"You what?" Her anger made Murphy's hackles rise.

"Keitha, you know how he gets. Look at him right now," Terran pointed at the dog. "He wouldn't have let me near you, and you would have hit your head on the floor if I hadn't grabbed you."

"You had no right."

Before Terran could continue defending his actions, Phelan ran into the room gasping for air. He saw Murphy and fell back against a wall and tried to talk, but all he could manage between gasps was, "He, he," pointing at Murphy until finally blurting out, "He's really mad."

Keitha studied Phelan for a moment. "Really?" she inquired sarcastically. Phelan sank to the floor.

"It was scary," the boy said as he struggled with his breathing for another moment before a rush of words came pouring out. "Murphy was pacing back and forth like crazy. Eddy and Brina were trying to calm him down, but he just wouldn't, and I asked them not to let him leave because . . ." He stole a glance at Terran. "Then all of a sudden he just burst past everyone, he knocked me down. I ran after him, but he was too fast for me to catch up, but I knew where he was going." He averted his eyes so he didn't have to look directly at Keitha.

Keitha was disappointed in Phelan, but turned and bore a hole through Terran. "Don't you ever instruct anyone to do anything to Murphy again."

"You're overreacting. Nothing happened to him."

"It's my fault. When Murphy started acting weird I should have," Phelan's voice caught as he looked at the dog. "I'm sorry, I should have paid attention to you."

Murphy went over to Phelan and nudged the boy's hand with his nose. They stared at each other for a moment until a small smile crossed the boy's face. Murphy returned to Keitha's side and resumed staring down Terran.

"The council needs to be told that Catherine's father died," Terran uttered, leaving the room.

Murphy laid down on the floor and expelled a dissatisfied grunt as Keitha realized that everyone else had made a surreptitious exit. She sat back down on the stool.

"It's very sad," Phelan said quietly.

Keitha looked at him confused, "What is?"

"Catherine's father," he replied, startled by her question.

"Yes, of course it is," she agreed, faintly discomfited by the boy's obvious compassion, which she lacked. "Come on, Phelan, let's get you to your classroom before I talk to the council."

The boy rose from the floor and they exited into the tunnel system. At the entrance to the classroom, Phelan turned to Keitha and Murphy with earnest eyes and said, "Should I say anything?"

"Let's wait until the council announces it to everyone."

He nodded at her, stroked Murphy's neck, and went in.

Keitha turned and continued down the tunnel to the great room, a large cavernous space that could accommodate everyone in the colony with ease. But when it was just the council in the room, it seemed like an enormous, empty place. The nine members of the council sat around an oval table with Terran standing to one side. As Keitha and Murphy entered the room, a man with a gray beard indicated a chair where she could take a seat. Murphy stayed by the entrance.

"The woman's father died," she stated bluntly. "I'm sure Terran already informed you."

"You need to use her name," Clara insisted.

"Catherine's father died," Keitha rephrased, but with the same brusqueness.

"Can you tell if this will affect her abilities?" the bearded man asked.

"It just happened. How could I possibly know how it might, or might not, affect her," Keitha replied, summarily dismissing the question.

"Her mother's death affected her abilities," he reminded her.

Keitha shrugged. "Not for long."

"Nevertheless, young lady," his voice grew impatient, "you need to be prepared."

"For what, Donal? You think this will finally wake her up? Or break through her complacent, narrow minded, closed off . . ."

"Enough," Clara boomed, locking eyes with Keitha. "This is an opportunity to actually connect with her, and you intend to waste it."

"Well, Clara, why don't you regale us all with how you connected with her after her twin sister died?" Keitha retorted coldly.

"How dare you!" A flush rose in Clara's face.

"I dare because you failed."

"Is that the best you can do?" Clara began laughing callously and rose from her chair. "Just remember, Keitha, I failed because I took a risk; you fail because you refuse to try."

Keitha slid her chair forcefully backwards as she flew to her feet.

"Stop it, both of you," Greer barked.

The two women stared at each other for a moment, but then both sat down.

"The rest of the colony needs to be told about Catherine's father," Greer said taking control. "Donal will call the meeting and the two of you will behave in a civil manner."

During the meeting of the entire colony, as Keitha told of the death of Catherine's father, people held each other and wept. When she was done, several of the council proposed a formal celebration to honor the man, but the final decision rested with everyone. None of the normal daily activities could be left undone, so preparations meant long days with little sleep, and yet, there was complete concurrence in favor of the idea. Clara suggested that the celebration be in conjunction with their summer solstice celebration, because the people of Catherine's time had once set aside a day each year, close to the beginning of summer, to celebrate all fathers.

A murmur of agreement arose and the people immediately split into smaller groups, each with a specific task: most dealing with food preparations that they were responsible for completing. Keitha was part of the group responsible for sweets, made only for formal celebrations. All of the other groups decided on their plans and left, while the half dozen people in her group had barely spoken a word to each other.

They were all pondering the significance of having a dual celebration, and they knew that if the sweets failed to live up to expectations, the day would be marred. Keitha did not feel that she had the right to speak first. Since she had only been a member of the group for two years, she still considered herself an apprentice. However, the longer the silence endured the more the other members turned to look at her.

Knowing that their repertoire of desserts was limited, she proceeded cautiously. "Does anyone have an idea what sweet would be appropriate?"

"I was hoping you could tell us what they had in Catherine's time, something we could adapt," a large formidable man stated, the others nodding in concurrence.

"I don't know, Morris," Keitha said, reluctant to be the one to decide. "They had so much, and our sweets aren't really the same."

"I know," Morris stated undaunted, "but we're pretty ingenious, and I think this celebration needs something special."

"Yes, definitely," a young woman enthusiastically agreed.

"Lily," Keitha said rationally, "I know how talented you and Morris are with sweets, but shouldn't we stick to something we know we can do well?"

"Keitha, you can't look at it like that," Lily's voice bubbled with excitement. "Think of this as an opportunity for us to prepare an utterly unique treat for everyone. It will make the celebration unforgettable."

"That's what I'm afraid of." Keitha's physical exhaustion had spread to her brain, and Lily's unabashed perkiness was getting on her nerves.

"Please, tell us about their sweets," Lily prodded, her eyes sparkling with anticipation, "so we can make something wonderful."

Keitha could see Lily's infectious nature starting to sweep through the group, so she gave in. "All right, all right."

Keitha described items she had found in the archives, after hearing Catherine talk about desserts. Cakes. Everyone shook their heads. Cakes required eggs, and eggs could not be wasted on sweets. Cookies had the same problem. When she brought up ice cream, their eyes grew wide as she described how the frozen dessert was made.

"You need to tell us about their ordinary desserts, not the ones reserved for important celebrations," Morris requested.

"These are their ordinary desserts," Keitha replied quietly.

"Well . . . my . . ." Morris said, flustered by the statement. Recovering, he continued undeterred. "There must be something we could use from that time."

"Morris, it's just not going to work."

"Keitha, don't give up so quickly," Lily cajoled. "Think about it some more. Please."

"Look, I'm telling you," Keitha said, feeling drained and irritated. She stopped when she saw the look of disappointment on the faces surrounding her. "All right, give me a minute."

Lily smiled encouragingly at Keitha, who shut her eyes tightly to keep from screaming.

"They made pies." Keitha's eyes shot open.

"Pies?"

"They would make a dough, place it in the bottom of a dish," Keitha used her hands to demonstrate the shape of the dish, "and then they would put some sort of blend of fruit and sweetener, or something else with sweetener, on top of the dough. Then they topped the . . . filling with another piece of dough," she explained.

"And that's it?" Morris pressed.

"That's how they're made," Keitha said and saw the group brighten. "But they're baked." There was a collective groan. The ovens would be in high demand, and there would be a strictly enforced time limit.

"How long do they have to bake?" Morris asked.

"I have no idea."

"If we use something in the center, say a fruit that doesn't need to bake, we could bake the bottom and top separately and fairly quickly," Morris said, not willing to give up.

"If you say so," Keitha responded in admiration; "you're the expert."

"What about currants?" Lily asked.

"It would take too many," Morris noted.

"What about grapes?" Lily proposed.

"Grape pie?" Keitha questioned with a wince. "I don't know if they made grape pie."

"Well, what would you suggest," Lily said defensively.

Although Keitha found Lily to be overly gregarious, she did not intend to impugn her skill with sweets. "If anyone can make a grape pie work, it would be you and Morris."

Lily smiled at the complement. "What else did they use besides fruit?" she asked brightly, her hurt feelings completely vanquished.

"Actually, they had sweet potato pies and some other vegetable pies," Keitha stated. "But I think they used eggs in the vegetable pies," she reluctantly added.

There was another collective groan.

"Wait, wait," Lily asserted, "they didn't use eggs with fruit." She looked to Keitha for confirmation.

"No, at least not that I recall."

"So who says we have to use them with a vegetable? We can adapt." She looked at Morris, her eyes sparkling. "We'll adapt."

Keitha watched as the rest of the group wholeheartedly concurred and marveled again at how contagious Lily could be.

Morris, as the senior and most gifted member of the group, assigned each person a task before turning to Keitha. "You'll ask George for the needed amount of the sweet plant?"

George was the head grower for the colony. His knowledge of horticulture and agronomy, combined with an uncanny amount of common sense and ingenuity, resulted in many more successes than failures over the years. Although a genius when it came to plants, George was brusque and easily irritated by people requesting special allocations, even for celebrations. The difficulty for their group was further complicated because the sweet plant that Morris referred to (the moniker had been bestowed upon the plant long ago by the children and adopted by nearly everyone else) was in trouble. The last of the older plants were showing increasing signs of stress at the same time George was losing a higher and higher percentage of yearling and second-year plants. If the current crop of year-old plants continued its downward rate of survival, then there was a very good probability that the seeds of the older parent plants would no longer be viable. The most promise George had seen was with the cuttings, but if the losses turned out to be a systemic problem, or if a mutation had occurred, there would be little that anyone could do to prevent the inevitable.

"George knows the request is coming," Keitha said. "I saw him at the back of the room when I made the announcement. He gave me one of his 'don't you dare' looks, but he'll give it to us," she stated with certainty.

After everyone left, Morris asked Keitha, "How can you be so sure? I would expect him to be more difficult than in the past."

"There's really no point in not giving us some small portion. Who knows how many more desserts we'll be able to make."

The look that passed between her and Morris was so grave that he instinctively reached out and placed his hand on her shoulder. Keitha patted it, but moved away from him. "I'll let you know how it goes."

CHAPTER 4

Henry woke up and rolled over. He could tell she wasn't in bed even before he opened his eyes. "Please let her be watching the TV," he implored, getting up. He found her upstairs in the spare bedroom, searching for something he knew she would not find.

"Catherine?" he questioned gently.

She turned toward him, but there was no recognition in her eyes.

"Catherine," Henry repeated, slightly louder, his tone remaining tender.

She looked away from him and then, as though she had forgotten something, she turned back. "I'm looking . . ." but her voice drifted away.

"It's all right," Henry reassured her, but his heart ached because he knew what she would say next.

"He was here. I felt him." She sighed in frustration but then adamantly repeated, "He *was* here."

"Catherine," Henry said as he wrapped her in his arms. "This has been tearing you up for over two months."

She stepped away from him. "I know how long my father has been dead, Henry."

"You know what I mean, Catherine."

"No, why don't you tell me what you mean."

It was Henry's turn to sigh. "Never mind."

"You think I've been imagining this." Her voice sounded strained as she waved her hand around to encompass the room where her father always stayed on his visits. "You think it's just grief, or stress, or wishful thinking."

"I do not, Catherine," Henry said indignantly. "I'm just worried about you."

She nodded her head and sank onto the edge of the bed. "I can't see him, Henry. Why can't I see him?" she asked, her eyes gazing up at him in desperation.

Henry sat next to her and wrapped his arms around her again as she buried her head in his chest. As he held Catherine he realized that she wasn't crying, even though he had seen the tears forming in her eyes. Henry could hear no sound at all. He had thought that nothing could be worse than the horrible agonizing sound that escaped her when she was unable to control her grief, but this was far worse. He could feel her body shuddering, could feel the tears against his bare skin—but no sound—not even a muffled sob or gasp of breath seeping out of her, which began to unnerve him.

Ever since they returned home after her father's funeral, Catherine's sense of humor and purpose seemed to be gone. She went through each day on autopilot; everything that needed to get done got done, but without heart or spirit. He knew better than to suggest medication or therapy, but he worried about her depression worsening, and as he sat on the bed with her crying, but not crying, he began to panic, failing to notice that she was staring at him with concern.

"Henry, are you all right? You're very pale," she said, stroking his forehead with the back of her hand.

"Am I all right? Am I all right?" he repeated, stunned. "Catherine, you weren't making a sound. Not a sound, but you were crying."

He looked at her face. Her skin was blotchy from the tears, her eyelids had puffed up, as though she was actually having an allergic reaction, and the whites of her eyes were bloodshot. Henry hadn't seen anything except pain, anxiety, or dullness in her eyes for what seemed like forever, but now what he saw was concern.

He hugged her tightly. "You scared the behomies out of me."

"They're behemies, not behomies," Catherine said quietly. "Not to be picky, but if you're going to use the word my dad always used, it should be the right one. Even if it isn't really a word." She tried to smile but her lip quivered.

"You really did scare me, Catherine," Henry stressed.

"Sorry." She let out a ragged breath.

"Something changed, didn't it?" Henry asked.

She looked around the room and her eyes began to glisten. She flicked her hand at the tears in annoyance and cleared her throat. "I'm not going to get to say goodbye."

"Maybe you will," he said, trying to comfort her.

"No, I won't," she said, swallowing hard.

The certainty in her voice sounded so much like the very first time Henry witnessed what Catherine experienced. Of course, he had no idea what was actually happening.

CATHERINE AND HENRY MET AT A PARTY in the summer of 1992, yet it wasn't until eight months later that they finally began spending the night together. Not that they hadn't made love before that, but Catherine always seemed to plan everything so that either he or she had plenty of time to go home. At first Henry thought he was being paranoid, but after several months he asked her why she never wanted to spend the entire night with him. She shrugged it off, saying she felt more comfortable in her own bed. It was a feeble excuse, since Henry actually felt more comfortable at her townhouse than at his pathetic apartment, which he had barely furnished since his divorce five years earlier, but he didn't push her. After several more months, Catherine finally asked him to stay the night.

One night, a couple of weeks after he began sleeping at Catherine's, Henry woke up to find that he was in the bed alone.

He looked at the alarm clock, 2:35, so he assumed that Catherine was in the bathroom. But when she did not return, he got out of bed to look for her. He found her crouched at the top of the stairway staring down into her living room. "What are you doing?" Henry asked.

Catherine placed a finger over her lips, got up and retreated into the bedroom, beckoning for Henry to follow.

"What's going on?" he asked in confusion.

"Lower your voice or they'll hear you," she whispered adamantly.

"Who'll hear me?" Henry whispered back, his heart racing at the prospect of intruders.

"Brigit and Barry."

He stared at her blankly until the names finally registered. "Your sister and brother-in-law?" he asked, not at all sure that he was understanding her correctly.

"Brigit and Barry are downstairs," she replied. "Something is wrong."

She sounded so certain that Henry began to wonder if they had arrived at the house in the middle of the night without his knowledge. He told her to stay where she was, left the bedroom, and carefully made his way down the stairs until he had a clear view of the entire living room. No one was there. He returned to the bedroom to find Catherine fast asleep. As Henry watched her, he thought he finally understood why Catherine had not wanted him to spend the night.

The next day, Catherine was unusually agitated, but before Henry could broach the subject of her sleep-walking, the phone rang. Catherine snatched it up.

"Hello . . . Slow down . . . When did it happen?"

Henry could only hear Catherine's side of the conversation, but her solemn tone and pained expression told him something was very wrong.

"I'm so sorry, Brigit," Catherine said.

At the mention of her sister's name, Henry felt a tingling sensation at the base of his neck.

After Catherine hung up the phone, she turned to Henry and said, "Barry's nephew has been killed in a motorcycle accident."

Henry was stunned. He had no idea what to say. Catherine just waited. He knew he had to say something and managed to ask, "When?"

Catherine stared directly into his eyes for what seemed a very long time. Henry had never had anyone scrutinize him so closely; he felt as though she was searching for something deep inside him and was relieved when she finally said, "Early this morning." The tingling returned and, when Catherine added, "The police think it happened around 2:30," spread down his spine.

Many months later Henry asked Catherine what she saw in him that day that made her decide to tell him about the timing. She smiled and said, "I saw you."

HENRY CLOSELY WATCHED CATHERINE as she continued to gaze around the room. Despite the certainty of her last statement, he knew she still had some hope.

"Are you sure you won't get a chance to say goodbye?" Henry asked. "I mean, this has lasted for a long time and has been so intense."

"There's no reason that this time should be any different."

"Yes there is. He was your father."

"You think that matters? When has any of it ever mattered?" she replied.

Henry's heart ached. They had been together for twelve years, married for nine, and Henry had felt her fly out of bed on many occasions because something in her "dreams" had been so disturbing or out of place that she had been compelled to act, only to find herself standing beside the bed staring wide eyed at seemingly nothing. Once he woke and found her kneeling next to Connor's bed crying so hard she was having a hard time catching her breath. He never forgot the agony in her voice when she said something was wrong with Connor, nor did he forget the look in Connor's eyes,. One of the constants throughout was Catherine's belief that what she felt, what she saw, never did anyone any good because what she "dreamt" was always too convoluted, or too little, or too late.

"I just thought maybe this time," Henry said.

"Yeah, well if there is one thing I've learned, it's that the length of time means nothing."

"I'm sorry, Catherine," Henry said, knowing she had been through this before. "I don't think you ever told me how long it went on after your mother died."

"Not quite this long." She shrugged.

"I can't imagine what it must have been like for you when you got back here after the funeral . . . all by yourself."

"You make it sound . . . I wasn't frightened, Henry. I could just feel her in my apartment. It was a comforting feeling, actually, and I just wanted to find her." She waved her hand around. "Sort of like now. This is ending the same way," she said, her voice tinged with regret.

"Are there any similarities to when Maria died?" he asked, daring to raise the subject.

Catherine stared at him without responding. Her fraternal twin sister had died when they were fifteen. Catherine was the uncoordinated scrawny sister, more at home with a book than a ball, and yet it had been Maria, the natural athlete, who drowned. For years after Maria's death, Catherine would make her way in the middle of the night to her twin's bedroom, the one Maria moved into after Brigit went away to college. Catherine's mother or father would find her in the room, awake but not awake, searching and calling Maria's name.

The trips down the hall to her twin's bedroom stopped when Catherine began to wake up in her own bedroom with the sensation that someone was there. Some nights Catherine was even sure that she caught a glimpse of a shape, a movement in the darkness. She was convinced it was Maria—after all, they had shared the room for thirteen years, and it comforted Catherine to think that Maria was saving her from worried inquiries of their parents every time they found her in the other bedroom.

Then the dreams began, and as they intensified, she became even more convinced that Maria was trying to reach out to her, until one night Catherine bolted upright in bed with the clear knowledge that what was with her in her room was not her sister. She screamed, a horrible, tortured sound that pierced the night, causing her parents to burst into her room in a confused panic.

The dreams, and the screaming, continued, and Catherine's parents, who decided she was having problems dealing with her grief, began to talk about sending her to a psychiatrist. Catherine, who had decided the dreams were *not* a manifestation of grief, devised her own means of stopping the dreams, and when the dreams stopped, the screaming stopped, and so did any discussion of a psychiatrist.

"Why are you bringing that up?" Catherine glared at Henry, but he was not going to be deterred.

"I was just wondering if you were experiencing anything else?"

"Experiencing?" Catherine repeated.

"You know what I mean."

"You make it sound almost normal. I'm having an experience," she fluttered her hand in the air, trying to make light of the situation.

"Are you having the same type of dreams that you had when Maria died?" he asked directly.

She didn't answer; she seemed to be contemplating.

"Catherine?"

"Did I ever tell you that I started having . . . odd dreams when I was around ten? Not all the time, mind you, just every once in a while," her voice sounded distant.

"No," Henry said, surprised by the revelation.

"The dreams I had after Maria died were . . . more disturbing. I mean I never remember screaming as a child, I just remember how . . . unusual they seemed."

"Unusual?"

"Not ordinary."

"Not funny. What do you mean?"

"I don't know. I was young, Henry, and you know how your imagination can be when you're young. I still remember how real some of them seemed. I felt captivated by what I was being shown."

"Shown?"

She furrowed her brow. "Sort of like standing in the wings of a theater watching a play. I wasn't part of the production, the action, but I wasn't part of the audience either because my perspective was more intimate." She cocked her head to one side. "You know, I never thought about it like that before."

"Do you remember what you saw?"

"They were dreams, Henry. Who remembers dreams?"

"Well, most people don't remember what they dreamt the night before, let alone thirty years later, but—"

"Hey, twenty-nine," she corrected, trying to grin, but then she turned serious. "You know, thinking back on it, I never did feel scared, even when the dreams seemed the most real, the most vivid. I always felt like someone was with me, protecting me." She shook her head. "God, how weird is that?"

"So, nothing like the dreams you had when Maria died?" Henry asked, watching as her eyes grew more intense. "Catherine?"

"They sort of started off the same; I mean, I thought Maria was with me but—" She stood up. "I don't want to think about any of this anymore."

"Just answer one more question for me, please?" he implored.

She scowled at him but then gave up, holding up one finger. "One more."

"Did you have any dreams when your mom died?"

"Yes, all right. Are you happy?"

"Was there any similarity to the others?"

"You said one question."

Henry raised an eyebrow.

"Oh, fine, *if* I had to describe them I would say that the ones after my mom died were jumbled, unfocused." She paused for a moment. "It reminded me of this time I saw a group of children playing some game I didn't recognize, and this one child, who was massively overexcited, rushed up to me and started explaining what was going on, but she just ended up tumbling over her words, and then she rushed back off, so I never really did understand." She looked pensive, but then shook herself. "Anyway, they weren't anything like the other ones, they didn't last very long, and no, I haven't had any dreams like any of them since my dad died. Just the ones that have gotten me up in the middle of the night in search of—" her voice caught, but then she cleared her throat and said, "I don't know about you, but I'm going to bed."

Henry looked disappointed.

"Jeez, Henry, what did you think? That you were on the verge of cracking the case? That somehow you would be able to connect the dots and all of this would suddenly make sense."

"There has to be some reason, Catherine," Henry insisted.

"There is no *bloody* reason," she yelled and then stopped herself. "Henry, I realize that you're looking for a logical explanation. Something that ties everything together, and obviously death is a common denominator."

"Don't do that, Catherine."

"Do what?"

"Don't put words in my mouth. All I'm trying to do is better understand what you've experienced. You're not exactly overflowing with information when it comes to this part of your life."

"Part of my life," she scoffed.

"It is part of your life."

"Well, I don't want it!" Catherine said, and then she turned and left the room.

Chapter 5

Keitha succeeded in persuading George to give the dessert group some leaves from the sweet plant, and the word soon spread throughout the colony that the celebration would include a special sweet.

The great room underwent a transformation for the occasion. The food was arranged on a long table in the center of the room, each dish surrounded by a decoration made by the children. The pies were on an elevated platform in the middle of it all. Everyone circled the table making grand gestures, proclaiming the splendor of every plate or bowl of food. Most of the children just gazed in awe before complete silence fell over the gathering to allow each person a chance to reflect in his or her own way. Then, based upon a longstanding tradition, the eldest person in the colony walked up to the table with one of the youngest children and took the first portion of each dish, which the two shared.

Groups of people followed in no particular order, while others stood patiently around the room conversing leisurely until it was their turn. As people ate, there were more declarations about the superb taste of all of the food and, although no one had ever eaten a pie, all agreed that these pies had to be the best that had ever been prepared by anyone, ever.

After the last morsel of food was consumed, the long table was moved to the far wall, and everyone sat on the floor in concentric circles, leaving an open space in the center. A group of young children entered the space and sang a song laced with images of oceans and rocky shorelines, things that no one had actually ever seen. Next came a short play, led by Lily, and after that a drum solo. Finally, Keitha stepped into the center. It was her responsibility to end each celebration with a story.

"In honor of Catherine's father," emphasizing the woman's name for the benefit of Clara, "I've been doing some research into her ancestors."

Excited murmuring filled the room. Everyone knew that even for someone like Keitha, with a connection to the past, researching the records could be time consuming, because only a portion of the extensive data had been reviewed and cataloged.

After the archivists were established, Clara and the two other young people began reviewing the data based on what they saw in the past. Records that corroborated an event were saved in files organized and cross-referenced by date, place, and/or subject matter. Records that indicated a completely different version of events from what the young people saw were kept per the same organizational structure but were placed in a sub-directory entitled "suspect," no matter how many other records said the same thing. After seven years, they had barely made a dent in the vast compilation of records. To further hinder the situation, after three years the two young people working with Clara began to lose their abilities, and by the time they turned sixteen they could no longer see the past.

Clara's ability never faded; it actually intensified when she was pregnant with Keitha, and she began to use more and more computer time to try and track down everything she was seeing. Donal finally had to tell her to scale back because her searches were requiring more and more power, which could not be justified when there had not yet been any direct benefit to the colony. Clara insisted that there was a reason she continued to see events from the past, but she concurred that the searches were too cumbersome and proposed using some of the older students to help compile the records into usable subsets that could then be searched with far less power. The teachers thought it was a wonderful learning opportunity and assigned students to help sift through the data.

Students usually began reviewing records when they were fourteen or fifteen, when they had enough maturity to understand the material and not become bored by some of the tedium. However, recently, a student had shown an amazing aptitude for finding and following information. At ten, even though she did not have the ability to see the past, Skyler became the second youngest person to work on the records. Only Keitha began at a younger age.

"I'd like to ask Skyler for a little help with some background information on Ireland," Keitha said.

Phelan spoke-up, excitedly exclaiming, "She's researching more than just Ireland."

A petite but forthright voice stated, "Only because I'm going through records from when Ireland was part of the United Kingdom of Great Britain, and I'm only looking at the Great Britain stuff that has to do with Ireland. The rest of it could take a person *forever.*"

Keitha tried not to grin. "Can you tell everyone about the Penal Laws?"

"You mean from the beginning? The Henry the Eighth stuff?"

"Yes, please." Keitha said.

The young girl drew herself up to her full height, which brought the top of her head up to Phelan's elbow.

"Henry the Eighth, they reused names for the kings and queens so they had to number them, was the king from the beginning of the 1500s to about the middle, so around 1550. He was married, wanted a divorce so he could marry another woman, but he was Catholic, and the Pope, the guy in Rome, Italy, that was the head of the Catholic Church, said no. So, Henry the Eighth ended up starting his own church and tells everyone, including the Irish, that they need to change to his church. Except everyone didn't change, so laws, called Penal Laws, were enacted that favored Henry's new religion and made it more difficult for the people who didn't change to do ordinary things. The Penal Laws in Ireland weren't really used for a long time until there was this war at the end of the 1600s. This other guy who had been king of England, and was Catholic, at least at that point he was, tried to get the throne back. Most of the Irish Catholics supported him, but he lost to the reigning king and queen who were Protestant . . . another really bizarre story . . . but not for right now," Skyler noted when she saw the look on Keitha's face. "Anyway, after the war the people who ran Ireland, who were Protestant, even though most of the people who lived in Ireland were Catholic, passed even more Penal Laws."

"Can you give some examples of the Penal Laws?" Keitha asked.

"The Irish Catholics couldn't teach or run schools in Ireland, but they also couldn't go somewhere else and be educated, they couldn't buy or lease land or practice law, they couldn't be involved in politics and eventually lost the right to vote." Skyler knitted her eyebrows together. "There was a bunch of them, do you want me to keep going?"

"No, I think that will do. Thank you, Skyler. That was very informative. You've really done a lot of research in a relatively short amount of time."

The young girl blushed, but acknowledged the compliment with a tilt of her head.

"The reason I asked for that brief background is because Catherine's ancestors were impacted by the Penal Laws, most of which were enacted between 1691 and the early 1700s," Keitha explained. "Her paternal ancestors lived in the rural southern region of Ireland, and like the vast majority of the people on the island, they were Catholic and farmed the land they lived on. Some of them actually owned a moderate amount of land. Under the Penal Laws, however, Catholics could no longer buy land, and what land they already owned had to be equally inherited by all male children. The result was smaller and smaller parcels for each successive generation until finally there just wasn't enough land to support a family. Most Catholics ended up selling to Protestant landowners and either stayed on the land and became tenant farmers working for the landowner, or moved within Ireland to try and find other work, or left Ireland altogether. Catherine's family did all three.

"Another thing that greatly affected Catherine's ancestors was the potato. The potato was not a native plant of Ireland but did extremely well in the soil and in the climate. So much so that by the 1700s the potato had become a staple in the diet of the rural people in Ireland, and as we know, it is never a good thing to rely on just one crop, because if something happens, it can be devastating for the people.

"From the end of 1739 and lasting into 1741, there was a sharp change in the mild winters that had been the norm for Ireland and other European countries. In Ireland the bitter cold caused the potatoes to freeze, making them inedible. They couldn't even be used as seed for the next growing season. Adding to the crisis was a drought, which occurred in the spring of 1740, decimating the wheat and barley crops as well as herds of sheep and cattle. The people in the rural areas began to starve, and many fled to the more populated cities seeking food."

"Keitha," Donal inquired uncertainly. "I'm no Skyler, but I thought the Irish Potato Famine was in the 1840s."

Keitha saw Phelan unsuccessfully try to tousle Skyler's hair, but the girl deftly dodged her head away from him.

"That is a different famine, which I'll be getting to," Keitha explained before continuing. "The Irish referred to the worst part of the first famine as 'the year of the slaughter' because of the number of people that died, and the failure of the potato crop wasn't the only crisis that the dramatic shift in the climate caused. The coal trade, a chief fuel, was affected because the harbors froze, so shipments couldn't dock. The coal yards in the country also froze, creating an even greater shortage of fuel. The water that powered mill-wheels froze disrupting grain processing and other industry; the cost of food soared, which led to food riots. As living conditions worsened, diseases like dysentery, small pox, and typhus spread.

"The official documentation of the number of deaths during the first famine wasn't very accurate at the time, but historians, who attempted to piece together information, estimated that the total number of deaths throughout Ireland was somewhere between 300,000 and 500,000. The fractious political response during it all led to economic turmoil, and it took a very long time for Ireland to recover. The potato crop became *the primary* diet of the rural poor by 1845, when it was ravaged once again, this time by a fungus that caused the potatoes to blacken and rot in the ground. That famine was called The Great Irish Potato Famine."

"Why would they go back to the same diet?" George asked disheartened. "Didn't they learn?"

"They really didn't have options. Crops that yielded more money for the landlords were sold or shipped out of Ireland. The same happened with the livestock. Potatoes were easy to grow, people didn't need a lot of land to grow them, and they were rich in nutrients.

"Now, let me give you a little background on the paternal side of Catherine's family. Her paternal grandfather's family lived in the rural southwestern part of Ireland, and her paternal grandmother's family lived over towards the eastern side of the island. They never came into contact with each other even though they had many things in common. Both sides of Catherine's paternal family ended up selling their land and becoming tenant farmers; both families had so many deaths during the first famine that their numbers were almost cut in half; and even before the second famine hit, both families were having an increasingly difficult time paying the rent on their tenant farms. Because of that, several of Catherine's grandfather's family left to work in the copper mines on the west coast if Ireland. At the same time, Catherine's grandmother's great-uncle, Daniel, left their farm to find work in the copper mines on the eastern coast.

"I've finally come to the story of the person I really wanted to tell you all about: Catherine's paternal grandmother, Molly. She was a very unusual woman for several reasons. First of all, she could read and write. Even after the Penal Laws forbidding the education of the Catholics were repealed, an education was not something that the poor could afford. However, Molly's great-uncle Daniel worked in a copper mine on the east coast alongside an old man who had once been a hedge master.

"A hedge master was a person who taught the Irish Catholic children when it was illegal under the Penal Laws to have Catholic schools. They were sort of renegade teachers, breaking the law but educating children. As the Penal Laws on education were repealed, hedge masters found themselves without jobs and had to look elsewhere, like the mines," Keitha explained.

"The old man taught Daniel to read and write, and Daniel taught Catherine's great grandfather, Cornelius, who then taught his only child, Molly. Molly was born in 1891, when her father was forty-seven years old. He died eight years later. Molly's mother, who was much younger, re-married and in quick succession gave birth to four more children. She died of respiratory failure shortly after the last child was born.

"Molly dutifully took care of the younger children and her stepfather until she turned sixteen, when he informed her that it was time for her to marry him. Molly refused, so he quickly married another woman and ordered Molly to leave his house. He openly berated her to anyone who would listen, saying how out of kindness and respect for Molly's dead mother he had offered to wed the girl, even though she was lazy and dimwitted and what thanks did he get? She spit in his eye, said she was too good for him. It was all horrible lies by a vindictive man who wanted nothing more than to see

Molly begging on the streets, and for that, he needed to make sure that no other man in Wexford County would even consider marrying her. But he underestimated Molly's tenacity. She was hardworking, resilient, and her stepfather never knew, because her mother had kept it a secret to the day she died, that Molly's father had taught her to read and write.

"Molly left Wexford County with two precious belongings that she had kept hidden from her stepfather. A journal that contained the stories that her father, Cornelius, had read to her every night while he was alive, stories committed to paper by her great-uncle Daniel about their family and heritage, and a small box. The key to the box was on a chain around her neck, where it had been since her father laid it and the box in her hand the night he died. Molly's father told her that Daniel had given him the box, and he was passing it on to her, with one condition: that the box couldn't be opened unless she truly was in need. Mere hardship wasn't enough—she was strong enough to get through hardship. He hoped she would never need to open the box, but if she did, she was to use whatever was inside wisely.

"Molly made her way to the city of Waterford and then to the city of Cork, finding work as a cleaning woman in some of the most appalling places, but even that work became so intermittent that the meager amount of money she was able to make was barely enough to feed her every other day. The night before she faced eviction from her small shabby room, the likelihood of ending up on the streets, just as her stepfather had wanted, was looming in front of her. She comforted herself by reading the journal from beginning to the end. As Molly absently flipped past a blank page that she always thought was the end, she was surprised to see additional writing that was not in her great-uncle's hand. It was her father's, and his words made her feel like he was sitting in the room next to her. She began to cry. At the end of his entries there was another blank page. She hesitated but felt compelled to turn past it, and found herself staring at more writing by a decidedly feminine hand.

"As Molly read, she realized it was her mother's writing. Her mother had been such an unassuming woman, meek even, especially around her stepfather, and Molly never knew that her father had also taught her to read and write. Molly read about the deep despair and longing her mother felt after Molly's father died, and then the tough, deliberate words of a woman determined to make a good life for her small daughter. The final entries described her mother's years with her stepfather, and Molly began to cry again, both for her mother and out of guilt for not knowing how much her mother had sacrificed. She stared bleary-eyed at the blank page at the end of her mother's entries, knowing there could be no more; there was no one else. Yet she once again felt compelled to turn the page. Her breath caught as she saw her own handwriting. She shook her head and looked up at the tattered ceiling, and when she looked back down, the page was empty.

"Molly fell into a fitful sleep that night and woke with a start, staring around her room. She swore she had heard her father's voice. Her eyes were wide with dread but when her heart finally slowed, she found herself repeating the words, 'You'll know.' She got out of bed, taking the box from its hiding place, and walked over to the dingy window that was letting in a little moonlight. Molly touched the key hanging from her neck, and with trembling fingers tried to open the clasp on the chain but failed, not once but three times. She cried out in desperation, yanking the chain over her head. But she could only stare at the box. Was she really in need or only weak? Her father had never found it necessary to open the box and here she was, ready to after only a year on her own. She started to slide the chain back around her neck when she heard, 'It's time.' This time Molly knew it was her father's voice, and the sense of dread returned, only to be quelled by the same calm, reassuring feeling that her father imparted to her whenever she felt afraid as a child.

"Molly stared down at her palm, which bore the imprint of the key that she had been clutching in her hand. She took the key, opened the box, and stared, stupefied at the sight of money, sure that at any moment it would all vanish and she would wake up. No matter how many times she shut her eyes, the money was still there when she opened them, until finally she saw a slip of paper. She took it out and read the simple note that her great-uncle Daniel had written, 'for a better life,' and wept for the third time that night. There was more than enough for passage to America, something she had never allowed herself to hope for. She wondered why her father hadn't used the money himself. Then she remembered: he never opened the box. He saved it for her, as if he knew.

She left Ireland on her eighteenth birthday, in 1909, and when she reached America, she used the remaining money to travel from New York City to a town out in the western part of the country, one that her father had told her about when she was little: Butte, Montana.

Michael, Catherine's paternal grandfather, also left Ireland in 1909, after his mother's death. He joined his two older brothers working in the copper mines in Michigan, but after three years, Michael decided it was time to strike out on his own and went to Butte, Montana, and there he found Molly. Michael would often remark that he had to come to a country one hundred times larger than Ireland to find his Irish sweetheart. He said it was as though she had been waiting for him all along, and Molly would just smile and pat his hand.

"They married in 1915. Catherine's father was born in 1925, Michael and Molly's third son, whom they named after Molly's great-uncle Daniel," Keitha finished.

There was silence, followed by raucous applause.

Keitha turned to face her mother. "What is it, Clara? You've wanted to say something all night."

"You found all of that in the historical records?" Clara asked skeptically.

"Of course not. I verified the historical information through the records, but the specific information about Catherine's ancestors came from a different source."

"What source?"

"I found Molly's journal," Keitha stated triumphantly. "At least part of it."

The room was stunned into an eerie silence.

"There aren't any paper documents," Terran stated. "And even if there were—"

Keitha cut him off. "Someone at some time transcribed the handwritten journal onto a computer, and I found it, even though it was stored in the oddest location. I could just as easily have missed it entirely."

"How did you even know to look for it?" Greer asked.

"Catherine told Henry about it at her father's funeral. She said it contained not only Molly's family history, but also Molly's transcription of the entire oral history of her husband Michael's family, as he relayed it to her and—"

"And you didn't think that was worth mentioning to us before now?" Clara interrupted.

"I've been looking for it. What good would it have done to tell you about it if I couldn't find it?" Keitha countered.

"Keitha, what did you mean, you found part of it?" Greer broke in.

"The last entries were from Molly and Anna, Catherine's mother. There were no entries after that, none by Catherine, so there must be another document somewhere."

"Or Catherine didn't add to the journal," Greer stated.

"Catherine probably didn't even have the journal." Terran said. "Wasn't it the tradition to pass on something like that to the eldest? You said Daniel was Molly and Michael's third son."

"Did you also hear me just say that the last entries were by Molly *and* Anna, Catherine's mother?"

"Why would Catherine's mother have entries in a journal about Catherine's father's family?"

"If you would just let me finish," Keitha snapped.

"Sorry," Greer said. "Please go on."

"Molly and Anna were very close, perhaps because Anna's mother, Maria, died when Anna was only ten, or perhaps because Molly wanted to have a complete record of both families for the child she wanted the journal passed on to," Keitha said.

"Catherine," Clara stated.

"Catherine," Keitha concurred. "Molly made it clear to Anna and Daniel that she wanted the journal to be passed on to Catherine."

"Why?" Greer asked.

Keitha shrugged. "I would only be guessing."

"So guess," Clara insisted.

"Maybe Molly knew that Catherine had inherited—" Keitha began.

"Her ability?" Terran interjected fervently.

"And more," Keitha said cryptically.

CHAPTER 6

"What the hell does that mean?" Terran demanded.

"There was a person in Anna's family with a comparable ability," Keitha stated bluntly.

"Who?" Clara asked, but before Keitha could reply, a tremendous snoring concerto resounded throughout the cavernous space. Everyone whipped their heads around and stared into a recessed alcove were Murphy and several other dogs were sound asleep.

"They wore themselves out playing with the kids," Keitha noted as the children began to giggle.

"I think we're all a little worn out," Clara stated.

"Would you rather I not continue?" Keitha inquired, arching an eyebrow.

"Noooo." The protest arose from the people in the room.

Clara sighed deeply and shook her head. "I don't think you can leave everyone in suspense. Do you?"

"I'll make the story as succinct as I can," Keitha said as a compromise.

Clara tilted her head in acknowledgement but said nothing. "Anna's grandfather lived all of his life in the northern hills of Mexico, and it was there that he married Anna's grandmother." Keitha commenced the story of the maternal side of Catherine's family. "They had five sons, and after a gap of twelve years, Maria, Anna's mother, was born. Maria grew up calling her mother Shi`Ma, but only when her father was not around. Shi`Ma said it was a special name, just for the two of them, but would say no more."

Keitha paused to make sure no one, especially the smaller children, looked sleepy before continuing the story.

"The first time Martin, Catherine's grandfather, asked permission to marry Maria, she was fourteen and he was sixteen, and both of Maria's parents vehemently said no. He had no job and no land, was just too poor. Martin went to work on a large ranch in New Mexico, terrified that Maria's parents would marry her off before he could prove himself worthy of their daughter. After two years he returned, relieved to find Maria still living with her parents, and again asked for permission to marry her, but again her parents said no. He tenaciously returned each year to ask for Maria's hand, and every year her parents turned him away. But the fourth year he noticed that, although her father continued to say no, her mother stood by silently. This gave him hope. Martin did not realize that in an act of defiance unheard of at the time, Maria had refused all suitors, and her father was threatening to throw her out of the house if she did not marry a man of his choosing. Shi`Ma knew that he would follow through on his threat if Maria continued to defy him, but she also knew that her daughter loved the strange young man who kept returning year after year. Shortly before Martin was due to return yet again, Shi`Ma sat down with Maria and began to speak to her daughter about the Tindi people, also known as the Lipan Apache, Shi`Ma's people.

"The Lipan Apache had migrated from the far north, eventually settling in what became Texas. They were expert hunters, adept at foraging for edible plants, and even grew their own corn and squash. The people felt a deep connection to the earth and everything that lived upon it. They approached hunts, whether for animals or plants, with great respect. Other tribes entered the same region, and the Lipan become warriors. They fought many battles and eventually broke into two separate bands. By the 1850s, the once united tribe had splintered into over ten individual bands, spread out over what became Texas, New Mexico, Colorado, and even into Mexico. Of course, for the Lipan people, these artificial boundaries meant nothing; however, they were acutely aware of the significance the white eyes placed on the borders, and the Apache people, as well as other tribes, played important roles in many of the land battles that occurred between the United States and Mexico.

"Maria felt the palpable weight that Shi`Ma's words carried as she told her daughter, 'You need to know that there were many falsehoods spread among the white eyes about our tribe, which were used, as they had done with so many other tribes, to seek out the Lipan Apache people and kill them. The Army of the United States even pursued the Lipan across their border into Mexico, where the Mexican government, under a man named Diaz, assisted them in their mission to destroy the Lipan. I am proof they did not succeed, even though I married and blended into the world of your father.'

"Maria's heart was beating so fast she thought it would seize in her chest, but Shi`Ma was not done.

"'I heard some say as little as twenty Lipan were left alive and were forced to live in a place called Oklahoma, on land called a reservation. I have also heard people talk about our tribe in hushed voices, as though we no longer exist on this earth. But we do. You do. What you must pass on to your children is that our people were great hunters because we knew how to blend into the land, and when we became the hunted, we used those same skills. Our people are still out there, and there will come a day when they will let themselves be seen again.'

"Maria stammered out half-formed questions, but Shi`Ma stopped her, as though she already knew the questions, and said, 'I'm telling you about our people now because you will be leaving me soon. I have seen it. Your brothers do not know these stories because they are completely of your father's world. They were the moment they were born. Now I would like to tell you more about our people.'

"Maria nodded without speaking, and realized from the instant her mother spoke the words 'our people' that she felt connected to something beyond the people and the place she had always called home.

"Shi`Ma talked all night about the traditions, the history, and the legends of the tribe. It was more than she had spoken during the entire twenty years of her daughter's life. Her words painted dazzling, powerful pictures for Maria. She felt as if she could see and hear it all: the men, as they headed out in search of buffalo; the women with their woven baskets, bending to gather agave; the prayers and dances when the people communicated with the spirit world and the natural world; the warriors in battle; the suffering as the people died from a disease called smallpox; and the anguish of being pursued to the edge of extinction.

"Only as the sun began to tinge the night sky with silvery light did Shi`Ma's words come to an end, as she quickly rose to begin her daily tasks. Maria grasped her mother's hand.

"'Are you a medicine man ... I mean woman?' Maria asked in a solemn voice, using a term she had once heard.

"'My daughter, I am nothing but a poor old woman.'

"'But, you hear things ... you see things.' Maria's voice shook as she added, 'You saw that I would be leaving.'

"Shi`Ma cradled her daughter's face in her calloused hands. 'All that makes me in this world is a poor, crazy old woman.'

"Martin arrived the next day. Shi`Ma greeted him at the door, her father nowhere to be seen, and before Martin could speak a word, Shi`Ma told him that she knew he was working in a mine in Colorado and that he had saved enough to buy Maria a small house. Martin was surprised and asked her if she had talked to his grandfather, Jorge. Shi`Ma shook her head and told him that he could marry Maria, but only if the two of them left that very day. Martin felt paralyzed by the divergent sensations of shock and delight that pulsed through him, but managed to move when Shi`Ma commanded him to go and find her daughter."

Keitha paused again, and this time she could see many of the children fighting to keep their eyes open, so she decided to end the story quickly. "Martin and Maria left that very same day and were married in Texas on their way to Colorado. Maria had three miscarriages before Catherine's mother, Anna, was born in 1930. As I said, she was their only child, and Maria died ten years after Anna's birth. Martin was heartbroken, and although he tried, he just could not remain in the house that they had shared together. So in 1941 he took his daughter and moved to Montana to work in the copper mines in Butte, where Catherine's parents met. They married in 1954."

The room erupted in thunderous applause and calls of appreciation, the slumbering dogs leaping to their feet and joining in with their own barks and howls. When the din died down the young children were ushered out of the room by Eddy and Brina, while the older children and remaining adults cleaned up.

Greer, Terran, Clara, and Keitha stayed after everyone else had gone.

Keitha turned to the other three. "What else do you want to know?" she asked them.

"Catherine's grandmother Molly and great-grandmother Shi`Ma . . . both had abilities?" Greer asked in amazement.

"It certainly seems so, from the accounts of their lives."

"Speaking of that," Clara stated, "I noticed that you have repeated conversations and things that people thought. I can understand that when it comes to Molly, she wrote down her own story, but Anna obviously wasn't there when Maria and Shi`Ma had their talk, so how can you be so precise?"

"I'm just reiterating what I read in the journal. You should know that there is a lot more information in the journal, on both sides of Catherine's family, which date back to before anyone could read or write."

"How can that be?" Clara questioned.

"Oral history handed down through the generations," Greer reasoned.

"Right," Keitha concurred. "Molly wrote down what Michael told her about his family, and Molly's great-uncle Daniel wrote down his family history. And Anna wrote down stories she had been told."

"So why are you furrowing your brow?" Clara asked.

"I can't find Catherine's stories," Keitha replied. "She must have added her own stories to the journal, and if I can just find them, they would solve a lot of problems."

"You think you can find everything we need if you find Catherine's part of the journal?" Clara probed.

"Not everything, but maybe enough," Keitha responded evenly.

"So you won't have to make an actual connection with her," Clara stated.

"Look, Clara, in case you hadn't noticed, I haven't been able to connect with the woman," Keitha barked. "Not any more than you were able to."

"You have an opportunity to do so now," Clara insisted.

"Because her father died? You think that will open her up? Be serious, look at what happened when her sister died, and her mother. She shuts down."

"I pushed too hard when Catherine's sister died. I should have known better: she was too young, and you were too young when Catherine's mother died. I should never have let you try."

Keitha was stunned by Clara's statement: her mother never talked about either instance. "Well, none of that matters at this point anyway. The fact is, Catherine is too old now. We lost our opportunity to connect directly with her, so the journal is our only chance."

"She's not too old," Greer stated.

"Really, Father, even now abilities can fade as a person ages. Abilities that people acknowledge and use, neither of which she has ever done."

"She has," Greer said.

"What? You mean what she calls her dreams." Keitha raised an eyebrow. "That's hardly an acknowledgement."

"It is for her."

"I don't want to talk about this anymore. I'm going to spend my time trying to track down Catherine's part of the journal and stop wasting my time on this ludicrous idea that I can somehow get through to her."

"The only reason you even knew to look for the journal was because of what you *heard* her say to Henry."

"Catching bits and pieces of someone's life is not the same as talking to them. I don't know where you even came up with the idea that it would be possible."

"Because Oscar did," Greer noted.

Clara's head snapped in Greer's direction, and she shot him a warning glare.

"Who's Oscar?" Keitha asked.

"No one," Clara stated firmly.

"Who's Oscar?" Keitha repeated, addressing Greer.

"Oscar is just a story," Clara said sternly, turning her back to Keitha and staring at Greer.

Greer looked at Clara incredulously, but when he saw her eyes beseeching him, he said, "I think it's time for all of us to get some sleep."

Keitha stared at her father in disbelief.

"We'll talk about this later, Keitha," he said resolutely.

Keitha knew she wasn't going to get anywhere so she spun away, calling to Murphy as she exited the room. The dog jumped up and shook himself awake before trotting after her.

"You brought up Oscar on purpose," Clara accused Greer as she came up behind him.

Greer turned to face her. His eyes were intense, his voice unyielding. "I'm giving you a chance, Clara, but if you don't tell her what happened, I will."

CHAPTER 7

As Keitha crossed the threshold into her parents' room, she knew immediately that they had been arguing. They were sitting at the old wooden table that Greer told her dated back to before Catherine's time. It wasn't a big table, slightly oblong with a scar right in the center, which Greer believed was some sort of burn mark. What fascinated Keitha, and most other people, was that two of the legs were hinged and could be rotated 90 degrees. This allowed the rounded pieces on each end, Greer said they were called leaves, to drop down creating a compact rectangular tabletop.

"So what is so important that you couldn't wait until my shift ended to talk to me?" Keitha asked, as calmly as she could. "And why did you insist that Murphy couldn't be here?"

The mere fact that Terran had approached her to say that she could have a long lunch because her parents wanted to speak to her had activated her internal alert system. When he added that Greer insisted that she come alone, her nerve endings began firing, causing her skin to tingle.

"I did not want Murphy getting upset. It wouldn't be good for him, it would distract you, and I need you to be focused," Greer stated.

The look on his face matched the strident tone of his voice, which only served to intensify the tingling sensation, and when she saw the strained look on Clara's face, she actually considered bolting from the room.

"Shit, Greer, what the hell is going on?" Keitha demanded, her voice quivering.

"When I was ten . . . I . . . wait a minute, just wait a minute," Keitha said, clearly unnerved. "I remember when I was ten. You both told me I was dreaming, but I wasn't, was I? Answer me!"

"I told you this was a bad idea," Clara told Greer. "She's becoming hysterical."

"Don't talk like I'm not here," Keitha yelled directly at Clara. "You are fucking unbelievable."

"I told you not to use archaic, vulgar terminology when you're talking to me," Clara said coolly.

"Father, tell me, was I really . . ." Keitha began to ask as she turned to Greer, but he was no longer in the room. "See what you did?" Keitha said whipping around to confront Clara.

"Please leave," Clara stated as she turned back to the shelf and took down an old teapot.

"Don't you dare make tea," Keitha said menacingly.

Clara continued her tea preparation as though she had not heard Keitha.

"You're wrong if you think this is over, Clara. Greer will tell me what happened."

Clara did not turn around until she heard Keitha leave. Only then did she allow herself to slump over from the physical exhaustion of keeping her emotions under such tight control. She stumbled over to the table and collapsed into a chair, her chest heaving with anguish. Clara knew that Greer would tell Keitha everything, that her daughter would never understand the choice she had made, and that she would lose Keitha forever.

CHAPTER 8

Keitha stopped at the archives to tell Terran that she would not be coming back for the remainder of her shift, and then she headed to the only cage that descended to the deepest levels where the reservoirs for the colony were located.

During active mining, the ground water was pumped to the surface to keep the working area dry, but those pumps had been abandoned in the latter part of the 20th century, and once that happened the ground water sought a new equilibrium, partially flooding the mine, which in turn contaminated the ground water. The founders designed and constructed an intricate system to intercept the ground water before it could come into contact with the exposed rock. The water was then conveyed to a series of lined holding ponds, and from there to one of two reservoirs.

Keitha carefully made her way along the tunnel that led to the drinking water reservoir. There was no lighting in this area to guide her, and she had been in such a rush that she had forgotten to grab one of the portable lights, so she kept her hand on the wall for support and reassurance. Even though she had no claustrophobia, the dark was so impenetrable she began to feel like the very air was closing in on her. She stood at the entrance to an immense, cavernous area, allowing her breathing to return to normal and giving her eyes a chance to adjust. Her father was sitting on an elongated rock, worn smooth by the behinds of generations of solace seekers. The small lantern propped against it provided the only source of light.

"I'm sorry about letting Clara get to me like that," she called over to him.

Greer motioned for her to come sit on the rock next to him.

"There's only one rule down here: whoever is telling the story can only be interrupted if something is unclear or if a question is asked in a constructive manner."

"How long have you had that rule?" Keitha asked.

"About two minutes now."

"It's a good rule," she said with a slight grin.

"One that I expect you to adhere to." He watched her out of the corner of his eye. "Are we clear?"

"Yes, Father."

They sat, listening to the whoosh, whoosh of the water entering the reservoir, and then there was silence.

"Why do you like it here so much? It's so much more austere than the lake." Keitha was referring to the other reservoir, constructed by the founders to mimic the habitat found in surface lakes to support the aquatic and amphibian species that they had brought with them.

"Austerity has its advantages," Greer noted without elaborating.

They lapsed back into silence. After several minutes, Keitha gave her father a furtive glance and asked, "Why did you leave?"

"What I was telling you was distressing your mother too much."

"Clara wasn't distressed."

Greer shifted his position so he could look directly at Keitha. "You really don't know her at all, do you?"

"Whose fault is that?"

"Keitha, you're a grown woman; it's unseemly to act like a petulant child." Keitha's face clouded over, and Greer reached out and took her hand. "You have to stop punishing your mother."

"Humph," Keitha snorted. "Nothing I say or do has any impact on her."

Greer stood up. "If that's what you truly believe then there's no reason for me to tell you anything." He turned and started to walk away.

"Wait."

He continued walking.

"Please."

He was almost to the entrance.

"Damn it, Greer!" She jumped to her feet.

He turned and faced her. "What do you want, Keitha?"

"I want . . . I mean, I need to know what happened when I was young. I'd like to understand why Clara—" Keitha cleared her throat, as if that would clear away the emotion she was feeling, but it didn't. "I've never understood why she pulled away from me the way she did."

"She had no choice."

"Please, Greer, don't feed me the platitudes about how my mother was one of the most skilled perceptives in the colony and she was needed by others."

"It's true, Keitha."

"That has *never* explained why she completely stopped training *me*."

Greer lowered his eyes. "Clara felt—"

"I swear, Greer, *do not* tell me that Clara felt she had taught me everything I needed to know," Keitha said angrily, as tears began clouding her eyes. She turned away from Greer, wiped the tears away with her hand, and took a deep breath before turning to face him again. "I've always known that was a lie," she said quietly. "I just didn't want to hurt your feelings by telling you I knew. For a long time I thought I did something terribly wrong."

"Keitha," Greer said, saddened.

"It seemed like the only plausible explanation for why she changed towards me the way she did. She was so withdrawn."

"I know your mother changed; I tried to tell you about the pressure she was under."

"I needed her reassurance, Greer, but all she would say was that I was too young to understand what she was dealing with, and I just had to leave it alone. She was so cold about it."

"You were young, Keitha."

"I was fifteen, Greer." She shook her head. "It doesn't matter anymore anyway."

"All we ever wanted to do was protect you," Greer said. "I tried to tell Clara there had to be a better way, but your mother can be so obstinate."

"Protect me from what?"

Greer walked back over to her. "Sit down, please." She did what he asked, but he remained standing.

"It can't be that bad," Keitha ventured, warily. He held her eyes, and she felt a prickling sensation move down her spine. She hated when that happened.

"When you were born, Sylvia told Clara that you possessed an unexpected energy."

"What did that mean?"

"She said you had the ability to be a remarkable perceptive. But you would need to learn control, sensitivity, and discernment."

"Discernment?"

"Sylvia said the aggressive, obsessed people she sensed could present false faces to people."

"False faces?"

"Like the masks that Lily sometimes has the children use in the plays she helps them perform."

"So they can pretend to be something they're not."

"Yes, but the people Sylvia sensed weren't pretending. They were using deception and manipulation to get what they wanted."

"What did they want?"

"Power."

"That's kind of general, don't you think? Power over what . . . or who?"

"Yes, well, that was, and still is, the critical question."

"Sylvia didn't know much, did she?"

"She knew enough to warn your mother."

"Did Sylvia think that one of these other people might be in our colony?"

"That possibility was raised."

"Oh come on, you or Clara would have known."

"How would we know?"

"You would have sensed the deception."

"Sylvia said they were very good, and we were very naïve."

"So what did you do?"

"Sylvia kept trying to get a glimpse of their location or hear something that would help identify what they really wanted and how they planned to get it. Unfortunately, by the time you were nine, she had made little progress toward either, and she was becoming increasingly uneasy. Sylvia was convinced that one of the Machiavellians, a name she and your mother used when referring to them, was beginning to discern her presence, and she feared that the person was beginning to sense *you*."

"Me?"

"Do you remember when Catherine's twin died?"

"I was only five, Greer."

"Yet you felt the death of Maria as strongly as Clara did. You told your mother that someone had to help the other girl, who couldn't stop crying."

Keitha furrowed her brow, "That was Catherine?"

"Yes, and when Clara told Sylvia, she said your energy was intensifying faster than she had thought was possible." Greer placed a hand on his daughter's shoulder. "Sylvia feared it would lead the Machiavellians right to you."

"Was I the reason Clara pushed so hard with Catherine? Because I said someone had to help her?" Keitha felt a flush of regret.

"No, even though you were really upset, Clara wouldn't have tried if she didn't believe that there was an opportunity to connect with Catherine. Catherine never questioned that she was sensing Maria, which opened her mind. Clara worried that it might be the last opportunity to get through to Catherine because, at that time, the older a person became, the less open they were to unusual situations. Unfortunately, Clara ended up overwhelming Catherine."

"Still, if I had known that the girl was Catherine, I wouldn't have been so harsh with Clara about failing."

"I doubt that it would have made any difference to you." Greer held up his hand to stop her protest. "Your mother redoubled her training efforts with you, hoping above all else that you could succeed where she had failed. Sylvia continued advising Clara for the next five years, and you really began to flourish, but during that same time Catherine succeeded in closing herself off completely to Clara, and all you could sense was an occasional impression of her life."

"That was when Clara taught me how to conduct historical research. She could still see images from the past, but they had no point of reference for her. Clara said it was like having an entire room full of people talking at the same time, and she was unable to join any of the conversations, so she got various bits and pieces, like the woman in Ireland." Keitha paused. "You know that had to be Molly."

Greer shrugged.

Keitha stared at Greer. "So you're trying to tell me that when Catherine shut Clara out, Clara lost her ability to focus?"

"Catherine grounded everything your mother saw and heard, and without her it was chaotic."

"Catherine? You can't be serious."

You don't think she's good enough," Greer stated.

Keitha remained silent.

"Catherine was able to block out your mother, *your mother*, but you don't think she's *good enough*. No wonder you can't get through to her."

Keitha couldn't remember the last time her father had rebuked her so vehemently. He was disappointed in her, but more than that, he sounded . . . offended.

"I'm sorry."

"No you're not. That's how you feel, isn't it?" Greer insisted, watching his daughter's face for any hint of a reaction. He spotted an almost imperceptible tensing of her jaw. "Or are you trying to dismiss Catherine because you're afraid you will fail, just like Clara did." He saw her jaw tighten even more. "Keitha," he said ardently.

She couldn't deny it, but didn't want to admit it, so instead of responding she prodded him, "Are you going to finish telling me what happened or not?"

Greer stared up at the ceiling, even though it was far too high for him to see clearly in the muted light. He needed a moment to compose himself. There was no point in demanding an answer, not yet.

He dropped his gaze back onto Keitha. "When you were almost nine, Sylvia found the second perceptive that she knew could be trusted. His name was Oscar and he had made a remarkable connection with one of his genetic ancestors from the early 17th century."

"The Oscar that you brought up at the end of the celebration."

"Yes."

"What does he have to do with you and Clara protecting me?"

"I've allowed you leeway concerning my new rule about not interrupting, but now I think it's time for you to listen more and ask questions less," Greer said.

"You said questions could be asked if something was unclear, and I'm unclear."

"New rule, no more questions."

"But—"

"Do you want to hear what I have to tell you or not?"

"I want to hear," Keitha conceded.

"Oscar and his ancestor, her name was Rebecca, connected because they were both very powerful neurotransmitters."

Greer used the same terminology that he knew Clara had used during Keitha's early training. Clara compared the brain's chemical messengers, which formed in the neurons and transmitted impulses across synapses to a specific receptor, to what she and Keitha could do. They transmitted impulses across the synapses of time and space in hopes of finding a unique DNA receptor, an ancestor who would be able to pick up their messages. Clara told Keitha that countless mediums, psychics, and clairvoyants, whatever people called them in the past, were actually receptors who were able to pick-up on impressions that someone else had transmitted, somewhere in time. Unfortunately, if the person on the receiving end did not understand and/or did not receive a clear impression, the images and the source were many times misinterpreted.

"When Rebecca was a child," Greer continued, "she would spend hours in the woods on her own, and in that solitude, with nothing but the earth and the animals, she could see things, wondrous things, but also, at times, disturbing things. By the time she was twelve she had warned her family several times to avoid specific situations, but, to their detriment, they ignored her. One brother broke a leg, while another had his home catch fire because of a careless ember. All of her brothers started avoiding her, and that was when Rebecca's mother told her she had to stop going into the woods, and she had to stop talking about things that might happen. Her mother was so completely terrified of what her husband might do to the girl that she made Rebecca swear on her immortal soul that she would stop.

"Rebecca honored her promise to her mother and stopped going to the woods. She never again said a word to anyone about her visions of the future. Soon her family forgot, or chose to forget, about the odd things she had said when she was a girl. Oscar didn't connect with her until she was a young woman, and he did it while she was asleep so he wouldn't frighten her. She knew immediately that he wasn't a dream, that he was real. Rebecca told Oscar that she had been waiting for him to figure out how to talk to her for a very long time."

"What? She couldn't . . . I'm sorry, Father, but are you actually trying to tell me she knew about Oscar before he knew about her?"

"Yes, Keitha. I told you they were both very powerful neurotransmitters."

"Then why didn't she reach out to him?" she countered skeptically.

"She tried, but before she was able to find him she promised her mother not to go into the woods. Apparently the tranquility and harmony she felt in the woods enhanced her ability, and without that she had to wait for him to find her."

"And she told him that? I mean she actually talked to him?"

"Yes, Keitha."

"Wasn't that a breach of her promise to her mother?"

"She remained true to her promise. She didn't go into the woods and she didn't talk about the future."

"I'd say that was the proverbial splitting hairs. Her mother obviously didn't want her using her ability."

"Can you imagine spending your entire life as an outcast, being ostracized by everyone including your family? What it must have been like having no one to talk to, and being prevented from using a skill that could actually help people, if they would only listen? Can you imagine how lonely she must have been?" Greer challenged.

"No," Keitha admitted.

"And then Oscar comes along. Someone who understood who she was and what she could do, and he treated her as an equal whenever he talked to her." He stared at Keitha, who averted her gaze.

Greer continued. "Oscar and Rebecca communicated with each other for almost a year, when Rebecca suddenly told Oscar that she had seen a bridge giving way, killing her father and all three of her brothers. She told Oscar that she just couldn't let them leave on their journey without warning them, but when she tried her father pushed her away. He told Rebecca that, as soon as he returned, he was going to send her away because she had the devil in her."

"The devil!" Keitha exclaimed.

"Why are you so surprised? People believed in possession long before the 17th century and long after."

"I know, but her own father? That poor woman."

"Yes." Greer was glad to see Keitha empathizing. "Rebecca's father and brothers never returned, and her mother couldn't bring herself to send her only remaining child away, but she never looked at Rebecca again without fear in her eyes. Rebecca was so devastated she wept uncontrollably, and Oscar couldn't comfort her."

"Comfort her?" Keitha asked.

"I guess you could say that they began meeting in the synapse between their two times." Greer replied.

"Really?" Keitha asked skeptically.

"Yes, really. And Clara thinks you and Catherine can do the same thing." Greer answered emphatically.

Keitha frowned but didn't comment on the possibility. Instead she asked, "So what happened to Oscar and Rebecca?"

"Sylvia sent a message to your mother when she figured out that Oscar loved Rebecca. She asked Clara's advice on how to proceed, but your mother had no idea. What do you say to a man who's in love with someone who has technically been dead for centuries?" Greer stated matter-of-factly.

"More to the point," Keitha responded, "what do you say to someone who's in love with his own great, great . . . *grandmother*?"

"Having *some* DNA in common doesn't mean there is a close familial relationship," Greer said in an authoritative voice.

"But in order to make the kind of connection you're talking about, they would have to have a *lot* of DNA in common." Keitha maintained.

"Why?" Greer argued.

"You're talking about crossing, what . . . five hundred years or more?"

"Why would the amount of time be relevant?" he countered.

"Because . . . because Oscar had a hell of a lot of ancestors in those five hundred years, and yet something drew him to Rebecca. It had to have been the amount of DNA they had in common," Keitha fired off.

"You haven't been listening to me, Keitha."

"Yes I have, Greer," Keitha insisted.

Greer sighed. "Let me finish the story," he said, not wanting to get distracted again. "Shortly after Sylvia sent Clara the first message, another one followed saying that Oscar was becoming increasingly agitated about what was happening to Rebecca, and Sylvia feared that he might do something rash. It turned out she had a valid reason to worry. Oscar had been busily researching Rebecca's time and discovered a research paper about unusual weather events. From there he found a very old newspaper article about a terrible storm that had swept inland along the eastern coast of the United States, devastating Rebecca's small township. Oscar warned Rebecca, and she begged her mother to take shelter with her deep in the woods. Rebecca's mother was so afraid of her daughter, and the woods, that she refused to go, and Rebecca refused to leave without her. Oscar was horrified. He tried reasoning and pleading with Rebecca, but she just continued to tell him she would not go without her mother. Oscar was astonished when Rebecca's mother told her she had to leave."

"Her mother?" Keitha asked, similarly surprised.

"You see, in her mother's mind, Rebecca's soul was already lost, and she couldn't let her daughter stay and die knowing that she would be damned to hell. Not when Rebecca could leave and live.

"Rebecca sought shelter in a cave she remembered from her childhood and survived. Her mother died along with most of the other people in the town, and when Rebecca returned to find her mother and bury her, she was confronted by survivors who wanted to know why she had been in the woods. Several recalled the incidents from her childhood and began flinging accusations at her. The hysteria mounted." Greer stopped.

"And?" Keitha asked, not sure if she wanted to know.

"They hanged her for being a witch," he replied somberly.

Keitha inhaled sharply.

"Oscar told Sylvia that it was his fault, that he killed her, because when he went back and checked the records, he found an article about the hanging. He swore to Sylvia that it hadn't been there before, and she tried to tell him that he must have just missed it the first time. The last message he sent her was 'I didn't miss a thing.' Sylvia never heard from him again."

"Do you know what happened to Oscar?"

"We didn't find that out for many more years, but after Oscar's final message, Sylvia's unease about the Machiavellians intensified. She finally told your mother that they had to cease communicating with each other because it was becoming too dangerous. Sylvia had her own mental defense against them, but they were getting stronger. She felt her only option was to break off all communication. She thought if she could isolate herself, she might be able to effectively hide from them and keep them from using her to get to you or your mother. You had just turned ten."

"So the nightmares I had when I was ten, they were about Sylvia?"

Greer stared into the reservoir in silence.

"Damn it, Greer! Were they about Sylvia?" Keitha asked shrilly.

"Yes."

"How could that be? I've never sensed people in our own time."

"Sylvia said you were remarkable."

"I could feel her panic, it was terrifying." Keitha's eyes were wide in remembrance. "Why didn't you and Clara tell me it was real? I could have helped her!"

"We were trying to protect you. We knew you were picking up images from Sylvia, and Clara was afraid that if you understood and tried to reach out to Sylvia, it would lead the Machiavellians right to you."

"But—"

"No buts, Keitha. You were too young to protect yourself, let alone help Sylvia."

"Nothing remotely like that has happened since."

"It isn't uncommon for an ability to fade," Greer said offhandedly.

"Uh-huh," Keitha said unconvinced.

"Clara made it stop. That's what was important."

"You don't think whether Sylvia is alive or dead is important?"

"Of course it is," Greer snapped. "I'm sorry, Keitha, but Sylvia was the one that told your mother we needed to protect you."

Keitha furrowed her brow. "How did Clara make it stop?"

"You remember the nightmares, but not what your mother did?" Greer shook his head. "Are you really that angry with her?"

"Just tell me what she did, Greer."

"She stayed with you every night. You would lay your head in her lap and she would sing to you softly until you fell asleep. If you started to stir, at all, she would stroke your hair and start singing again. Clara didn't get a good night's sleep for a month, but finally you began sleeping straight through, and your mother knew it was over. She knew that either Sylvia had found a safe place or that she had died."

Greer waited patiently as Keitha grappled with the information.

"I don't remember Clara singing to me. Why don't I remember that?"

"I don't know, Keitha. Maybe you haven't wanted to remember."

Keitha grimaced but then asked, "Why would these Machiavellians want to harm a ten year old? What could I possibly have done to them? And why, if Clara protected me so lovingly then, did she push me away five years later?"

Greer's face darkened.

"What happened when I was fifteen, Father?"

CHAPTER 9

G reer finally sat down next to Keitha, but didn't say anything. He just stared around the large cavernous space. Keitha realized that even though his eyes seemed to be searching as if something would suddenly appear from one of the small, hidden recesses in the protruding rock, his mind was really somewhere else. She waited for her father to compose his thoughts, and when Greer spoke, he sounded bleak.

"Your mother never used the telegraph to send out another message. She was too worried about the Machiavellians, but she would check each day to see if something came in, and one day something did."

"At first it was just a rush of noise because it had been so long since Clara had translated the dots and dashes into words. She silently implored the person to send the message again so she would have another chance to decipher the content and, as though the person heard her plea, the message began repeating. I walked into the room, as I had so many times, expecting your mother to look at me with a combination of disappointment and relief; instead, her face was ashen. She began gesturing at me wildly, pointing at her computer pad. I handed it to her, and she began keying in letters and words. She stopped and frantically scanned the screen on the pad as she listened intently to the message for the third time. Finally, Clara took the earpiece out and stared at me. She looked completely despondent. I reached out and took her hand." Greer shuddered involuntarily. "It was cold and I could feel a slight tremor. I managed to say Sylvia's name, as if it was an all-encompassing question. Clara stared past me, her eyes glazed. I wasn't sure she heard me until suddenly she said the message wasn't from Sylvia and handed me the pad."

Keitha's neck muscles tensed. "What did the message say?"

Greer took a small pad from inside one of his deep pockets and held it out to her. "I'll be back in a little while," he said walking away.

Keitha stared at the device and had a fleeting thought of setting it aside, but when her eyes fell on the screen that contained Clara's transcript of the message, she automatically began to read.

My identity is not important, but what I'm about to tell you is. If you pick up this transmission and can understand what I am saying, then I know you will believe me. The code is cumbersome for me so I will make this as short as possible. There are people alive somewhere today that are seeking to establish a mental bond with people from the past so that they can change events that occurred. They are frustrated because, so far, they have not been successful, but they are not going to stop.

Keitha began to pace. Was this message about her and Clara? It couldn't be; they didn't want to change the past. Keitha came to an abrupt halt. Could this person be talking about Oscar? No, no. Whoever sent Clara the message said they had not been successful, and unfortunately, Oscar had changed how Rebecca died. Could this person possibly know about the people Clara and Sylvia called the Machiavellians?

Keitha continued to read.

I know there are other perceptive people out there but for some reason you are hidden, which is why I am risking sending the message out the way my brother taught me.

Even though Keitha had a death grip on the pad, she almost dropped it as she read the voiceless plea contained in the last lines of the message.

Something must be done to stop them. I beg you, if you are still out there, help me.

Keitha's chest started to ache from her rapidly beating heart. She stood absolutely still, closed her eyes, and calmed herself by listening to the faint intermittent lap of the water against the edge of the impoundment. Just as her heart rate began to slow, she heard a noise and spun around. The entry was dark, and the muted illumination from the portable light sitting next to the bench cast eerie shadows where the rock jutted in and out. Keitha watched as one of the shadows pulled away from the wall and stepped forward.

"Jeez, Greer," she squeaked, her sense of dread getting the better of her.

"Sorry, I wanted to let you read it without me hovering over you, but I didn't want to leave you alone," he responded as he walked over to her. "Are you all right?"

"What do you think?" she asked, holding up the pad. "Who sent this? Were they talking about the Machiavellians? I mean, what the hell, Greer?"

"I know it's a lot to take in, Keitha. It was for your mother and me at the time. Clara never told anyone about the Machiavellians, except me, but the person who sent that," Greer gestured at the pad, "obviously knew about them. At least that was our conclusion, and you came to the same one. After all those years of Sylvia struggling to find out what the Machiavellians were trying to do, there it was, right in front of us. They wanted to change the past. Clara knew she had to help the person, but she was concerned about you, because even though she had been able to effectively conceal you since you were ten, at fifteen you were becoming increasingly headstrong, and that made it much more difficult for her."

"Clara concealed me?" Before Greer could respond, Keitha added, "I don't understand any of this. Why wasn't I told? I could have protected myself."

"You wanted us to tell you that you were a potential target for people that we knew little to nothing about? When were we supposed to do that, Keitha? When you were ten? All we wanted was to give you as much of a childhood as possible. Besides, you could never have protected yourself when you were ten."

"Maybe not at ten, but if I was as strong as Sylvia believed, then I certainly should have been told when I was fifteen when you got this." Keitha waved the pad at Greer.

"You showed a lot of skill when you were fifteen," Greer said, "but, as I said, you were also impulsive, Keitha, and like most young people, you thought you were invincible. Hardly the attributes necessary to ensure your own safety."

"I wasn't impulsive."

"How about obstinate and imprudent?" he offered.

"I was just—"

"Young, Keitha," Greer asserted. "You were still young, but you were also at that stage in life where you were so sure you knew the answers to everything."

"You're," Keitha pointed a finger at him, "exaggerating."

"Not by much."

Keitha looked as though she was going to argue but instead asked, "So what did Clara do to help the person, if she was so worried about me?"

"She came up with a plan to help the person and still protect you," Greer stated. "She completely isolated herself and then she lowered the mental barrier she had created. Clara said the barrier was like 'white noise,' a term used to describe—"

"I know what white noise is," Keitha stated.

"Do you also know how demanding, how remarkable, something like that would be to establish, let alone maintain for five years?"

"How would I know anything about how remarkable or demanding it was? This is the first time I've heard any of this." Keitha replied testily.

Greer stared at his daughter sadly. "I know it is, Keitha. I just hope you're beginning to understand why."

"Truthfully? I don't know, but I do want you to finish what you have to tell me."

Greer felt encouraged. "Your mother isolated herself in an area deep within the tunnel system, where no one had been for many years. She placed plugs in her ears, covered her eyes, and put herself into a deep meditative state. She cleared her mind of everything except the person who sent the message, thought only in Morse code, and let nothing else enter her consciousness. She completely blocked everything else out, which is how she protected you. It took two days for him to establish a connection with her."

"Clara can put herself into deep meditation?" Keitha asked surprised.

"She had a little help." Greer said in a deep tone.

"From who? One of the healers?"

"It was a long time ago," he replied, as nonchalantly as he could, because he did not intend to get into that part of the story.

Keitha stared at her father, puzzled by the fact that he didn't seem to remember that detail, but she let it go and asked, "You said he?"

"Yes."

"*He* established the link?"

"Yes, your mother just opened her mind so he could find her. Once he made the connection, Clara didn't need to keep her other senses muted, and it quickly became obvious to her that he needed to find his way here."

"What do you mean find his way here? He was already connected to Clara . . . I don't understand."

"Clara said she had to physically get him here."

"Physically?" Keitha asked stunned.

"Clara insisted that it was imperative that she get him to a safe place. It took her three months, and that whole time she stayed in isolation, away from you, because, above all else, she had to keep you safe."

"That was where she was when Catherine's mother died?" Keitha asked, but it sounded more like an accusation.

"Your mother didn't have any choice. He had already started the journey here, and she could tell he was getting weaker. Clara was afraid to break off the connection, because he wouldn't have been strong enough to re-establish it. He would have been out there alone," Greer pointed towards the surface, "and he would have died." Greer fixed upon his daughter with resolute eyes.

Keitha turned away from her father and walked over to the reservoir. She stared down into the iridescent green water surrounding the submerged ultraviolet light webbing and absently noted that the scheduled maintenances on the web and the ultrasonic equipment was coming up, making the reservoir area inaccessible.

"Keitha," Greer said, coming up behind her. But she would not turn around to look at him. "Your mother knew she could help you once he got here if I could get you to just wait, but you wouldn't. You were angry and determined to prove to your mother that you could do it by yourself."

"I tried because my mother told me that it was critical to try and get through to Catherine when she was the least guarded. When she was open to possibilities," Keitha seethed, "I told you that Catherine could sense her mother, that it was a perfect opportunity to try again, but I needed Clara's help. All you told me was that she was working on a very important project for the colony. A project that was more important than helping me."

"I told you it was critical and sensitive, not that it was more important than you," he said defensively, but when he saw the hurt in his daughter's eyes he added, "I realize that it must have sounded the same to someone as young as you were."

"Stop saying how young I was," Keitha roared. "Do you really think that excuses the fact that both of you hid the truth from me for *all* these years?"

"There is more to it, Keitha," Greer replied.

She didn't seem to be paying attention to him. "Where is this man that Clara helped? He's not in our colony. So where is he?" Keitha demanded, but Greer said nothing. "He didn't survive, did he? No one could survive a journey like that," she said with certainty.

"I traveled at night."

Keitha spun around and stared at the man standing in the entryway holding another lantern and said, "You!"

"And I had protective gear," Terran continued without acknowledging her astonishment. "I found shelters to use in the day with the help of Clara. I had some food, and amazingly I was able to find other sustenance to keep me going, again with Clara's help, but what with the amount of time it took me to get here, I was in pretty bad shape when I finally arrived."

Keitha stared at him without blinking.

"You're making me uncomfortable," Terran noted.

"I'm making *you* uncomfortable?" Keitha retorted.

"Yes . . . well, I'm sure you have a lot of questions. I think it would save time if I just tell you what happened."

"Shut up. Just give me a minute, will you," Keitha said, massaging her temples with her index fingers.

Terran glanced at Greer, who could only stare at him wide-eyed, trying to convey an approaching danger but unable to articulate what it was. Terran, baffled, turned back to Keitha, and there was such fierceness in her eyes that he took an involuntary step back, as though she had pushed him.

"So you were in on this conspiracy of silence with Clara and Greer," she fumed.

Terran stared at the older man.

"Don't look at him, you little shit!"

"Don't call me that," Terran said, biting back.

"What made you come down here, Terran?" Greer asked, in an attempt to diffuse the situation.

"Well, she," Terran indicated, pointing towards Keitha with a flick of his head, "looked pretty agitated when she came by the archives and said she wouldn't be back for the rest of the day. I went by your room to see if anyone knew what was going on and found Clara just sitting in her chair staring . . . at nothing really. She wouldn't talk to me, so I decided I had better find you. I tried the gardens first, and George told me to try here."

"So you decided to enter the lair without knowing what was going on? Either brave or foolish," Greer observed.

"I didn't know she'd be here. Let alone that you'd be talking to her about what happened."

"Does he know everything?" Keitha asked her father, tensely.

"I was directly involved. How would I not know?" Terran replied.

"I wasn't asking you," she stated.

"Keitha," Greer warned. "Terran needs to tell you his story."

Keitha narrowed her eyes but said, "Fine, tell me your story."

Terran looked over her shoulder at Greer.

Greer nodded.

"Well?" Keitha pressed.

"My brother Oscar was an amazing man." Terran began, his voice faltering slightly, but remaining in control. "He was ten years older than me, and I think he always had the ability to perceive the world without boundaries.

He was certain that I would experience what he did and wanted to prepare me, make me better than he was." Terran shook his head. "He was mistaken, I couldn't be better because I never had all of his abilities."

"He could perceive the past and the present, and your perception is limited," Keitha deduced.

Terran nodded. "Oscar told me about everything he saw in the past, and he saw so many things, but never in context, until he made contact with Rebecca." Terran said the name with obvious affection.

"Just like Clara and Catherine," Keitha noted.

"Yes."

"And Oscar felt strongly toward Rebecca?" Keitha asked, raising an eyebrow.

Terran's eyes hardened. "She was the love of his life. I know what you're thinking. How can a man today love a woman that lived centuries before he was even born? All I can tell you is he did, and I'm sure she loved him as well."

Keitha fidgeted uncomfortably.

"What is bothering you?" Terran asked bluntly.

"It's just . . . well . . . they were related."

Terran's barking laugh took Keitha by surprise. "That's what you're focused on? Really?"

"Well, he could have been in love with his great-great, whatever, grandmother."

"Rebecca died, childless," he said harshly, "and not that it matters, but Oscar said they didn't share very many genetic markers." Terran turned to Greer. "Didn't you tell her?"

"I told her about the DNA; I thought the fact that Rebecca died childless was obvious."

"All right, so I misspoke about the great grandmother lineage, but I just don't see how Oscar could have been so sure that they didn't share very much DNA," Keitha insisted.

"He wasn't, Rebecca was," Terran said.

"She understood genetics?" Keitha asked, astonished.

"Not in those terms. Oscar was like you, he thought there would have to be a substantial linear familial connection, like the branches of a single tree.

Rebecca told him that she thought it was more like puppies. Some puppies obviously belong to a specific breed, like spaniels. However, if a spaniel bred with a hound, and a puppy from that litter bred with a third breed, eventually there would be a puppy who didn't look at all like a spaniel, but the puppy would still have a little spaniel in it, somewhere. Rebecca said some people needed to be a spaniel in order to recognize another spaniel, but some people who were spaniels could recognize the traits of a spaniel, even in the most mixed mutt."

"So she was the spaniel and your brother was the mutt?" Keitha tried not to grin.

"Oh yes, that was definitely the case."

"She recognized the spaniel in Oscar."

"Yes, not only recognized it, found it." Terran stared at Greer. "Didn't you explain *any* of this to her?"

"I did," Greer stated. "You see, she doesn't think Catherine is capable, so I think she would rather also believe that Rebecca wasn't."

"Well, believe me when I tell you this," Terran addressed Keitha severely, "I was in awe of my brother's abilities, but Oscar said they paled in comparison to Rebecca's. He said she was a nexus: everything just came together within her. She understood how things interacted in the world around her and the world beyond her, and that she was truly amazing. I suppose that's why Oscar felt compelled to save her." Terran looked away for a moment to compose himself before proceeding. "Rebecca told Oscar that it was very important for me to 'know my time.' Even though he had been training me, when Rebecca said that, he really started to push, but I was fifteen, and you know how it is when you're fifteen." He stared at Keitha, his face creased with sorrow. "I thought I had plenty of time. I didn't put in the hours that Oscar wanted me to, and a year later Rebecca died, and Oscar walked away from our colony."

"Walked away?" Keitha asked.

"Oscar was racked with guilt. He told me that his interference in her life caused Rebecca to suffer needlessly."

"She would have died in a horrible storm in any case," Keitha noted rationally.

"With her mother, not alone, on a gallows with people she knew scream-ing at her . . . cursing her," Terran's voice caught, "spitting on her. Oscar saw it all."

"Then she wasn't alone. Oscar was with her."

Terran gave Keitha a miserable look. "Oscar saw what was happening to her, but he couldn't feel her, couldn't feel her emotions, so he was sure she couldn't feel him."

"I don't understand."

"Rebecca shut him off."

"Because she couldn't forgive him?" Keitha conjectured. "She must have blamed him for telling her about the storm."

"She didn't blame him!" Terran yelled. "She loved him and wanted to keep him from experiencing something that she thought would devastate him."

"You can't possibly know that!" Keitha yelled back.

"She told him that it was her last wish that he not witness her death," Terran said through clinched teeth." She must have known he wouldn't be able to fulfill it, that he would want to be with her, so she shut him out of her mind to try to spare him. She didn't know that Oscar would be able to see everything, and that alone destroyed him. He was practically out of his mind with grief and guilt. I didn't know how to help, and then one day I just couldn't find him. I searched the entire colony. He was gone, but nothing else was missing, no protective equipment, no food, no water."

Keitha gasped.

"I told you I wasn't the best protégé," Terran continued, without acknowl-edging Keitha's astonishment. "All I ever seemed to get was flashes every once in a while, nothing clear. But afterward there was nothing, absolutely nothing. I convinced myself that I was better off. Years went by, and one day I started to hear bits and pieces of conversation, actual conversations. The bits and pieces gradually became more cohesive, but even so, all I could tell was that the people talking were perceptives, and that they were very intent on planning . . . something; for all I knew it could have been a celebration. Until one day I heard them very clearly. It was like getting hit by a blast of hot, putrid air, but once I understood what they were attempting to do, and why, I knew they had to be stopped. I also knew, because Oscar told me about the messages from Sylvia, it had to be the perceptives she called aggressive. I had to warn her, so I scrambled to relearn enough of the code they used to send her a message. I got Clara instead."

"According to what Greer told me, that would have been after Sylvia stopped communicating with Clara and blocked her out," Keitha said.

"I wasn't aware of that, not then. Clara and Greer told me when I got here."

"Your message wasn't just meant for Sylvia."

"It was meant for anyone who knew the code."

"So Sylvia told Oscar about Clara, which is why you said you knew there were *more* perceptives. You couldn't sense us, because Clara's white noise kept everyone out."

"Are you just thinking out loud or do you have a point?"

Keitha studied him. "Why did you risk the journey here? You and Clara could have continued communicating through the telegraph."

"I decided he needed to come here." Clara's voice floated over to them from the entrance. "He needed help before the Machiavellians sensed him. That kind of training couldn't be done over the telegraph."

CHAPTER 10

Terran and Keitha turned in unison and saw Clara enveloped in a surreal glow. They stared blankly as Greer stepped from behind Clara holding the lantern in his hand.

"When did you leave?" Keitha asked, when she found her voice.

"While the two of you were bickering. You didn't even notice that I took one of the lanterns with me."

"We weren't bickering," Keitha asserted.

"Really? Then you were doing a very good impression."

"This was a mistake," Clara commented to Greer as she turned to leave.

Greer held her shoulders as he addressed Keitha and Terran. "I convinced Clara to come down here so that she could tell both of you the rest."

"The rest? You don't want me to finish?" Terran asked perplexed.

"I thought you would be finished," Greer stated.

"Let's get this over with," Clara said in a disembodied tone that made Keitha's skin crawl. "Have you told her about the timelines?" she asked Terran.

He shook his head.

"Then tell her," Clara instructed.

Keitha turned slightly so that she could face Terran.

"I had no idea that Clara would attempt to open her mind up to me. I was expecting a coded message. I didn't want to send my message again; repeating it the way I did seemed like enough of a risk. So each day I just sat by the telegraph and waited. I was ready to give up when I was inexplicably overwhelmed by this prickly sensation."

"Clara," Keitha said with certainty.

"No, it wasn't her." Terran's face contorted.

A chill ran through Keitha, causing her to shudder.

"The sensation kept escalating," Terran went on, "as though needles were being stuck all over my body, my nervous system was firing uncontrollably. Then it stopped and I was suddenly seeing two things occurring at the same time, one right on top of the other, and because they overlapped, neither was completely in focus. I became locked in this endless cycle where the two distorted impressions just kept whirling in my head. It was horrible. I thought I would lose my mind when," Terran glanced at Clara, "fortunately, I did sense your mother, so serene and confident. I was on the brink of collapsing into a mental abyss, and Clara anchored me. The chaos began to stabilize as one of the images became clear, and the other faded into the background until it disappeared entirely."

"You saw two timelines?" Keitha asked skeptically.

"Yes."

"How?"

"I told you, with the help of Clara, and because I had more of my brother's abilities than I thought."

"He said he knew that the article about the hanging wasn't there when he looked through the records the first time," Keitha said with eyes wide open. "He saw both timelines."

Terran nodded.

"So what did you see?" Keitha asked excitedly.

"I saw them, but I didn't retain both."

"Wait a minute, if you didn't retain both, how can you be sure there were two?"

"Because I remember the chaos, and the second timeline is still somewhere in my mind; I just can't get at it. I guess you'd call it a defense mechanism."

"A defense mechanism? Against what?"

Terran looked away.

"Tell her," Clara instructed.

"When I felt the Machiavellians attempt to change the past . . . I wasn't the only one that had a problem. I heard a person screaming for someone to 'make it stop.' I could feel, for an instant that seemed to go on forever, what was happening in the person's mind. It was like seeing someone else's nightmare," Terran said softly, "but one that you've had yourself. The person was having the same problem separating the two timelines, but they didn't have anyone to help them, and everything just kept replaying, looping, interweaving."

"It must have ended, it couldn't possibly go on and on like that, it would drive a person mad." Keitha stopped abruptly.

An uneasy silence filled the room.

"Why did you say they attempted to change the past, if you saw two timelines?" Keitha asked warily.

"How about their attempt didn't get them what they wanted. Is that better?"

Keitha's eyes started to flick back and forth and her heart started to race. She pointed an accusing finger at Terran. "Are you saying that this," Keitha waved her hands around as her voice grew hostile, "is not the way things were . . . originally. That we've been living this life because of something the Machiavellians caused when I was fifteen?"

"No, I'm not saying that. I don't think what they did drastically changed anything."

"You can't know that. If you felt two timelines, and one went away, then the one that was left had to have changed." Keitha was trying to maintain control but she was close to screaming at him.

"Yes, but it doesn't mean there was a significant change. Oscar tried to keep Rebecca from dying, yet all he managed to do was change the way she died, that and the newspaper account of what happened."

"That isn't all that changed," Keitha said incredulously. "Your brother died because he was so guilt ridden, and who knows what his death may have changed."

"You don't think I thought of that?" Terran stated harshly, his face clouding over. "I've gone over every conceivable scenario so many times," lowering his voice. "My brother might have been just as racked with guilt if he had done nothing to try to save Rebecca. I'll never know, and since I can't remember the two timelines I sensed, you're right: I have no idea how much might have actually been changed. What I do know is that the Machiavellians are not done, they want power, and they did not achieve that goal."

"Once again, how can you be so sure, if you don't know what changed?" Keitha asked, challenging his contention.

"If they succeeded, why would they still be trying?" he countered, arching his eyebrow at her.

"Stop arguing about it," Clara said edgily. "We'll never know, not with any certainty, so just finish telling her your story."

"You're right," Terran said. "When I got here I was in pretty bad shape. Malnourished, dehydrated, and even with protective gear and some form of shelter during the day, I still sustained skin damage. I have some permanent souvenirs, and no one knows what will happen as the years go by, but I was extremely lucky that this colony had such accomplished healers. After I regained some of my strength, Clara began to train me. She said it was all a matter of concentration, meditation, and discipline."

"I know how Clara trains people," Keitha said impatiently. "What I don't understand is why she couldn't train us both?"

"It was my fault," he said. "I was so raw and inexperienced, and when I told Clara that I knew the Machiavellians weren't going to give up, she knew she had to concentrate on developing my skills."

"Please," Keitha scoffed. "Clara could have trained ten people, if she wanted to."

"Please, yourself, Keitha," Greer retorted. "How was your mother supposed to train you when you refused to talk to her after she returned. You went so far as to move out of the rooms we shared back then."

"She was gone for five months without any explanation," Keitha observed coolly. "Now I know that the first three were spent getting him here"—she pointed a finger in Terran's direction—"and I assume the other two were spent getting him immersed in training."

"The other two were spent helping the healers with Terran's recovery and starting his training."

"Yeah, all I did was spend those five months wondering why my mother couldn't spare some time to help me try to get through to Catherine. Oh yeah, I almost forgot, I also turned sixteen while she was gone."

Greer saw Clara grimace, and his voice became rigid. "After Terran told Clara everything he knew about the Machiavellians," he hesitated, "I've never seen your mother so frightened."

"Greer, don't," Clara said, reaching out to grab his arm.

"She needs to know," he said, patting her hand before directing his attention back to Keitha. "The Machiavellians' plan is insidious. They don't want the person they connect with in the past to know who they really are. They want the person to believe that they are a manifestation that is guiding them."

"A manifestation of what?"

"A divine being, a beloved person who has died, it doesn't matter, as long as the person accepts the false face they present."

"Why would they do something like that?" Keitha asked.

"If the Machiavellians convince the person to trust them unconditionally, then that person might do whatever they ask, no matter how objectionable they might otherwise find the task."

"If a person would object to it under normal circumstances—"

"A being from their belief structure, or a trusted loved one, talking to them," Terran broke in. "There wouldn't be anything remotely normal about it."

"Especially if the Machiavellians told them that if they didn't carry out the task there would be dire consequences," Greer added.

"You mean for the person?" Keitha asked. "You think the Machiavellians would threaten the person?"

"They would threaten whatever meant the most to the person," Terran stated. "Not directly, mind you: the *danger* would lie in what would happen if the person failed to act."

Keitha still looked uncertain, so Terran continued, "Remember that paper you ran across, the one about whether people back in Catherine's time, knowing what happened in World War II, would have killed Adolph Hitler if they were given the chance?"

Keitha nodded hesitantly.

"What if a person who lived in Hitler's time was told what would happen and that they could prevent all the atrocities, but the person who had to die to avert the violence was Albert Einstein?"

Keitha began to feel nauseous. "All right, all right, I can understand how that would scare Clara."

"Scared her? It terrified her." Terran glanced at Clara. "If they are willing to do that, can you imagine what the Machiavellians would be willing to do if they ever found out that there were other people, living in this time, who could also reach into the past and who wanted to stop them?"

Keitha shuddered and closed her eyes.

"Clara knew it was more important than ever that you be protected," Terran said.

Keitha rubbed her temples. She seemed to be contemplating what Terran had said, but then her eyes flew open. "Why do I remember you being in our colony before I was fifteen?" she asked.

"I think maybe we need to take a break. This has obviously been a little too much for you to process all at once," Greer stated.

"Don't patronize me, Greer. I remember when Terran left to work on the reserve reservoir project. I was twelve."

"I was the one who convinced your father that it had to be done," Clara said. "If you want to blame anyone, blame me."

"Blame you for what? What had to be done?" Keitha asked anxiously.

"You said you wanted her to know." Clara stared at Greer with compassion in her eyes. "This is part of it. You had to know it would come up. Keitha forgets only what she wants to forget."

Keitha felt the familiar, irritating prickling that occurred whenever Clara's words struck her as unkind or harsh, but she wasn't about to let it distract her this time.

"What is Clara talking about, Greer?"

Greer didn't look at his daughter; instead he stared at Clara, who merely raised a challenging eyebrow. He dipped his head to her as though conceding, but then turned to Keitha and said, "Terran understated his condition when he said he was in pretty rough shape when he finally got here. He was close to dead, drifting in and out of consciousness for days, ranting incoherently. That was why your mother stayed to help the healers. They thought she could help calm him, but he just kept repeating, 'They can't know, they can't know; too many minds, too much risk.' It wasn't until his fever broke that he was finally able to explain to your mother his fear. Terran said that if everyone in our colony knew about him, about what he could do, and why he was here, the sheer number of collective minds would be enough to alert the Machiavellians, and if they found him, they would find the two of you. Clara could only see two options: seclude Terran from the rest of the colony, which wasn't practical, or ask me for assistance."

"I don't understand how could you assist?" Keitha asked.

"Have you ever run across any reference to people from the past called hypnotists?"

Keitha shook her head.

"Some hypnotists were performers that used relaxation techniques to 'put people under,' a term they used for putting people into a type of trance. The hypnotist would then make suggestions, usually silly ones, meant to entertain an audience. Clucking like a chicken when a specific word was spoken seemed to be a favorite."

"You're joking." Keitha said.

"I'm not," Greer assured her. "However, hypnosis was also used in areas like dentistry and child birth to relieve pain, and by some in psychoanalysis to help people recall repressed memories, events buried in their psyches. The practice came under intense scrutiny in the later 1900s when critics charged that people weren't recounting actual events but events suggested by the therapist."

"You mean they believed something that wasn't really true?" Keitha asked warily, suddenly uncomfortable with the direction of the conversation.

"People respond to suggestion differently. At one point psychologists or researchers actually ranked people high, medium, low; or 1–10, you get the idea. They thought that some of the difference had to do with whether or not the person was actively involved in the process, if they were open to the suggestion," Greer said.

"What are you saying, Greer?" Keitha asked, edgily. "Are you saying you can hypnotize people?"

"I was almost thirteen," Greer said, wanting his daughter to understand, "when, right in the middle of math class, one of the other students asked the teacher a botany question just as I was thinking about the gardens. I thought it was a weird coincidence, but it kept happening, so I decided to design an experiment. I made up an outlandish story in my mind about an event that we were studying and thought about it over and over on the day the teacher was quizzing us. Every student answered every question incorrectly but every answer matched my made-up version. What made it worse was that our teacher, who was obviously puzzled by the answers, didn't know why he was puzzled. I went to Donal—who as a council member oversaw the course work—and asked to be relieved of my final schooling. I had no family to object, and both of the teachers agreed that it would be the best thing for me . . . because I wanted them to agree. I needed them to let me go because I couldn't be around my classmates anymore.

"I didn't understand why at the time, but Donal agreed, even though no other child had ever been allowed to quit. He even got me the internship in the gardens, where he worked at that time. The quiet tranquility and the friendship of two very important people helped me suppress the ability for a while. But two years later I lost control. That was when Donal took me to see an old woman." Greer's voice grew very soft. "She looked ancient. She was blind, her body contorted by arthritis, and she was remarkable. I pleaded with her to destroy the ability, rip it out of me, but she told me that was impossible, it was a part of me, ingrained in my very being; I had to learn how to control it instead of letting it control me. She taught me everything she knew, and when I returned to the colony, I used her training to bury the ability deep within me. I didn't want it to be a part of me, and I lived as though it never was, until Clara came to me and asked for my help."

Keitha stared back and forth between her parents. She felt numb, and yet her head throbbed painfully. "By help, you mean she asked you to get everyone in our colony to believe that Terran had always been here," Keitha asserted. "You hypnotized everyone? Planted a false memory?" She was starting to sound more and more distressed. "How could you do that?"

"Your father did it to help," Clara insisted when she saw that Greer was not going to respond. "Just as our healers use the power of the mind to control pain and help in the healing process."

"You're comparing what the healers do to what the two of you did?" Keitha asked in disbelief.

"What they did," Terran said testily, "was save me and you and possibly this entire colony."

"Saved? That's a bit melodramatic, don't you think?"

"You're still alive and sane, thanks to them," Terran said, glaring at her.

Keitha's arms tingled, and she could feel an almost palpable charge in the air. "Sane?" her voice shook.

"You were so absorbed with being the tragic teenager, you had no idea how dangerous the situation was," Terran said.

Keitha's eyes flashed. "I would have known," she roared, "if I had been told!"

"That is exactly why you couldn't be told," Terran retorted. "You were too volatile then and you're still too volatile."

"I'm not the one who couldn't control his emotions after his brother died, the one who couldn't hold onto two timelines." Keitha was jabbing her finger at him, as though it was a sword. "The one responsible for making Greer do whatever it was that Greer did to make us all think you were a member of our colony."

"Stop it!" Greer yelled so loudly that he startled Keitha and Terran into silence. "I'll tell you exactly what I did, Keitha. The emergency reservoir and conduit system along with the connecting tunnel was under construction when Terran arrived. The project took four years, and the crews were rotated with the people living at the construction site, not in the main colony. There were three people there from start to finish. I added one more, and when the construction was completed the colony welcomed four people back instead of three."

"You created the idea that Terran had been working on the construction for four years and everyone thought it was real." Keitha was simultaneously impressed and alarmed.

"Terran actually worked on the project for several months, so the idea had a basis in reality," Greer stated.

"But he never actually lived in this colony before that," Keitha said, struggling to grasp what had transpired.

"The perception was that he did."

"Everyone thought they knew him?"

"There were some people that weren't as responsive to the suggestion and didn't recognize him, but so many others did, they just decided that he had changed or they just hadn't known him very well because he was young."

"They went along with the recollections of everyone else even though their memories were actually correct?"

"Group memory can be a strange thing."

Keitha shook her head and asked, "What about the three people he supposedly was with during the four years? What about them?"

"Terran had a very specific assignment that meant he only interacted with them occasionally."

"You say it like it was real," Keitha said, disconcerted.

"For a little while it was."

"Don't dismiss it that way, Father. You made people believe he had been working on the reservoir system the entire time."

"I did not *make* anyone believe it. I suggested it."

"That's just semantics."

"No it isn't, Keitha," Clara stated firmly. "I read documents that talked about brain washing, mind control, or reprogramming. Manipulating a person's mind by exploiting a weakness or, in the extreme, breaking a person's mind using drugs or torture that was mental, physical, or both. Although your father has a very strong ability, he suggests, he does not make."

"Well, his very strong ability means that everyone thinks that Terran has *always* been a part of our colony, including me." Keitha couldn't hide the resentment in her voice.

"Not everyone," Clara said, refuting Keitha's statement. "The healers were not influenced by Greer either directly or through the group memory. However, they have their own means of shrouding their minds, and once they knew about the Machiavellians, they agreed with our course of action. As for you, your perception wasn't altered."

"I remember him," Keitha insisted.

"Really? Tell me what you remember."

Keitha's face twisted into a scowl. "I just remember him being . . . around."

"You really don't have any memory of Terran 'being around.' You just didn't care enough to figure that out."

"All these years you let me believe a monumental lie," Keitha said reproachfully.

Clara raised an eyebrow. "You let yourself believe, and monumental or not, it was necessary, and I will not apologize for asking your father to do something that in the end protected everyone."

"Really, Clara?" Keitha inquired. "The ends justify the means?"

"Tell me, Keitha," Clara countered, "who was harmed?"

"People believe something that isn't true."

"That I lived here longer than I did," Terran said. "What difference does that possibly make?"

"No matter how benign you think the lie was, the fact remains that an entire group of people believe something that isn't true, all to keep you hidden from the Machiavellians."

"Stop insisting that what Clara and Greer did was just to keep me safe," Terran snapped. "They did it to keep the Machiavellians from finding a way into the minds of the people of this colony, to keep everyone safe. You were the most vulnerable of anyone."

"Why don't you stop insisting that Greer did it because of me?"

"I did it," Greer stated firmly, "because I feared that if the Machiavellians found one of us, they would find all of us. That they would do anything they could to stop us from interfering with their plans. I feared that if they had someone like me, they wouldn't hesitate to break a person's mind. You may judge me for having done what I did, but I could not stand by and do nothing. I could not bury my head and hope that nothing bad happened, when it was clear to me that inaction would make things so much worse."

"And no matter what you would like to tell yourself, Keitha," Clara said quietly, "you were especially vulnerable. You were so angry with me that you refused any type of training, you stopped meditating, you weren't sleeping well—you just kept spiraling out of control." Clara stared at her daughter with regret. "No one could get through to you."

"Why didn't you just tell me what was happening?" Keitha implored. "If you had, everything might not have become so broken."

"Terran asked me to tell you, and Greer has badgered me for many years. I refused, and I made them swear not to tell you."

"Why?" Keitha's voice broke.

"It took you a while to get yourself under control, but when you finally let your father help, you managed."

"I know what Greer did for me, but you could have helped me even more. Why weren't you there?"

"I wanted to be there for you . . ." Clara's throat tightened with emotion. She tensed and took several steps back, as if trying to distance herself from the pain.

Greer continued for her, "The bond you and Clara shared when you were a child was amazing. You could sense each other so effortlessly." He smiled at the memory.

"I remember the connection Clara and I shared, Greer. That's what made it so difficult for me when I couldn't get through to her when I needed her most."

Greer's face clouded over. "I told you that Clara had to be in complete isolation in order to get Terran here."

"I know that now," Keitha said sadly.

"Well, you also need to know that it was the reason why Clara developed and maintained the mental barrier in the first place. She was not about to let the Machiavellians find you through her, even though the emotional and physical toll on your mother was unbelievable." Greer looked around for Clara, who had wandered over to the reservoir. "Getting Terran here weakened her even further," he said quietly.

"Weakened? Clara?" The idea stunned Keitha.

"Yes, and because of that Clara was afraid she wouldn't be strong enough to re-establish the mental barrier when she got back to the colony. It didn't take long for her to realize that your anger was continuing to block your connection, and she also knew that if the connection between the two of you remained severed, it would be virtually impossible for the Machiavellians to find you. It was the best possible protection Clara could give you, so she did nothing to stop you from hating her."

"She did more than that, Greer," Keitha said unhappily. "She grew distant, cold."

"Clara was afraid you'd forgive her, so she drove the wedge in very deep."

"What?" Keitha asked. "Why? Surely she could have re-established the barrier once she recovered her strength. There was no reason for this to go on for this long," Keitha said, distressed.

"She tried, Keitha." Greer stared at his daughter. "Clara expended too much energy between maintaining the barrier and rescuing Terran. It's why she doesn't see the past any longer."

"I thought she just couldn't see Catherine."

"When is the last time you've heard Clara mention anything that she saw or heard."

"I . . . I . . ." Keitha stammered, turning toward the reservoir, but her mother was nowhere in sight. Confused, Keitha turned back to Greer. "Why now? Why are you telling me all of this now even though Clara didn't want you to?"

"You were developing into a remarkable perceptive, just as Sylvia said you would, but your anger interfered. It has made you less than what you should have been. Clara said you were still strong enough to establish a connection with Catherine, but she was wrong. We need you to get through to Catherine, and you need Clara's help to do it, but you would never have agreed, so you needed to be told."

"Why is it so important to get through to Catherine? Why doesn't Clara help me connect with Molly or Shi`Ma, at least they understood their ability?"

"No, Keitha, it has to be Catherine."

"Why?"

"Because Catherine is somehow connected to what the Machiavellians are trying to do."

CHAPTER 11

Henry woke up and realized Catherine was already up. Her night roaming had tapered off and finally ceased entirely by the end of July, and with it, he thought, went some of her grief. But he was wrong. He didn't know that when Catherine stopped sensing her father she would experience a different kind of sorrow, one laced with despair.

Henry got out of bed and started up the stairs, which led to the main floor of the house. Before Catherine and Henry decided to get married, in the spring of 1995, they jointly bought a bungalow style house in an old neighborhood on the southern edge of downtown Denver. It was, more or less, in its original configuration, except that the previous owners had converted the basement into a family room. It only took one summer in the house for Catherine and Henry to decide that they didn't need a living room upstairs and a family room downstairs; what they needed was a cooler bedroom. They had the house revamped, replacing the family room downstairs with a master bedroom, half bath, and laundry. Upstairs they kept the living room, dining room, kitchen, spare bedroom, and main bathroom, but they reapportioned the main bedroom into a combination office/library and small second bathroom.

Henry plodded down the hallway and around a corner. Catherine was at the kitchen table sipping coffee and idly thumbing through the newspaper.

"Bad night?" he asked, kissing the top of her head.

Catherine looked up from her coffee and shrugged. "Sort of," she said. The deep circles under her eyes made her face look haunted.

"Nothing to do with . . ."

"No, nothing to do with my dad," she replied with a lingering sadness. "Just kind of a weird dream; I don't really remember it, except I swore I heard my name being called. It made it hard to go back to sleep." She gave him a lopsided, half-hearted smile.

Henry had never known Catherine not to remember at least part of her dreams, but he decided not to push her. "What would you like for breakfast?" he asked brightly.

"I'm not all that hungry."

"You need something. Toast, cereal, popcorn?" When Catherine found most food unappealing, popcorn would sometimes come to the rescue.

"I'll try a piece of toast."

"Sounds good." Henry knew she was only trying to appease him but placed two pieces of bread in the toaster anyway and turned back to her. "So what should we do to celebrate Labor Day?"

"Hmmm, let me think. How about the same thing we've always done on Labor Day."

"A hike?"

"Don't sound so surprised."

"I just didn't know if you'd be up to it." Henry extracted a jar of jelly from the refrigerator and held it up. Catherine nodded her approval. "Where to?" he asked, just as the toast popped up.

"Well, it's not like we've gotten out a lot this summer. What with me being a blob and all. So I think we can go pretty much anywhere."

Henry spread the jelly on the toast, placed one piece on a napkin, and handed it to her. "The goal should be just to enjoy the day. Agreed?"

"Agreed." Catherine managed an actual smile. "How about we find a completely new trail? Somewhere we never went with Connor. I couldn't stand thinking about him and my dad." Her eyes brimmed with tears.

"How about we head up 285 and just see what looks good," Henry said, trying to divert her attention from thoughts of their greyhound, but his own mind strayed.

Back in 1996, after all of the renovations to their house were complete, Catherine said it was time to add a dog to the household, one that needed a home. Henry knew "one that needed a home" came from an article Catherine had shared with him about greyhounds that were often sold to laboratories or outright killed after their racing days were over, and even though he had never had a dog in his life, he was game. They submitted an application to an adoption group, and in March of that same year, they brought home a big, beautiful five-year-old red brindle greyhound.

One of the first things that struck both Catherine and Henry about the dog, besides his stately bearing and large responsive brown eyes, was that he didn't respond to his racing name or the nickname he had been given at the track kennel. Catherine said they had to figure out what his real name was, and because Henry knew the story of the dog she grew up with, he knew what she meant.

The dog Catherine grew up with was found abandoned on a ship docked in California and, through a convoluted series of events, ended up with her family in Montana. The veterinarian that examined him said that the dog had some old wounds that looked like he had endured numerous cruelties, in addition to being left to starve. Catherine's family had no idea what breed or mix of breeds the dog was, but his size, a robust twenty pounds when he filled out, belied the fact that he had the survival instincts and self-confidence of the leader of a wolf pack. It made the moniker Skippy, which he had been saddled with before he came to live with them, completely absurd. Catherine's dad started calling him Murphy, and the dog responded as if it had been his name all along. And many years later, when Catherine happened upon the meaning of the name, she understood why. Murphy meant sea warrior.

After almost a full afternoon of research and trial and error, Catherine and Henry determined that their greyhound was Connor, with an 'o,' because it meant 'much wanted,' which he was, and when he died of bone cancer at ten and a half, it broke their hearts.

"How does that sound?" Catherine was staring at him, her head cocked to one side.

"How does what sound?" Henry had no idea what she had said.

"Where were you?" she inquired.

"You know . . . just thinking."

"Yeah, I know," she concurred. "I've been thinking . . ."

"About?" he prodded.

"Maybe it's time we adopt another dog."

"Are you sure?" he asked, stunned by the sudden turn of events.

"You don't want to?"

"It's not that. It's just . . . are you sure you're ready? I mean what with your dad, and everything else, are you sure it's the best time?"

"You don't think it is?"

"I think your heart has to be in it."

Her eyes misted. "You're right, it wouldn't be fair to bring a dog into our house right now."

Henry's heart lurched as he watched her dab at her eyes with the napkin he had put the toast on. "No, no, don't listen to me. You just took me by surprise, that's all. If you're ready, hell yes, I'm ready," he said enthusiastically.

"We'll think about it." She got up slowly and took her coffee cup over to the sink. When she turned around Henry was standing in front of her.

"Catherine, we should call the adoption group."

"It's been too long, they won't remember us. They won't have our original adoption papers."

"So we'll put in new papers."

"Look, Henry, I know what you meant by the 'and everything else' statement. When Connor lived with us you were a professor teaching atmospheric science, and you were home almost every night. Now you're sometimes gone for weeks at a time."

"I know. I'm sorry."

"Don't be. There's a reason why you kept being asked to provide your expertise. Between your early work on dispersion modeling and the research you did at the university, people would have been crazy not to continuously tap you for your opinion. And, don't forget, I agreed completely when you decided you had to consult full time."

"I'm not sure either of us realized the full extent of the time commitment that it would turn into."

Catherine patted his face, actually his beard, which time had turned from dark brown to white, and yet, the inexplicable red that had always outlined the beard remained, although time had also seen fit to dampen that once red fire down to an auburn ember. His red hair had also cooled to the same auburn color. The change prompted Catherine to remark that he was looking more and more like the endangered Red Panda with each passing day. Henry's mother, a geneticist, after looking up a picture of the animal, had agreed. Henry rebuffed the idea as pure exaggeration and made them swear not to repeat such slander to friend or foe. Secretly he knew that if his eyebrows ever turned white there would be no denying the resemblance and the beard, at the very least, would have to go.

"I wouldn't worry about it; it isn't like where I work is low key," she said lightly. "I'm just lucky that I get to work behind the scenes."

"Seriously, Catherine, if we adopt right now, I'm afraid you would end up with a lot more of the responsibility."

"I know that."

"Have you considered all of the long hours you've had to put in lately?"

"Lately? My hours have never been nine-to-five, Henry."

"Catherine, you know what I'm talking about."

"Maybe we won't have to put up with a second term of the merry environmental deregulators and the let's-deny-the-science gang that occupy the White House, and our work lives will slow to the old frenzied pace."

Henry looked skeptical.

"Hey, it could happen."

"I doubt if his stance on the environment is going to be the make or break issue for the voters."

"Tell me, Henry, when has the environment *ever* been the make or break issue in a presidential election? I'm not delusional, but I do think that this administration has more than just a stance on the environment: they have actively ignored, watered down, or outright blocked the science from being reported. People need to remember that practically right after he got into office, he asked the National Academy of Science to go back and re-evaluate the issue of human activity and greenhouse gases. And when that report stated, and I quote, 'Greenhouse gases are accumulating in Earth's atmosphere as a result of human activities, causing surface air temperatures and subsurface ocean temperatures to rise,' his administration hung their hats on another statement in the same report that said, and I quote again, 'but we cannot rule out that some significant part of these changes are also a reflection of natural variability.' The intent was to point out that science has to address all aspects of a problem, not just one, and just because other contributions are acknowledged, that acknowledgement doesn't lessen, or negate, one of the primary variables. And that variable is human beings. Yet, the administration twisted the statement into meaning that the science was uncertain."

"I know, Catherine," Henry offered. He also knew that because of her memory—which she steadfastly refused to call photographic—whenever she specifically quoted something it was almost, if not completely, verbatim.

"Do you think people will care that the administration stated that the Kyoto Protocol was dead even before that report came out? Or that they *removed* the entire chapter on global warming from the EPA report in 2002?"

Henry cocked his head to one side.

"Yeah, neither do I."

"I thought we were talking about adopting a dog."

"You were the one that brought up my work schedule."

"Both of our schedules," Henry corrected. "I just wanted to talk about what it could mean for the dog, because, and don't shoot the messenger, I don't think you can hope for a change that may not occur."

"I have a plan B, Henry."

"Of course you do." Henry had learned over the years that Catherine would sometimes have these trains-of-thought that appeared to be taking them completely off topic only to have her return to the point she had intended to make all along. He often wondered what it would be like to see her brain when it happened. Would it be a firework explosion bursting outward from the originating subject into copious tendrils that hit her all at once, or would it be more akin to a trail system where she followed various divergent paths that eventually led back to the main trail?

"I took an informal poll at the office, and nobody would object if a well-behaved dog spent some time in my office," Catherine said.

"I see." He gave her a shrewd look. "So I guess it is time to adopt another dog."

Catherine kissed him on the cheek and headed into the bathroom to take her shower before going to work. Henry turned back to the table and stared at her uneaten piece of toast.

CHAPTER 12

C atherine's office, located less than two miles from their home, was in a once-elegant house that had slowly deteriorated over the years until it was finally converted into an office space. The group she worked for bought the entire building ten years ago, and Catherine found the eclectic space more to her liking than traditional office buildings. She also loved the fact that she could walk to work, and even though it was good exercise and saved on car emissions, the overriding reason was the uninterrupted time it gave her to sort through the myriad of projects and issues that would need her attention that day. Oftentimes it turned out to be a futile exercise, as she stepped over the threshold of the expansive front porch into the house and found herself bombarded with the latest crisis, but she continued the practice, nonetheless. However, on this particular day, she could not stop thinking about the year leading up to Connor's adoption.

The year 1995 had been full of major life changes for Catherine. She had grown steadily more frustrated with the political influence on environmental decisions and by her own lack of any meaningful way to change the status quo in her work at the State of Colorado. Shortly after she married Henry, Catherine started looking for a new job but found that most of the opportunities were not in situations that she found appealing. Just as she concluded that her only option would be another government job, an acquaintance called, out of the blue, and asked her if she was free for coffee. Zachary had been the lawyer for an environmental group working on a lawsuit that involved her division, but she hadn't seen or heard from him for two years. She couldn't imagine what he wanted to discuss with her and accepted his invitation purely out of curiosity.

As Catherine entered the coffee shop she began scanning the tables for a man in his early forties, bald but for a ring of fluffy, light brown hair that stretched around the base of his scalp, ear-to-ear. She spotted Zachary at a secluded corner table and was surprised to see another man seated with him. Catherine approached the table, and the two men rose to greet her. The man with Zachary appeared to be in his late fifties or early sixties. He had a full head of snow-white hair, was impeccably dressed, and had a clean-shaven, strong face and penetrating brown eyes that held hers as he reached out to shake her hand.

"Catherine," she said, introducing herself.

"Ford," he responded in kind, before sitting back down.

Catherine turned her attention to Zachary and shook his hand. "Hello, Zachary." She tried not to stare at his mustache and goatee, which were new. She really didn't like too many goatees. A lot of them looked like the person had a smudge on their chin instead of hair. Zachary's was no different.

"Hello, Catherine," he replied.

"So, Zachary, why the invite after so many years?"

"I see you're still as direct as you always were," Zachary noted, as he glanced at Ford. "Can I get you a cup of coffee while Ford explains the purpose behind the invitation?"

"I suppose so," Catherine said, perplexed. "Just plain black coffee," she added, when she realized Zachary was waiting for her to tell him what she wanted.

After he left she said, "I feel like I've just been hit with a bait and switch."

"I apologize for that, but if I had called you, well, you wouldn't have known who I was. Zach works for my organization. He came to me when he heard rumors that you might be looking to leave your current employment. It was logical for him to call and arrange a meeting."

"You mean this is about a job offer?"

"Yes. Please have a seat." Ford gestured to the third chair.

"What company are you with?" she inquired as she sat down.

"I said organization, not company, and I said it was mine, not exclusively mine, but I have a vested and majority interest."

"So you did," Catherine acknowledged. "I'm obviously at a disadvantage. So please explain your organization to me."

Ford smiled a genuine, but disarming smile as he sized her up before proceeding to tell her about the Global Resources Research Institute that he, and a select few like-minded individuals, had established in 1987—a financially independent institute that conducted technical and legal evaluations of regulations, policies, and practices that could adversely impact the environment.

"You must be very busy," Catherine said when he was done explaining.

"We are, and we can't look at everything, so we're forced to triage. Some issues are obvious, but we also try to identify rising issues or ones that don't get as much attention. Of course the more you look the more you realize—" Ford paused.

"It's all connected," Catherine noted.

"We tend to compartmentalize the environment with the way we set up laws and regulations, and that leads to compartmentalization inside and outside the regulatory agencies."

"You mean like the one I work for?"

"Precisely. However, I understand that you are now looking for something else, or is it something more?"

"That's a curious way to put it."

"Not really. I understand you've been offered several environmental engineering jobs that you've turned down, even though the salaries that you were offered were well above what you make now."

Catherine leaned forward in the chair. "Really? May I ask where you are getting your information?"

Ford looked at her intently. "I've made you uncomfortable. You'll have to forgive me, but I am a very thorough man, and I'm interested in more than just your work history. I'm interested in what motivates you. The fact that you turned down offers with higher salaries tells me it isn't money, or at least money is not the deciding factor for you. So if you would indulge me, Catherine, please tell me what more are you looking for?"

People rarely surprised Catherine, but this man was turning out to be an exception. "I want a chance to win against the windmills," she answered.

"Don Quixote," he said, nodding thoughtfully. "All I can promise you is that we put up a gallant fight and, at times, we do win."

"I have to tell you that I've never heard of your institute, so I have no idea what your win/loss record is."

"Our work is primarily done in the background, but we make sure our research finds its way into the right hands. So if you're looking for published statistics you won't find them."

"I don't understand? Why not use the research yourself? You must want your group to establish a reputation and have credibility."

"We have a reputation, just not in the public eye. There are enough groups in the spotlight, and we don't need to be, because we don't rely on contributions to survive," Ford replied, as he reached down into a briefcase that was at his feet, extracted a file, and handed it to Catherine. "We're highly credible. Look this over and we'll talk again. Let's say Friday, if that works for you. Otherwise it could be a while. I'm afraid I have other commitments."

"Friday is fine," she said, surprised by how comfortable she felt even though she had only the vaguest idea what the Institute did, and had no idea what kind of a job she was being offered.

"Good, we'll meet back here. Same time?"

She nodded.

"One other thing: I don't mean for this to sound conspiratorial, but I have to ask you not to share the contents of this file with anyone."

Catherine raised an eyebrow but nodded.

That evening she read the file and spent the rest of the night searching the web using Henry's computer, which had Netscape Navigator. She was looking for corroborating evidence of what the file contained, or at least for crumbs that might lead her in the right direction because, although the number of sites on the web had grown significantly between 1994 and 1995, there were still documents that had to be accessed at a library, be it public, university, or governmental.

By Friday, Catherine had been able to confirm a majority of the information in the folder. It hadn't been easy, but she had found oblique references to Ford's group within the maze of articles and reports that she had pored over. Catherine concluded that the institute was like a stealth environmental agency that didn't answer to any bureaucratic chain of command. She couldn't imagine why they wanted to offer her a job.

Catherine sat opposite Ford at the same corner table in the coffee shop and placed the file between them.

"Interesting reading," she began.

Ford took the file, placed it back in his briefcase, and waited for her to continue.

"The assumption being that your organization had a role in each of the cases you provided."

"You assume we did, but you don't know?"

"The assumption was a place to start; it gave me something to look for, and you left a trail—an overgrown, almost completely hidden trail, but a trail nonetheless."

"Why don't you tell me what you found," Ford said.

"On which topic?"

"Start with the first one."

"Well, there certainly was an international conference in Toronto in 1988 on the Changing Atmosphere. The recommendations that came out of the conference pretty much established the International Panel on Climate Change. Yet none of the scientists or policy makers in attendance were affiliated with your group."

"So we weren't there," Ford said in a neutral voice.

"I didn't say that. There was no affiliated listing, but there was reference to an obscure report that traced back to a group called GRRI."

"What about the second case?" he inquired.

"The Khian Sea incident," she paused and cleared her throat. "I have to tell you, I'd never heard of it, never even heard any reference to it."

"Not surprising, you've been working on state water quality issues."

"That would be one excuse, but it would be just that, an excuse. In the summer of 1986, I was in the middle of getting my Master's degree, and had just finished the painful process of going over the Resource Conservation and Recovery Act in all its glory, including the Hazardous and Solid Waste

Amendments of 1984. The Khian Sea would have made an interesting case study, since New Jersey stopped accepting Philadelphia's solid waste incinerator ash for disposal in 1984, which meant Philadelphia had to find another means of getting rid of the waste. So they contracted with a company, and the Khian Sea set sail for the Bahamas with fourteen thousand tons of incinerator ash."

"Out of sight out of mind," Ford noted.

"Yeah, I guess they didn't expect the Bahamas to change their mind and turn the ship away, which led to the ship roaming around the Atlantic looking for somewhere else to dump its cargo. I mean, you read the accounts and it's like a keystone cops performance, albeit a grotesque interpretation. The ship ends up in Haiti, the crew starts unloading the ash when the Haitian government demands that the waste be reloaded onto the ship, but instead the ship just takes off, leaving the Haitians with about four thousand tons of the ash. The ship continues to wander around, even returning to the United States at one point, getting turned away each time it tries to unload. The ship, which had changed names twice, is now called the Pelacano, but that apparently doesn't fool anyone, and in November of 1988, while it was going from Singapore to Sri Lanka, as if by magic, the cargo disappears. Greenpeace, who has been involved in tracking the ship for a long time, firmly believes the ash was dumped, but the crew remains silent until, drum roll please," Catherine began tapping the top of the table, "the captain admits to dumping the ash into the Atlantic and Indian Oceans. Anticlimactically, it wasn't until 1993 that charges were brought against two of the owners of one of the waste disposal companies originally hired by Philadelphia to dispose of the waste." Catherine stared at Ford, and cringed inwardly when she realized that she had actually imparted the information as though she were recounting a Faustian tale, instead of in a matter-of-fact manner.

"Sorry, sometimes I get carried away," she said, trying not to sound as mortified as she felt.

"No reason to be. I find it indicative of the extent of your review," Ford said staidly, which did little to curb her discomfort.

Catherine composed herself and, in her best professional tone, continued, "That incident, along with others, resulted in the United Nations

Environment Programme convening a diplomatic conference in Basel, Switzerland, in 1989. The result of the conference, known as the Basel Convention, was an international agreement to control the movement of hazardous waste between countries and to prevent illegal dumping by companies in developed nations on developing areas. The agreement entered into force in 1992, but some of the signatories, including the United States, have yet to ratify the treaty. There were several references to GRRI reports."

"Did you find the research difficult?"

"Not that difficult. A little digging, a little perseverance. I mean, the cases were outside of what I normally work on, but you know, it wasn't too bad." She stopped abruptly, to keep herself from rambling.

"Really?" Ford pressed.

"The conference and the convention weren't difficult to research," she noted. "Finding anything that actually cited your organization was where the perseverance came in. As I said, you don't leave much of a trail, but there was enough."

"You could have accepted the case studies as proof of issues we became involved in without going through the additional research. It would have saved you time and effort."

"You wouldn't still be talking to me if that's all I did. Accepting without attempting to verify accuracy is imprudent."

"You don't believe in unbiased reporting?" Ford asked.

"A group of people witness something first hand, yet when asked to retell the event, each person will tell it somewhat differently based on their own preconceptions."

"Did you find that in your research?"

"There was some of that; sources varied on some of the particulars, but there were basic facts that remained consistent."

"Tell me, how do you decide what to accept and what to dismiss?"

"Good question. I wade through the information provided by each source. I look for similarities and differences. Are the differences critical? If the answer to the last issue is yes, I need to know why one source would report it differently than another, and that comes down to knowing the source."

"Trusting the source?"

"No, knowing the source doesn't imply that you trust the source. Everyone has a motivation, and you can learn a great deal by understanding a source's bias. Actually finding a source considered to be on the opposite side of an issue can be very insightful. After I'm done gathering information, I weigh everything I've learned. Sometimes it comes down to making a call."

"Gut instinct?"

"It's much more involved than just gut instinct," Catherine said, feeling a little offended. "I would equate it to being on a jury, in a civil case. You find as much evidence as you possibly can, both pro and con, and then weigh how much rings true based on how the information is presented, how much supporting documentation there is." She shook her head, "I can't explain it any better."

"It's one of the best explanations I've heard," Ford said in frank admiration. "Before I leave I'd like to know what you thought of the Yablokov case."

"Yes, the Yablokov Report," Catherine said, raising an eyebrow. "I couldn't find the report itself, but what I did find was enough to give a person nightmares."

"What did you learn?"

"The Yablokov Report came out in 1993, prepared by a team of Russian scientists. Very interesting, since it detailed how the Soviet Union handled nuclear waste for decades, dumping over 2.5 million curies of radioactive waste into the Arctic Ocean and other marine environments. The waste included eighteen nuclear reactors from submarines and one nuclear ice-breaker. Apparently the report also stated that there were an additional 10 million curies of radioactive material stored aboard vessels in Murmansk Harbor. Some people think that figure is low." Catherine carefully watched for a reaction, but Ford remained expressionless.

"The trail in this case led me to the London Dumping Convention, which has been meeting since 1972, and specifically to the international treaty intended to limit the disposal at sea of wastes generated on land. The dumping of high-level radioactive waste was included in the 1972 treaty that entered into force in 1975, when 15 nations ratified the treaty, including the United States. In 1983, the parties adopted a moratorium on the dumping of low-level radioactive waste. Two years ago, in 1993, the treaty was amended and included a ban on the dumping of all radioactive waste. That amendment became legally binding at the beginning of 1994, so now that something is in place—"

"Russia formally objected, so they still are not legally bound," Ford interjected.

"What? No, wait a minute, the amendment is in force now," her eyes widened. "Are you telling me that even with the amendment becoming legally binding there's some loophole where dumping can still occur?"

"If a party formally objects they are not legally bound to comply. That is how the treaty was set up. Five parties abstained from the vote on the amendment, but Russia was the only one that filed a formal objection."

"I didn't know." Catherine silently berated herself for failing to dig deep enough.

"Did you find a record of us?"

"Nothing specific," she said, regaining her composure. "I found the listing of the nations that are a party to the treaty, references to scientific groups, Greenpeace International, but no mention of your group's involvement. But you were involved."

"What leads you to that conclusion?"

"You mean aside from the fact that you gave me the case study?" she quipped, noticing that the muscles surrounding his mouth did not move, not even a fraction. His entire face seemed locked in a neutral expression. She had no idea what possessed her to try to lighten the situation. This man obviously did not appreciate it.

"Is that your reason?" he asked evenly.

"No," she said, clearing her throat self-consciously. "Comments were made by 'credible' individuals who weren't associated with any of the parties, independent sources if you will. That fit the pattern of the other two cases without directly naming your group, leading me to conclude that you either made sure you didn't get cited or someone didn't want to cite your group because they didn't want to give you any credit."

"Credit is only important if your group or agency lives or dies by the perception of others. The omission therefore is meaningless to us, but let me assure you, we would never conspire to have a reference to our group purposely removed. That would be disingenuous."

Ford never raised his voice, but Catherine knew she had been admonished. And yet, for some strange reason, she did not feel affronted. "I stand corrected," she said, and then asked, "May I ask you a question?"

"Certainly," Ford responded.

"How long has your group had the Yablokov Report?"

"Since it was released." He then added subtly, "We have resources."

"It would appear you have a great deal more than that," she mused.

"You dug out an impressive amount of information in a short period of time. You are a tenacious tracker."

"You provided the crumbs."

"I think, young lady, you need to learn how to accept a compliment." Before Catherine could react he asked, "Are you interested in coming to work with us?"

"Doing what?" she asked. "What can I possibly contribute? I've been working on state water quality issues for the last seven years. I don't think that qualifies me to work on global environmental issues."

"You would be wrong," Ford said simply, nodding imperceptibly to Zach as he rose. "You need to stop being so hard on yourself, young lady." He gave her a wry smile before turning and walking out of the coffee shop.

Zach watched Catherine's stunned response before noting, "He can be a bit disarming."

"Ya think?"

Zach sat down. "So are you going to come to work for us or not?"

"That's blunt."

"If anyone should appreciate someone getting to the point, it's you. Besides, I don't have a lot of time, and Ford thinks you will be an excellent addition to the group."

"How can you possibly know that?" Catherine asked in confusion. "The two of you didn't exchange even one word with each other."

"He talked to you for forty-five minutes, he didn't look around. He never once looked displeased."

"Well, he should have, because I made a fool of myself a couple of times."

"Doubtful. I would have seen a reaction."

"*He* didn't show any reaction. Until the end."

"Like I said."

"This is the weirdest interview I've ever had," Catherine commented, more to herself than Zach.

"Do you want the job, Catherine?" he asked.

"I don't even know what the job is. I assume you wouldn't be talking to an environmental engineer unless that was part of the job requirement."

"Engineering is certainly one of the attributes you'll be bringing to the job. Another is your research skills."

"All right, but what *exactly* would I be doing?"

"Whatever is needed, based on your skills."

"What's the job title?" she asked, trying a different tack.

"The institute doesn't work under the guise of specific job titles. Ford finds that too limiting."

Catherine realized she would have to make a decision based on the information she had and on her instinct. "I have no idea if I can be of any use to your institute, but I have a feeling that I shouldn't turn down the chance to try."

"So that's a yes?"

"Yes."

Catherine and Zach spent a half hour discussing the minutia of salary, benefits, and office logistics before Catherine finally asked Zach, "How much did you have to do with this offer?"

He held up his hand and formed a zero with his thumb and index finger. "Other people brought you to Ford's attention, and based upon their recommendations he decided it would be worth sitting down with you. You're the first person in five years that has gotten an interview with him."

"Five years? You must not have much turn-over."

"We don't, but turn-over isn't the issue. You're not being hired to replace anyone," Zach clarified.

"Why am I being hired?" Catherine asked.

"Because Ford thinks you fit." When he saw the perplexed look on her face deepen, Zach asked, "Did he talk to you at all about why he started the institute? I mean the impetus behind it?"

Catherine shook her head.

Zach sighed heavily. "I don't know why he leaves this to me."

"Leaves what to you?"

Zach studied Catherine for a minute before saying, "Ford is short for Fordon. He's . . ."

Catherine's mouth gaped open, "Fordon? The business mogul, the Fortune 500 business mogul?" she asked, recalling something she had read. "I remember when I was in college . . . oh my God, his son died suddenly, it was an aneurysm. The article said he was their only child."

"He was. Fordon was certain the boy would grow up, follow in his footsteps, take over the business that Fordon built, which had indeed made him a very wealthy man—a Fortune 500 business mogul, as you put it. As it turned out, his son wanted nothing to do with the business. You see, Ford, I'm referring to the son, he was also named Fordon, but everyone called him Ford. His father took up the moniker after he died. Anyway, when Ford started high school the Environmental Protection Agency was just being formed, and his biology class read *Silent Spring* as an ode to Rachel Carson. The book itself, and Carson's resolute defense of the findings contained in it, impacted him profoundly. It wasn't that he thought his father's business was environmentally a bad actor, but he didn't see his father doing anything to make a difference in the world. He wanted his father to stand for something other than massive wealth.

"While Ford was in college, he joined various environmental groups looking for the one that 'fit him.' After he graduated he went to work full-time for the one that did, against his father's strong objections. The strain between them became so bad that father and son stopped talking for several years. Ford's mother intervened at just about the same time that their son decided to go back to school and get his law degree. Fordon thought his son was finally coming to his senses and would stop wasting his life— until Ford quietly informed his father that his desire to go to law school stemmed from the fact that the environment had to be protected through legal actions.

"Fordon was dismayed, yet at the same time he finally realized that Ford was not indulging in a youthful rebellion against him, so he began to appreciate his son's dedication. Fordon decided to evaluate the evidence about what was happening to the environment for himself. Up to that point he had treated the issue of protecting the environment as a fad, something from the sixties, which along with flower power and free love would fade with time. In 1981, Fordon and Ford began to have long, in-depth debates about a variety of environmental topics. They debated each other for two years, Fordon always trying to find the flaws in his son's arguments, until finally Fordon told Ford that his intellect and passion would make him a great environmental lawyer. Ford died the next year, his last year at law school."

"The article said he was in law school, but there was no mention of his environmental work," Catherine noted.

"Fordon's wife controlled the press release. She never did understand her son's 'obsession'—her word for the environment."

"Yet you said she was the one that intervened, got the two of them to talk again."

"She wanted the family back together so the gossiping would stop."

"Oh."

"She died less than a year after Ford, in 1984. The funeral was very private. She had begun to set up a foundation for one of her pet projects in honor of their son, which Fordon went along with, even though he knew it wasn't what their son would have wanted. After her death, Fordon scrapped the plans for the foundation and decided to do something for the environment. The years of debate and discussion with his son convinced Fordon that the environment needed a different sort of advocate."

"So the institute is funded solely by Fordon?"

"You need to call him Ford; he left Fordon behind a long time ago," Zach insisted. "To answer your question, though, Ford's a very persuasive man. He convinced some very wealthy people to take a stand, just not in the public eye."

CATHERINE WAS APPROACHING her tenth anniversary with GRRI. The institute was involved in a broad scope of environmental issues and had a formidable reputation amongst the people and organizations that they dealt with directly, yet the name remained unrecognizable to most others. Each year Catherine's assignments had become more complex, making her job increasingly demanding, and the politics still made her want to run screaming down the street. But she had learned that you can't run from politics. Despite the stress and setbacks, Catherine never regretted her decision to join the institute because, as Ford had promised, there had indeed been times when they triumphed over the windmills.

"Morning, Catherine."

She was at the bottom of a wide set of stairs. "Morning, Zach," she said, looking up.

He was holding the main door open for her, so she quickly climbed up to the porch. Zach still sported the mustache and goatee. However, over time the facial hair had thickened and grayed, making him look less ratty and more distinguished.

"Any profound revelations on your morning walk?" Zach asked as Catherine reached the porch landing.

Zach's question had become his standard greeting ever since Catherine told him about her musings on her walks to work. "Not today, sorry."

"Really?" Zach looked perplexed. "You looked like you were deep in thought."

"I was thinking about an event that changed my life," she said wistfully. Catherine felt the air suddenly cool and shivered.

"Are you all right?" Zach asked.

"Yeah, yeah, I'm fine," Catherine said as she turned around and looked to the west, towards the mountains. She could see the craggy peaks against the blue backdrop of the sky. "That's weird."

"What's weird?"

"For a minute, it felt like there was a storm coming in."

CHAPTER 13

K eitha rushed into the eating area with Murphy leaping jubilantly at her side. She quickly scanned the room, which was full of rectangular and square tables, the same tables that the founders had brought with them, made from recycled plastic bottles and jugs. It was always difficult for the children to believe that there could ever have been so many cast-off beverage containers, until they saw the pictures of the mountains of material that people once threw away.

Keitha finally spotted Clara, Greer, and Terran, but she cursed under her breath when she saw Donal sitting with them. Murphy, having already honed in on the group, happily loped up to the table. Keitha deliberately took time to stop and talk with a few people, and to pour a glass of water for herself, before strolling up to the table.

"Hello everyone," she said nonchalantly, taking a seat.

"What's going on?" Donal inquired in greeting.

"Nothing much," she replied. "How about with you?"

"You were excited about something when you came in. The way you were looking around to find these three"—Donal waved a hand to encompass Clara, Greer, and Terran—"made it appear fairly important."

"It really wasn't."

Donal raised his bushy eyebrows, which dominated his narrow face, making him look like he had a mustache on his forehead.

"What?" Keitha asked nonchalantly.

Donal kept gazing at her relentlessly.

"There is something I've been wanting to talk to you about," she said. "I've been wading through a lot of articles and documents on the presidential election that is coming up . . . in Catherine's time. It's time-consuming. So much of it sounds like propaganda, for one side or the other, and I don't think it's a good use of my time when all you have to do—"

"Keitha, we've gone over this," Clara stated, trying not to sound annoyed.

"Seriously, Keitha, you need to give it up," Terran chimed in.

"All I'm asking is that Donal approve opening up a couple of records so I don't have to wade through all the rhetoric. All I need to know is who ultimately wins."

"I can't believe you're bringing this up . . . again. We are not accessing records ahead of Catherine's life. She has to live through the events first," Clara said.

"I think Donal is the one who makes that decision, Clara," Keitha said politely.

"When you establish an actual connection with Catherine, you cannot have knowledge of events that will happen in what will be her future. It's a precautionary but necessary measure."

"I appreciate your confidence in me, Mother, but I doubt I'll connect with her any time soon, so who cares if I skip over all the gruesome details and just find out who wins the stupid election." Keitha gave Clara a genuine smile.

"The point, Keitha, is that we err on the side of caution because we have no idea when you might have a breakthrough," Clara said with finality, although hearing Keitha use the term "mother" warmly made her heart flutter slightly.

Clara knew that daughter and mother were still treading on patchy ground, which could crumble at any time, as they tried to repair their relationship in the wake of all the revelations at the reservoir. The last thing Clara heard that night was Keitha saying how distant and cold Clara had become. Clara had been unable to catch her breath under the crushing weight of sorrow that threatened to overwhelm her and left before she lost control. Because of that, Clara failed to witness Greer's unyielding determination to get their daughter to understand what happened all those years ago and was shocked when Keitha tracked her down to talk. There had been more than a few tears shed, but their relationship was gradually being repaired.

Keitha surreptitiously looked at her mother across the eating table. Clara was obviously deep in thought, but Keitha doubted that it had anything to do with the historical records. After Greer's final revelation to Keitha at the reservoir, about a potential connection between Catherine and what the Machiavellians where planning, she was speechless. This lasted for about five minutes, before she unleashed a firestorm at Greer and Terran.

She reiterated all the facts, previously unknown to her, about Terran, Oscar and Rebecca, the Machiavellians, and, for crying out loud, Greer's second ability. The fact that they had all known these things and didn't inform her offended her deeply. Greer and Terran let Keitha vent all of her frustration, and when she was done, Greer completely stunned her when, without a word, he hugged her. Wrapped in Greer's arms Keitha felt like she was ten years old again, when nothing could harm her because she knew her parents loved her and were there to protect her. In that moment of utter clarity, she knew she had to go to Clara. Keitha glanced across the table at her mother again and knew it was a defining moment in her life.

Terran was watching Keitha and Clara from the end of the eating table. He still found himself uneasily waiting for the two women to start arguing with each other, but outbursts were becoming the exception instead of the rule. He thought back to the night at the reservoir and how, as Clara and Greer took over to finish telling Keitha about the threat from the Machiavellians, he had imperceptibly separated himself from the discussion and physically backed against the wall. The rest of the colony believed that the reason Keitha was trying to reach Catherine had to do with untangling the menagerie of records from the past to help them understand the history that led the founders to establish the colony. No one besides the healers and the three, now four, of them, knew the Machiavellians existed.

Terran knew Keitha should have been told much sooner, but Clara was a force to contend with under normal circumstances. She was an unmovable power when it came to protecting her daughter. Even when Terran told Clara that he could sense the Machiavellians growing stronger, she refused to say anything to Keitha. She insisted that the knowledge wouldn't help Keitha connect with Catherine, and if Greer hadn't interceded, they would still be arguing about it. And so far, Keitha had still been unable to establish a viable link with Catherine. So why had she been so excited when she came into the eating area? Terran's eyes widened and he examined Keitha's face more closely.

Greer had been observing everyone at the table from the moment Keitha sat down. Terran needed to learn how to control his facial expressions. He had obviously just deduced that Keitha had wanted to talk about something, and it was not opening the records. Clara, to whom self-control was like breathing, undoubtedly knew immediately that Keitha was using the issue of opening the records to distract Donal and was merely following her daughter's lead. Greer smiled inwardly.

He had hugged his daughter at the reservoir—even though she admonished him fiercely about keeping so many secrets from her—because he saw the spark of understanding behind the indignation. And when he let go of her, he saw a woman who could forgive.

"What are you staring at?" Keitha turned to Terran.

"Was I staring?" Terran replied, sounding like a child who had been caught doing something he shouldn't.

"Yes." She bugged her eyes out at him.

"Your mother is correct, Keitha," Donal said, forcing her attention back to him. "We established the safeguard so that you don't reveal anything."

"Of course," Keitha concurred knowing that the real reason behind the safeguard was what happened to Oscar and Rebecca.

"That's it?" Donal looked at her skeptically.

"I'm not going to fall on my sword over it," Keitha answered. She saw the disconcerted looks around the table. It was just an expression from the past, but the idea of using a weapon, which the colony did not possess, unnerved people. "Sorry," Keitha said. She then widened her eyes just enough to get Clara to intervene.

"Yes, well, I think Keitha understands the risk and won't bring up the idea again, Donal," Clara said rising from the table.

Everyone else rose in unison, including Murphy, who had curled up at Keitha's feet.

Keitha and Murphy were the last to arrive at Clara and Greer's room, the unofficial meeting place for the four of them when they had something to discuss.

"What took you so long?" Terran said the minute they came in.

She held up a cup.

"You actually stopped to get yourself a cup of chicory?" Terran asked incredulously.

"I actually did," Keitha retorted.

"Keitha, what were you and Murphy so excited about?" Clara cut in.

"Catherine has a dog," she replied, feigning complete composure.

Murphy stood next to her leisurely wagging his tail back and forth. The other three stared at Keitha in stunned silence before they all started talking at once.

"When?"

"Are you sure?"

"A dog."

"That could make all the difference."

"Are you sure?"

"Stop, stop," Keitha shouted excitedly. When they halted the barrage, she began filling them in. "Catherine and Henry talked about another dog in the latter part of August."

"You didn't tell us that," Terran stated.

"Because it was only talk, no reason to get everyone excited," she noted. "Until now, less than a month later, when," she said, indulging in a pregnant pause, "a dog has come to live with them."

"You're sure?" Terran asked.

"I am," Keitha arched an eyebrow, "and so is he." She placed a hand on Murphy's muscular neck.

Terran looked at the dog. "You're absolutely sure?"

"Stop asking that," Keitha said impatiently. "I wouldn't be telling you if I wasn't *absolutely* sure."

"This could be the additional catalyst that we needed, especially if Murphy and," Clara looked at Keitha earnestly, "what is the dog's name?"

"Addy."

"Addy," Clara said, savoring the word. "The name means noble." She smiled. "This is very good news, the best we've had in a long time."

"I didn't think I should tell anyone else unless something comes of it."

"Absolutely correct, Keitha. We need to be prudent," Greer agreed.

"Of course," Clara nodded.

"Any suggestions on how I should proceed?" Keitha asked.

"Let Murphy take the lead and see if Addy can influence Catherine," Greer said.

"Definitely," Clara agreed. "But in the meantime, keep calling Catherine's name, soothingly so that she won't be startled."

"If Addy does open a means of access, how would you suggest I proceed?" Keitha asked intently.

Clara nodded. "That is critical," she said. "I would suggest neutral ground."

"Neutral ground?" Keitha asked perplexed.

"It didn't go at all well when I tried to enter her world, and you can't bring her here. So that leaves neutral ground."

"What the hell is neutral ground? Where the hell is neutral ground?"

"Keitha." Clara shook her head.

"Sorry." Keitha had ceased swearing just to get under Clara's skin, but the habit was hard to break. "I just don't know what you're talking about."

"You need a place where she will feel comfortable," Clara elucidated.

"You will also need to show her something that will intrigue her enough to make her want to stay and talk to you," Greer added.

"Oh, well, if that's all I have to do," Keitha said.

"You can't approach this lightly," Greer said. "It's crucial that you approach her correctly."

"I am not approaching this lightly, Greer. With trepidation, yes; lightly, no."

Greer cupped Keitha's face in his hands and searched her eyes with his. "We just need you to be thoughtful and receptive, not reactive. This may be our last chance to succeed."

"But—" Keitha stopped when she saw the fateful look on Greer's face. "How? Just tell me how?"

"Training, my dear," Greer replied earnestly. "You and Clara have to finish the training that you started so many years ago."

CHAPTER 14

Catherine was sitting on the couch in front of the television when Henry came in to the house through the front door.

"I just saw Richard. He wanted to know if I voted today and informed me that he voted early because he didn't want any problems with his ballot, like there was in Florida four years ago." Henry laughed and shook his head.

Catherine looked up scowling. "The hanging chad debacle? Are you kidding me? He has a Bush/Cheney sign on his lawn, and he thinks *he's* going to have a problem. Besides, we don't even use punch-card paper ballots here."

"Catherine, you're being too touchy."

She sat up straight, keeping her legs folded underneath her. "That butthead complained to the city when we took out the sod in the front yard and replaced it with xeriscape. He told them it was an eyesore, and when that failed he tried to get the rest of the neighbors to sign a petition to force us to put sod back in."

"No one listened to him."

"When Connor came to live with us he accused me of letting him poop on his front lawn. I had the blasted bag of poop in my hand, but he continued to insist that a pile of shit on his lawn was Connor's."

"As I recall you furiously waved the poop bag at him while you lectured him."

"All I said was that since I worked in water quality for years I was well aware of the health and pollution problems associated with people not responsibly picking up after their animals."

"As I recall, you also told him that you would have the crap on his lawn tested for DNA, and when it didn't match Connor's you were going to sue for defamation of character. Not your character, Connor's."

Catherine raised one eyebrow. "Yeah, well, he made me mad. He should have been ragging on whoever actually left the crap on his lawn instead of accusing us just because Connor happened to be with me." A slight grin crept onto her lips. "So maybe I embellished a little about what I was going to do."

"DNA matching?"

"That butthead didn't like Connor from the moment he came to live with us," she said, once again irked by the memory.

"Catherine."

"He said Connor was weird looking."

"Richard never saw a greyhound before."

Catherine scowled. "Hello! It was rude."

"He's an old man, set in his ways, but he has mellowed over the years."

Her eyes narrowed. "Being old doesn't give a person the right to be a butthead. So you go ahead and play peacekeeper all you want, but Addy and I don't want anything to do with him."

"God you're a hardheaded woman," Henry said, placing his briefcase on the floor before scratching the ears of the dog who had quietly come up to stand beside him.

"About some things, yes I am," Catherine admitted, her expression resolute, yet as she watched the interaction between Henry and Addy, how at ease Addy was becoming, a broad smile spread across her face.

Catherine had contacted the adoption group after Labor Day weekend and was happy to find out that they still had all of the paperwork from when Henry and she adopted Connor. After confirming that they still didn't care about the dog's sex or color and that they would still be willing to accept a dog with "challenges," Catherine had hung up with the understanding that it might be a month before they heard back. Five days later, they got a call and were asked if they would be interested in a four-and-a-half year old female greyhound whose racing career had ended due to an injury. The dog had been returned by the first family that adopted her for what they termed "unacceptable behavior."

Even though Catherine and Henry knew that they would adopt the dog after the initial telephone call, they also knew that they would have to go to a required get-together. The day Catherine and Henry met Addy she was lying in the shade of a crabapple tree. They didn't even see her until she raised her head to look at them. The dog was lying in a perfect sphinx position, head held high, ears alert. A beautiful brindle so like Connor that Catherine and Henry froze for a moment. As they drew near, however, they could see that the shade had given the illusion that her coat was darker than it actually was: she was a blond brindle, not red, but the resemblance had been striking. Catherine and Henry took the dog for a walk and sat with her under another tree as she studied her surroundings before turning her eyes on the two of them, with what could have been misinterpreted as aloofness but was really apprehension.

The three of them returned home that day and the dog began following them from room to room, needing to keep them in sight at all times. At night her breathing never slowed to the steady rhythmic breathing that they remembered with Connor. Instead her breathing was rapid and uneven. She slept like someone who could not relax for fear of what might happen next. The poor dog was deeply stressed and clearly suffered from separation anxiety, which they immediately began to address. And when it became obvious that the dog was not responding well to the name she had been given, Catherine started researching.

Henry walked into the office. "Have you found a name?" he asked.

"Well," Catherine stared at the computer screen, "I kind of like the name Addy."

"Addy," he said rolling the name out. "That's nice."

Catherine raised an eyebrow. "Nice," she said, tilting her head sideways as she examined him. "So you don't like it," she concluded.

"I love it, it's the most beautiful name I've ever heard," he said with a flourish of his hands.

"I'm serious, Henry. Your first reaction was 'nice,' and nice is, well, nice."

"I like the name, Catherine. What does it mean?" he asked.

She scrunched up her face but answered, "It means noble, but I don't want people to think we mean she's aristocratic or snobby, or anything like that."

Henry didn't want to point out that the odds of anyone caring what the name meant, let alone knowing what the name meant, were at least a thousand to one. "You mean she's dignified," he said instead.

"And gracious, kind, and her eyes are so . . ."

"Kind."

"Yeah, some of the sites actually said noble and kind."

"So, now it's up to her," Henry said, shifting his gaze down to the floor where the dog was lying with her head between her paws, staring up at the two of them.

Catherine watched Henry pick up his briefcase and walk into the office, Addy close on his heels. He emerged without the briefcase or his coat, but with a prancing Addy. They disappeared into the kitchen—it was treat time after all. Catherine smiled. Every animal that she had been privileged to share her life with had taught her something. Henry and she would never know exactly what event, or combination of events, had scarred Addy's spirit, but her gentle dignity had endured and the hope that filled her eyes, even in her most frantic moments, was remarkable. She was living proof that you couldn't give up, because you just never knew when things would turn around and life would get better.

Catherine heard Henry saying "good girl" several times and then heard the telltale thunk, thunk, thunk as the treats hit her bowl.

Henry poked his head out of the kitchen and said, "Let's eat at the dining room table with the TV off. We'll have plenty of time to see the results without agonizing over every moment."

"Fine," she agreed, glancing at the map on the screen. "The exit polls in Florida and Ohio look promising."

"I heard."

"Hope springs eternal."

By midnight hope succumbed to the need for sleep, but several hours later Catherine catapulted herself out of bed before fully waking up and realizing she was in her own bedroom.

"It's all right," Henry intoned from his prone position.

He was definitely still asleep. Long past was the time when Catherine startled the hell out of him. Now Henry could sleep right through her dreams, most of the time anyway. It was amazing what people could get used to, what became ordinary.

A slight stirring in front of the dresser caught her attention.

"Sorry, girl." Catherine's eyes had adjusted enough to see Addy standing at alert. "Guess you haven't been here long enough for this to seem routine." The dog slowly advanced toward the head of the bed and drew up next to Catherine, who stroked Addy's head reassuringly. "It's okay, really." Catherine felt the slight trembling under her hand as she continued to stroke the dog. "You poor thing, your first adoption home is with people that should never have taken a greyhound in the first place and they gave you back. You, one of the sweetest dogs in the world, and then what happens? You end up with a nutty person with crazy dreams." she said this in such a light, happy voice that Addy started to wag her tail.

"Are you two going to break into full play mode at . . . what time is it?" Henry's groggy, muffled voice wafted up from his pillow.

"Sorry, it's probably late or early, depending on how you want to look at it."

Henry raised his head to look at the clock on the nightstand in the corner of the room. "It's 2:40," he said without surprise. "Did you have a bad dream or are you just getting up to pee?"

"Well, now that you mention it, I guess I will pee," she responded.

"Catherine?" Henry asked drowsily.

"Go back to sleep," Catherine said as she went into the bathroom.

She sat on the toilet staring at the tile floor under her bare feet and thought about the damn voice that kept calling her name, over and over. It was beginning to drive her . . . no. It was really starting to piss her off.

As Catherine walked back into the bedroom she could hear Henry's deep, even breathing. She never failed to be astounded, and a little jealous, at how quickly Henry could drop off to sleep.

Addy was laying back down on her bed. Catherine bent to pat her again. "You stay here, sweetie." She carefully opened the door and went upstairs.

Catherine sat on the couch with a glass of water in her hand and turned on the TV, quickly turning the volume down low. She stared at the image on the 24-hour news channel, the one they had been watching the election coverage on before giving up and going to bed. Behind the commentator was the familiar map of the United States, and it appeared to be glowing red.

She sighed, a defeated, disheartened sound. How could the exit polls in Florida, New Mexico, and Ohio have been so wrong? Why would people say they voted for Kerry only to have the numbers indicate the support was for Bush? It didn't make sense, but hell, nothing made much sense anymore.

Catherine was a registered Independent, and even though there were a gazillion parties, most elections still came down to the big two. What she couldn't understand was why strong candidates from other parties didn't run for Congress. She longed for a Senate made up of 49 Democrats, 49 Republicans, 1 Libertarian, and 1 from the Green Party, or some variation thereof—that would begin to break the two party stranglehold. She glanced at the TV again, decided there was no sense in continuing the self-torture, and began surfing the channels. As a station flashed by something caught Catherine's eye. She went back. A large wormlike creature appeared on the screen.

"Perfect."

Catherine stretched all the way out on the coach, propping her head up against a throw pillow and began to drift in and out of a half sleep, waking at various points in the movie or during commercials. She started dreaming about a worm that was eating a map of the United States until she heard the voice calling her name from far away . . .

CATHERINE FOUND HERSELF standing on the edge of a rock ledge looking out over an expansive canyon. She carefully backed away from the precipice, as though any sudden movement would send her tumbling over the brink, and felt a presence behind her. She turned around quickly and gasped.

Plants and animals crowded the plateau that stretched out in front of her. Catherine slowly scanned the area without moving anything other than her eyes. To her left, maybe 100 feet away, there was a grey wolf standing next to a grizzly bear. Their beauty was riveting, but at the same time, Catherine felt the hair on her arms prickling her skin as inherent self-preservation warned her to get the hell out of there. Something else, something more powerful, told her to stay where she was as her eyes shifted downward and she stared at the animal, at the unmistakable mask and legs of a black footed ferret, standing in front of her, in broad daylight. Daylight? She stared into the sky, not unheard of, but definitely unusual. A quick movement to her right caused Catherine to whip her head downward.

A Sage Grouse. Its small head delicately nestled in a bloom of white, like the collar of a coat that elegantly draped down the front of the bird's chest, with brown and white tufts rising dramatically from the back of the collar. Camel colored wings tucked beneath the mottled brown-and-white body. A spectacular tail exploding in an array of dark spikes. As the bird turned, Catherine saw that from the back, the tail looked like a fan, the spiked feathers framing a core of coffee colored feathers tipped in white. Haute couture, eat your heart out.

Catherine heard a splash and turned just in time to catch sight of several spotted fish leaping in the air and disappearing into . . . water? There was no water, and yet she had definitely heard a splash. There they were again. Catherine pointed, for her own edification, when the fish leapt into the air again . . . trout, Bull and Cutthroat, so where were the Rainbow? More movement, the plateau pulsed with life. Catherine then focused her attention on another speckled bird striding toward her with long, graceful legs; she watched it pass a light-green plant with two distinct stalks, one of which appeared to have a cluster of small peas on the end. Peas? Catherine furrowed her brow as the name Slender Moonwort sprang into her mind. The bird, in the meantime, had come to a halt several feet in front of her, its bill so long and thin it reminded Catherine of an elongated writing quill. A Long-billed Curlew, of course.

"There is no possible way I know any of that," Catherine declared, startling herself and causing all movement on the plateau to stop.

"Damn," she exclaimed softly. "I'm going to ruin this." A sensation at her feet drew her attention.

A small, greenish-gray frog was almost sitting on top of one of her bare feet. She absently wondered why she was barefoot before realizing it wasn't a frog at all: it was a toad with the distinctive bumps that made toads so much more prehistoric looking than frogs, and which also lead to the myth that toads caused warts. This small creature also had dark, irregularly shaped blotches on its body and small dark markings on its milky throat . . . a

Wyoming Toad. Next to the toad was a plant with wispy white puffs, which could probably be blown away by a gentle breeze, and spires of yellow jutting out from amongst the white. It was Desert Yellowhead.

Catherine drew her head up and let her eyes scan the plateau. There was a sea of creatures . . . species covering the expanse, and even though she knew they shouldn't all be present in this ecosystem, the one she was standing in, somehow they all belonged.

"Why? Why are they all here, Addy?" she whispered to the dog patiently waiting at her side. As her mind grasped the significance of what she had just said, Catherine calmly asked, "How long have you been here?" Addy smiled and wagged her tail.

Without warning, the plants and animals began to disappear, leaving in their place scorched images on the earth. Catherine, in despair, looked up at the sky. It looked alive—and enraged.

"Wake up, wake up!" Catherine demanded, without making a sound. Addy stepped closer to her. Catherine laid a shaky hand on the dog's head just as the sound of gravel being scraped by a foot made her eyes snap to her left. She yelped in astonishment when she saw a woman and an animal, which Catherine could not distinguish clearly but looked like some sort of dog, standing on a long rock shelf that rose on the opposite side of the plateau.

Every nerve in Catherine's body began to tingle. It felt the same as the sensation that came over her one night when Henry had been in D.C. after Connor had died. The power in the house had gone out. Thrust into the dark, with no candle or flashlight to assist, she carefully made her way from the couch to the front door. Just as she reached for the curtain, to see if the rest of the street was also dark, she heard a thud coming from the direction of the kitchen. She jerked around and pressed her back against the door where she tried to get her heart rate to return to normal as she vacillated between investigating the noise and running for the neighbors. Logic, and the fact that she was not the type of person to run screaming for help just because of a noise, forced her to move toward the kitchen. However, another part of her kept thinking of all the horror movies she had seen: the expendable characters always went off in search of the noise only to be . . . well, that was why they were the expendable characters. As she neared the kitchen, her heart rate began to increase again, and she could hear her own rapid breathing as she forced herself past the kitchen and down the hall to the pantry, where they kept the candles and matches. She searched the kitchen with the quivering light of the candle she held in her unsteady hands.

Catherine watched the woman closely, trying to calm her racing heart as the familiar fight-or-flight response started to overtake her. Addy nudged her hand gently. Catherine looked down at the dog—she wasn't alone this time. Catherine took a deep, cleansing breath before looking back at the woman. Suddenly a thought struck her cold and she furiously shouted across the distance, "Are you the asshole that has been yelling my name?"

Catherine sat up with a jolt. Henry was hovering over the couch.

"Sorry, I didn't mean to startle you, but it's 6:45."

"What?" Catherine stared at him, her tongue felt thick.

"It's 6:45. Last night you said you had a meeting at eight o'clock."

"Shit. Why did you let me sleep so long?" She wiped her hands over her face and twisted her stiff neck back and forth.

"You wouldn't wake up the first time," Henry stated as he handed her a mug of coffee. "I thought I'd give you a little more time before trying again."

Catherine wrapped her hands around the mug, letting the warmth seep into her chilled skin. She smelled the aroma and sipped, and the hot coffee acted like a sponge absorbing the remaining fragments of sleep. She struggled off the couch and made her way toward the office.

Henry followed her. "Aren't you going to take a shower?" he asked, perplexed. "You really don't have a lot of time."

Catherine sat at the roll-top desk, reached for a pen, and began jotting down notes on a scrap of paper. Henry started to speak again but she held up a finger. "Just a sec." She made a short list of names and after concentrating for a minute said, "That's all I can remember."

"Remember?" Henry took the piece of paper from her hand and read the names. "Were you watching something on the Animal Planet last night?"

"No."

"So these are work related?"

"No." Catherine looked around. "Where's Addy?"

He pointed back to the living room. "She finished eating an hour ago and sacked out in the sun. She was sleeping as hard as you were when I came in."

Catherine's face creased in contemplation.

"What are you thinking about?"

"It's just . . . nothing . . . never mind," she replied.

"Catherine?" he insisted.

"What did I do with my coffee?" she asked absently.

"It's right here." Henry reached over her and snagged the mug off the desk, handing it to her.

"Thanks." Catherine looked at her watch and then at the list in Henry's hand. "Can you do me a favor while I'm in the shower?"

"Sure," he said, knowing she was preoccupied and therefore not concentrating on his questions.

"Could you get on the Fish and Wildlife website . . . I have it bookmarked under my work stuff."

"And look up these names?" He waved the piece of paper in the air.

"Never mind, I don't know what I'm thinking, you don't have time."

Henry frowned at her. "I'll decide if I have time, thank you very much," he said, then adding, "I'm working here this morning, so I can take a quick look."

"Thank you. I'd really appreciate it if you could look up at least some of them."

"So these don't have anything to do with work?" he queried again.

"No," she said. "I'll explain later. I need to get going or I am going to be late." She kissed him on the cheek and headed for the bathroom.

Catherine placed her coffee mug on the sink after taking a long sip, turned to start the shower, and almost fell over Addy.

"You are the quietest big dog, I didn't even know you were here . . . or there," Catherine said, motioning with her head in the direction of the couch. Addy looked at Catherine affectionately before backing out of the tight space.

Catherine hopped in the shower but left the bathroom door wide open so Addy could lay on the runner in the hall with her front paws extended just over the threshold of the bathroom on the tile floor. It had quickly become the dog's favorite vantage point when either Catherine or Henry showered.

Catherine was in the process of shaving her legs, cursing because of yet another nick she had just inflicted on herself right above the anklebone, when Henry stepped over the prone dog and entered the bathroom.

"Are you using my razor?" he asked.

"Damn it, Henry, can't you make some noise," Catherine protested, her nerves still slightly raw.

"Sorry, I thought I did make noise."

"I'm in the shower," she said. "How much do you hear when you're in here?" she asked, peering out at him through the glass.

"So, is that my razor?" he reiterated, ignoring her irritation.

"Maybe," she said ambiguously.

"So it is," he said with satisfaction.

"So it is," she mocked lightly.

Henry closed the lid of the toilet and sat down. "So what is up with all of these different species?"

"What did you find?"

"What's it for?"

"Me."

"Not an acceptable answer, and since you're using my razor and I looked all these up for you . . ." He waved the piece of paper at her.

"Blackmail?" Catherine asked in feigned shock as she pressed her face against the glass.

"Not blackmail so much as payment for goods and services rendered," he noted.

"Oh fine, be that way," she said, moving to her other leg. "I have no idea what the list is for."

"How can you have no idea? This is a very specific list."

"Yeah, it is," she mused, pausing with the razor suspended over her knee. "Why don't you tell me what you found out and maybe I can figure out what it's for?"

"That's backwards, Catherine," Henry noted but proceeded to fill her in on what he learned. "All of them have either been listed as a threatened or endangered species, or there has been a request for listing."

"Hmm." Catherine rinsed the razor under the stream of water from the showerhead and then shut the water off.

"Is that a *hmm*, I knew that, or a *hmm*, that's interesting?"

"It's a, hmm, I had a funny feeling, but I needed confirmation." Henry lifted her towel off the rack and handed it to her as she opened the shower door. "All right, well, stop me if you know this: the last one I looked up was the Colorado River Cutthroat Trout. The request to list was just denied in April."

Catherine directed the razor at him. "Yeah, yeah, I know the basics," she waved her makeshift pointer, "not enough evidence, blah, blah, blah, same old, same old." She looked at the razor and then at her decidedly nicked legs. "To hell with it, I'll wear pants."

"Catherine?"

"What?" she asked, as she began to brush her teeth.

"How did you come up with this specific list?" he asked, holding the piece of paper up.

Catherine spit into the sink and then leaned against it with both hands.

"What did you see?" he asked carefully.

She shook her head. "It was just one of my weird dreams. That's all . . . except . . ."

"Except you knew all of these names," he finished for her.

"It's possible, you know. I probably ran into the names somewhere along the line."

"Possible? Yes, but have you?" Henry knew she must have been racking her memory to answer that question while she was showering. It explained why there was such a proliferation of nicks on her leg, instead of the usual one or two. Her mind was elsewhere.

"No," she said uneasily.

"So, what do you think it means?"

She looked down at him, her eyes shining. "I don't know, but you should have seen them, Henry. An entire plateau filled with all these different species. I only had time to focus on," she pointed at the list in his hand, "those few, but there were hundreds, probably thousands." The sparkle in her eyes dimmed. "One minute teeming masses and the next . . . poof, nothing but scorched images on the ground." She shook her head. "Crazy damn Freudian dream," she concluded before walking out of the bathroom and heading downstairs.

After getting dressed for work, Catherine went into the office and found Henry back on the Fish and Wildlife page. "Henry, you don't have to keep looking."

"I'm done. I just wanted to see if there was something that the species had in common."

"Did you find anything?" Catherine inquired. "Aside from the big one you already confirmed."

He swiveled around in the chair so he could face her. "Not so far."

"Don't waste your time looking."

"It's my time."

Catherine raised an eyebrow. "Do you think you're going to find some hidden meaning to the dream?" She clapped her hands together excitedly. "I know, I know, I bet it's a premonition about threatened and endangered species dying out completely. I must be clairvoyant."

"In addition to being a smart-ass?"

"I know, so much talent in one person. How lucky can a person get?" Catherine leaned down and kissed him. "I have to get going. Don't waste any more of your time," she said definitively.

Henry rose out of the chair and escorted her through the doorway without acknowledging her commentary.

Addy raised her head up from her prone position. Fortuitously, their bungalow did not have a front porch and therefore no overhang to impede the sun's rays from streaming in through the east-facing living-room window. As long as there was sun, Addy was content to stay in the living room, even if they were in the office. Addy yawned and stretched out her front legs, extending her long neck and head up to the ceiling while raising her butt off the floor into the air. A downward-facing dog pose that any yoga instructor would envy. Catherine and Henry continued to watch as Addy effortlessly brought the front of her body up, extending her shoulders and chest upward as she lowered her butt slightly, her whole body shuddering.

"Stretcher dog," Henry said with delight as the dog walked toward them, gently wagging her tail at the sound of his voice.

"You're staying with Henry this morning, sweetie." Catherine smiled as she patted the dog on the top of her head and scratched behind one of her ears.

Henry kissed Catherine at the front door. "I'll talk to you later about dinner."

"Uh, huh," Catherine replied, shutting the screen door behind her and waving at Henry. She heard him close the front door as she headed down their walk. She turned left at the main sidewalk and strode northward until she knew that even if Henry was watching her from the front window she was well out of sight. Only then did she stop.

"Damn," Catherine said aloud, as she stared down at the sidewalk, noticing a crack that had just begun to make its way across the slab. "What the hell was that all about?" she pondered. "Weirdest . . . well maybe not weirdest," she began correcting herself as she started to step off the sidewalk. A car horn blared and Catherine stopped abruptly, traffic hurtling past her.

When Catherine made it safely to her office, she threw her coat across the back of a chair, circled around the desk, and dropped her small backpack onto the floor. She booted up her computer and began rapidly typing an email. Only after she hit the send button did she stop to think that she shouldn't be wasting anyone's time chasing after something literally out of a dream, but it was too late to recall the message. Knowing Hal, she would have an answer soon.

Catherine was on the phone when she looked over and saw the person standing in her office doorway. She held up a finger to indicate that she would only be a minute more.

"Yes," Catherine spoke into the mouthpiece, motioning to the chair in front of her desk before noticing her coat still slung over the back. She gestured to the coat and to a chair in the corner. The man moved the coat, as instructed, before sitting down.

"I know, Bernie. It's just that they need to review your evaluation and time is getting short."

Catherine listened for a moment.

"Right . . . no, I'll let Zach know, you don't need the aggravation." Catherine hung up the phone and looked at the man across from her.

Hal was a tall, lanky man, which meant he couldn't fully extend his legs in the space between the chair and the front of her desk, but he steadfastly refused to move the chair to accommodate his frame. He had shoulder-length, wavy gray hair and round, wire-rimmed glasses, always looking to Catherine more like a laid-back English professor than one of the best aquatic biologists in the country. Ford had personally recruited Hal to come work with the Global Resources Research Institute, something Zach said he had done with only one other person—it wasn't hard to deduce that Zach was that other person. Before Hal would agree to any salary proposal, he had insisted on a laboratory space. In response, Ford had a state-of-the-art lab built to Hal's specifications in a separate building across the street from the main office. That was four years ago.

"Hal, you didn't need to come over here."

Hal shrugged. "Your question intrigued me." He stopped and waited for her.

"I just wanted to know what you can tell me about the determinations on threatened and endangered species listings by Fish and Wildlife under the Bush administration?" Catherine said, reiterating what she had written in her email.

Hal leaned forward, putting his elbows on his knees. "What exactly are you looking for, Catherine? Is there a specific case you're interested in?"

"No, no," Catherine said quickly, realizing he thought she needed information for some project she was working on, one he hadn't been informed of. "There's no work-related issue. I just ran across something and, you know, I got curious. Should have just looked it up myself instead of bothering you," she said apologetically. "It's not like you have spare time."

"Neither do you," he said bluntly, motioning at the phone.

Catherine instinctively looked in the direction he indicated and then stared down at a piece of paper on her desk. The symbol for the United Nations held her attention for a moment as she absently scanned the announcement of the UNFCC Framework Convention on Climate Change, Conference of the Parties, Tenth session, Buenos Aires, 6–17 December 2004.

"Yeah, well, what else is new, we all have our priority projects don't we?" she said, shrugging.

Hal looked more relaxed as he leaned back in the chair and asked, "What caught your attention?"

"If I wanted to look up some more information on, say, the Cutthroat Trout denial, could you give me a list of resources? Just to save me a little time?" Catherine ventured.

"Which one?" he asked.

"What?"

Hal raised an eyebrow. "Colorado River? Yellowstone? Coastal? Rio Grande?"

Catherine held up a hand to make him stop. "I guess I was thinking Colorado River Cutthroat," she replied uncertainly, "but then again, that's pretty much the only one that I'm familiar with." Catherine paused when she saw the look on his face and then added, "Go ahead, say it."

He gave an exaggerated sigh and then said one word, "Engineers."

"Thank you, we do what we can," she said in mock appreciation but then asked, "How many have had a request for listing that has been denied?"

"As with so many things, Catherine, the answer is more complicated. I'll send you a list of resources. If you have questions after you read the material, I'll answer them when you take me out to lunch."

Hal got up. As he left he passed Zach, who was waiting in the doorway, and the two exchanged nods, but no verbal greeting. Theirs was a relationship based solely on professional work; they had abandoned what each deemed unnecessary courtesies years ago. Catherine had always sensed the underlying rivalry between the two men—which they vehemently denied—knowing that it stemmed from their standing with Ford.

Zach stepped into Catherine's office. "What was that about?" he asked casually.

"Nothing," she replied without elaborating. "What do you need?"

Zach paused and Catherine knew he was debating whether to pursue his question further, but he merely said, "What's the status of Bernie's review? We're running short on time."

"I just talked to her and she said she'd have the evaluation of the emission inventory methodologies for international aviation and maritime transport fuel emailed to me within the hour."

Bernie was the only person Catherine had ever recommended for hiring. She had been one of the best graduate and doctoral students that Henry had ever taught and distinguished herself in the field of atmospheric science after receiving her Ph.D.

Catherine stared back down at the United Nations letterhead on her desk.

"What about the rest?" Zach asked impatiently.

She looked up at him, trying to quell her irritation, "Do you know how many issues there are related to the greenhouse gas inventory?" Catherine proceeded to tick off the complex issues as though she was reciting a grocery list: "The rationale for recalculations, including methodology for emission factor changes; omissions or inconsistencies between the amounts reported by any Party and what the UN Secretariat calculated; emission trends and sources—"

"Everything that was in the UNFCC executive summary that was distributed in October," he said, interrupting her.

"Yes, but we only have two people working on it."

"And you," he noted.

"I'm only the compiler, not one of the experts."

"We're leaving in less than three weeks, Catherine. The meetings before the conference provide the best chance to solidify strategy and provide talking points for representatives."

"I'm aware, Zach."

"This is important, Catherine."

"It's always important, Zach."

"I would venture, based on the election results, that it is now more important than ever."

"Right, as if the Congress was ever behind the Kyoto Protocol," she snapped.

"Touchy."

"Tired," she corrected. Before he could say anything else she added, "I'll have everything to you by Friday."

Zach got up and left without another word.

Catherine stared at the entrance to her office, daring someone else to appear. Like the woman and her dog. The unwanted thought caught her off guard and she sat straight up in her chair as a tingling sensation spread down her spine.

CHAPTER 15

T erran hesitated at the entrance to the older couple's room until Greer looked up from his tea and waved him in. "You're early."

"I am?" Terran sounded baffled. "Keitha came by the archives and said she needed to talk to the three of us right away."

Clara came over to the table with her cup of tea. "So you thought she'd already be here."

"I guess so." He looked around as though he expected Keitha to materialize.

"Well she's not. So you may as well sit down and stop looking so anxious."

"But she made it sound important."

Clara and Greer looked at each other knowingly and nodded.

"Do you want some tea?" Greer asked as he got up.

"Yes, please," Terran said, delighted by the offer.

Greer had a special blend of herbs that were renowned in the colony, and although he shared them with everyone, no one could quite match the remarkable flavor that he was able to obtain. This had created an ongoing debate amongst the tea aficionados in the colony. One group insisted it was Greer's careful attention to every detail that made the difference, while the other group insisted it was the apparatus he used. Technically two separate apparatus, an old teakettle and a white ceramic teapot, which had a ceramic cylindrical basket infuser with vertical rows of holes equally spaced around the entire circumference.

"Do you have enough water?" Clara asked.

"Yes," Greer replied as he reached for a container underneath the ledge and poured just enough water into the kettle to make another cup.

"What about Keitha? Won't she want some tea when she gets here?" Terran asked.

"I'm sure Keitha stopped for some chicory," Greer said. Even though it was an herb, chicory required a different brewing technique than tea and over the years had become the province of the central food preparers.

"Which, of course, is why she's not here yet," Terran stated. "Even though she made it sound really important."

"You know her routine," Clara said.

"She should be more courteous," Terran replied.

"Hmm."

"What's that mean, Clara?" Terran asked.

"Nothing."

"That wasn't a nothing 'hmm.' That was a something 'hmm.'"

"I just find it interesting how easily Keitha can irritate you at times," Clara said nonchalantly.

"She does not irritate me," Terran protested. "I just think she should be more considerate of everyone's time."

"I see," Clara said, taking a sip of her tea.

"Stop doing that, Clara," Terran said in exasperation.

"I'm not doing anything." Clara sipped her tea again, but this time she couldn't suppress a grin.

"Greer," Terran said, turning to the man for help.

"You're on your own, young man," Greer replied as he turned back to the task of making tea with a grin on his own face.

Greer relished the warmth of his restored optimism as he opened the container that held the herbs. He had watched helplessly over the years as Clara's capricious side, which harbored her droll sense of humor, all but disappeared and she hardened—forever, he had feared. But now he was witnessing her coming alive again. His grin turned into a wide smile as he measured out precisely the amount of herbs needed for a cup and deposited the dried leaves into the ceramic tube, absently touching the slight chip on its lip before carefully placing the diffuser into the teapot. Greer instinctively knew when to remove the teakettle from the small heat pad so that the water did not come to a full boil, but this morning he was distracted. He was as anxious as Terran to find out what caused Keitha to rush into their room and say something about a breakthrough before running out, yelling that she had to go get Terran.

"Greer, the water," Clara cautioned, causing Greer to glance over at her. "The water," she repeated, motioning to the kettle; "don't let it boil."

"No, of course not," he said, but his mind had not been on the task and Clara knew it.

Greer carefully poured the water over the leaves to let them steep, and just as he set the hot cup of tea in front of Terran, Keitha appeared with Murphy at her side.

"She showed up," Keitha said evenly, as the other three stared at her in astonishment. "Clara, your insight about a neutral area was inspiring and, Greer, showing her various species to keep her interest—"

"Catherine showed up?" Clara asked, not entirely sure she was hearing her daughter correctly.

"Yes, she showed up," Keitha reiterated.

"You were able to talk her?" Clara asked.

"Not yet."

"Why don't you sit down and tell us exactly what happened," Greer instructed his daughter.

Keitha sat down and relayed everything that happened, and when she was finished, the other three just sat, contemplating.

"Why the scorched earth?" Clara asked, a little disturbed. "We didn't talk about anything that intense. We need Catherine to stay, Keitha. Scorched images and an angry sky? That's risky."

"You weren't there, Clara. It seemed to me like she needed something more. Something that would keep her coming back."

"Something more than seeing the species?"

"I thought stressing that they could all be gone in an instant was what was needed."

"They are not *gone*, in her time, Keitha," Greer stated.

"She needs to feel like they could be. She needs to feel the immediacy."

"Talk about risky," Terran noted.

"I am only showing her species that have been determined to be in crisis or dying out in her time."

"I don't know, Keitha, it could backfire if she becomes aggravated by it."

"She's already aggravated. She called me an asshole."

"What!" Terran shouted. "She saw you!"

"Yes!" Keitha shouted back, but then lowered her voice. "She saw me and Murphy."

"What did you do? Why did she call you an asshole?" Terran demanded.

Keitha stared at him for a moment before turning to Clara and Greer. "She knows I was the one calling to her. At least she thinks she knows."

"That's what she said?" Clara asked.

"More or less, then she and Addy left."

"All right, all right," Greer spoke sharply to get everyone's attention. "I think the pertinent point is that she stayed, even with the sky changing, even after the species . . . disappeared. That is incredible progress."

"Your father is right," Clara concurred, "Catherine stayed, through it all, she stayed. She's obviously intrigued. Which makes it that much more important that you engage her further."

"How exactly do you propose I do that when she's clearly mad about me calling her name? I don't get the feeling she's open to listening to me."

"She only thinks you were the one calling her name," Greer noted.

"Not a huge leap in logic, Greer."

"You don't have to tell her it was you," Clara stated.

"You want me to lie to her?"

"I want you to have the opportunity to gain her trust. I don't want her to hold something against you that I suggested."

"The minute I say something, Clara, she'll know it was me."

"Then don't say anything," Greer instructed.

"Just how do you expect me to gain her trust if I don't talk to her? Do you want me to hand her something to read?" Keitha said facetiously, but then stopped. "Wait a minute, that isn't a bad idea: I could take one of the palm devices to communicate with her."

"You can't take technology with you," Clara said firmly.

"Why not? They have . . ." Keitha started snapping her fingers. "What do you call them?"

"Mobile phones," Clara offered.

"No, no, those other things. Sort of like an early version of ours . . . what were they called?"

"It doesn't matter. Clara is right, you can't take any of our technology with you," Greer stated.

"Well, what else is there?"

"You could always draw in the sand or use pantomime," Terran suggested.

"Draw in the sand? Are you serious?" Keitha scoffed at the idea. "I can't draw and I'm certainly not going to do any pantomime."

"Why not?" Terran asked.

"Don't even try that innocent crap with me," Keitha said, glaring at him. "You know perfectly well what happened at the last game day, when I was cajoled into playing." She turned her glare on Greer and then whipped around at Clara who had risen from the table and was heading over to where Greer had made the tea. Keitha could see her mother's shoulders shaking and asked, "Clara, what was it you guessed?"

Clara turned back to her daughter, trying to quell her laughter. "I really did think you were doing an excellent deranged chicken."

"A deranged chicken," Keitha said, earnestly. "When the whole point of the game is to inform people about some of the interesting things we run across in the archives, but in a *fun* way. Isn't that right, Greer?" Keitha pivoted and pointed an accusatory finger at her father.

"Lily is the—"

Keitha cut him off, "You, my dear father, found out about charades, and it was you who asked Lily to modify it."

"Everyone loves that game," Clara said. "The children particularly love it when your turn comes around."

"A deranged chicken. How in the world would that be something that I found in the archives?" Keitha asked indignantly.

"I thought you were trying for a comic moment," Clara replied, "based on some of the old archival footage. I thought you were very good."

"Except, I was acting out the Apollo moon landing," Keitha declared, the other three burst out in laughter.

"That's it, I am not doing pantomime," Keitha stated with as much dignity as she could muster.

Greer restrained another laugh and said, "You have to be able to communicate with Catherine, somehow."

"I'll talk to her."

"And if she recognizes your voice?" he asked. "You are so close, Keitha, we just can't risk her walking away because we may never get her back."

"If that happens I'll just have to work harder to reach someone else. Molly or Shi`Ma."

"We need Catherine," Greer insisted.

"Why? What makes you so sure we need her?"

"It's the only logical conclusion," Greer stated resolutely.

"The only logical conclusion," Keitha repeated, baffled. "To what?"

"To why you and Clara reached the same person."

CHAPTER 16

Catherine tried to tell herself that she did not want the dream on the plateau to recur, and to reinforce that decision she began to employ the methods that had helped her stave off unwanted dreams in the past. However, she did not have the same commitment to ending it as she did when she was young. She had Henry and Addy for support. No one, not even herself, was talking about needing to see a psychiatrist to find out what was *really* causing the dream. So it did not surprise Catherine when she found herself back at the edge of the plateau at a steadily increasing frequency.

The dream always started out the same as the very first time. Catherine would find herself on a rock ledge looking out at the spectacular vista with a mix of awe and dread. Addy was always by Catherine's side and the dog's gentle reassuring presence made her feel, for the first time in her life, that she wasn't facing the unknown all alone. As Catherine's trepidation subsided, Addy and she would simply turn, but not walk away, from the edge, as they waited for the scene on the plateau to unfold.

Each repetition of the dream brought with it more and more species of plants, animals, and insects until the vast plateau that they stood upon rippled with life. After that, Catherine saw the floor of the canyon and the nearby mesa and buttes begin to fill, even before she and Addy had a chance to turn away from the edge. The tableau on the plateau always ended with the scorched marks that all but blackened the earth and, at that point, Catherine would always wake herself up.

She told Henry one morning how curious it was that there was never any creature in the sky high above her. He had incisively proffered his opinion that if all of the winged creatures were in flight they would block the light from the sun, which would interfere with her ability to observe what was around her.

Catherine was fascinated to find that every time they turned around, on what she began to think of as Addy's and her plateau, the species that would appear immediately in front of her would be something completely new. She would get on the computer right away when she woke up and, not surprisingly, find almost every species either already listed or on a petition to be listed under the United States Endangered Species Act—all but three.

The first was a harlequin toad that had waves of bold black lines filled in with bright yellow and orange. The small creature looked as though an impressionistic painter had used it as a living canvas, even down to the long and slender black toes accented with yellow tips. Catherine went to Hal after she was unable to find it anywhere on the websites she had grown accustomed to perusing, and he produced his hard copy of the *2004 IUCN Red List of Threatened Species, A Global Species Assessment*, flipped to a page, and handed it to Catherine. She found herself staring at an amphibian mug shot of the toad, listed as critically endangered.

The second was a shark ray—the back end looking like a shark; the front end, a ray, with the most spectacular dots along the body—listed as vulnerable by the IUCN. Yet neither Catherine nor Hal could find much data about them in the wild, except that their fins commanded quite a price for use in soup. That was how Catherine found out that the devastating toll from shark fin soup was not limited to the literal shark populations.

The third species was an Indian White-rumped Vulture. Even before she heard the name resounding in her head, she knew it was a vulture. There was no mistaking the bare head, powerful hooked beak, and the long turkey neck that protruded from the collar of white feathers, but when the bird spread its wings she gasped in amazement.

Catherine found various websites describing devastating declines in the vulture population: reports of over 99 percent loss in India, Pakistan, and Nepal in the last decade. Initially, various causes were suggested, including a decrease in one of the vulture's primary food supplies, cattle carcasses, but nothing could account for the near annihilation. Research then began to focus on some sort of viral disease rapidly spreading through the population of three species of vultures, but there was little supporting evidence. In May of 2003 there was evidence presented at a conference that pointed to the use of a non-steroidal drug, diclofenac, in livestock. When vultures did what all good carrion eaters did, and ate the carcasses of dead cattle treated with the drug, the birds developed visceral gout and died of renal failure. The devastating decline in the vulture population meant the carcasses were not efficiently and effectively eaten, and health and environmental concerns were beginning to emerge. In response to the plight, India decided to phase out the veterinary use of diclofenac and explore an alternative that did not cause mortality in vultures, but there was a growing concern that it might be the proverbial too little, too late.

Henry found Catherine just staring at the computer screen the morning she was compiling the information on the vulture. He came up behind her, and when she turned to face him, his hand, holding a piping-hot mug of coffee, froze in mid-air. Her face was pallid, making the blotchy red of her cheeks more predominant. But it was the distant, desolate look in her eyes that sent a shiver down Henry's spine.

CATHERINE FOUND HERSELF, once again, gazing across the expanse at the multihued red, tan, and purple mesas rising up from the green-speckled, semi-arid floor of the canyon. She stared at the brush either gathered in lush grove like clusters or standing singly as if someone had casually tossed a handful of them across the landscape. She had begun to relish the view, which possessed a certain familiar comfort, although the incongruous aspects made it too surreal for her to believe it actually existed anywhere but in the dream. As the vista in front of her began to brim with life, she reached down and stroked Addy's neck. They turned in unison.

Catherine felt something on her foot and looked down; she had ceased wondering how she could feel and smell in the dream. A small insect had landed on the top of her right foot. She tried not to wiggle her toes. She was always barefoot in the dream, even though in the real world she never went outside without shoes or at least socks on. But this too she had stopped wondering about.

She focused on the small creature—obviously a bee, though not yellow. Why did she think bees were always yellow? The little creature, making its way across her foot, was more of a burnt orange. Catherine absorbed every detail she could distinguish before the inevitable happened, and all that was left was a smudge of soot on her big toe. She raised her head and saw the blackened earth, which was not at all comforting, before lowering her hand to feel Addy's soft fur under her fingers. Before Catherine could wake herself up, Addy let out a loud yip and began to trot off.

Catherine's heart raced with anxiety as she called out, "Addy, Addy."

The dog swiveled her head and calmly looked at Catherine, and then swiftly closed the distance between her and the other dog. Catherine watched, dazed, as the two animals formally greeted each other, as dogs will do, their hind ends coming first and then their noses. Addy then broke away from the other dog and went back to Catherine.

"Don't do that," Catherine admonished, her voice shaking. "You scared the shit out of me." She stroked Addy's neck before finally looking over at the other woman.

Catherine started to wake herself up, just as Addy took several steps toward the other pair. Catherine reached out to grab Addy's collar but the dog was just beyond her reach. Catherine carefully stepped forward, to keep Addy from bolting off, and just as she drew near the dog's rear end, Addy moved forward again. This slow advancement continued several more times until Catherine finally yelled at Addy in exasperation.

"Stop!"

Addy turned and came back to Catherine's side, whereupon Catherine immediately hooked her hand around Addy's collar and asked, "What has gotten into you?"

Catherine looked up. She and Addy were within several yards of the woman and her dog, which was when Catherine realized that as Addy was moving her forward, the other pair had also been moving forward. The four of them were standing in the middle of the plateau.

Catherine took a deep breath before saying, "I guess I must be making you both up. Mixing up pieces of various people, various dogs," Catherine said, motioning toward the animal next to the woman.

The woman shook her head. Catherine placed a hand on Addy's head. "It's time to go now," she said with quiet force.

Addy looked up at her with tranquil, tender eyes before moving away from her.

"No!" Catherine cried, stunned that she had somehow let go of Addy's collar.

Addy and the other woman's dog met midway between the two people and calmly laid down together, heads between paws.

"Addy," Catherine beckoned cheerily, but when the dog did not move she raised her voice to a command, "Addy, now."

Addy did not stir.

"I'll leave you here," she said, but it was a hollow threat. Catherine would never abandon the dog.

"Why are you being so stubborn?" Catherine asked in defeat before looking back at the woman whose startlingly translucent eyes were fixed on her.

"He's amazing," Catherine couldn't keep from remarking, as she motioned to the dog, and then asked, "What kind of a dog is he?"

The woman seemed puzzled by the question.

"Addy is a greyhound," Catherine said pointing at her dog. "What kind of dog is he?" she reiterated before saying, "Gad, what am I doing? There is no answer because I made you two up so he has no breed."

The woman patted her own chest, obviously agitated, and then pointed emphatically at her dog and then back at her own chest again.

Catherine knew the woman was trying to indicate that they were tangible. "Yeah, well, you may think you're both real but that don't make it so, Pinocchio."

The woman crinkled her brow quizzically as she cocked her head to one side.

"What? Don't tell me you don't know who Pinocchio is."

The woman shook her head.

"I know, so you have to know," Catherine insisted.

The woman shook her head again.

Catherine narrowed her eyes and scrutinized the woman, who looked back at her guilelessly. "All right, let's say I'm willing to suspend my skepticism for a moment. Since, apparently I can't leave yet,"—Catherine glanced over at Addy—"here's your opportunity, convince me."

The woman stared at Catherine, bewildered.

"You know, prove that you're not a figment of my subconscious."

The woman waved her hands around.

"Nope, doesn't prove a thing."

The woman glared at Catherine and waved her hands around wildly.

"Why don't you talk to me?" Catherine challenged. "If I hear your voice and confirm that you were the one calling my name, it might make me reassess my conclusion."

The woman rolled her eyes, but then opened her mouth to speak, and nothing came out. She looked horrified.

"Now that is weird," Catherine said and looked around. "And in this land of weird that is saying something."

Keitha could not believe it. All those hours of working with Lily had been a complete waste of time. It all came down to proving to Catherine that she and Murphy were not figments of her imagination, and the proof that Catherine was demanding was that Keitha speak. So why couldn't she? Keitha stroked her throat and tried again but all that came out was a whoosh of air. She felt helpless, which turned into indignation as she jabbed an accusatory finger at Catherine.

"It isn't my fault you can't talk," Catherine said dismissively.

Keitha narrowed her eyes. The tension between the two women caused the dogs to leap to their feet, barking.

"It's all right, girl," Catherine reassured Addy, who had gone to her side.

Keitha looked down at Murphy, who was now by her side, and when she lifted her head to face Catherine, her expression was benign. Keitha touched her throat and shrugged her shoulders.

"Okay," Catherine said slowly, staring from Keitha to Murphy. "For some reason you can't talk so we really can't communicate very effectively . . . unless . . . why don't you just write out what you need to tell me?" Catherine proposed, as she bent over and drew some letters in the dirt.

Keitha grimaced, what was this woman asking her to do?

"You can write?" Catherine inquired uncertainly.

Keitha grimaced.

Catherine straightened up. "You can't write?" she asked surprised.

Keitha pointed at the letters Catherine had drawn but couldn't figure out how to explain.

"I didn't mean to offend you," Catherine said sincerely. Maybe I could just ask you some questions and you can try to answer the best you can."

Keitha fought to keep her aggravation from showing. She closed her eyes, took a deep breath, opened them again, and slowly nodded her head.

"All right," Catherine said, obviously pleased that she had come up with a solution. "What is the point of all of this? I don't work on threatened and endangered species. I work on a lot of other things, but not that."

Keitha watched Catherine closely and then carefully folded her hands together.

"Interconnected?" Catherine asked cautiously.

Keitha nodded.

"Of course it's all interconnected. That doesn't explain why I keep dreaming about all these species. I don't even know how I know all of them."

Keitha shook her head, leaned over and pounded the ground, patted her own chest, and then pointed at Catherine.

"Oh yeah, right. I forgot, we're going on the premise that this is not my subconscious. So, you're trying to say that you're the one showing them to me," Catherine said, trying not to sound as skeptical as she felt. "And why is that?"

Keitha folded her hands together and then opened them, carefully keeping the edges of her palms on the pinky side together.

"A book?"

She leaned over her hands and pretended to scan the imaginary book.

"Research?"

She nodded.

"Well, I've been researching the species I see, and I get the fact that we're losing species that we don't even know exist. I am painfully aware that more will be lost because of climate changes and a whole host of other reasons. I really don't need anyone *showing* me how vast the problem is,"

Catherine stressed, "or goading me with the fact that there are so many different stressors, we'll never be able to control them all."

Keitha shook her head emphatically and laced her fingers together again.

"I said I know it's all interconnected!" Catherine shouted. "Stop telling me what I already know." She paused, glaring at Keitha. "If you really want to be helpful then tell me how I stop the inevitable from happening? That would convince me that this is more than just a dream."

Keitha's hands flew up in unison, and then she shook them as though she was strangling someone. She pointed at Catherine and made an exaggerated sad face, taking a finger and running it from her eye down her cheek before putting her hands on her hips in disgust.

"Oh really?" Catherine replied testily. "You want to strangle me? Well, let me tell you something, sister, the feeling is mutual, and for the record, I am not feeling sorry for myself."

Keitha slapped her own head incredulously and stomped one of her feet on the ground.

"Do not yell at me unless you're willing to YELL AT ME!"

Catherine woke up with a start and looked over at Addy's bed, her eyes quickly attuned to the dark, and she saw the raised silhouette of the dog.

"Sorry, girl, but she was really getting on my nerves."

Addy emitted a deep groan before lying back down on her bed. Catherine glanced over at Henry, heard his steady deep breathing, and laid back down on her own pillow. She stared at the ceiling for a long time, refusing to give in to her own curiosity, because that would somehow mean the woman had won, but when it was obvious that sleep was not going to come, Catherine slid out of the bed. She held her fingers to her lips as she passed Addy and motioned for the dog to stay where she was before making her way up the stairs into the office. Catherine woke the computer from its standby mode and began searching for honey bees.

"What can you tell me about honey bees?"

"Good morning to you too," Hal said without looking up from his microscope.

"Sorry." Catherine apologized as she stood on the opposite side of his lab bench. "Should I come back later?"

"No need, I'm almost done." He raised an eyebrow but not his head. "Did you bring me coffee?"

"Out on your desk." Catherine was well aware of the strict protocol that neither food nor drink could ever be brought into the lab.

"I'll be right out. You're welcome to sit in here if you want, j—"

"Just don't touch anything," she finished for him as she walked over to the door. "I'll wait in your office."

The benthic laboratory was Hal's domain and Catherine was one of the few people, aside from research assistants, allowed entry. Hal insisted on the lab space so he could complete his own taxonomic identifications whenever he found it necessary. Although the samples he worked with didn't require a huge amount of space, the building that housed the rest of the staff could not be retrofitted with the proper ventilation system, so Ford bought the vacant commercial building across the street that had previously housed a small veterinary clinic.

Hal emerged from the laboratory into his office within minutes and settled into the chair behind his desk. He picked up the container of coffee and examined it.

"This isn't my to-go cup."

"It's a spare."

"It isn't mine, Catherine," he reiterated.

"I know, Hal, but your cup was over here and the coffee was over there."

"You could have come and gotten it."

"The cup has been washed, Hal," Catherine noted evenly.

He took a reluctant sip before questioning her with her own question, "What do you know about honey bees?"

"Well, I know they aren't threatened; however, I found some articles that talked about declining numbers, but there seems to be a lot of uncertainty over what's causing the decline."

"You understand that this is way outside my area of expertise."

"You know plenty about stuff outside your area. All I'm asking is whether you've heard or read anything about what might be going on."

"Stuff?" His brow creased. "That's how you refer to the biological world?"

"Think of it as a catchall."

Hal stared at her over the cup, "What *exactly* do you want to know?"

"If I knew that, I wouldn't be over here talking to you," she replied.

"You know, Catherine, if I didn't know you better, I'd say you were thinking about changing professions."

"I'm sorry, you lost me."

"You've been showing this real passion lately for learning about a wide array of species. It could make a person think that you were considering going back to college."

"Yeah, well, I'm not. Besides, I'd make a lousy biologist."

"So why the sudden interest?" he inquired. "It isn't related to anything you're working on, and since you think you'd make a lousy biologist, it can't be a personal passion, so what is it?"

"Hey, it can still be a personal passion," Catherine corrected him.

"Is it?"

"In a way, yes . . . let's just say I'm searching for the canary in the coal mine."

"You think that you're going to find a species that warns of what exactly?" he pressured.

"I don't know, Hal," she replied, exasperated.

"I'm only asking because every one of the other species I've helped you with has been listed as threatened or endangered, or a request was made, but now you're asking about honey bees. Did you read or hear something that connects all of them?"

"No," Catherine sighed. "It's all just random shit that I keep seeing. There is nothing that connects them."

"Where do you keep seeing them?" Hal asked, intrigued.

"You know, here and there," Catherine said ambiguously. She was not going to talk to Hal about her dreams. "I've been imposing on your time and expertise way too much and I shouldn't be," she said getting to her feet.

Hal stared up at her. "You're not imposing on me. I've just pointed you in the direction of some resources, and it's been fascinating seeing the progression of your interests. So I have to admit a certain curiosity about the impetus."

Catherine looked down at her watch. "Damn!" she exclaimed. "I'm going to be late for a conference call. I'll have to talk to you later," she called over her shoulder as she hurried out of his office.

Catherine mumbled to herself as she crossed the street to go back to her office. "Why couldn't I just leave it alone for a while? No . . . ," she drew the word out, "I just had to bug him again. So of course he's going to wonder what's prompting my sudden, very specific interest."

She started to parody a conversation with Hal.

"Gee, I'm sorry, Hal, haven't I told you about this woman and her dog from my dreams? What dreams you ask? Well, you see, that's where I keep seeing all of the species I talk to you about. Yes, yes, I know. Isn't it fascinating how my subconscious seems to be working?" Catherine paused and lowered her voice, "Except I don't recall ever running across a lot of the species, but when I see them their features are meticulously detailed. Explain that."

She deepened her voice as though she were Hal. "Obviously you're exhausted, Catherine. You need a good long rest, a convalescence really; there are some fine facilities."

Catherine stood on the sidewalk in front of the main GRRI building and absently gazed at the lilac bushes that stood, like guards, on either side of the stairway leading up to the porch. A plethora of buds on each of the sentries finally commanded her attention and Catherine knew that if there wasn't a late freeze, she would soon be greeted by the heady smell of the purple blossoms.

Catherine was at her desk reviewing a letter late in the day when she sensed Addy shifting on her bed. She looked up.

"Hal, what brings you over here?" she asked, trying to sound casual.

"I didn't think you had Addy with you today." He leaned down and perfunctorily patted the top of the dog's head.

"She was with Tobias most of the day," Catherine said, referring to the institute's computer wizard.

"It was a shame about his mother."

"Yes, yes it was," Catherine agreed but wished Hal would get to the point of his visit. "What can I do for you this evening?"

"I just wanted to come by and let you know that something about honey bees came to my attention after you left this morning."

"Hal, really," she said shifting in her chair, "I was serious this morning. I've imposed way too much lately. I can do my own research."

"This is very new, Catherine," he said cryptically, watching for her reaction.

"What are you talking about?" Catherine asked.

"Penn State has been researching the drastic number of deaths that have been occurring in bee colonies across the country. They just published their findings."

"Just?" she asked as normally as she could.

"Today, Catherine," he stated, as he handed her a sheet of paper. "That is the May 17th on-line version of the Proceedings of the National Academy of Science."

Catherine nodded as she took the sheet from him and was relieved to see that her hand wasn't shaking. "How strange, even a bit Twilight Zoneish. I mean, what are the odds?"

He watched her as though she were a specimen under his microscope. "They're looking at a non-native bee mite but said something else has to be involved. Healthy colonies of honey bees are becoming ill, and the hives are collapsing within two weeks. They suspect a combination of increased mite infestation, virus infection, and bacteria."

"Thanks, Hal, I really appreciate this," she said, keeping her eyes focused on the synopsis but not concentrating on one word.

"Do you have any questions?" he asked, noting that her eyes were not moving across or down the page in front of her.

Oh yeah, she had some questions, but not for Hal. "Not right now," she said, as her head began pounding from the pressure of keeping her emotions in check. "I'm sure I will once I have a chance to study this," she said, flapping the paper in the air, "but I have to focus on work first." She pointed at her computer monitor, shrugging apologetically. "Deadline."

Hal got up and headed toward the door.

"I really appreciate you bringing this to me," Catherine said.

Hal waved away her thanks as he left.

She leaned back in her chair and rubbed her temples. Hal clearly had wanted to talk to her, otherwise he could have just emailed the information, but what could she possibly have said to him.

"Shit, I think I screwed up, Addy."

The dog raised her head. Catherine's left eye began to twitch, a sign of her mounting stress. "What the hell is going on?"

Hal, who had hesitated outside Catherine's office, made his way silently down the hall wondering what she thought she screwed up. What possibly could be going on that made her so distressed, and what did it have to do with her uncanny inquiry about the honey bees?

Catherine sat staring at her computer screen, which was beginning to look blurry. It had been a long day. The synopsis Hal brought her about the honey bees had caught her off-guard, and she found her focus drifting several times when she should have been concentrating on her work.

"Good evening, Catherine."

She jerked her head up, startled by the booming greeting. "I'm sorry, Catherine," Ford said from her office doorway. "I didn't realize you were concentrating so deeply."

Ford had a small office space set aside on the third floor of the building so that he had a place to sit and a door to close on the rare occasions when his schedule allowed him an opportunity to stop in. He had developed the deserved reputation of showing up without warning and at odd hours. He liked to "pop in" and talk to people about the projects that they were working on and to provide his own insight and encouragement.

Catherine rose from her chair as Ford came around the desk to give her a big hug. It had taken her awhile to reconcile the distinguished comportment of the man with the relaxed, affectionate hug that he now, always, gave her whenever he came into her office.

A deep bond had developed between the two of them over the years, the seed of which began one night shortly after Connor had died, when Henry was back in Washington. Catherine had lost track of time and Ford had passed by her office door before doubling back to comment on the fact that he thought he was the only one in the building. Catherine, who was just as sure that she was the only person left in the building, let out a reflexive squeal as she held her chest and told Ford that he scared the behemies out of her. Ford earnestly apologized, asked her what exactly a behemie was, and then proceeded to inquire about what Catherine was working on as he settled into the chair across from her desk. They found themselves discussing a broad range of environmental subjects into the early morning hours. Many similar evenings transpired over the intervening years, and as their conversations evolved to include not only the scientific but also the philosophical, their friendship flourished. A month after Catherine's father died, Ford began to talk to her about his son. He began by reiterating what Zach had told her the day in the coffee shop about his relationship with his son and how it had evolved, devolved, and was finally transformed into something stronger than he had ever thought possible. Then Ford took the conversation in an unexpected direction.

"I was sitting in a meeting with my board of directors when suddenly my head began to ache and my ears started ringing. I could see the people in the boardroom moving their lips, but I couldn't hear anything they were saying, and then I heard my son's voice." Ford paused, scanning Catherine's face before continuing. "The next thing I knew, several of the board members were standing on either side of my chair repeating my name over and over. I stood up and said, 'Something is wrong with my son,' and left the room.

"I called his apartment, but there was no answer. I thought about calling my wife, but something stopped me. I called his friends, but no one had seen him. An hour later my assistant entered my office to tell me that a doctor I had never heard of was insisting on speaking with me. I already knew what she was going to tell me, that my son was dead. I had known from the time I heard his voice, but my mind refused to allow me to believe it." Ford paused again and waited for her to speak.

"What did your son say to you?" Catherine asked calmly.

"I don't know," Ford said, continuing to watch her carefully. "I've tried for many, many years to remember, but to no avail. I still hope that one day I will know. I believe it was something important because for a month after he died I could still feel him in our house." He thought he saw Catherine's hand twitch, but she seemed so composed he couldn't be sure. "Some people said it was like an amputated limb: I thought he was there because I wanted him to still be alive. Others, including my wife, said I was in denial, and when I accepted the fact that he was dead, the sensation would stop. They were all wrong."

Catherine remained attentive but silent.

"Of course I should never have said anything, to anyone, let alone people who perceive the world through a very narrow range of possibilities. There was even speculation about my mental health. Apparently, and unbeknownst to me, the stress of my son's dying so suddenly caused me to suffer a breakdown," Ford said, smiling sadly. "Better late than never, I learned to stop talking about what I was sensing. Everyone let out a collective sigh of relief that I was finally moving on with my life." Ford stopped for a moment and Catherine saw the pain in his eyes. "It wasn't long before I really couldn't sense him anymore."

Ford sat back in the chair and waited for Catherine's reaction.

Catherine had been trying to keep the prickling sensation, which was propelling small electrical tremors throughout her body, under control so that she would not shudder in front of Ford.

"Why are you telling me all of this?" she managed to ask.

"You have such a unique way of evaluating situations, and I think your perspective encompasses more than a lot of people see or want to see. Besides, I trust you."

"I believe that you heard your son and that you felt him in your house," Catherine whispered, and as the tension in her body began to dissipate, several tears escaped and ran down her cheeks.

Catherine opened one of her desk drawers and extracted a tissue to wipe her eyes and blow her nose. When she looked back at Ford, he was staring at her with concern.

"I'm sorry for upsetting you," he said. "I shouldn't have burdened you."

"It's not a burden. It's just—" She took a deep breath to collect herself before saying, "Thank you for confiding in me. It means a lot."

"I pride myself on being very discerning when it comes to people, my lapse in judgment after my son died notwithstanding," Ford said assuredly. "I also thought that if I told you about my experience you might find it easier to talk about yours," he added gently.

Catherine felt taken aback.

"Don't look so surprised," Ford said. "I recognize your haggard countenance. You haven't been getting much sleep lately, have you?"

Catherine shook her head and the tears began rolling down her face. Ford came around her desk and placed a comforting arm around her shoulder. "You can tell me," he said, and so she did.

Catherine found herself not only telling Ford about her father, but also about what happened after her sister and her mother died. She stopped short of mentioning anything about the weird dreams, which had woken her up for much of her life, because she refused to risk the chance that a look of incredulity would pass across Ford's face. Perhaps someday she could tell Ford, but she would have to trust him as much as Henry, and that level of trust was rare for her.

Catherine smiled at Ford as he released her from his hug. He stared at her computer screen, confusion spreading across his face.

"Personal research, not work related," she explained quickly. "I was just getting ready to forward it home."

"I've told you more than once you're welcome to do whatever research you want at this office," he responded absently, while continuing to stare at the screen.

"Because you never know where an idea might spring from," she quoted him before sitting down and hitting the forward option on the email.

"Henry in D.C. again?" Ford asked, walking around the desk to bend down and scratch Addy behind her ears. The dog looked up at him contentedly.

"No, he's actually here."

"That's good." Ford straightened and then sat in the chair in front of her desk. "Catherine, I'd like you to come with Zach and me to the London meetings in July before the G-8 Summit."

"You don't need me to be there."

"I'd like you to be there."

"I'd rather not," she said simply.

"You should meet some of these people."

"That's what you and Zach do. I like the behind-the-scenes work."

Ford knew it was her preferred role, but it was not the role he thought best suited her. "I wish you would reconsider."

"Really, Ford, I'd rather not."

"Catherine, what's bothering you?"

"I don't know. I've just been feeling disheartened."

"About?"

"All of it."

Ford lifted one of his eyebrows questioningly.

"You realize the United States is never going to ratify Kyoto," Catherine stated in a fatalistic tone. "Certainly not this administration and not this Congress. Hell, the last administration didn't submit the protocol to Congress for ratification even though they supposedly believed in it. The preemptory 95-0 vote from *that* Senate stopped that from happening rather effectively."

"You know perfectly well that Kyoto was ratified by enough nations after Buenos Aires and went into force on February 16th of this year, even without the United States."

"It only went into force for the nations that ratified it, so the United States isn't being held to any standard."

"More nations will ratify the protocol now that it is in effect, wait and see."

"This nation will *not* be one of them, not in the foreseeable future. Look at what Bush said in September. 'I've asked my advisors to consider approaches to reduce greenhouse gas emissions.' Consider. The Russian Federation was ratifying the approach that had been developed, while Bush was talking about *considering approaches*. At the same time he said that 'our actions should be measured as we learn more from science and build on it.' *Measured*? This administration doesn't care what the consensus amongst the scientific community is as long as they have something, no matter how inconsequential, that they can point to and say, 'Not all the scientists agree.' Yet did Bush note any disagreement in the speech he gave in 2003 about the *healthy forest policy*? No, what he said was that the policy was a consensus amongst the scientists, but there were scientists that disagreed with the policy, enough to write the President voicing their concerns. Apparently the definition of consensus changes, like everything else, depending on how much power you have and what the agenda is."

Ford sat patiently waiting for Catherine to return to her original concern. It did not take long.

"The United States is losing ground when it comes to greenhouse gas emissions, you know," she said. "You saw the inventory data. The United States reported an increase in greenhouse gas emissions in 2002 compared to the base-reporting year of 1990. Except for methane, and that should be exciting news, right? After all, methane is twenty-one times more effective at trapping heat in the atmosphere than carbon dioxide. However, it wasn't much of a decrease, and even when the difference in global-warming potential of twenty-one was taken into account, methane ended up accounting for only around eight percent of all greenhouse gas emissions in the United States, while carbon dioxide accounts for at least eighty percent.

"Tell me this, Ford, why is it that people latch onto the fact that methane has more global warming potential without looking at the full picture? It would be like a pawn shop saying they'll pay twenty-one dollars for each gold ring and one dollar for every silver ring. It looks like anyone with a gold ring is going to come out with more money, which is obviously true if two people walk in at the same time with only one ring each. But if one of the people has thirty gold rings and the other person has 6,300 silver rings, who comes out on top? And speaking of enteric fermentation . . ."

"I didn't know we were," Ford said politely, even though he had a worried look on his face.

Catherine continued as though she hadn't heard him, "Or should I say the 'exhalation from the digestive tracts of domesticated animals.' Why not just say that animals with more than one stomach burp methane? I know, not technically accurate, since it comes out in their breath but . . . where was I?" She furrowed her brow.

Ford had no idea, so he remained silent.

"Right . . . right, did you see where the EPA identified production-enhancing agents as a management method to reduce enteric fermentation? The document stated that advances in science and biotechnology could reduce emissions because they increase production efficiency. Bovine growth hormones, anabolic steroids, and polyether antibiotics were specifically noted."

"Catherine," Ford said, trying to focus her attention, "what is your point?"

"My point is that we don't look at the whole picture . . . the whole vista of what's in front of us."

Ford saw her eyes glimmer.

"We don't consider whether a solution is consistent with another program or concern or could cause another problem or exacerbate an existing one. Did you know that the United States has decreased our available 'sink' of land and forestry areas that could help absorb some of the greenhouse gases? It just doesn't make sense to me. Bush calls for more funding under the Tropical Forest Conservation Act, and believe me, I have no argument with relieving the debt of developing countries in exchange for their agreement to protect their forests. So you would think that the *Climate Change Strategy: A New Approach* that came out in 2002 would have a similar commitment to protect our forests. What's more, there was a Forest Stewardship Program to provide technical and financial assistance to non-industrial, private forest owners. But apparently there wasn't a similar need to promote stewardship on industrial or government land. So there will be help for farmers to conserve and improve soil, water, air, and wildlife resources by removing environmentally sensitive land from agricultural production, while at the same time there are continuing efforts to open up the Arctic Wildlife Refuge to oil exploration. It's contrary."

"It's our energy dependency."

"So that makes it all right?"

"Of course not, Catherine," Ford said sternly.

"I know you're not saying that it's all right, Ford, but that's what it boils down to, and there is nothing we can do to stop it. The power lies with the energy."

"Catherine," Ford began.

"You know it's true," she interrupted, clearly dismayed. "The so called 'New Approach' is just smoke and mirrors, sleight of hand. They say the President's yardstick is so much better than Kyoto because it's based on 'greenhouse gas intensity' that takes into account economic growth. Because, as we all know, a rapid reduction in emissions would be costly and threaten economic growth. Yeah, right. Give me a break. Do you remember the study that the Department of Energy completed on the impact of Kyoto on the U.S. energy market and economy back in 1998? You know, the one the House committee on science asked them to do?"

"I'd bet most of my money I don't know it as well as you," he said, in reference to Catherine's ability to recall information.

"I've just been going over a lot of this stuff lately," Catherine said self-effacingly while rummaging through items on her desk. "Here it is," she said, pulling a piece of paper out of a stack. "I made some notes. They used 1990 as the base case, which is appropriate, and then they evaluated different scenarios. Take the case of a 3 percent decrease in greenhouse gas emissions. The DOE said the average price of gasoline would peak at slightly more than $1.80 a gallon by 2009. Now, if we were so audacious as to implement a 7 percent decrease, the DOE said that the price of gas would almost reach $2.00 a gallon by 2009. If I remember correctly, they were using 1996 adjusted dollars. Not being an economist, I don't know exactly how that sizes up with today's dollar, but when I filled up at the beginning of the week, regular gas was at $2.16, and last I looked it was still 2005, not 2009. You know, if gas prices keep going up . . . well, I guess I could look at the bright side. At least they can't blame it on trying to decrease greenhouse gas emissions; but just wait, if prices do keep going up, you can just bet someone will try to place the blame on environmental regulations or on not drilling in the Arctic."

"Catherine, we've been dealing with these same problems since you came on board, and even before that," Ford said, concerned over what was triggering her meltdown.

"I'm sorry, Ford, you shouldn't have stopped by today. I'm afraid I'm just tired of it all."

"You're losing sight of what has been achieved. You need to focus on the fact that the Kyoto Protocol was put into effect without the United States. That's a major achievement, and there are states within these United States that are moving forward on their own."

"It's piecemeal."

"It's progress."

She shook her head. "Overall the decisions in the United States aren't being made based upon the weight of scientific evidence but by special interests that are paying for the 'science' that the administration chooses to promote to the public. And, to add insult to injury, the administration is editing the science that the government releases."

"Because history is written by the winners," Ford remarked.

"I can't accept that, Ford. There are always witnesses. Their evidence has to be recorded. Otherwise how will future generations know what actually happened?"

"Every account is tainted by the observer."

"So you're saying there is no real truth," she said dejectedly, "there never has been."

"Catherine, we do the best we can to put down the facts as accurately as we can, but they are the facts as we know them. There is so much more that we don't understand that could influence our perception of what you refer to as the truth."

"I think I need a drink," she said, sounding demoralized.

"I'm sorry, I shouldn't be waxing so philosophically," Ford said. Although he longed to have an in-depth conversation with her, he did not think she was ready. "Go home and have a glass of wine with Henry."

"Yeah," she said giving him a waning smile, "I'll be sure to let Henry know you saved him from an evening of hearing me rant."

"Before you go may I ask you something?"

"Of course," she said without hesitation.

"Why are you looking at honey bees?"

"Oh, that." She had almost forgotten the information that had been in the email on her screen when Ford walked into her office. "It's just something that came up last night that I wanted to look into a little more. Nothing work related."

"So you said, but what specifically caused you to look into honey bees?" Ford asked, looking directly into Catherine's reluctant eyes. "That's all right, you don't have to tell me."

"It will just sound weird, that's all," she said, not wanting to offend Ford.

"Not much in this world strikes me as weird anymore. I would consider it a great compliment if you would trust that I will have an open mind about anything you would tell me," Ford said so genuinely that Catherine lowered her guard.

"I had this odd dream," she hesitated, still wary about broaching the subject.

"And there was a honey bee in it?" Ford asked encouragingly.

"Yes."

"And you're sure it was a honey bee?"

"Yes. I knew it was . . . in the dream I mean, but I double-checked."

"Of course you did." Ford said this as a complement.

"Do you know anything about them?"

"I know a little. For instance, I'm aware of that same report," he stated, pointing at her computer monitor. "When did you have the dream about the honey bee?" Ford added as casually as he could.

Catherine felt her left eye twitch. She bent her head away from Ford so he couldn't see it and shut off the computer before turning to grab her small backpack from a drawer.

"It was just a dream, Ford," she said getting up. "I'm going to head home. I'm exhausted. Come on, girl," she said to Addy as she came around the desk heading toward the door.

Ford took her hand as she passed by the chair he was sitting in. She stopped and stared down at him.

"We will talk some more," he said, making it sound like a pledge.

"Of course we will," Catherine replied, but the weight of his words concerned her.

"Say hello to Henry for me," he said brightly, patting her hand before releasing it.

"I will," she said. She was so tired she didn't even have the energy to worry about whether she had made a mistake bringing up the dream.

After Ford heard the front door of the building close with a resounding thud, he took a cell phone from his breast pocket and dialed.

Without any prelude Ford said, "What exactly do we know about the honey bees?" The person on the other end of the phone responded, and as Ford listened, his posture grew rigid as his eyes constricted.

CHAPTER 17

"**S**he yelled at you because you weren't yelling at her?" Terran asked Keitha in confusion.

"That's what I said. You know I warned everyone how bad I was at pantomime, but none of you would listen. It annoyed her."

"If I understand you correctly," Clara stated, "she was annoyed because she knew you could talk, yet you weren't."

"I *couldn't* talk," Keitha asserted, "and the pantomime annoyed her."

"You were able to communicate with her," Greer noted optimistically.

"That was Addy's doing," Keitha said with obvious gratitude. "Catherine would have been out of there if it hadn't been for her. You know, I think this would go a lot better if Addy and Murphy could just act as our interpreters."

"Because now you really can't talk," Terran said.

Keitha glared at him menacingly before directing her next remark to Clara and Greer. "She knows I'm the one that's been calling out to her, so there really was no point in remaining silent in the first place or sitting through all those lessons with Lily."

"Apparently there was a point," Clara noted. "When you found yourself unable to talk, pantomime was your only means of communicating with Catherine."

"All right, I'll grant you that. The only other choice Catherine gave me was to write out what I wanted to say . . . in the soil," Keitha said, still mortified by the idea.

"You mean draw?" Clara asked, perplexed. "As Terran suggested?"

"No," Keitha stated emphatically, "write. She actually started making letters . . . with her finger."

"Fascinating," Greer remarked.

"Fascinating? How about archaic," Keitha paused. "If she wants to use written communication then she could bring one of her computers."

"You expect Catherine to bring an object with her?" Greer questioned.

"Why not? You don't want me to bring one of ours with me because she can't see our technology, but it doesn't matter if I see hers."

"I believe your father's point is that you can't expect Catherine to bring an object with her when she still doesn't understand exactly where she is."

"Maybe Addy could bring one."

"Keitha, could we be serious for a minute?" Clara said. "If Catherine wants you to write in the soil it might be a better means of communicating with her, one that would make her feel more comfortable."

"I don't know how to write, Clara. No one does because it is an obsolete means of communication."

"Freehand writing was very artistic, in its own way, and you could learn how to do it. I'm sure it wouldn't be that complicated," Greer said, encouragingly.

"Oh no, no," Keitha said, wagging a finger at her father. "I've seen some of the writing you think is so beautiful and it took me hours to decipher what some of it said."

"If you can read freehand, you can learn to write it," Greer observed.

"One has nothing to do with the other. Just because I look at an image of a painting done in the 14th century doesn't mean I can paint. Besides, why would I even try to learn how to write when all I have to do is talk?"

"You said you can't talk."

"But I will."

"I wouldn't be so sure if I were you. There has to be a reason why you can't," Greer pressed.

"I suppose you know what that reason is," Keitha challenged.

"I have a pretty good idea," Greer replied pointedly.

"If you're just going to start in about how I don't understand her or her time, you can just save your breath."

"It's why you can't speak," Clara noted. "Can you imagine what you would say to her? You would insult and anger Catherine long before you had a chance to get her to trust you."

"Oh, please, she gets irritated even when I don't talk."

"Don't you understand," Greer bellowed, "that it is your responsibility to get Catherine to listen to you? To get her to believe you? You will fail if you irritate Catherine, or if you let her irritate you and allow your temper to take over so that your brain and mouth don't communicate with each other."

"That is not fair, Greer," Keitha objected. "Catherine refuses to believe what's right in front of her, what's been right in front of her for her entire life. How do you expect me to change that?"

"I expect you to change her because you have to. We need her," Greer said sternly. "Do you understand?"

"Do I understand?" Keitha replied angrily. "It's what I've been told practically my entire life, but no, Father, I don't understand."

Greer turned away from Keitha and stared at Clara. They were standing in the great room where the celebration for Catherine's father had occurred. When Keitha found her parents and Terran conferring after the conclusion of a council meeting, she couldn't contain herself and had blurted out the events on the plateau.

"I think we need to talk in private," Clara said to Greer, understanding what he wanted to discuss without his saying a word.

"Talk about what?" Keitha asked impatiently.

Greer slowly walked towards Clara. "Yes, I think we do," he said, and they made their way toward the entrance to the room. Greer paused for a moment. "Meet us at the reservoir in an hour," he instructed before disappearing from view.

Keitha turned to Terran, who shook his head and sat down behind the oval table that the council used.

Clara and Greer walked into the cavernous space and switched off their lanterns when they saw that Keitha and Terran had already illuminated the area. Terran was sitting on the rock bench and Keitha was marching around the reservoir with Murphy keeping pace at her side.

When Keitha heard her parents enter, she whirled around and asked, "Where did you two go? What did you need to discuss before you could tell us?"

"Why don't you come over here and sit down," Clara said, motioning to where Terran was sitting.

Keitha made her way over but refused to take a seat. "What the hell is going on?"

Greer shook his head.

"That is not helpful, Keitha," Clara stated. "What your father and I have to tell the two of you is going to be very difficult for you to accept. We've shielded the two of you from this information because—"

"Not another secret," Keitha said sharply.

"Our world has been changed by something the Machiavellians did in the past," Greer said stoically, ignoring Keitha's reaction.

"Greer, I don't know if that is the best way to approach this," Clara said calmly.

"How would you have us tell them?" Greer asked wearily, but Clara didn't answer.

Keitha and Terran stared at the two older people, stunned.

"What do you mean changed?" Keitha demanded.

"Our world has been altered," Greer replied.

"You mean when the person went mad?" Terran asked, surprised.

"Greer isn't talking about when you sensed the madness," Clara clarified, "he's talking about an instance that affected our time when you were only a child."

"What are you talking about?" Keitha asked in agitation.

"When Clara was pregnant with you, she sensed something unsettling," Greer explained, "which we dismissed as nerves. Clara never mentioned it to Sylvia, which was a mistake because Sylvia probably knew what your mother was really sensing. It wasn't until Terran got here and described the double imaging that he experienced with the two timelines that Clara began to reconsider what she sensed."

"You think you experienced a shift?" Terran asked skeptically. "You couldn't have, you don't have the capability of experiencing two timelines."

"Not before I was pregnant with Keitha and not after she was born, but there must have been some sort of synergy created while I was carrying her, because I did sense a shift."

"If you experienced a shift you would have known it at the time. You would have seen two timelines," Terran insisted.

"I didn't remember the images, any more than you did."

"I knew there were two timelines."

"And I remember the sensation, and I knew there was something just beyond my grasp."

"Something in the shadows," Terran said, obviously shaken.

"Yes," Clara said. "Did the same thing happen to you?"

Terran inhaled as though he couldn't get any air.

"Terran, are you all right?" Keitha asked.

His eyes were wide but he managed to whisper, "I was six."

"And Clara was pregnant with Keitha," Greer noted steadily.

Terran nodded but then shook his head. "I was just a child and Clara is assuming that she experienced two timelines based on what I told her. It could just as easily have been an aberrant episode related to the fact that she was pregnant."

"Hormones? Really?" Keitha scoffed at him.

"It wasn't hormones," Clara stated definitively.

"I'm sorry, Clara, no disrespect intended, but you are one of our most skilled perceptives and the changes that occur with pregnancy might have affected you differently from other women," Terran said, refusing to believe that a shift occurred when he was too young to be fully cognizant.

"I believe I've already said that it was because of the pregnancy that I was able to feel the shift."

"That's not what I'm saying," Terran insisted.

Clara held up a hand to stop him from continuing with his argument. "I know I felt a shift because Greer helped me recover a remnant of what I saw."

The two younger people looked dazed as they turned their attention to Greer, but it was Clara who continued to speak. "After Terran relayed to me what he experienced, I asked Greer to help me try to access the part of my mind that contained the imprint of what happened. After a fair amount of arguing, I finally convinced him that we had to try. Terran woke something inside me, and I had to know what it was. Greer helped me reach a meditative state where my mind was uncluttered and I was thinking so incisively, with absolute control. I recalled events that I hadn't thought about in years, some that I didn't even remember, but it was as though I was living them all over again. I could feel that I was getting close, that I just needed to focus my awareness." Clara heaved a sigh. "I don't know if some sense of self-preservation took over but suddenly I froze. I could see people stirring all around me, but I was unable to move or interact. I desperately wanted to reach out and touch them, because I could sense that there was something different about them, but they were just beyond my reach."

"So you concluded that it was an imprint of another timeline?" Terran questioned. "Did you consider any other possibility that would explain what you were seeing?"

"What are you implying?" Clara asked harshly.

"You have to admit, Clara," Terran responded, "that what you're talking about could just as easily be erroneous recovered memories. That would be much more logical than your sensing a shift in our timeline."

"First of all, young man, if you are saying that Greer influenced my memories, you should be ashamed of yourself," Clara stated.

"I'm not saying he did it on purpose. It could have been unintentional, like when he was in class or after Daniel died."

Clara was incensed. "Do not bring up what happened when he was young," Clara warned. "Greer has had complete control over his ability for over thirty years, and in all that time he has only used his ability to help and only because I asked him. I was able to open my mind so that you could reach me because he helped me attain the deep meditation I needed. He saved your life, not once but twice, and he saved all of our lives when he shielded you from the Machiavellians."

"Clara, it's all right," Greer said, taking her arm.

"He is accusing you of deliberately planting false memories in my mind."

"I am not," Terran protested.

"That is the *only* way it would happen. Are you understanding me?" Clara demanded.

Terran nodded his head.

"My memories were true, and there was definitely a shift in our time when I was pregnant with Keitha. I could feel the fracturing." Her tone left no room for discussion.

"If you really did sense something—" Terran began. Keitha threw her hands up in the air as Clara glared at him. "All I'm saying," Terran continued cautiously, not wanting to incur any more of Clara's wrath, "is what difference does it make? If the Machiavellians changed something in the past, it's done. There isn't anything we can do about it, except continue to live with the consequences."

"What we can do is make sure they don't succeed in the first place."

"If our timeline has been altered, Clara, they have already succeeded."

Clara did not respond. She was staring at something over Terran's shoulder.

During their exchange, Greer had surreptitiously gone over to the reservoir, opened a storage bin, and withdrew a small rod. He selected an area on the floor of the cavern where rock had slaked off and been nearly pulverized into a sandy texture and used the rod to score a circle into the sand.

Keitha was the first to notice what Greer was doing and walked over to watch. When Clara and Terran joined them, Greer proceeded to draw two more circles.

He pointed to the first circle and said, "This is the original event." Then he drew a line directly from the center of the circle and connected it to the center of the second circle. "The original event brought about the second event." He drew the same sort of line to connect the second circle to the third. "And the second brought about the third. I could draw more and more circles, but you get the idea."

He stared at the other three and they all nodded.

"The Machiavellians altered the original event, perhaps only a little." Greer traced another circle almost directly on top of the first one but they could all see that there were small slivers of each circle that did not overlap. "This caused the second event to be slightly off and then the third." He drew the lines and circles that were all slightly askew of the originals.

He continued, "Or perhaps the change that the Machiavellians created was significant and everything that followed bared little resemblance to the original events." Greer drew another set of circles and lines, but this time there was only a sliver of the first set of circles that did overlap the third set.

Terran was shaking his head.

"You don't agree, Terran?" Greer asked.

"It's too simplistic. A small change could end up creating a substantial shift in the events that follow or a large change to one event could have relatively little impact on the final outcome."

"It was meant to demonstrate what we could be dealing with," Greer said in a serious tone.

"Which brings us back to the point I was trying to make with Clara," Terran reiterated. "If the Machiavellians did change something in the past, it has already happened. We are living with the consequences and there is nothing we can do about it."

"Unless, as Clara has said, we keep the Machiavellians from interfering with the original timeline in the first place," Greer quickly shot back.

Terran ran a hand over his head in frustration. "All right, let's just say that it's possible. How are we supposed to find that one thing that got changed? For that matter, what makes you think there haven't been hundreds, or thousands, of changes to the past? We can't possibly correct them all," Terran said in exasperation. "Maybe we should just accept that this is how it all works and live with how things turn out, just accept it as our fate."

"All roads led to Rome?" Clara asked enigmatically.

"What?" Terran asked, perplexed.

"The journey taken may vary slightly, with different routes, but you still end up in Rome," Greer interjected.

"Yes," Terran agreed.

"Except that we're not talking about deciding to take one road over another to reach the same destination," Clara pointed out. "We're talking about someone blocking or removing a road, actively interfering with the past so that we miss Rome altogether."

"Bringing us right back to how in the world you expect to find, let alone correct, all of these interferences," Terran remarked.

"There probably hasn't even been a handful," Clara stated.

"That's just more speculation," Terran maintained.

"Think about it, Terran," Clara insisted. "We're not talking about a thought sent out from someone here that just happens to be picked up by someone, somewhere in time, who happens to share some common DNA. Think about how much focus, how much energy, it takes to consciously connect with another person across spatial and temporal distances." Terran's posture told Clara he was not accepting her argument. "Young man," Clara snapped, you know what it has taken to connect with Catherine and you know what it took for your brother to connect with Rebecca. Yet that pales in comparison to what it must take to make a connection while maintaining a 'false face' in order to sway the person in the past." Terran's eyes flickered. Clara continued, "You have never sensed any other group besides the Machiavellians, and you sense them the strongest when they are in the process of actively seeking to form a connection." Terran furrowed his brow. "What do you think they are doing in the dormant times? They need time to recharge, otherwise the amount of energy . . . their minds could never withstand the stress."

"I agree that they have been dormant," Terran conceded. "I have assumed that they were training, learning . . . and they also had to find someone else who could remember two timelines. The person I sensed would not be able to help them any longer . . ." Terran paused before finishing his thought. "Their mind was too badly damaged, and the Machiavellians need to know how successful or unsuccessful they have been so they can hone their skills and not make the same mistakes over and over."

"Mistakes?" Keitha asked.

"If we accept that Clara felt something, that means they have connected with someone in the past twice, and both times their efforts have failed."

"Failed?" Keitha asked in amazement. "You and Clara each felt a shift. How does that equate to failure?"

"*No one*," Terran stressed, spreading his arms out wide, "would purposely want this world. Besides, I would not be *sensing* them organizing for yet another attempt if they already got what they wanted!"

"Terran is right about that," Clara interjected.

"Thank you," Terran said in relief. "That is what we should be concentrating on, stopping them now."

"I said you were right about the Machiavellian's not achieving what they wanted," Clara said forcefully. "I did not say anything about not trying to prevent the incident that occurred when I was pregnant with Keitha."

"Great," Terran said in frustration, "we circle right back to the point that we don't even know what the Machiavellians changed or when the change happened. So how the hell are we supposed to prevent it?"

Greer glanced at Clara. "Clara is convinced that what happened, what caused the shift, is linked to Catherine."

"Why?" Keitha asked, suddenly apprehensive.

"I believe I heard her voice when I retrieved the event while I was in deep meditation," Clara answered.

"I thought you said you were frozen and all you knew was that you were surrounded by people you couldn't touch."

"That's correct, Terran, but I heard Catherine."

"Are you sure? Why didn't you bring this up in the first place? What did she say?" Keitha asked fervently.

"Keitha," Greer said, trying to get his daughter's attention and keep her from firing off even more questions. "Your mother heard Catherine's voice. Regrettably, she could not make out what she was saying."

"You have got to be kidding me!" Keitha exclaimed.

"Wait a minute," Terran broke in. "Are you proposing that we proceed on the presumption that Catherine was involved in what the Machiavellians changed and that Keitha can find out precisely how?" Terran asked.

"Yes," Clara said.

"This is why you have always insisted that Catherine was so important," Keitha said.

"Yes," Clara acknowledged.

"So why in the world didn't you tell me before now? I could have been trying harder this entire time to get through to her."

"If you had pushed too hard, she could have blocked you out the same way she did me."

"So what's changed?"

"You have," Greer noted. "You're back in training; you're getting your temper under control, as you proved by not haranguing your mother and me. You now need to understand how important Catherine is so you can approach her correctly."

"Correctly?" Keitha asked apprehensively.

"You can't be condescending," Greer said.

"I understand," Keitha said evenly.

"You'll have to quell any urge to lecture her."

"I understand," Keitha said, chewing her lip.

"Or disparage her time."

"Oh, come on!"

"Keitha," Greer said, shaking his head in disappointment.

"All right," Keitha conceded. "I will try not to irritate her."

"You irritated her without even talking," Greer said.

"Maybe you just shouldn't talk," Clara said.

"I need to talk, Mother," Keitha insisted.

"She has to, Clara," Greer said, agreeing with his daughter. "You have to discuss things rationally with Catherine," Greer instructed Keitha. "Take it slowly. Remember that you need to convince her to help us, and for that, you need to tell her who you are, but not yet."

"Right," Keitha said thankfully. "I'll begin by talking about the species that I've shown her, about the losses that are happening in her time, common ground. I'll start with the latest one I showed her because it will be fresh in her mind, and she seemed really interested in the honey bee." Keitha's confidence disappeared when she saw the startled look on Greer's face.

"The what?" he exclaimed.

CHAPTER 18

The reedy ringing jolted Catherine, causing her to almost fall off the couch as she struggled to clear her mind and grab the cell phone. She fumbled wildly before realizing it was no longer on the arm of the couch, where she had deliberately perched it, but was instead next to the throw pillow that she had fallen asleep on. Fallen asleep! She could not believe that she had actually dozed off for even a moment, her nerves had been so raw after receiving the phone call from Ford's personal assistant, James.

It was just after three in the morning when James called to notify her about the bombings that had occurred in London. Three underground trains and a double-decker bus were involved. It was horrible, but the fact that Ford and Zach were in London made her heart race out of control and her stomach began to churn. Catherine knew that Ford, unlike almost all other exceedingly rich people in the world, liked to take public transportation. He said it made him feel close to his son. Not only that, Ford had told Catherine that deep down he was a people watcher. He said it helped him gain insight into the human condition.

Catherine also knew that Ford and Zach had been meeting for weeks with a cross section of influential people to present information relative to the climate discussions that would occur at the G8 summit. On this particular morning, they had yet another meeting, even though the summit was already underway in Scotland.

The draft statement about global warming prepared for the G8 summit and the Bush administration's edits to that statement, along with some other administration documents, had been leaked to the media in the middle of June. The British newspaper *The Observer* reported that the leaked documents showed the Bush Administration's attempt to undermine completely the science of climate change. The documents also revealed that the White House was withdrawing from a crucial United Nations commitment to stabilize greenhouse gas emissions. Specific changes that Washington officials had made to the draft statement included the removal of all reference to the fact that climate change is a serious threat to human health and to ecosystems; the deletion of any suggestion that global warming has already started; and the expunction of any suggestion that human activity was to blame for climate change.

Ford had gone to London hoping that the public revelation of the extent of the White House's considerable efforts to exert influence on the other members of the summit to water down the statement would finally embarrass the Bush administration. Zach had merely stated that "nothing embarrasses this administration."

"Yes . . . hello," Catherine yelled into the phone when she finally got hold of it. She had been unable to reach either Zach or Ford, and the waiting had heightened her already anxious state of mind.

She heard crackling and then a muffled voice.

"Hello, hello," she repeated, exaggerating the words as though it would somehow make the connection stronger.

"Catherine?" It was Zach's voice.

"Zach," she began to shout. "Are you both all right?"

"We're both all right."

"Can you hear me, Zach?"

"Barely, the connection is really bad, but Ford wanted me to let you know, as soon as possible, that we're both all right."

"Thank God," she yelled. The relief made her slightly lightheaded. "Zach, is there anything I can do?" she asked looking over at the television, which was tuned to one of the 24-hour news channels. She pressed a button on the remote control to bring up the channel guide. It was 5:00 in the morning, noon in London.

"No, nothing, and I need to cut this short. I'll call again later when—"

"Zach? Zach?"

The connection was gone.

Catherine looked around the living room in a daze. She had to call Henry to let him know Ford and Zach were all right. His was the second phone call that she received at half past three, which was half past five in D.C., where Henry had seen the breaking news. Henry knew Ford and Zach were in London, and that Catherine was one of a handful of people that Ford had instructed James to call in the event of an "unusual circumstance"—Ford's terminology, which she had never asked him to explain—and he had hoped he would get through to her first.

The adrenaline that had surged through her body when she answered the call from Zach was still coursing through her system. Suddenly, without any warning, she began to cry. Addy, who had been lying on the floor propped up against the far end of the couch watching Catherine intently, scrambled to her feet, wedged herself between the coffee table and the couch, and leaned directly against Catherine, who wrapped her arms around the dog and let the tears flow.

Keitha and Murphy stood on the rock outcropping, waiting for the other pair to turn toward them. Keitha was anxious. Her inability to talk to Catherine back in May had already made her wary of rushing back too soon, but then Greer's revelation that at the beginning of the twenty-first century the honey bee wasn't listed as threatened or endangered stunned her. She showed the honey bee to Catherine after talking to George about the sweet plant earlier that same week, and pollinators were in the forefront of her mind, but Keitha knew she had failed to review the listings before contacting Catherine. It was a flagrant error that raised the likelihood that Catherine would actually believe she was experiencing premonitions.

The possibility of the damage she may have caused plagued Keitha, and she found herself unable to return to the plateau. Ultimately, Murphy was able to quell her apprehension and guide her back.

Keitha stood looking across the plateau at Catherine and Addy. Clara had advised her to keep the images exactly the same as before, including showing Catherine new species, up close, to distract her from the honey bee. It was a good plan, but Keitha still felt anxious. She glanced down at Murphy for reassurance, expecting to see the dog eagerly waiting to greet Addy, and was startled to find his hackles raised. Before Keitha could determine what was causing *his* apprehension, Catherine turned and started to sprint toward them. Addy was matching her stride for stride and they closed the distance in seconds.

"What the hell good are you?" Catherine roared, as she slid to a stop no more than a foot from them. Addy stood at her side making no move to greet Murphy.

Keitha instinctively took a step backwards, momentarily losing her balance even though physically she wasn't actually there.

"Did I scare you?" Catherine fumed. "Good."

Keitha recovered herself enough to turn both hands upward and shrug her shoulders, a sign of confusion at the outburst.

"You don't know why I'm pissed off, is that it?"

Keitha was sure that it had something to do with the honey bee, but she controlled her trepidation and waited for Catherine to elaborate.

"You know, in May I actually started to think that maybe, just maybe, somehow . . . I don't know . . . but I actually thought this was all supposed to mean something. You showed me a honey bee right before that bloody announcement. I knew nothing, absolutely nothing, about the plight of the honey bees. So why did I so clearly see the bee on my foot? Did it mean that somehow the two of you are some sort of . . . messengers, that this is a premonition?"

Keitha recoiled from both the verbal assault and Catherine's conclusion, which confirmed her failure.

"Well, forget it." Catherine cut the air with a swooping motion of both arms. "I am such a fool, thinking you have some sort of valuable insight for me. The truth is you are worthless and all of this is meaningless because it doesn't help."

Keitha froze. If she remained silent, Catherine might interpret it as acquiescence of their worthlessness, but at this stage, if she tried to tell Catherine that, in their own way, they were messengers, just not of the paranormal variety, it could prove disastrous.

"Can't say or mime a damn thing in your own defense, can you?" Catherine railed.

Keitha could only blink.

"You don't even know what I'm talking about, do you?" Catherine was so incensed her voice seemed to electrify the air around them.

Keitha opened her mouth to try to explain about the bee but nothing came out.

"That's what I thought. Well, let me tell you, a hell of a lot of people just got killed in London because of terrorists." Catherine's voice was hard but solemn. "Two people I know, Ford and Zach, were in London," her voice caught, "were heading for the underground but somehow . . . no thanks to you. It was sheer luck, that's all. I cannot believe I was so naïve. None of this means anything."

Keitha felt numb, "I . . ." she managed to rasp but Catherine and Addy were gone.

KEITHA SAT UP WITH A START. She looked over at Murphy and could see his ears pinned back against his head. She got up, scrambled into her clothes, and went careening down the tunnel, Murphy sprinting next to her, which caused everyone in his path to hug the wall, effectively paving the way for Keitha's mad dash. They burst into the archives, and Keitha immediately took over one of the workstations, furiously searching through the newly opened files for the beginning of July in the year 2005. Terran came up behind her and watched silently.

"And?" he asked, when Keitha finally paused in her feverish quest.

"Ford and Zach were there," she snapped, pointing at the headline that was still emblazoned across the screen, "and Catherine is outraged that I didn't warn her."

"You mean they're—"

"No," Keitha cut in. "Apparently by sheer luck, as Catherine put it, they weren't in the underground when it happened."

"Why would she expect you to warn her?"

Keitha tilted her head sideways to stare at him.

"Oh," he understood, "the honey bee."

"Yes, the honey bee," Keitha said, annoyed.

"Don't get mad at me."

"We need to find Clara and Greer," she said as she disconnected a hand-held device from the workstation and left.

"She was furious with me and I mean furious," Keitha stated as her parents read the articles she had found, "and I didn't have a clue about what she was talking about."

"Keitha, calm down, your upsetting Murphy," Greer said quietly, looking at the dog's ears, which were stiffly upright, as though a strong wind was blowing. Murphy never held them like that for more than a few moments, and only when something startled him or piqued his curiosity, but this time Murphy was obviously unsettled.

"He's already upset. He knew something was wrong back at the plateau, his hackles were up the entire time."

"How bad did it get," Clara asked.

"Bad," Keitha replied, repeating the gist of the encounter. By the time she finished, an uncomfortable quiet had descended over the room.

Murphy laid down with his front paws stretched stiffly out in front of him and lowered his head onto the floor whining softly.

"It's my fault for showing her the honey bee," Keitha said, agitated by the dog's distress.

"We don't have time for recriminations," Greer noted. "What we need is a plan on how to go forward."

"She won't be back," Keitha said, miserably staring down at her bare feet. "She thinks it's worthless. She thinks I'm worthless."

"She needs time to calm down," Clara stated. "Time to think about things rationally, not emotionally."

"I'm telling you she won't be back no matter how long we give her. You didn't see her, she was so angry. She sounded . . . betrayed."

"Because she was actually considering the idea that you and Murphy were more than figments from her subconscious."

"Clara, she was considering whether or not we were part of a premonition."

"That might not be as bad as we thought," Greer mused.

"Really, Father, you can't be serious. You and Clara have always said that we *don't* want her to believe in psychic messengers or portents or premonitions. We need Catherine to understand that I'm a person, just like her, and that Murphy is a dog, just like Addy."

"I think your father's point," Clara said, "is that perhaps we have been too unrealistic. Catherine is trying to understand what is happening to her and she is using the concepts from her time, narrow though they may be, at least she is seeking an answer. It gives you a place to start the discussion and to explain who we really are."

"Are you listening to me, Clara? She feels betrayed." Keitha looked away from her mother. "She could stay away for a long time, time we may not have."

"Keitha," Clara said gently, "she wants to know. That's why she keeps returning to the plateau."

"Well, I think her anger is going to override her curiosity."

"It isn't curiosity that's driving her, it's the desire to understand. Catherine is on the verge of awareness; she won't be able to turn back," Clara stated with certainty.

ZACH WALKED INTO CATHERINE'S OFFICE and threw a bundle of papers on her desk. She looked up at him and then down at the document.

"It's the final communiqué from the G8 Summit," Zach said bluntly.

"Gee, and I didn't get you anything," Catherine responded.

Zach and Ford had answered a myriad of questions when they returned from London, but after the initial onslaught they made it clear that they did not want to continue discussing what had occurred. Catherine respected their request.

"Very funny," he said, but his face conveyed no humor. "We got nowhere."

"Not true. Bush conceded that there is an issue that has to be dealt with and that human activity bears responsibility," she replied, trying to sound encouraging.

"You know perfectly well that during the BBC interview he merely said human activity was 'to some extent' to blame, but this," Zach picked up the pages and then let them drop back on her desk, "says climate change is a serious long-term 'challenge' and that we should 'slow and, as science justifies, stop and then reverse' the growth of greenhouse gases. Blair went into the G8 Summit saying climate change was a threat, not a challenge, apparently with the support of the other leaders. Everyone but Bush, that is, and yet what happens? This." He picked up the sheaf of papers again and threw them down on the desk. Catherine snatched them up as Zach continued, "It's the same old bullshit. Challenge my ass, the G8 acquiesced to Bush." He reached down to grab the pages again and saw that Catherine held them in her hands.

Catherine had only seen Zach show this much irritation a few times in all the years she had known him and wondered silently how much of the outburst was due to the unsatisfactory outcome of the summit and how much was due to latent stress over the bombings.

"Well?" he asked edgily.

"What do you want me to say, Zach?"

"Don't you have some more encouraging words for me?"

"You're mad as hell. I get it."

"You're damn right I am. Do you want to know what makes me even madder? Having you try to put a positive spin on that." He pointed at the papers still clutched in her hands.

"Fine, I won't."

"Fine."

They stared at each other.

"You, of all people, acting like Little Mary Sunshine," Zach said.

"I get it, Zach."

"No, you don't. If you start sugar-coating things, who the hell do I go to when I want an uncensored, incisive observation?"

"Yeah, well," Catherine mumbled self-consciously before emphatically stating, "By the way, I can be downright optimistic about some things."

"Right, and Nietzsche was a religious man."

Zach started to leave but turned at the doorway. "You know what else was disheartening?"

Catherine shook her head.

"The communiqué also says that 'oil demand is currently projected to continue its strong growth.'"

He looked so tired.

"You should go home and get some rest."

"Watching out for my health are we? Next thing you know pigs are going to start flying." He left her office without saying another word.

Sadly, Catherine wasn't surprised by the content of the communiqué. What did surprise her was Zach's response. He was usually such a realist, but it was obvious that Ford was not the only one that had expectations going into this summit; Zach had just hidden his. Before Catherine had time to ponder Zach's reaction any further, Ford appeared in her doorway.

"I didn't know you were here," she said in surprise. "Zach didn't mention it when he stopped in to give me this." Catherine held up the communiqué.

"Ah yes, not our finest hour." Ford looked around the office. "Where's Addy?"

"Tobias is taking her for a little walk around the block," Catherine replied.

"They're getting to be close friends. It was a good idea of yours."

When Tobias' mother died, after complications from what was supposed to be a minor surgery, he had become uncharacteristically depressed. The apparent senselessness of how she died had made him question many of the beliefs she had raised him with, and despite the effort of his family and friends, he remained disconsolate.

People around the office began to avoid him. There were growing comments that he needed to get on with his life. That was when Catherine decided to ask him to take a walk with her and Addy. He had been reluctant. They were colleagues, not friends, and had even butted heads on several occasions over the format and programming for a critical database. However, when it was completed, they both gained an enhanced respect for each other's work. Whether it was that, or something else, Tobias got up and went with Catherine and Addy. They walked in complete silence until they returned to the office.

Before mounting the stairs, Catherine turned to Tobias and said, "Anyone who tells you they know what you're going through is full of shit. No one knows exactly what you're going through. Every death is of an individual life that was unique, and so is the grief of the ones who are still living. I know people are saying you should be over it by now, moving on with your life. Personally, I don't think you ever get over the death of someone you love. You live with it and it changes you, sometimes subtly, sometimes deeply.

You just have to fight to make sure the best parts of yourself don't get lost in the process." Then Catherine bounded up the stairs with Addy, leaving Tobias at the bottom. She turned at the top and added, "We go for a walk whenever Addy is here. You're welcome to come whenever you want."

He did. The three of them—the elegant, graceful greyhound, the man, who had played right tackle for his high school and college football teams, and the woman, who had no idea how diminutive she looked next to him—began setting out in whatever direction Addy chose. For days upon days, not a word passed between the two people, until finally Tobias began to talk.

He was named after his father who died when Tobias was a sophomore in high school. Tobias's mother, who was just a baby when her parents emigrated from Haiti, worked so hard to help put him and his two sisters through college and then, just as she was getting ready to retire, she died and he was angry. Catherine saw that his anger began to subside as the weeks of walks with Addy and her grew into months.

"What was a good idea?" Catherine asked Ford, perplexed.

"Taking Tobias with you on your walks with Addy," Ford said.

"Oh, that. Well, you know, Addy is like a therapy dog. She relaxes people. They can open up around her," she said adroitly, deflecting any credit from herself.

Ford nodded and then inquired, "May I ask you something, Catherine?"

"Fire away."

He raised his eyebrows as he moved into the office and took a seat. "Why did you not want to go to London with Zach and me?"

"I told you when you asked me, I prefer working in the background." The way he was scrutinizing her made Catherine uncomfortable.

"Yes, I know, but was that all there was to it?"

Catherine felt pinpricks on her skin. "What more could there be?"

"I was just wondering if something else made you not want to go. Something unusual," he said gently, knowing he was treading on dangerous ground.

Catherine could feel her throat constrict as the pinpricks grew in intensity until they felt like electric pulses firing through her nerves. She swallowed, but her throat was dry. She grimaced.

"I'm sorry, Catherine, truly I am, but if you are experiencing something I might be able to help."

"Don't you think I would have said something to you if I knew anything about . . . anything at all," she rasped.

"Of course, of course you would have. If you understood."

"What do you mean?"

"After we discussed the honey bees I made some inquiries."

"The honey bee has nothing—" Ford held up a hand and Catherine stopped talking.

"Are you aware that the French experienced a massive die off of their honey bees in the late 1990s after the pesticide imidacloprid was used extensively on their sunflower crops? That they then banned most applications of the pesticide in 1999? And in 2003 the Comité Scientifique et Technique, convened by the French government, declared that the treatment of sunflower seeds with imidacloprid produces a significant risk for bees? That same year the German government suspended their approval of eight pesticides, mainly neonicotinoids, used for seed treatment after they had a die out of their honey bees."

Catherine's head was pounding so badly she couldn't concentrate. "I don't understand. You think that has to do with—"

"Are you aware?" he repeated.

"Yes, I found that same information," she acknowledged and without thinking added, "Imidacloprid is a neonicotinoid, a synthetic derivative of nicotine, and it's an approved pesticide in the United States sold under various brand names. It is used not only on crops, but on flowers, lawns, trees, even in flea collars."

"So you continued to research even after you saw the report Hal gave you? The one that indicated a bee mite was compromising the immune system of the bees, leaving them vulnerable to virus and bacteria, which was causing the deaths they were seeing in the colonies in this country?"

"I know what report you're talking about, Ford," Catherine said, her voice tight. "I wanted to know if any other nation was seeing a decline in their bee population and, if so, what the symptoms were and what they were identifying as the likely cause. Initial theories don't always end up identifying the primary cause of a problem." She thought about the vultures, and not for the first time. The similarity was uncanny.

"Yet you didn't know any of that before you had the dream about the honey bee."

"For God's sake, Ford, what do you think the damn dream with the honey bee was? Some sort of premonition?" She almost choked on the word. "Do you seriously think I somehow am . . . through dreams. Give me a fucking break." Catherine was so distraught she didn't care that she was swearing directly at him. It was all that damn woman's fault.

"Catherine, I'd like to be able to discuss this with you, calmly, if you'd let me," Ford said, although the intensity of her reaction was making him feel anything but calm.

"There isn't anything to talk about," Catherine said unequivocally.

"I realize how hard this must be for you."

If it had been anyone else, Catherine would have ripped into them, but it was Ford, and there was a reason she had told him about the damn dream in the first place. So she waited for him to continue.

"I've done a lot of traveling, as you know, and I've had the privilege of meeting a rather unique conclave of people who have graciously shared experiences with me over the years." He was watching her closely. "Experiences that can't be explained within the construct of conventional thought."

Catherine blinked. "What does that mean?" she asked stoically.

"Catherine, these people I'm talking about, people I've spent a great deal of time with, all have a perspicacious reasoning that allows them to view their experiences with open minds untethered by what people routinely accept as feasible. Through their discussions of the concepts of reality and the ability of the mind, I believe I have a better understanding of what is possible for people who utilize their cognitive ability more extensively than most, with an awareness of what is possible."

The pounding in Catherine's head increased.

"I'm just asking you," Ford added, "to consider that the dream about the honey bee may have been more than just a dream."

Catherine's hand went into a spasm and she knocked over her coffee mug, spilling the cold liquid and congealed cream onto some papers.

"Damn it!" She leapt out of her chair, grabbed the mug, and growled as she opened the top drawer of her desk and began pulling tissues out of the box she kept there. She blotted the papers, furiously flinging each saturated glob of brown tissue into the wastebasket.

"Catherine," Ford rose to his feet to assist, but when she held up her hands, as if shielding herself, he paused.

"Don't, Ford, just don't," she insisted and left the office.

Ford sat back down and sighed heavily. He would give her some time before he tried again, but he had to get her to listen to him.

CHAPTER 19

"Hi, Keitha. What are you looking at?"

Keitha pivoted on her stool to find Skyler standing at the entrance to the archive room. "Aren't you supposed to be in bed?"

"It's still early."

"So you decided to come down here to do some research?" Keitha asked, having seen no name on the schedule.

The girl blushed. "No."

"So you don't have permission to be here and yet here you are." Keitha raised an eyebrow. "Did you need to look up anything in particular?"

Skyler's cheeks bloomed crimson. "I peeked into the eating area and saw Terran and the other archivists, but I didn't see you, so . . ."

"So you thought I might be here and thought you might check and see what I was looking at."

"Well, yeah," Skyler said, looking briefly down at her feet and then back up into Keitha's eyes. "So, can I see?"

"I'm just going over some documents that have been released by the guardians of the records," she replied wryly.

Skyler laughed lightly, but her voice turned serious when she asked, "Will it help you talk to Catherine?"

Keitha flinched. She hadn't seen Catherine or Addy for months now, and she was still not convinced that she ever would again, but she just replied, "It could."

"Why do you sound so sad?"

"It's nothing."

Skyler wrinkled her brow. "Phelan told me you and Clara were getting along a lot better, way before anyone else in the colony started noticing. He says you and Greer and Clara and Terran have been talking a lot lately and that sometimes all of you seem excited but sometimes you act jumpy, especially lately. Phelan also says that Murphy isn't very happy lately and it's because of whatever is going on with the rest of you."

"Phelan said all that, did he?" Keitha asked, trying to hide her discomfort.

Keitha knew that the two were fast friends. Skyler was now eleven and Phelan was thirteen. At first blush they appeared to be opposites: Skyler was still slightly small for her age while Phelan was having a growth spurt; her hair was a curly raven black while his was an uncontrollable auburn; she was focused and direct while he was more easily distracted.

"Yes, he did," Skyler said proudly.

"I had no idea he was keeping such a close eye on us," Keitha said casually. "Doesn't he have better things to do?"

"Seriously, you adults," Skyler said, shaking her head in disapproval. "You don't think anybody our age pays attention to anything because we're too young and too distracted, when the truth is you're so caught up in what you think is important you don't see what's right in front of your nose. Phelan says you've all been so worried that another adult will overhear you that you hardly ever notice him, and when you do, you don't think he understands what's going on, so you don't care if he hears what you say. I care, though, and I listen, and then we talk about it, about what it all means."

"That's . . . I suppose that's true . . . some of the time," Keitha admitted uneasily.

"Sure. Right. Some of the time."

"Skyler, it's not that we don't think Phelan or you would understand. It's just complicated."

"That's what adults always say."

"Not *always*," Keitha said. Looking annoyed she asked, "What did you and Phelan conclude?" Keitha hoped that Phelan really did not understand what he heard if he had indeed heard more than they had intended.

"Something good happened and then something bad."

"Care to elaborate?"

"Do you?" Skyler replied.

"I'd like to hear what the two of you think."

"Why?" Skyler asked carefully.

"So I can tell you if you're right or not."

"Why don't you tell me what's been going on and then I'll know if we're right," Skyler countered.

"If you don't want to tell me, that's fine," Keitha shrugged, feigning indifference.

Skyler tilted her head to one side and studied Keitha before responding. "You and Clara haven't gotten along for as long as I can remember." Skyler made it sound like forever, and for her it was. "Everyone else is just happy the two of you are finally talking, but Phelan and I think something major had to have happened. You put that with all of these talks the four of you have been having and add to that the fact that you haven't briefed the colony for a while about Catherine, it makes Phelan and me think that something is going on with Catherine. Maybe it's something that got the four of you excited, but you weren't sure enough about it to tell the rest of the colony."

"Did you consider that maybe I haven't briefed the colony simply because there isn't anything to report?"

"No," Skyler said with the forthrightness children have before they start to censor themselves. "You'd still be telling us stories about Catherine's time, and you haven't been. You and Murphy haven't visited the classroom, and you didn't share a story at the solstice celebration."

"Murphy and I can't always visit, and the play was longer than usual this year, and the younger children had to get to bed. Besides, I really haven't had any good stories to tell."

"Any *good* stories? So something did go wrong with Catherine and that is why Murphy has been so . . . despondent," Skyler stated, finding the adult word she wanted to use so that Keitha wouldn't treat her like a child.

It was true, after Catherine's hostile dismissal, Murphy had not been himself. His daily activities had not changed. He was eating, drinking his water, and going to the archives with Keitha, but he did everything with an underlying sadness. Keitha knew it was because Addy was loyally following Catherine's lead and Murphy missed her.

"So what went wrong?" Skyler asked bluntly.

"I . . . Murphy and I . . . Catherine is a difficult . . . it's complicated," Keitha faltered as she tried to answer.

"Seriously," Skyler raised an eyebrow in disdain, "you're going to use 'complicated' again?"

"Skyler, really—"

"Does it have anything to do with all of that?" Skyler pointed to the screen where the myriad of documents that Keitha had been perusing were still in full view. Dozens of documents were arranged so she could view them all together. Before Keitha could remove them from the screen, there was a noise at the entrance to the room. Murphy, who had been dozing in a corner, slowly got up and walked over to Phelan.

"I knew I'd find you down here," he said to Skyler as he scratched Murphy behind his ears before walking over to her.

"The other archivists will be here soon, and you two should both be in bed," Keitha said emphatically as she began dropping the documents into a file folder.

"You were showing her that," Phelan said accusingly, pointing at the screen while he read.

"No," Keitha replied, continuing to move the records off the screen as rapidly as she could. "I forgot I had them up."

"She doesn't need to see all that," he said, waving his hand.

"You can stop," Skyler said to Keitha. "I saw most of them already." She turned to Phelan, "You don't get to say what I can see and what I can't. I'm not a child."

"I was only—" Phelan began defensively.

"We said we were going to do this together," Skyler interrupted him. "I want to know as much as you do and I think that was part of it. You needed to wait awhile longer."

Keitha's eyes narrowed as she stared at the two young people in front of her. "So this was all a plan that the two of you concocted. Skyler starts the questioning and you," she pointed at Phelan, "come in after she's gotten me to tell her everything, or are you the back-up in case she didn't get me to crack under interrogation?"

"I wasn't interrogating you," Skyler stated, glad that she knew the word but bothered that Keitha had used it in reference to her.

"Really? It felt like you were."

"I was just trying to get some answers."

"And what makes you think you're owed any answers?" Keitha flared, feeling as though she had been manipulated.

"Because he's miserable!" Phelan yelled, pointing at Murphy, who had gone back to the wall to lie down.

"I know he is," Keitha stated bleakly. "I'm just as worried about him as you are."

"Then why aren't you doing something to help him?"

"What do you suggest?"

"We don't have any suggestions because we don't know what's going on," Skyler replied. "Not for sure."

"Shit." Keitha threw her hands up in the air.

"Clara doesn't like it when you use—" Phelan began but stopped when he saw the desperate look on Keitha's face. "Never mind," he murmured. "Does it have something to do with all those people and animals being left in that city after the storm?"

"It wasn't just any storm, it was a *Katrina* hurricane," Skyler explained to Phelan, thinking she had pieced together some of what the documents meant. "Hurricanes are really bad storms, so a Katrina hurricane must be the worst type of hurricane."

Keitha shook her head, "No . . . I mean yes, Hurricane Katrina was a horrible storm, but back then each individual hurricane was given a person's name. Katrina was the name of the storm, not a type of storm."

"Really?" Skyler said, puzzled. "Why would they name each hurricane like that?"

"I think it was a way to keep track of them. Tell them apart. I'm not sure really."

"Why were all of those people and animals abandoned for so long? Why weren't they helped?" Phelan asked.

"I haven't been able to find anything that really explains it. Everyone blamed everyone else," Keitha replied.

"Didn't people care?" Skyler said anxiously.

"A lot of them did, but the government had the primary responsibility to help, along with certain specific groups. Ordinary people weren't being allowed to just go into the area."

"So they couldn't do anything?"

"According to the articles, people volunteered for the relief efforts, and a lot of people sent money to various groups to help—"

"The articles?" Phelan broke in. "What about what you saw and heard through Catherine?"

Keitha didn't answer.

"Can't you . . ." Phelan saw the troubled look on Keitha's face. "Oh," he said with a mature comprehension.

Keitha sighed heavily. Not only had she driven Catherine away, she had failed to detect and appreciate Phelan's growing acumen.

"What happened?" Skyler asked softly. "Did it have something to do with the hurricane?"

"No, Catherine got really mad at me because she thought I should have warned her about something else that happened in her time, but now she probably thinks I should have warned her about the storm, too."

"So this other thing and the hurricane happened pretty close together?" Phelan asked.

"July of 2005, and then the hurricane at the end of August, same year."

Phelan whistled and Murphy's head shot up. "Sorry, boy," he said.

Skyler poked Phelan in the ribs.

"Ouch! Geez, Skyler, you've got boney elbows. I already told Murphy I was sorry."

"I think you're missing the BIG thing," she said, ogling him.

"Keitha isn't going to tell us what Catherine got mad about," Phelan stated, thinking he understood.

"Catherine got mad at Keitha, which means Catherine and Keitha talked," Skyler offered shrewdly.

"Oh, that big thing," Phelan said self-consciously. Keitha closed her eyes and contemplated kicking herself for saying too much, but an overwhelming urge to take the two young people into her confidence suddenly gripped her.

"Not exactly talked," Keitha said and then very seriously added, "What I'm about to tell you is just between the three of us."

"And Clara and Terran and Greer," Phelan noted.

Keitha began to wonder if she was being too rash. They were just children, after all.

"We can't tell anyone else," Skyler said, giving Phelan a withering glance. "We get it, Keitha. You can count on us. Can't she?"

Phelan nodded fervently.

"All right, all right, don't hurt yourself," Keitha said. The compulsion to tell them about what transpired on the plateau was so strong that she knew if she ignored it, it would be a mistake.

"Wow! Catherine has a dog," they said almost in unison when Keitha had finished.

"Yes," Keitha said, intrigued but not surprised by what had grabbed their focus.

"No wonder Murphy is so upset," Phelan noted.

"He isn't the only one," Keitha stated.

"What are you going to do?" Skyler asked intently.

"I don't know."

"Catherine shouldn't blame you for not warning her about London: you weren't allowed to know."

"Thanks, Skyler, but she doesn't understand who we are, so she thinks we're part of some sort of premonition." When Keitha saw the puzzled look on the girl's face, she added, "A vision, or dream, of what is going to happen."

"That's not good," Skyler said wide-eyed.

"No, it's not," Keitha concurred. "I'm afraid this whole thing that is occurring with their Endangered Species Act is just going to reinforce that impression, make her even madder, and I'll never get a chance to explain who we really are."

"What are you talking about?" Phelan asked.

Keitha tapped an icon on the screen and a whole series of new documents appeared. Phelan and Skyler began to read in earnest.

"I don't understand this Pombo person," Phelan said.

"Well, how should I explain this? He represented the people that lived in one of their states," Keitha began.

Skyler rolled her eyes at Keitha and pointed at one of the documents. "You mean he was a member of their Congress?"

"Sorry, I didn't know you had already learned about . . . sorry." Keitha enlarged a document. "Pombo argued that the existing law was failing because only a handful of species had recovered over the thirty years from the time the law was first enacted."

"That's what I mean," Phelan stated. "Thirty years doesn't seem like a lot of time."

Keitha touched another folder icon and a completely new set of documents covered over the others. "There were people and organizations that tried to point that out." She gave Skyler and Phelan a chance to read.

"Yeah, look," Phelan said, pointing at the screen. "This says species typically didn't get listed as endangered until their numbers were critical, and it takes time to bring a species back from the brink. Now that makes sense."

"Did you see this one?" Skyler asked, pointing to another document. "It says Pombo's bill would change the law so that recovery plans couldn't be enforced by the courts." She looked at Keitha and informed her, "We learned about their courts too. They were there to make sure if someone didn't do what they were supposed to do, or did something they weren't supposed to do, then the courts would make it right." Keitha nodded and Skyler asked, "So I don't get it. It wouldn't be right if the recovery plans couldn't be enforced. Where would the people who were trying to save the species go if someone didn't do what they were supposed to do? Look," she elbowed Phelan lightly, "it says that protection of threatened species wouldn't be mandatory either. And look," she elbowed him a little harder, "this Walden person added something onto the bill that would take away the ability to stop the use of a pesticide if it was shown to be harmful to a threatened or endangered species. Wouldn't that mean that if a pesticide was killing off a species, no one could stop it and no one would be held responsible? Oh no, look!" Phelan surreptitiously moved behind Skyler so that her elbow caught only air when she went to elbow him yet again. She spun around.

"My ribs needed a break," Phelan said.

"They passed the bill!" Skyler said, infuriated as she turned back to the screen.

"The House of Representatives passed it," Keitha corrected.

"You mean the Senate didn't?" the girl asked hopefully.

"I don't know. That information is still in the unopened archives. You now know as much as I do."

"You think Catherine will think that you showed her all those species because of this?" Skyler asked, furrowing her brow.

"I'm afraid so."

"Shouldn't she be glad that you sort of warned her, even though you didn't mean to?" Phelan asked.

"Sort of warning isn't the same as telling," Skyler said.

"Keitha couldn't tell Catherine because she couldn't talk," Phelan noted.

"You know what I mean," Skyler replied.

"I don't want Catherine to think it was a warning to her at all," Keitha interjected. She needs to know who I am, but she doesn't want anything to do with me."

"You're not going to give up?" Skyler asked in dismay.

"She has completely blocked me out, so what do you suggest I do?"

"I suggest you try another way. Just like the people who were trying to help after the hurricane. If they couldn't go into the city themselves, at least they tried to help the people who could get through," Skyler said assuredly.

"Yeah," Phelan chimed in. "You need to help the one that can get through."

"Murphy," Keitha stated knowingly, shaking her head. "You don't seem to understand. He can't reach Addy because she's being loyal to Catherine."

"That's just lame," Skyler professed.

"I agree. Addy shouldn't be prevented from seeing Murphy."

"I mean, *you're* being lame. Murphy could get through to Addy, if you let him."

"Yeah," Phelan concurred. "You need to let him go."

"I'm not the one preventing him," Keitha insisted.

"Yes you are," Phelan said, just as stubbornly, with a squeaking voice. He blushed, embarrassed by the obvious sign of puberty, yet he resiliently continued, "Murphy can't get through all the crap you and Catherine have put in his way, but if you back off, Catherine won't be able to keep him out."

"Don't be ludicrous, Catherine is the only one blocking anyone out," Keitha said evenly.

"Don't you get it?" Phelan slapped his own head in frustration. "Addy isn't the only one who is loyal. Murphy isn't going to try and get through Catherine's barrier if you don't let him!"

"I'm not stopping him," Keitha reiterated. "Besides, if she can block me out, Phelan, what chance would Murphy have of getting through?"

"Catherine can block you out. How hard can that be?" Phelan blurted. His knees beginning to tremble when Keitha's eyes narrowed, but he pushed on. "I mean, you're people, and people let crap get in their way. Murphy and Addy are a whole different story. He can get by Catherine, if you just let him," Phelan pleaded.

"You have no idea what you're talking about," Keitha said dismissively. "Even if Murphy could 'get by' Catherine, there is still Addy's loyalty to her."

"You think you know everything because you're an adult," Phelan said accusingly. "Well, you don't. Catherine is mad at you, and you're just as mad at her, but Addy isn't mad at Murphy and he isn't mad at her. So just get out of his way!" Phelan yelled. Keitha glared at him, but Phelan didn't care; Murphy was depending on him. "I'm right and you'd know so if you weren't being so stubborn and, and . . ." Phelan fumbled for the right word, "petty."

"Yeah, Murphy needs you to get over yourself," Skyler interjected, employing an old saying she had overheard Keitha use. She was not about to let Phelan endure Keitha's ire alone.

Keitha focused on Skyler, who stared back unflinchingly, spreading her feet out and crossing her arms in a further show of defiance. Phelan moved next to Skyler and mimicked her stance.

Keitha turned away from both of them and looked at Murphy, still in the corner, his nose tucked under his paw. He looked miserable. Keitha went over and knelt down in front of him. He lifted his head and gazed at her sadly, but expectantly. Phelan was right, she was letting all sorts of crap cloud her mind. When Catherine told Keitha she was worthless and then left before Keitha had a chance to respond, she had been outraged. That Clara and Greer encouraged her to just keep trying to reestablish the connection with Catherine only aggravated and unnerved her further.

What if she could never reestablish a connection with Catherine? What if their only hope of determining what the Machiavellians changed was gone?

"I am so sorry," Keitha said as she wrapped her arms around Murphy and whispered to him softly. Murphy tucked his head into the crook of her arm, and she buried her head in his neck.

Phelan and Skyler looked on. It amazed them how adults could spend so much time worrying about what might happen and so little trying to make the right thing happen. As they continued to watch, Skyler reached out and took Phelan's hand.

Murphy bounded into Clara and Greer's room ahead of Keitha.

"Murphy," Greer greeted the dog heartily. "You're looking more like yourself today."

"He is," Keitha commented dryly and then eyed Greer. "Would you like to explain to me why you didn't tell me what was going on with him?"

"We tried," Clara answered, leaning on the ledge.

"No you didn't."

"Keitha, we did," Greer stated unequivocally, as he scratched Murphy's neck, to the dog's delight. "You just kept cutting us off or leaving the room."

"I just couldn't stand hearing you tell me the connection could be reestablished, when I was sure it couldn't be."

"You also never gave us a chance to talk to you about Murphy."

"So you sent two kids to do your work for you," she stated.

"We didn't send them. It was their idea. They felt so strongly about helping Murphy and thought they might be able to get through to you. They said something about adults not wanting to listen to other adults. Apparently they were right."

"Phelan yelled at me."

"An interesting, although naïve, tactic," Greer noted.

"Did you scold him?" Terran asked.

"Keitha, please tell me you didn't," Clara said. "They were only trying to help."

"You can relax, Mother, I didn't. Although I was tempted to when he said I was stubborn and petty."

"Wow, I would have expected something like that from Skyler," Greer said.

"She said I had to get over myself."

"Where in the world did she get that from?" Clara asked.

"Me, I'm afraid. The two of them hear a lot more than we realize—and understand a lot more than we give them credit for."

"Speak for yourself, my dear daughter."

"Oh, I think even you, my dear father, might be surprised."

Greer looked contemplative. "You might be right."

CATHERINE WAS SO TRANSFIXED by the document on her computer that she didn't notice Zach hovering in the doorway to her office until he started tapping impatiently on the door jamb like a flicker on a tree trunk.

"Stop that," she demanded, snapping her head up.

Zach moved into the office as Catherine turned back to the computer. "What are you so engrossed in?" he asked.

"Nothing," she replied, minimizing what was on the screen.

"Anything to do with Pombo's House Bill?"

Catherine sat back in her chair. "Hal sent me an update," she responded matter-of-factly.

"Why?"

"Why not?" she replied calmly, though his demeanor made her edgy.

"Did he mention that it passed, 229 to 193?"

"Yes."

"And that it didn't break along traditional party lines?"

"Yes."

"Why have you been researching threatened and endangered species?" Zach inquired. His voice was even, but Catherine saw him scrutinizing her like a lawyer cross-examining a witness.

"I have an interest in the issue. You know: climate change, species decline," she involuntarily intertwined the fingers of her hands, "there are connections being made." Catherine stared down at her hands, as though they weren't hers, before yanking them apart. She saw Zach slightly lift one of his eyebrows and berated herself for reacting so fervently just because she made the same gesture as the woman from her dreams.

"Hal said that you started delving almost a year ago."

"You and Hal getting to be buddies?" Catherine tried to jest, but her nerves began to jump as she wondered whether Hal had also told Zach about the honey bee.

"We just happened to be talking about the Pombo bill, and he mentioned the coincidence."

"I see." Catherine decided that if he was going to treat her like she was on the witness stand, she was going to respond in kind, no volunteering information, just answering the questions.

"You have to admit it's an interesting coincidence," he pressed.

"Not really," Catherine replied, staring at him blandly.

"It's not a coincidence?"

"It's not interesting."

Zach nodded his head shrewdly. "I think it is."

"Good for you."

"You're not a biologist."

"I never claimed I was."

"So who identified the specific species you've been researching?"

"I ran across them," Catherine said stoically while thinking to herself, *on a plateau, in a dream, along with a strange woman and her dog.*

"Hal said you knew the scientific name of each one."

"The internet is a wonderful thing, Zach. You should try it some time."

"Come on, Catherine, did someone let you in on something?"

"Just what exactly are you asking me, Zach?"

"Do you have a source?"

"A source?" Catherine was confused. The woman wasn't a source, she was . . . well, Catherine didn't know what she was. Then Zach's meaning, as it related to the 'real' world, not her dreams, hit her. "Oh my God!" she exclaimed. "You think I have a source that told me something was going to happen to the Endangered Species Act," Catherine said in disbelief. "How could you think that I could have that kind of information, for a day, let alone a year, and not say something?" Suddenly Catherine felt nauseous. What if the dreams had been a warning? No, they couldn't have been, there were way too many species, and some of them weren't even found in the United States. It couldn't have been about the Act.

"Catherine, I didn't say your source told you what was going to happen to the Act. I'm just saying that any information you get should be shared with the right people in the organization. There are those of us who understand the potential implications of a tip, no matter how vague, better than others," Zach stated.

"There are no tips, Zach, because there is no source," Catherine insisted.

"I understand."

"Don't say it like that."

"I said I understand."

"Yeah, right, in that condescending way that means you're humoring me but don't really believe me."

"If anything should come up in the future—" Zach urged.

"Oh my God," Catherine said, exasperated. "Get out of my office."

CHAPTER 20

Henry could hear Catherine plodding up the steps, so he got up to pour her some coffee.

"Good morning," he greeted her as she appeared in the archway to the kitchen.

"Morning," Catherine grumbled, sagging into her chair.

"Bad night?" he asked, placing the coffee in front of her before sitting back down.

As Catherine wrapped her hands around the mug, she stared up at him through her bangs, part of a new haircut that she had tried on impulse, hated, and was currently in the process of growing out.

"What do you think?" she asked tepidly.

Addy trotted into the kitchen, stood next to Henry, and stared at Catherine.

"Don't talk to me, you," Catherine said to the dog.

"I don't think she was going to," Henry stated, rubbing Addy under her chin. The dog elongated her head and neck in obvious delight.

"Are you encouraging her?"

"Encouraging her in what? I'm just rubbing her."

"You know perfectly well that she keeps bugging me."

Henry did know. Addy had been Catherine's watchful companion for months after the bombings happened in London, and her soothing presence helped relieve Catherine's stress. However, as the months wore on, Addy began exhibiting some unusual behavior. She began barking sharply in the morning when Henry let her out in the backyard, as though she saw something in the alley, although nothing was ever there that Henry could see. Then, just as abruptly as she had begun the strange barking, Addy stopped and started to inexplicably dart around the house before coming to a stop in front of Catherine, whom she would stare at expectantly. For the past month, all the waking signs of Addy's restlessness stopped, but she began to whine in her sleep, her pitch varying between soft and vociferous. Henry's sleep was rarely disturbed. The same could not be said for Catherine's.

"I don't think she's trying to bug you; she's asleep."

Catherine glared at Henry. "She's trying to bug me all right. I'm the one that wakes up in the middle of the night while she"—Catherine pointed an irate finger at Addy—"sleeps right through, just like *you.*"

"Sorry."

"Look at her," Catherine said accusingly. "She's so damn happy."

"Don't you want her to be happy?"

"Oh for God's sake, Henry, that isn't the point!"

"What is the point, Catherine?"

"She's talking to that other dog."

"I see."

"No, you don't. You don't believe me, but I know what she's been doing."

"Catherine, I didn't say I didn't believe—" Henry began in his most soothing voice.

"Don't start with me, Henry."

"I'm not starting with you."

"Look, you might think it sounds crazy, but I know what I know. Addy is communicating with that dog and conspiring to get me to go back there with her."

"Conspiring, Catherine?"

"I'm telling you, I've woken up just in the nick of time. I can see Addy standing on that goddamn plateau, but I'm not going to join her," Catherine said, scowling at Addy, who looked back placidly.

"Catherine," Henry said gently.

"What?" she barked, whipping her head in his direction.

"I think you need to consider going back with her."

"You have got to be kidding me," she replied. "Have you been listening to me at all?"

"Yes, I have, but when was the last time you got a good night's sleep?"

"I don't know, Henry, probably 1978."

"How many times in the last several months have you had the dream"—he used his fingers to encase the word in air quotes—"about being on the highway?"

"What does one thing have to do with the other?" Catherine challenged.

"You haven't had that particular dream," he said, using air quotes again.

"Stop that." Catherine cut him off and using her fingers to mock him said. "I get it, they're not 'really dreams.'"

"Well, you won't let me use any other word, but your contention that Addy is communicating with the woman's dog, conspiring against you even, means they are definitely more than dreams, unless you're trying to say that Addy is communicating with something from your subconscious."

Catherine cocked her head to one side and stared at him disapprovingly. "Are you done?"

"Just trying to make a point."

"Really? And that point would be that I should go back with Addy because I keep dreaming about being on the highway in Wyoming, just like I dreamt right before I got the call from Brigit about my dad? One thing has nothing to do with the other."

"You said these dreams were more vivid and felt like when you were actually on the highway in Wyoming on your way to Butte when you saw the faces of the people."

"I haven't seen any faces."

"Because you've been waking up screaming before it gets to that point."

"I have yelled, I have not screamed. Believe me, you would know the difference if you had ever heard me scream."

"Catherine, I'm just trying to help."

"How is telling me to go back into that dream helpful?"

Henry sighed deeply. "I think if you go back with Addy, the other dream might stop."

"The dream on the plateau and that woman have caused me nothing but grief," Catherine said bleakly. "Need I remind you that both Hal and Zach are wondering about the coincidences that have occurred, first the honey bee and then the bill to gut the Endangered Species Act?"

"I know."

"Hal and Zach are talking about me, Henry. Zach thinks I have a source, a real live source, and I'm sure Hal does too. I, myself, would have the same suspicion about me because it has all been too fucking coincidental for it to be just a coincidence. So where does that leave me, since there is no way I can tell them about the dreams? Look at what happened with Ford when I told him I saw the honey bee in a dream. He thought I knew something about the London bombings, Henry, and I knew nothing because that woman showed me nothing." Catherine shook her head and sighed. "It wouldn't have mattered anyway. If there really are some hidden meanings to the dreams, they are too enigmatic for me to decrypt."

Catherine got up, scraping her chair on the floor as she did. As she turned to leave the kitchen, Henry stood and blocked her way. "Take a cue from Addy and talk to the woman. Maybe then you will understand what she's trying to tell you. If you could just stop worrying so much about how things work, or might work, maybe you could find out how they actually work."

"You have no idea what you are talking about," she insisted, stepping around Henry and striding toward the bathroom.

"Are you coming to the airport with me to pick up my parents?" Henry asked, just as she closed the bathroom door. He turned to Addy saying, "That went well, don't you think?"

Addy cocked her head to one side.

"Yeah, I know, not an auspicious start to the Thanksgiving holiday, but I had to try." Henry patted the dog on the head. "Don't worry," he added brightly. "She will want to know, she won't be able to help herself, so just hang in there, little girl."

Addy wagged her tail happily.

CATHERINE WAS BACK ON THE PLATEAU with Addy at her side.

"Bloody hell! Stop doing this," Catherine demanded, glaring down at Addy. "I'm not staying." She closed her eyes and started chanting, "Wake up, wake up, wake up," but when she opened her eyes she was still on the plateau. "Damn it, Addy," Catherine said crossly. She then noticed how still it was and couldn't stop herself from looking over the edge and seeing . . . nothing. There was no mammal, reptile, amphibian, bird, fish, insect, or plant. The canyon, plateaus, and mesas that had always teemed with life at the beginning of the dream were now completely barren. She turned around. The plateau was equally deserted. There wasn't even a wisp of wind to swirl the sand. The woman and her dog were standing in the middle of the plateau instead of on the opposite side. Catherine instinctively felt for Addy, taking comfort from the dog's presence.

"I'm not happy about this conspiracy," Catherine whispered, looking down at Addy, who wagged her tail gently. Catherine groaned. "Fine, you win. Let's just get it over with," she said and began walking over to the other two, Addy by her side.

"What the hell is going on?" Catherine asked abruptly.

The woman looked puzzled.

"This," Catherine waved her hand around. "I mean, before it was weird, and the incineration was just overwrought, but I was getting used to it. So why nothing now?" she asked, waving her hand around again. "It's just downright creepy."

"I thought the way it was before made you uncomfortable."

"I said I was—" Catherine's mouth fell open. "You're talking," her voice squeaked in surprise.

"I thought you wanted me to talk to you," the woman replied.

Catherine rubbed her hand over her face and then said, "I think this was a mistake."

Addy went over to the woman's dog and sat next to him.

"Addy doesn't think so, Catherine," the woman noted.

Catherine's eyes narrowed. "How do you know my name?"

"Why wouldn't I know your name?"

"Why wouldn't . . . how about because you don't know me," Catherine replied.

"Yet, I know your name."

"Yet, I don't know yours," Catherine noted sharply.

"My name is Keitha."

"What?"

"My name is Keitha."

"I heard you the first time."

"Then why did you say what?"

"I was just—"

"His name is Murphy," Keitha interjected.

"What?" Catherine said, stunned, and when Keitha opened her mouth, Catherine waved her hand in a dismissive gesture. "I heard you, I heard you."

"Is there something wrong with his name?" Keitha asked.

"No. I like his name. As a matter-of-fact, I had a dog named Murphy when I was growing up," Catherine mused. "So did his name come from my subconscious?"

"My mother named him."

"Your mother? All right," Catherine said warily before addressing Addy, "Come on, girl, it's time to go."

"Why are you leaving?" Keitha asked anxiously.

"Because bringing your mother into this is just too much."

"Too much? Too much of what?"

"You show me all those different species and then melodramatically scorch them, without any explanation. In fact, at first you don't talk at all. So I do my own research, and find they're threatened or endangered species. Then you do the mime thing about everything being interconnected, and, by the way, I am already well aware of that fact. What I didn't know, what you didn't bother miming, was that the Endangered Species Act itself was being threatened. First it was the honey bee, then the Endangered Species Act. I don't understand why you made it so cryptic instead of just telling me what was happening."

"I was only trying to get and hold your attention. The honey bee was a mistake, and I had no idea that your Endangered Species Act was at risk."

"A mistake?" Catherine paused. "And what do you mean *my* Endangered Species Act?"

"I don't think you're ready for that discussion."

"Why?"

"Because it is a difficult concept to understand."

"And I'm not capable of grasping it, is that what you're saying?" Catherine asked, annoyed by the condescending tone. "After all the grief you've caused me, now you're insulting me?"

"How am I causing you grief?"

"Because of all this, people I work with have been asking me questions, uncomfortable questions. What caused my interest in the honey bee? Did I know anything about what was going to happen in London? Why did I have such an interest in threatened and endangered species? Why was I researching specific species? Wasn't what happened with the Act an interesting coincidence? Did I have a source?"

"A source?" Keitha queried.

"Someone providing me information," Catherine explained brusquely.

"I didn't mean to provide you any information that you didn't already have. It all really was just a coincidence."

Catherine glared at Keitha. "Do you understand the position you've put me in? Do you understand the grief you've caused me?"

"Somewhat."

"Somewhat," Catherine threw her hands up. "Great, that's just great. Look, lady, I've about had it, so you had better tell me what is going on, right now."

"Mentally, you're not ready to listen to me," Keitha said matter-of-factly.

"First you insult me by saying I'm incapable of understanding, and now I don't have the mental capacity to even listen. You're a real diplomat, you are," Catherine said sarcastically.

"I don't mean to be insulting."

"And yet, you are," Catherine noted harshly.

Keitha looked at Murphy and shrugged before saying, "Fine. You want to know what is going on? I'll tell you. This is a means of communicating with you, but it is not a means of providing insight into your future. We are not some sort of premonition."

"I never said you were."

"You implied it."

The two women locked eyes as though they were children waiting to see who would blink first. Two high-pitched yips made them break off the contest. Addy and Murphy were crouching low to the ground, ears flat against their heads.

"Addy, what's wrong?" Catherine asked, taking a step toward the dog. Addy and Murphy stood up at the same instant and yipped again.

"They're mad," Keitha said. "Can't you see that?"

"Yes, I see that," Catherine answered gruffly.

Addy and Murphy stood side-by-side, absolutely still, deep furrows evident on their brows.

"I guess they don't like the vibe coming from us," Catherine said.

"Vibe?"

"Yeah, you know, feeling . . . sensation."

"Ah," Keitha nodded. "No, I do not think they like our . . . vibe . . . at all."

Catherine turned to gaze at Keitha. "You are a strange person."

"I could say the same of you."

The two women sized each other up.

"Let's just say, for the moment, that what you've been showing me here just happens to coincide with what is actually happening. No intent, just really bad timing on your part." Keitha grimaced as Catherine continued, "Given that premise, you need to come clean about what this is all about." Catherine tried not to show any outward sign of the anxiety that was making her head pound.

Keitha blinked. "What does cleaning have to do with anything?"

"Sarcasm, oh yeah, that's a good idea," Catherine replied tersely until she saw the bewildered, exasperated look on the other woman's face.

"I don't know all your idioms," Keitha said bluntly. "Who possibly could? A lot of them don't even make sense."

"Interesting. However, I think the question is, who wouldn't know them?" Catherine reflected for a moment. "You're not from my subconscious, and by your own admission, this has nothing to do with premonitions, but it is about communicating with me."

"Yes," Keitha confirmed.

Catherine glanced at the dogs who were still standing like statues. "They communicate with each other."

"Yes."

"Without us."

"Yes. They have their own unaffected way of communicating. It's not clouded by suspicion or doubt. They believe that what they sense is real, is real."

"Touché," Catherine said, waiting for the confusion to return to Keitha's face. "That you understand?"

"Of course."

"Of course." Catherine shook her head and stared at the dogs again. "You say they have their own unaffected way, but they are affected by us. Addy didn't start dream . . . communicating with Murphy . . ." she hesitated. Saying the name in reference to this dog felt strange to her, that is, until she saw his ears wiggle slightly, which made her smile. "It took a while, and I think that's because I was so mad about all of this."

"So mad at me, you mean. I wasn't too happy with you either," Keitha admitted. "They empathize with us—perceive our vibe, as you put it—and because of that we can hinder them."

"Yet Addy has been talking to Murphy for well over a month, and during that time, my attitude toward all of this, including you, didn't change."

"But mine did. Murphy was able to reach out to Addy because I stopped insisting that he shouldn't."

"You were stopping him?"

"It was pointed out to me, by some insightful people, that I was impeding him."

"And how I felt became irrelevant?" Catherine asked, a little offended.

"Not irrelevant. I'm sure Addy tried to tell you Murphy was back before she came here on her own."

"How could she tell—you don't mean when she was barking at nothing, and running around the . . . ?" Catherine's voice trailed away. She looked over at Addy, who trotted over and leaned against Catherine's leg. "I guess I wasn't listening the way I needed to," Catherine said, stroking the side of the dog's head.

"It can be difficult," Keitha acknowledged as she rubbed Murphy's neck. "Addy senses the complexity of what goes on around you, even when you are blocking it out. That's why she helped bring you here in the first place and why she insisted you come back."

"Why did Addy bring me here? What is it you want?" Catherine asked apprehensively.

"Will you let me tell you a story?"

"A story?" Catherine asked in surprise.

"I think it would help explain."

Catherine realized she was holding her breath and let it out in a shudder, nodding her head up and down like a marionette.

Keitha pointed at a rock. "Maybe you should sit down."

Catherine turned slightly and stared in the direction Keitha was indicating, at a rock that hadn't been there before. It had a slight indentation that made it look like a backless chair. Catherine sat, and Addy settled down in front of her, lying so her head was just barely touching Catherine's feet.

"There was this woman named Rebecca who lived in the early 17th century. When Rebecca was a child, she would spend hours in the woods on her own. And in that solitude, with nothing but the earth and the animals, she could see things that were wondrous, but also, at times, disturbing. By the time she was twelve she had warned her family several times to avoid specific situations, but to their detriment, they ignored her. One brother broke a leg and another had his home catch fire because of a careless ember. Rebecca's mother told her that she had to stop going into the woods and that she had to stop talking about things that might happen. She made Rebecca swear on her immortal soul that she would stop. Rebecca honored her promise to her mother, stopped going to the woods, and never told anyone anything else about something that would happen to them. Soon her family forgot, or chose to forget, about the odd things she said when she was a girl. Then one day, when Rebecca was a young woman, a man named Oscar began communicating with her."

Keitha proceeded to tell Catherine about Rebecca and Oscar. She carefully wove the story around the two people without mentioning anything specific about how and where Oscar lived. She said only that he lived in a time different from Rebecca.

Catherine gradually leaned forward as Keitha's story unfolded until she was perched on the edge of the rock. Then Keitha concluded that, "Oscar blamed himself for causing Rebecca to die so horribly, and so he left. He walked away from all of the people he knew, including his own brother."

Catherine didn't move and didn't say a word when the story was done, her eyes searching Keitha's face for any hint of deception. Keitha didn't flinch under the relentless scrutiny, and Catherine finally spoke.

"That was quite a story."

"I thought so, when it was told to me."

"Who told you the story?"

"My father."

"First your mother, now your father, who it seems is quite the fanciful storyteller."

"No, he isn't actually, not at all."

"So is it a parable? A tale to prove a point?" Catherine asked, feeling the need to define the term.

"I know what a parable is, but no, it isn't. It's a story about what happened. I believe you call it a true story."

"I see." Catherine's eyebrow shot up.

Keitha could see that Catherine didn't see, so she attempted to get the point across by saying, "It really happened."

"I heard you, it's a *real* story," Catherine said as she touched her temple.

"I said it was a true story."

Catherine stared at Keitha with one eye. "Yeah, well, real and true are relative terms."

"I understand that many things that were purported to be real or true in your . . ."

"Go ahead, just say it." Catherine was still only looking at Keitha through one eye and, when she didn't respond, Catherine said, "No? Okay, let me. *In my time,*" she said drolly.

"What I told you is true," Keitha reiterated.

Catherine opened her other eye with difficulty. Her head was throbbing. "How do you know it's true?"

"My father told me it was, and so did Oscar's brother."

"Sooo," Catherine drew the word out in a low, almost inaudible voice as she closed her eyes and rubbed both her temples. "Did Oscar's brother tell this to you, face to face, or . . . you know?"

"Face to face."

"Sooo, Oscar lived in a different time from Rebecca and you live in the same time as his brother. How many years' distance from Rebecca's time are we talking?"

"About six hundred years, more or less. Forward."

"Yeah, I kind of thought that would be the case. So, doing the math, it means that you're from my future," Catherine said, putting the last two words into finger quotes, "about two hundred years, more or less. In keeping with the true story, it also means that you and I must share some genetic link."

"Yes," Keitha replied, but then said, "but you don't believe me."

"I think I'd rather believe that you are some sort of premonition," Catherine said.

"Why?"

"I don't know," Catherine said truthfully. "Maybe because it's sort of accepted, or at least considered possible, by some people."

"Will you at least consider that what I'm telling you is true?"

Catherine shook her head slowly. It felt like it weighed a ton. She couldn't think straight, and she just wanted Keitha to stop talking for a minute.

"No?" Keitha said incredulously.

"I wasn't shaking my head because I didn't believe you. No, I was shaking my head because . . . it is a lot to absorb."

Murphy nudged Keitha's hand, and she looked down into his insistent eyes.

"I understand, but you said you wanted to know what we want, and first you have to understand who we are," Keitha said in a calm voice.

"I wanted a rational explanation about who you are and why you're here," Catherine insisted.

"Rationality is merely a product of the time you live in."

"What?"

"Would you think it was rational for anyone to believe the earth was flat? Or that it sat on the shoulder of Hercules? Would it be rational not to believe in germs?"

"Very clever, but what you're asking me to believe is completely unverifiable, which makes it just a little bit more out there than any of those things."

"Out there?" Keitha asked, but before Catherine had to explain she said, "Oh, yes, I understand. New ideas almost always seem out there, at least to some people. Discovery comes about when someone says, I think things might work differently or better. Or they just say, what if? What if the earth isn't flat? What if the sun doesn't revolve around the earth? What if there are minute particles within atoms that can't be seen but must be there? Has anyone in your time seen an individual quark?"

"There have been experiments that show—"

"I said seen."

"No, not that I've ever heard of," Catherine admitted, but added, "It isn't the same thing."

"No, it isn't," Keitha said emphatically. "You can see me and Murphy. You can see this place and all of the different species that have been here."

"Again, very clever, but I need time to consider . . . everything, without you pushing your agenda."

"It is not an agenda," Keitha snapped, unable to control her temper. "I am telling you the truth and all you need to do is open your mind to the possibility. How hard can that be?"

Suddenly Murphy and Addy rose to their feet, ears twitching.

"You're upsetting them again," Catherine noted.

Keitha listened carefully before saying, "No, that isn't it. I don't think we have much time left."

"What are you talking about?" Catherine asked, just as she began to discern a persistent, muted noise, like a small fly buzzing around her head. She rubbed her ear and said, "You know, if I were to open my mind and believe you, then . . ." Catherine paused because the noise was getting louder, and it sounded more like a dump truck was backing up. She rubbed her ear again and thought, *Where is Addy?*

"Then what?" Keitha bellowed.

Catherine couldn't tell if Keitha was trying to be heard above the beeping noise, which was at a feverish pitch, or if she was just irritated.

CATHERINE BOLTED UPRIGHT IN BED and stared at Henry uncomprehendingly.

"Sorry," he said, shutting off the alarm.

Catherine continued to look at him vacantly.

"Catherine?"

"What? What did you say?"

"I said I was sorry."

"Why?"

"I forgot to shut the alarm off after I got up. Didn't you hear it?"

"Yeah, sort of," she said, bewildered.

"Sort of? Catherine, it was obnoxious."

She finally noticed that Henry was standing at the foot of the bed in his sweatpants and t-shirt.

"What is wrong with the two of you this morning?" he asked, concerned.

"What do you mean?"

"Addy was completely zonked, didn't even hear me when I got up, didn't wake up even when I called to her from the doorway. So I decided to let her sleep, and then you don't hear the alarm. And I hate to break it to you, but you look dazed."

"I told you I heard the alarm," Catherine asserted as she got out of bed, threw on her sweats, and stomped up the stairs. "Where's Addy?" she asked, looking around as Henry mounted the stairs behind her.

"She ran upstairs a minute ago so I let her out. I thought surely you would hear the alarm and get up."

"You really need to remember to shut that thing off when you get up," Catherine said. "It's really loud."

Henry threw his hands in the air and went to the back door to let Addy in. Catherine poured herself some coffee, glanced at Henry's laptop that was sitting on the table, and headed into the office.

"Catherine, what are you doing?"

She jumped in the chair that was facing the computer and whipped around. "Shit, Henry."

"Sorry, did I startle you?"

"Did you feed Addy?" she asked instead of replying.

"No, I've been sitting at the kitchen table staring at the ceiling for the last forty-five minutes," he said facetiously, making his way over to her chair. "Of course I fed her. I also sent off several emails while I was waiting for you," he said, staring at the computer screen.

Catherine quickly swung around to the keyboard and minimized the document.

"Hold it." He put a hand on her shoulder. "What was that?"

"Nothing. Just a mental exercise."

"Looked like a list to me."

"Yes, a list," she said dismissively and reached for the mouse.

Henry's hand covered hers, and he carefully lifted it off the device. "Catherine, I saw two lists. One titled 'reasons to believe her,' the other 'reasons not to.' Believe who?"

Catherine didn't respond.

"Okay, fine." Henry pressed the mouse, and the document sprang back onto the screen.

"Give me my hand back," she demanded.

He ignored her, keeping her left hand in his, as he scanned the lists. "What does that mean?" He pointed at the screen. "And what about that?" He jabbed at the screen in alarm. "What the hell is going on?"

She reached across the keyboard with her right hand and minimized the document.

"Oh no you don't," Henry said, reaching for the mouse.

"Henry, stop it."

"What's going on, Catherine?"

"The hell if I know. You're the one that wanted me to go back there."

"Was the woman there?"

"Yes," she replied curtly.

"Well? What happened?"

Catherine sank back in the chair. She felt exhausted. "She told me a story."

"A story?"

Catherine proceeded to tell Henry everything Keitha had told her. "Seems there was this woman named Rebecca . . ."

"Wow!" Henry said after Catherine finished. "Will you let me continue reading what you put down?"

Catherine leaned forward and opened up the document before getting out of the chair. "I need a refill."

Henry nodded absently as he sat in the chair she just vacated, completely engrossed in the lists.

Catherine left the office, walked into the kitchen, then over to the coffee pot to pour herself another cup. She sipped it slowly. Henry would need some time to ponder what she had written. No matter how broad-minded he purported himself to be, she doubted that he had conceived what the woman insisted was true. She filled up her mug again and slowly walked back to the office. She looked into the living room and saw Addy lying in her morning sun, completely at ease.

Henry was staring at the computer screen.

"Strange, huh?" she said, this time taking him by surprise. "Sorry," she said softly.

"Strange isn't the right word," he said honestly.

"How about impossible? I must be cracking up or something."

"You're not cracking up."

"Henry, for God's sake, I can't be talking to a woman from the future."

"Why not?"

"Oh, come on! You're a man of science, Henry. You can't tell me that this doesn't stretch things to the breaking point."

"What is wrong with stretching things—or breaking them, for that matter? We have to stretch to make strides. If we stopped with what we believed to be true we'd still think the world was flat."

"Don't try to use her arguments on me."

"Her arguments?" Henry asked, intrigued. "You didn't say anything about her arguments?"

"Let's just say she'd make a great attorney."

Henry raised an inquiring eyebrow.

"She threw a lot of shit at me about being open and about how discovery comes about when you ask 'what if?' One of the what ifs she used was the world being flat."

"Fascinating. What else did she say?"

"You know, I don't think you would find it quite so fascinating if you were in my shoes."

"I hope I would, but I would have to know more about what happened," Henry said.

"Oh, very clever."

A sudden pinging on the computer caught their attention.

"You have mail," Henry noted. "Were you expecting something?"

Catherine never turned on her email alert unless she was anxious to see a reply, and Henry knew it, so it was a rhetorical question.

"Would you like to sit down?" he offered.

"Oh for pity's sake, just open the damn thing."

Henry opened Catherine's email account and clicked on the new message. They read through it at the same pace, and then Henry opened one of the two attachments. As he opened the second, Catherine noticed that his hand was shaking slightly.

Henry sucked in a gulp of air and started choking. Catherine pounded on his back as he tried waving his hands in the air. He finally caught his breath and gasped, "Stop pounding."

She handed him her tepid coffee, and he took a drink before turning to face her.

"My God, Catherine!"

"It doesn't prove anything," she said.

"It proves that what the woman told you was a true story."

"It merely proves that there was an incident that closely resembles part of her story," she noted.

"Catherine, look at the evidence. You're the one that found it."

"I don't even know why I looked."

"Because that's who you are and you know it," Henry said emphatically. "How in the world did you track this down?" he asked with obvious admiration.

"I got lucky."

Henry waited for her to elaborate.

"I stumbled across an article about unusual weather events in the 17th century that contained a list of references. One paper sounded like it dealt with the right timeframe, but I couldn't find it, so I went back to the original document, and there was an email address for the person that wrote the paper. I sent an inquiry, giving the approximate date and location, and asked if there was any documentation about a severe storm event," she hesitated, "and if there was, I asked if there was any record of what happened in the aftermath of the storm. I thought it was a long shot. I really didn't expect to get any reply, let alone this quickly."

Henry nodded. "I'd say you got more than a reply. I'd say you got proof."

"Of what? That old article merely said a person was hanged for being a witch. It didn't say the person's name was Rebecca."

"'A young woman' was hanged because people thought she caused a storm that destroyed most of her village."

"Again, all that means is that part of the story was rooted in fact."

"You need to move Rebecca to the reason to believe list," Henry asserted.

"Not yet."

Henry shook his head but moved on. "You put the woman's name on your list of reasons to believe."

"Have you ever heard of the name before?" Catherine inquired.

"No. Keith I obviously have heard of, but not Keitha. So, what does the name mean?" Henry asked.

"I didn't have time to look it up."

"Let's look it up now." Henry closed the email, navigated to Catherine's favorites, and clicked on one of her links for researching names. When the website came up, he typed in the name Keitha and hit the search button.

"There it is. Let's see . . . female form of Keith, Scottish clan surname, and probably a variation on a couple of Gaelic names which meant woods." Henry clicked on another of her favorites.

"What's that say?" Catherine pointed at the screen.

"Celtic origin meaning knowledgeable."

Catherine snorted. "Well, she certainly thinks she is."

"You listed Murphy and Addy as reasons to believe, in bold."

"They are."

"I would agree."

"Then why the hell are you grilling me about what I put on the 'reasons to believe' list?"

"Because I want you to talk it through so you won't start talking yourself out of every single one of them."

"Don't start," she warned.

"Don't close yourself off," he countered, holding her stare.

"That's sure easy to say when it isn't your life. You don't have any idea what you're asking me to do."

"Not entirely, Catherine, but please, I want to help you figure out what's happening."

"I don't think you can," she said quietly, turning her back on him.

Henry shook his head sadly and rose from the chair. As he walked past Catherine, she reached out and touched his arm. Henry wrapped his arms around her as she fell against his chest. Her body heaved as she began to cry. Addy appeared in the doorway.

"Addy's here," Henry whispered into Catherine's ear.

"Of . . . course . . . she is," Catherine replied jerkily as she regained control and felt the dog's nose on her hand. She looked up at Henry. "I'm just so tired."

"Here," Henry led her over to the chair, "Sit down. Do you want some more coffee?"

Catherine shook her head, using her sleeve to dry her eyes, and took a shaky breath before asking, "How do you think you can help?"

Henry placed his hand gently on her cheek and then sat on the edge of the couch-cum-futon to gather his thoughts. "Living with you, seeing what you've gone through over the years, well, it does lead one to contemplate possibilities."

"Really? Contemplation about possibilities?" Catherine gave him a waning grin.

"Are you going to let me talk?"

Catherine nodded halfheartedly.

"I think that there are areas of our brains we know little to nothing about. I think that a person who could consciously access some of these areas would be more than capable of constructing a place, like the plateau, to communicate with someone else who was in a different place or time. But the person that they were trying to communicate with would have to have the key to breaking the code."

"Like the code that was broken during World War II? That kind of code?"

"Yes. The Allies intercepted all those messages, but they didn't know what they meant because it was in a code they didn't understand. They needed someone who could find the key. Once that was done, what looked like gibberish became meaningful. Now can you imagine cracking the codes that would allow a conscious communication between people across temporal and spatial barriers?"

"According to the story I was told, Rebecca didn't have to crack any code. Her genetics provided the key to picking up on Oscar's message."

"That, and her ability to understand what was happening," Henry added as he pondered. "So, really, the communication was more like the Navajo code talkers who used their own language to send messages. Since Navajo was a complex language, which had never been written down, only someone else who knew Navajo could understand what was being said, and only if that person knew the rest of the code. Out of all of Oscar's ancestors, only Rebecca heard, understood, and could communicate back to him. Which means . . ." Henry left the sentence hanging as he raised an anticipatory eyebrow.

"I know what you think it means."

"Tell me you don't believe you're related to Keitha, after everything you've thought about and confirmed," he said, pointing at the computer.

"You didn't even bring up genetics in your first cracking-the-code analogy."

"Very true. My analogy was missing the key piece. Genetics was just never raised as a possibility before." Henry drew in a quick breath.

"Why would it have been raised before now?" she asked, confused.

"I think you need to talk to Ford."

"Ford?" Her eyes widened. "You mean to tell me that you've been contemplating possibilities with Ford?"

"Theoretical possibilities, yes. He's—"

"Oh my God. Oh my God." Catherine pulled at her hair. "You're the reason why Ford asked me to consider that my dream about the honey bee was more than just a dream. How could you do that without telling me, Henry?"

"We *never* talked about you or your dreams."

"You didn't have to. Ford put two and two together," Catherine retorted before rushing out of the room.

"Please, talk to Ford," Henry yelled after her, then looked at Addy. "I think I'm making progress."

Addy stared at him, her ears quivering.

CHAPTER 21

K eitha sensed the presence next to her, even though the interloper had made no sound upon entering the room and was so nimble that Keitha barely felt the slight give of the cot under the weight of the other body. She felt no apprehension and waited patiently until there was a light tap on her hand. Keitha opened her eyes at the same time that the cat pounced on her stomach.

"Oomph!" Keitha grunted. "What is it about my stomach?" she asked the cat, which was hovering above her head, staring down at her with wide, lustrous eyes, framed in velvety gray fur.

There had always been a cat or two, when possible, assigned to the garden area to keep the rodent population in balance. Unlike the other growers, George, in his single-minded pursuit to maintain optimal health and productivity of the various plant species, treated the cats with courteous professional detachment, until the small creature, perched upon Keitha's chest, entered his horticultural world three years ago.

Keitha had stopped by to see how the sweet plant was faring, and George began to tell her how the latest cat was proving to be very astute and seemed to understand the intricate balance within the garden. As George was making his observations, Keitha spotted Murphy heading down one of the aisles and knew the dog would attempt his best canine greeting if he ran into the new arrival—a gesture that few cats in the colony had ever found the least bit decorous, much to the dog's, and in many instances his nose's, dismay.

Keitha took off after Murphy, hoping to head him off. She rounded the end of one of the planting beds, fully expecting to see a lone, forlorn dog or a standoff between the dog and a hissing cat with an arched back. Instead, she found the feline nonchalantly watching as the canine contorted his body as low to the ground as he was capable and leaned his head out toward the cat. Murphy's nose looked disproportionally huge as he touched the petite nose of the cat and wagged his tail happily. Buoyed by his success, he proceeded to try to smell the cat's rear end, at which point the cat sat down and stared at him with wide eyes.

"She looks startled, but she isn't running away," Keitha noted as George came up behind her.

"I made the same mistake when Clara brought her here. I asked how in the world a tiny, frightened little thing like her was going to be able to work in the garden. Clara told me that even though Slate looked perpetually alarmed, she really wasn't; instead, she was inquisitive and fearless."

"Slate?"

"A metamorphic rock—"

"A rock?"

"I wasn't finished," George remarked brusquely. "Clara said the name also was used for the color gray with a blue hue. So it was the coloration of her fur, and the fact that Slate is unshakable, like a rock, that led Clara to the naming."

Slate was weaving between Murphy's legs, causing the dog to lift one paw and then another in a dancing motion, until the dog gently nudged the cat with his head when she emerged from between his front legs. Slate rolled but quickly regained her footing and started to weave around Murphy's legs again, only to have the dog bump her again as she emerged.

"I think she's tickling him," Keitha said.

"I think he's letting her," George observed.

The dog and cat continued their play for several more minutes until Murphy lay down, and Slate curled up into his chest. Throughout the ensuing years, the elaborate play became their routine whenever the two friends met.

"How did you get past my ever-vigilant companion?" Keitha said, turning her head to look over at Murphy, who was watching the cat, his ears against his head. Keitha knew immediately that something wasn't right. "What's going on?" she asked the cat.

Slate sprang from Keitha's chest onto the floor and disappeared through the entry. Murphy scrambled to his feet and quickly followed. Keitha lagged behind the other two because she had to throw on some clothes, and her hurried attempt to get her pants only served to slow her down even more. As she emerged from the room, the cat and dog were nowhere in sight, but Keitha knew there was only one place they could be headed, so she took off at a sprint.

Keitha found Murphy and Slate in an elongated space separated from the main garden area by tall shelves that held a variety of tools and gardening supplies. George sat on a stool in front of a long workbench that ran along the rock wall. There were numerous pots containing various types of plants, in differing stages of growth, on the bench itself. On the shelf above the bench, there was an assortment of botanical laboratory equipment and one small gray cat lying like a sphinx, her eyes uncharacteristically hooded. George was holding one of the pots in his hands, staring hopelessly at the shriveled leaves.

"George?" Keitha approached him carefully as she looked around for Murphy before spotting him sitting at attention next to another stool, ears still pinned against his head.

George raised his head and stared at Keitha with bloodshot eyes. She recoiled.

"I can't save them," George said desolately.

Keitha drew up next to him and looked at the obviously dying plant. She put a hand on his shoulder, although she knew it would not comfort him.

"How could they?" he asked.

"I don't understand, George," Keitha said gently.

"Were they really that uncaring? Didn't they understand what would happen?" George asked vacantly, as though he hadn't heard her.

"Who are you talking about, George?" Keitha asked earnestly, shaking his shoulder to get his attention.

"Have you asked Catherine?" The pain in his eyes was more difficult for Keitha to bear than the anguish in his voice.

"I haven't—"

"I know you've talked to her."

Keitha felt exposed.

George stared at her, the pain in his eyes replaced by a fierceness that Keitha had rarely seen. "Have you asked her to explain how they could let it all happen?"

"You want Catherine to explain what's happening to the plants?" she asked, perplexed.

"I want you to ask her why they did what they did, which has led us to this." George picked up the pot with the dead plant.

"You can't expect her to answer for all the mistakes that were made."

"Mistakes," George said vehemently, slamming the pot down on the counter, causing Slate to hiss and arch her back and Murphy to leap to his feet.

"George, you need to calm down."

"They plundered and exploited anything they needed or wanted so that they could live a comfortable, indulgent life," he persisted.

"Not everyone, George." Keitha never thought she would defend the people of Catherine's time, but George was being too broad in his condemnation. "There were people trying to stop the downward spiral and help keep the same mistakes from being repeated."

"Stop saying mistakes," George roared. "They didn't care that they were condemning their descendants to a world . . . ," his voice cracked, "so broken."

Keitha had never seen George show so much raw emotion. She didn't know what to do, so she simply took one of his hands in hers.

"You need to intercede," he said, squeezing her hand. "The records need to be opened so you can find out exactly what happened."

"George," Keitha began, in an attempt to soothe him.

"You could, you and the other archivists." George's eyes darted around the room, landing briefly on different plants. "You could look at all the records, and surely a pattern would emerge that would point to what they failed to do or what they shouldn't have done. I could help pinpoint the causal factors, and then you could change them."

"You know what the records are like, George. Even with the insight from what we see in the past, it is difficult to separate the actual fact from the semi-fact and the lies that passed for fact back then. If we chose wrong we could make things so much worse."

"Worse than this? What could be worse than this?" George asked, frantically tightening his grip on her hand.

Keitha wanted to tell him that this world was probably, at least in part, a result of the Machiavellians interfering with the past, for no other reason than to make themselves more powerful. Even though George's motivation was more justifiable, it still meant interfering.

"Are you listening to me, Keitha? You have Catherine, and if everyone else helps narrow down the possibilities, you could use her for confirmation," George reiterated.

"No, George," she said adamantly, prying her hand away from his. "We don't have the right to intentionally interfere with their world like that. We don't have the right to make the choices for them."

George looked away, and Keitha saw his whole body slump, his head in his hands.

"I'm really sorry," Keitha said softly as Slate hopped down from her perch onto the bench. The cat came over to George and rubbed against his arm. He cupped his hand to allow Slate to nudge her nose against his palm.

"I'm afraid I'm a bit desperate, Keitha, because I've run out of ideas."

Keitha shuddered. "George, I . . ." Her voice trailed away. What could she say to this man who had tenaciously and skillfully kept the plants, for the most part, productive and therefore the colony healthy? Should she tell him about the shift that Clara had felt? Tell him that if she could convince Catherine to help her find out what the Machiavellians changed then maybe, just maybe there wouldn't be a looming crisis? Keitha knew that George wouldn't be reacting so strongly unless the other plants were under threat. What was happening to the sweet plant could be systemic. The wretched fact was that, even if she did convince Catherine to help and they could find the event that the Machiavellians changed, there was no guarantee that it would substantially change anything for them. It could turn out that the alternate road still led to Rome, which for her colony meant a food supply that was beginning to fail.

George stared at her, waiting, an awkward silence squeezing in between them.

"I guess we should get going," Keitha muttered; the emotionless look on his face disturbed her already uneasy feeling, as did his outburst.

After Keitha and Murphy left the area, George said, "How long have you been standing there?"

Greer emerged from a space where the shelving created an alcove.

"I came down to talk to you about the status," Greer said, pointing at the pots on the workbench, "and when I saw Keitha was here, I didn't want to interrupt."

"Did you hear what you expected?"

"You make it sound like I was intentionally listening."

"You were hiding," George said matter-of-factly.

Greer straightened his back, "I wasn't hiding."

George raised a disapproving eyebrow. "Maybe you wanted to hear what your daughter had to say to someone besides the three of you."

"I heard you yelling," Greer stated testily.

"This situation is extremely serious, as you well know."

"Putting more pressure on Keitha is not going to help."

"Slate brought Keitha and Murphy down here; I didn't go get them."

"Are you seriously trying to tell me you didn't orchestrate this little encounter?"

"What I'm telling you is this: we are running out of time."

"I know that," Greer barked. He then took a deep breath. "Keitha is an amazing woman. She'll be able to convince Catherine."

"No matter how amazing she is, she can't do this without your help," George said. Slate jumped off the bench and darted off.

"I am helping her."

"Do not feign ignorance with me," George stated firmly. "Keitha needs your ability. Val and I were there—"

"Yes you were, which is why you, of all people, know why I can't risk helping her that way," Greer said, cutting him off.

"Keitha will never find out what happened, if you don't help her."

Greer resolutely shook his head.

"Keitha is stronger than your mother was," George insisted. "She can handle it."

Greer's eyes flashed angrily. "Even if Keitha can, that still leaves Catherine? Do we just sacrifice her?"

"You're assuming the worst."

"I will *not* risk it," Greer bellowed and walked away.

CHAPTER 22

K eitha and Murphy looked out over the panoramic view. She glanced over her shoulder for the umpteenth time, but there was still no sign of Catherine and Addy. She continued to gaze at the vista, so astoundingly similar to the images she had found in the archives that she had relied on to craft the landscape.

"Where are they?" Keitha asked Murphy, who was sitting patiently waiting. "Do you think the story was too much?" Murphy's ears fluttered slightly. "I had to do something to dissuade her from the idea that we were part of a premonition. The honey bee was a mistake, granted a weird coincidental mistake for her, but the endangered species thing was pure coincidence. I guess that really didn't help her much, you know, with other people in her time asking awkward questions about it all. So I tried to explain how this really works using Oscar and Rebecca as an example, and she doesn't want to believe me. She would rather have us be part of a premonition. What sort of warped logic is that?" She stared at the dog waiting for a sign of support.

Murphy cocked his head to one side, then abruptly put his nose into the air and flared his nostrils, inhaling some unseen scent. Keitha was about to comment on the dog's uncanny ability to use his olfactory system like that, even though physically he was back in their room, when Murphy leapt to his feet and began running across the plateau.

Panic surged through Keitha. She sprang after Murphy just as he disappeared behind a protrusion of rock that looked like a flattened pillar. She ran behind the pillar to the same location, her feet somehow finding a vague path between the jutting sage bushes, the intermittent clumps of prickly cactus, and the strewn shards of large and small rock. Keitha caught sight of Murphy and yelled his name, but she watched helplessly as Murphy's tail fell away from her view. She then began descending off the tabletop of the plateau just as a more defined sandy depression appeared between the pitches of rock on one side and the shoulder of the ridge on the other.

Her lungs heaved in her chest as she continued her pursuit, only vaguely wondering why she felt the physical exertion, when suddenly she saw a large piece of vegetation looming directly in front of her. Keitha's mind quickly registered that it was a tree of some sort, but this one was protruding perpendicularly out of a crevasse in the rock edifice, suspended about five feet above the ground. The tree was far enough off the ground that Murphy would have been able to run unimpaired beneath it—except that, because she was taller, she was in imminent danger of smashing her face into what appeared to be very sharp needles. Her heart pounded wildly as she tried to stop, her feet skittering on the sand as she slid sideways toward the edge. Keitha scrambled in an effort to find firm footing and hit a patch of solid rock, propelling her in an uncontrollable lurch around the bizarre obstacle. She flayed her arms to keep from falling on her face and collided with the motionless dog.

Murphy's body withstood the impact, his powerful legs holding ground as Keitha fell on top of him, landing like a saddlebag over his flank.

Stunned, but relieved, Keitha hugged the dog's rear end from her prone position as he happily waved his tail in her face.

"Give me a minute," Keitha gasped, slowly righting herself by pushing off of Murphy's rear end. She glanced back up the path to the narrow strip of ground that she had slid across and could see where the edge fell away to the canyon floor. Keitha looked down at her trembling hands and tried to reassure herself that she would have woken up back in her own room if she had slipped off and felt herself falling through the air. Yet a nagging uncertainty caused the tremor in her hands to worsen. She clasped her hands together, studying Murphy.

"What the hell are you doing?" she demanded, in an unsteady voice.

Murphy continued to look down the path in front of him and began moving forward.

"Hold it," Keitha said harshly.

The dog stopped but did not turn around.

"You can't go running off like that." She heard the pleading in her voice and detested it, but she was unaccustomed to the panic that had overwhelmed her and did not want the dog to take off again.

Murphy's stance did not change.

"I know this setting is a means of interacting with Catherine and Addy, but you can't venture off the plateau."

Keitha approached Murphy carefully, examining the area he was standing alongside more closely. Her eyes widened as she stared at an open area on their left where the sandy surface was interspersed with something that resembled blackened clumps of rock. She bent over to examine the area closely. It looked as if something had eroded and stained the rock. She reached out to feel the surface but stopped just shy. The rock, or whatever it was, was coarse, yet porous, and she was afraid it would crumble if she touched it.

"Do you suppose those crevasses have something to do with weathering, Murphy?" she asked softly. "Real weathering, not what happens under the dome, what happens out in the open, when something is exposed to the elements."

Keitha straightened and stepped back. She rotated her head to the right as she tried to make sense out of what she was seeing and found herself gazing out over the landscape. For the first time she saw expanses where there was no foliage, expanses which appeared dark green. It looked as though someone had taken a brush and created streaks and dots. Keitha turned and stared back at the area close to her and Murphy. The black could look dark green and the intricate fissures unrecognizable from a distance. Could she be looking at the same thing, just from two different perspectives? An image of a painting she had seen when she was ten suddenly filled her mind. It was *Sunday Afternoon on the Island of La Grande Jatte*, a replica of the artist's original, and she had been fascinated by the imagery of people relaxing next to water. Some were lying down on the ground, others standing or walking, and there was even a child skipping. She was deep in thought when Eddy, who had also been Keitha's teacher, came up behind her and asked what she thought.

There was a lot about the picture that Keitha didn't understand. She pointed to a woman and man in the foreground and asked what the woman was holding onto. Eddy replied that it was an umbrella and explained that people had used them to shade themselves from the sun or to keep moisture off. Keitha had replied that there wasn't any sun, pointing to the darkened area where the figures stood, but before Eddy could respond, she jabbed her finger at another figure and asked what it was. Eddy told her it was a monkey, which confused Keitha because the depiction of the monkey did not correspond with her understanding of the animal, its habitat or habits. She had continued silently studying the painting until Eddy asked her if she liked it. Keitha informed him, in her best grownup tone, that she wasn't sure. At first, she thought everyone seemed very relaxed and happy, but not everything seemed to belong together and everyone wasn't really enjoying the day. Eddy instructed her to take a closer look at the picture. As Keitha moved nearer, she saw that the painting was made up of individual dots of specific hues. She walked backwards, away from the painting, until the dots again melded into each other, forming the various images and creating all of the various colors. Eddy told her that it had taken the artist, Georges Seurat, two years to complete.

It had intrigued Keitha that a person would invest so much time and painstaking care on something that, back when the painter was alive, could have been done with the stroke of a brush. Eddy tried to explain the significance of Seurat's use of the base components of colors and distance to accomplish the optical imagery that she had just experienced. Keitha, in her youth, had noted how unfortunate it was that Seurat did not have the use of a computer, which could have both generated the same illusion in a fraction of the time and provided distinctive facial features.

"I owe Eddy an apology, Murphy. How could I have been so completely stupid? A computer could replicate whatever was input, be programmed to imitate, but not envision the concept in the first place. Why didn't I see the skill it took to precisely place each dot to create the full picture? No wonder it took him years. And what if Seurat intentionally wanted the faces nondescript? What if that was part of what he was trying to convey? I can now see this anonymity amid a gathering of people. Nuance: a computer has no concept of nuance.

"You know, if over the years some of the dots on Seurat's original canvas had started to fade away, no one would probably have noticed at first. One, two, three dots disappearing would make little difference, but after a while, if the dots continued to disappear, the art experts, the really good ones, would have noticed. They would have tried to find out what was happening, what was causing it, to figure out how to stop it." Keitha stared down into Murphy's eyes. "When do you suppose everyone else would have noticed? Would it have been too late to save the masterpiece?" Images of the threatened and endangered species she had shown Catherine flooded her mind. "How many of the living masterpieces will be lost?"

Murphy's ears shot upright and then settled back into a relaxed position.

Keitha sighed heavily. As she continued to study the area surrounding them, the discomforting thought that had been trying to break through, finally did. "You know," she said apprehensively, "none of this detail is from me. I mean, I don't even know what that," she pointed at the bumpy area, "actually is."

Murphy tilted his head and studied her.

Keitha returned his look before blurting out, "Catherine cannot be doing this."

Murphy sat down and thumped his tail on the ground, creating a mini-sandstorm.

"She can't. Can she?" Keitha stopped for a moment, considering the implications. "This is why you ran off the plateau. You sensed the change, which means she did this recently . . . when we weren't here." Keitha's tone turned urgent. "Shit, we better get back up there."

Murphy did not move from his sitting position. "Come on," Keitha said sternly. She started hiking back up the slope.

Keitha turned and saw that the dog still wasn't moving. "Murphy, now!" She was losing her patience. "We need to be up there when they show up."

He regarded her with thoughtful eyes but didn't twitch a muscle.

Keitha walked the short distance back down to him. "What is your problem?" Murphy tilted his head to one side.

"What? What?" she insisted, pressing her lips together in a severe line. "What do you think I'm going to do? Just blurt out, 'By the way, how often have you two been here without us and how did you add all that stuff we just saw?' Please, I do know how to be tactful."

Murphy twitched one of his ears.

"I do so!" Keitha said in an aggravated tone but immediately calmed down. "I promise I will be the epitome of tact."

Murphy stood up effortlessly and trotted by Keitha, waving his tail in the air.

"You're a pain in the ass," she yelled, hurrying to catch up.

As Keitha and Murphy rounded the rock pillar, they saw Catherine and Addy looking at the place where they should have been.

Catherine jumped as she heard the scuffing of sand, which in the utter stillness sounded more like the hull of a boat scraping across a shallow reef. She spun to her right and Keitha saw the hackles rise on Addy's neck.

"Shit," Catherine exclaimed. "Are you trying to give me a heart attack?"

"No, why would I want you to have a heart attack?" Keitha inquired.

Catherine glared at her, obviously annoyed. "Where have the two of you been?"

"What do you mean?" Keitha asked, hoping that she sounded baffled by the question.

"Addy and I have been here, off and on, for the last couple of weeks, but the two of you have been nowhere in sight."

"I've been a little preoccupied."

"What about him?" Catherine pointed at Murphy, who was sitting down studying an immobile Addy. "He can show up without you."

"*He* has a name," Keitha said curtly.

Catherine ignored Keitha but leaned over to address the dog, "Sorry, I'm just not used to calling another dog Murphy."

Murphy's ears softened and Addy ran over to greet him.

"Do you know what Murphy's name means?" Catherine asked as she watched the two dogs.

"Sea warrior, Murphy means sea warrior," Keitha replied immediately.

"That's right." Catherine's eyebrows shot up in surprise. "I've never met anyone else who knew that."

"My mother named him."

"Yeah, so you said before. But why did she name him Murphy?"

"I don't know," Keitha replied. "I never asked."

"Oh," Catherine said, regarding her warily.

Keitha knew she had to tell Catherine more. "When Murphy was born, my mother and I weren't getting along very well, and the subject just hasn't come up recently."

"Oh," Catherine said again. This time there was no suspicion. "You're getting along better now?"

"Yes."

"So why didn't Murphy come without you?" Catherine reiterated.

"He was waiting for me."

"And what were you waiting for?"

"I thought you might need some time to consider what I told you."

"How long did you think I needed?"

"A while."

"It's been over two months."

Keitha frowned.

Catherine shook her head. "Mid-December 2005," she held up her index finger, "to mid-January 2006," she held up another finger, "to mid-February . . . wait a minute, I forgot, I guess I should be saying mid-December, what would it be again, 2205 or somewhere thereabouts?"

"Clearly over two months wasn't long enough," Keitha stated.

"Oh, sarcasm, that's good,"

"At least I wasn't disparaging you."

"Skepticism isn't disparagement," Catherine countered.

Addy and Murphy started barking and the two women turned in unison to stare at the dogs, who immediately calmed down. Catherine and Keitha reluctantly turned back to each other.

"Our vibe," Keitha remarked.

"Yes," Catherine concurred.

"I suggest we sit and have a rational, calm discussion," Keitha said.

"Agreed," Catherine replied.

"Over there," Keitha pointed to two rocks.

"No, not there," Catherine said sharply. "We don't want to walk on the soil crust."

Keitha stared at the soil surrounding the rocks where raised clumps of darkened matter, which had never been present on the table of the plateau before, were visible.

"What is that?" Keitha asked in wonder.

"What do you mean, 'what is that?'" Catherine asked, perplexed.

"That porous looking substance," Keitha pointed. "I saw the same thing down there," she twisted her torso and pointed over at the area where she and Murphy had appeared and, when she untwisted, Catherine was staring at her with hard eyes. "What? Why are you looking at me like that?" she asked.

Catherine's eyes softened, but her voice still conveyed a trace of doubt. "You *really* don't know?"

"I have no idea," Keitha stated frankly.

"That is just too bizarre."

Keitha realized what was happening, but knew it was not the time to tell Catherine, so she blurted out, "Would you let me tell you another story?"

"What?" Catherine responded, confused by the request.

"Can I tell you another story?" Keitha repeated. "It could help clarify things for you," she added quickly.

"Another true story," Catherine said steadily, her insides churning at the thought of Rebecca and the article about the hanging.

"Yes," Keitha replied.

"One more story," Catherine held up a finger and abruptly sat down on the rock that had doubled as her chair before. Addy and Murphy came over to lie down in front of her, nose-to-nose.

Keitha remained standing, took a deep breath, and began, "There was this girl who began having vivid dreams that she would try to tell her parents about when she woke, but she didn't always remember everything or understand what she saw, and so many times her stories sounded jumbled. One day she overheard her parents talking about what a strange imagination she had, so she stopped telling them about her dreams." Catherine shifted uncomfortably on the rock. Keitha was counting on the similarities between Clara and Catherine—how they both dreamt when they were young and how people did not understand—to intrigue Catherine. At the same time, Keitha knew she had to make it clear, and quickly, that she was not telling Catherine's story so that the other woman would not leave. "It wasn't until the young girl dreamt about events that were obviously from her past that she first began to wonder if there was something more to them, but she still had doubts. Then right before she turned thirteen, she dreamt about something that she knew, without a doubt, that she had never learned in her classes. She needed to find out if there was any evidence in the old historical records that the event she witnessed had ever actually occurred."

Keitha went on to recount the story of Clara and Greer that she had told so many times to so many children in the colony. Once again, she carefully left out the details of how the colony lived, although this time she found it much harder not to slip and say something that Catherine would find odd even though she was careful to replace the word "colony" with a term from Catherine's time.

". . . and the town council decided to open the records to the young girl, and several others who also were dreaming, to determine if they were seeing actual events from the past, and if so, why. They became our first archivists."

Catherine waited. "The end?" she inquired, when Keitha didn't continue.

"Yes."

"I would deduce that the girl and the young man in the story are your parents."

"That's very good," Keitha said.

"Elementary, my dear Watson."

Keitha stared at her in puzzlement.

"Sherlock Holmes, Sir Arthur Conan Doyle," Catherine said expectantly. Keitha remained puzzled. "Are you sure you people can read?" Catherine asked skeptically. "I mean you can't write, so it seems pretty—"

"You can't seriously be talking about when you wanted me to scratch in the sand in an archaic—" Keitha began before catching herself.

"Archaic?"

"We read," Keitha continued quickly. "We read volumes of information every day. Do you know how much drivel you people generated?"

"Yeah, I have a fairly good idea," Catherine stated, "but the Sherlock Holmes novels aren't drivel, they're classics."

Keitha stared at her for a moment. "Novels? You mean fictionalized work?"

"Yes."

"We don't have time to read fictionalized books. It's hard enough deciphering what part of your historical records were factual."

"I understand, and yet within fiction there is often a great deal of truth. Aside from that, fiction can convey a sense of the time the story is set in, give a glimpse into the mores of the day, offer what people thought, describe how they acted, and find out what motivated them."

"If you say so. Still, we don't have time to read anything but the historic records," Keitha stated.

"You keep repeating that."

"Repeating what?"

"That you don't have enough time."

"We don't have . . . ," she searched for the right term, "leisure time."

Catherine tilted her head in thought and Keitha wondered if she had said too much.

"So, why is it so important for your people to know about the past? And why were the . . . how did you phrase it . . . the records unavailable?" Catherine asked.

"I told you, we want to learn about the past, accurately learn about the past, and the records weren't unavailable. They just weren't being accessed because—"

"You didn't have the time?"

"I didn't say that," Keitha responded quickly.

"You didn't have to."

Keitha's skin began to tingle in alarm. She had been so careful choosing her words, what to include and what to leave out, but she had the sinking feeling that she had slipped anyway.

"What were your people so busy doing? Wait a minute, that's probably too much information for me," Catherine quipped.

"You think it's easy to try and tell you enough about us so that you will start believing me without telling you too much?" Keitha questioned bluntly.

"Touchy."

"Just tell me if you believe who we are?" Keitha motioned toward Murphy.

"Believe you? Based solely on your stories?"

"I see. You think your fiction informs, and yet when I tell you true stories about the people of my time, you dismiss them without any thought," Keitha noted indignantly.

"Unlike you, I can't research what you just told me. All I have is your word that it's true."

"Are you telling me you didn't research Rebecca?"

"I said I can't research what you just told me."

"So you did research Rebecca. What did you find?"

Catherine pinched her face into a scowl.

"You found out the story was true," Keitha said with more than a hint of triumph.

"I found a story about a storm and a hanging. That's all."

"That's all?"

"It doesn't prove it was Rebecca, and there is still no proof about Oscar."

"I am standing right here," Keitha snapped. "How much more proof do you need?"

The two dogs snapped their heads up in unison.

"You are not proof of Oscar, you're not proof of anything," Catherine said defiantly but without conviction.

"I am proof of myself, and I think you know it."

"Don't presume what I know."

"So tell me, what do you know?" Keitha asked.

Catherine tried to shrug off the question but couldn't. "I came back with Addy to figure it out, didn't I? We came, and you weren't even here."

"Yes, you did," Keitha murmured, her eyes drifting up to the sky. "The clouds are marvelous, aren't they?"

Catherine found herself looking up. "They're certainly unusual."

"Really? How so?"

"They don't seem quite real." Catherine lowered her eyes and stared at Keitha. "Because, of course, they aren't."

"What's wrong with them?" Keitha asked, still absorbed in examining the fluffy white shapes.

"They're just wrong." Catherine said, watching them along with Keitha. "For one thing, they don't move like clouds."

"What's wrong with how they move?"

"They don't look natural," Catherine replied in frustration, unable to explain exactly what it was that bothered her. "And they shouldn't all be so uniform," she added.

"They aren't uniform, they . . ." Keitha groped for the word she wanted, "they billow."

"There should be wispiness, or striation, to some of them. They shouldn't all be basically the same. I shouldn't have to explain it to you," Catherine began, pointing off in the distance. "There, that's what I mean, wispy."

"Oh, I see."

"What do you mean, you see? You did that."

"No, that cloud came from you." Keitha gave Murphy a sidelong glance, perhaps this wasn't the most tactful way to tell Catherine.

"It wasn't me," Catherine said, mortified by the idea. You said this was a way for you to communicate with me."

"It is. It just isn't a one-way communication. It was at first, because you were an observer, but you're not anymore. You come here of your own volition, and you make adjustments to the surroundings. The cloud and the substance on top of the soil," Keitha said.

"We're back to the biological soil crusts?" Catherine asked in amazement.

"Biological soil crusts," Keitha ruminated as she repeated the words. "See, you are a participant. It's really rather amazing."

"What's so amazing about it?" Catherine demanded, the affront trumping the mortification.

"I didn't think you had the ability or clarity of thought for either undertaking," Keitha said frankly.

"That is so rude." Catherine's body visibly tensed.

"It's not rude, it's the truth," Keitha replied.

Catherine's voice grew as rigid as her body. "The truth, you say. Well, let me tell you a little truth that I've figured out even with my inability to form clear thoughts. You need me for something."

The comment unnerved Keitha.

"How's that for clarity of thought?" Catherine asserted. "By the way, you should know that *in my time* it's considered impolite to insult a person that you need to ask for a favor. They might turn you down."

"I'm not here to ask you for a *favor*," Keitha said, appalled.

"I don't care what you call it, I'm not going to help you," Catherine declared without thinking.

"Now why doesn't that surprise me? This has been a complete waste of time. I told them there were other people better equipped to understand, who might actually be able to help. But you, you're a product of the selfish, self-absorbed time you live in."

"How dare you!"

"I dare plenty. The records are full of proof that you people ignore what is happening right in front of you and just hope that all the bad stuff will go away, so you don't have to sacrifice any part of your nice, comfy lives. Don't get involved, that's someone else's job. You don't even wait for things to wear out or stop functioning before you have to have the latest piece of crap. You are gluttonous about everything: food, energy, every resource imaginable, and you want it cheap and plentiful. Who cares what the ultimate cost is as long as you aren't the ones that have to pay," Keitha contended.

"You think you have it all figured out?" Catherine asked, arching her eyebrow indignantly. "Let me tell you something, just because you sit in your nice safe research library and read through a bunch of documents doesn't mean you understand a damn thing about my world, lady. You're just as bad as what our mass media has become: biased, unwilling to look at things with an impartial eye. You have no idea what it is like living with the daily bombardment of conflicting statements and reports that are produced by our so-called leaders of government and industry, the experts, and the pundits. Do not ask me what a pundit is," Catherine warned before continuing, "We can't count on our media to report the facts to us anymore because they're as partial as the politicians who were, once upon a time, supposed to represent 'We The People.' The politicians represent the lobbyists, the corporations, the greedy, and the powerful. The ones who want nothing more than to continue capitalizing on the bullshit that they've been peddling to the world for decades. So much for 'We The People.' What are we left with? We have to wade through all of it ourselves to try and decipher what is fact and what is manipulation of fact, because we don't have the advantage of someone dreaming the facts for us," Catherine said harshly. "So yeah, I'm painfully aware of the shortcomings of my world, without your pathetic, inaccurate attempt to lecture me, but I'm also aware that there are plenty of people who, despite how complicated and disheartening my world has become, still wake up every day and try to make a difference."

"I'm well versed in how things work in your time. Your system is set up on the principle of the majority rules. So if the majority of your country wanted to change, conserve, find alternative sources of energy, it would happen. The majority clearly does not," Keitha retorted.

"Like I said, you may have read about my time, but you clearly do not understand it," Catherine reproached.

"You," Keitha jabbed a finger at Catherine, "just don't want to face the degeneration of your society and what that will lead to. Just like you don't want to face who we are, who you are," she jabbed a finger at Catherine again, "and what you are capable of doing. You're not up to this, that's obvious. You're too scared to get involved."

Catherine's face contorted, and when she spoke, Keitha could almost feel the heat on her face. "Scared? Who the hell do you think you are, calling me scared?"

"Your descendant," Keitha bellowed, "the one living with the consequences."

"S<small>HIT</small>!" K<small>EITHA EXCLAIMED</small> as she sat up and looked over at Murphy who was standing with his ears straight up. He didn't look at all pleased.

"That was not my fault."

Murphy continued to stare at her without lowering his ears.

"I tried to be tactful."

Murphy refused to break off his stare.

Keitha leaned her whole body toward the dog and glared back. Murphy refused to yield.

"Did you hear her? She called it a favor and then said she wouldn't help," Keitha insisted in her own defense as she got up and went over to the pegs on the wall, yanking off a pair of pants and a shirt. She cinched the cord of the pants around her waist. "Stop staring at me," she said without turning to look at Murphy. "She was being completely unreasonable."

Keitha could feel the dog's eyes boring into her back. She rested her head against the wall in defeat and sighed. "I'm going to go brief the others right now. Are you coming?" Keitha turned but Murphy was already gone.

"Keitha," Clara said, dismayed, "how could you insult her when she was actually contributing?"

"I didn't think of it as an insult."

"You told her you didn't think she was capable," Terran noted.

"Did you hear what she said to me?" Keitha countered.

"What bothered you more, that Catherine is capable or that she figured out we need her help?" Terran asked.

"You're bothering me a whole lot more right now," Keitha warned.

"Keitha," Clara intervened, "you didn't think Catherine would ever be able to do either, did you?"

"What difference does it make? She said we needed a favor and then said she wouldn't help. She said I sit in a nice safe research library. She keeps calling me *lady*," Keitha said, emphasizing the disagreeable tone that Catherine used.

"We heard you the first time, Keitha, but no matter what, you were supposed to remain calm, not disparage her time, and you certainly never should have told her we were living with the consequences of their actions," Greer stated.

"I didn't say how."

Greer shook his head. "You squandered a perfect opportunity to get her to trust you by squabbling."

"Tell me, Greer, how would you have reacted if she told you she wasn't going to help us? Don't tell me that it wouldn't have upset you."

"I wouldn't have insulted her."

"Stop saying I insulted her."

"Catherine said you insulted her."

"Well, I didn't mean to," Keitha protested. "I was complementing her."

"It is not a complement to tell someone that they're not as stupid as you thought they were," Greer stated.

Keitha groaned. "All right, all right, I failed miserably, and there is nothing I can do about it now."

Clara's heart ached when she saw how truly miserable her daughter was and gently said, "You still can salvage this, my dear daughter, you just have to realize how troubling and frightening all of this must be for Catherine. She has figured out that we need something from her, but she has no idea what it is, and she has no idea what our motives are. For all Catherine knows, we could be like the Machiavellians, manipulating her for our own ends. It's natural for her to be wary and reactionary. You have to choose your words carefully. Think about how you would feel in her place. You and Murphy are the only ones of us she's met, you're our emissaries and you have to empathize with her."

"It's hopeless, Mother."

"No it isn't. You just have to control yourself, Keitha, and let Murphy help you," Greer said reassuringly.

Keitha glanced over at Murphy, who looked as glum as she felt. "Murphy has tried but there is only so much he can do."

"Well, you will just have to try harder," Greer stated.

"I can try and try, Greer, but we'll just end up in the same place. Catherine said it, I'm not a diplomat." Keitha hesitated and suddenly her eyes brightened, "But what if I take someone with me who is."

"I don't think taking your mother with you is a good idea. We can't risk Catherine recognizing Clara from back when she was fifteen. No offense, my dear," Greer said to Clara, "but that could cause a very intense emotional response."

"I wasn't talking about Clara going with me. I was talking about you coming with me, Father," Keitha clarified.

"I don't have that ability, Keitha," Greer said dismissively.

"I'll take you with me," Keitha said excitedly. "You're so calm and rational, you'll be able to defuse the situation quickly if things start getting tense."

"Keitha," Greer stated as reasonably as he could, considering how agitated he felt inside, "you can't just take me with you, it isn't that simple."

"I didn't say it would be simple, but I think I can bring your consciousness along, if you're willing to try. Please, Greer, clearly I'm not good at censoring myself, and I don't think there is time enough for me to learn."

"Clara," Greer beseeched her, "talk to your daughter."

Clara, however, was staring intently at Keitha.

"Don't tell me you think this is plausible," Greer stated in alarm.

Clara turned to him. "I think if anyone can get you there, it's your daughter. She needs you."

Greer got up without a word and left the room. As he made his way down the tunnel, he felt like he was in a dense fog. People were walking by greeting him, and all he could do was nod like an automaton, his feet taking him where his dazed mind needed him to go.

Greer stumbled into the garden area. George was kneeling in front of a row of plants, carefully examining the leaves, and raised his head when he heard Greer's footsteps. He recoiled at the sight of his friend. Greer's face was gaunt, his eyes vacant.

"Did you tell Keitha?" Greer shouted the accusation.

CHAPTER 23

"Tell Keitha what?" George asked in alarm as he began to rise stiffly from his prone position.

Greer instinctively reached out his hand to help George up and continued to hold on once George was on his feet.

"Did you tell her?" Greer implored.

The dull look in Greer's eyes was gone, replaced with dread. "What are you talking about, Greer?" he asked anxiously.

"Did you tell Keitha that I needed to help her with Catherine?" Greer looked so devastated that George began to fear for his friend.

"No, no, I would never do that," George avowed resolutely, studying his friend with the same intensity with which he had been studying the leaves on the plant. "Come, I'll make us some tea."

George gently led Greer over to a secluded recess that he had converted into his sleeping quarters. After George's partner Val died, he no longer wanted the room that they had shared for so many years. He said he preferred to be close to his work, but Greer knew it was because George couldn't stand the constant reminders amid the endless silence. Greer sat down on the only stool in the small space as George began making the tea. Neither man spoke a word.

George handed Greer a hot cup of the aromatic brew before sitting on the edge of his cot with his own cup. George waited patiently as Greer sipped from his cup. Slate sauntered in and, after giving Greer a look of minor curiosity, leapt onto the cot next to George. Greer began recounting the discussion that had caused him to flee from his own room in panic.

"When I talked to you about helping Keitha, I never envisioned her taking you with her. Do you think it's possible?" George asked, unable to keep the fascination out of his voice.

"It doesn't matter if she can or not, the risk would be too great. I'm not about to let her try." Greer's voice was rigid. "My mother was practically driven insane and I was . . ." He shook his head violently. "A latent gene could be triggered by Keitha linking her consciousness with mine, and I will not put her through what my mother and I went through."

Greer's mother, Ione, had been plagued by headaches most of her life. After Greer was born, their frequency and intensity increased. She hid her pain from her son, but she could not hide her nightmares. Every time she woke up screaming, Greer was there to try to comfort her, but he was just a young boy and Ione could not bear to let him endure her torment. She went to Val, who was an exceptional healer. He tried everything he could to help her, but nothing lasted very long, and Ione refused to tell Val what the nightmares were about. However, Val had begun to notice unusual incidents around the colony. People would suddenly start discussing a topic that no one else understood, or start performing a task they had never done before, almost perfectly, yet none of the people involved could recall what had happened afterward when he asked. Ione's nightmares became so terrible that she refused to sleep for days. When exhaustion finally overwhelmed her she would collapse and another incident would occur.

Shortly after Greer turned eight, he awoke one morning to find his mother gone, and Val and Donal standing in the entrance to their room, waiting. Donal tried to explain to Greer that Ione could no longer be near people, not even him, and as devastating as it was for her, she needed to leave. Greer lunged at Donal, pummeling him with his small fists, crying uncontrollably and screaming at Donal to tell him where she was. Val grabbed Greer and held onto him, reassuring the boy that they would always make sure his mother was well cared for, but she feared what living with her would do to him and made them promise not to tell him where she was. Greer had wrenched loose from Val's grip, staring at the man with cold, detached eyes.

After that, Greer became quiet and withdrawn, immersing himself in his studies, stubbornly refusing to allow anyone to stay with him in the room he had shared with his mother.

At thirteen, when Greer's ability to influence other people's thoughts manifested, Donal took him to the gardens and introduced him to one of the most influential people of his life: Daniel, the head horticulturist who adamantly told Donal that the boy was not ready, that he had to continue his studies. Greer just as adamantly said he would not go back. Daniel, after an extensive discussion with Donal, agreed to let the stubborn young man work in the gardens, but he would not allow Greer to apprentice, he just didn't have the necessary education.

Greer ignored the man's opinion and threw himself into the work. He found that the sheer physical exertion helped quell his tumultuous mind, and for the first time since his mother left, he didn't awake and fall asleep with the sense of being adrift. After a while, Greer began to notice that Daniel imparted knowledge to the gardeners as effortlessly as he directed the work. Greer started surreptitiously listening whenever he could, and it didn't take long before he realized that he lacked the ability to grasp most of the principles Daniel was teaching. However, the very thought of returning to class to expand his knowledge made Greer break out in a cold sweat, and he was too proud to admit to Daniel that he needed help.

Greer always suspected that, along with Val and Donal, George knew where his mother was living, so he treated all three men with equal contempt. Yet his desire to understand Daniel began to grow stronger than his disdain until he finally asked George, who was second only to Daniel in horticultural knowledge, to tutor him. Greer knew the man could easily refuse him, chastise him for his offensive behavior, but George agreed to help him without comment. Over the next year they worked diligently on Greer's studies, and despite their fifteen-year age difference, they became close friends.

Daniel, seeing how hard the young man was working, both in the gardens and at his studies, allowed Greer to begin his apprenticeship. Greer strove to emulate the brilliant yet unassuming man, who believed everyone could comprehend even the most esoteric of his theories—if he explained it properly and with patience. Daniel saw possibilities every day, sometimes in the simplest of things that others ignored, dismissed, or overlooked, and he saw vast potential in Greer. A year later Daniel died unexpectedly and Greer's grief tore him apart. His ability resurfaced, and with it, headaches and nightmares just like his mother endured.

"Why didn't you tell Keitha that the healer Donal took you to, when you lost control of yourself, was your mother?" George asked.

A shiver went through Greer as he thought of the day Donal took him to see her. Ione lived in a small cavernous area at the end of a long series of tunnels, which the miners, centuries ago, had hollowed out of the sheer rock as they followed the vein of ore they were extracting. The founders had structurally reinforced the entire area, the same as the rest of the colony, but it proved to be too remote to be practical and no one wanted to live so far beyond the infrastructure of the colony. Yet it was exactly that remoteness that kept everyone safe from Ione's influence.

In the seven years Ione had been gone from him, she had aged severely. Greer did not recognize his mother in the old woman, who was bent over with arthritis and whose hair had fallen out in clumps, leaving wispy threads hanging from scattered locations on her scalp. Then she spoke, and in that instance, Greer felt grateful. But then his gratitude turned to anger. He yelled at his mother for leaving him, and he yelled at Donal for keeping him from her. Ione clumsily reached out for him and Greer collapsed in her arms, sobbing. When he finally calmed down and was able to listen to her, Ione told him both why she had to leave, and about her own ability, which was now threatening him.

Greer sat down on a small stool and Ione went on to tell him that she had spent most of her initial solitary time reading about meditation and control of the mind from material that Val brought her. Then she began to practice the techniques, over and over, not because she expected to be able to return to the colony but because she wanted to be ready to help her son if he had inherited her ability. Ione vowed that Greer would never have to hide away from people as she had to, so terrified of what she was able to do. Her son would be able to live out his life without the anguish of not being able to control when and what part of someone else's mind would suddenly unlock and allow him entry. After so many years of dedicated training, and with the willing assistance of Donal, Val, and George to test her progress, Ione was confident that she had achieved absolute control over her mind. The cost she paid was the loss of most of her sight, whether because she read by her solitary lantern or because she spent so much time in the dark to conserve fuel didn't matter to her. All that mattered was her son.

Ione spent the next year imparting all of the knowledge and skill she had acquired to Greer, who became happy and content for the first time in his life. Greer also learned how much Donal, Val, and George meant to his mother. Every week one of them would make the trek to bring her food, water, clean clothes, and fuel for her lantern and take back all of her waste to the main colony for processing. The most treasured things they brought her were their company and news of how Greer was doing.

When Ione was certain that Greer was as skilled as she was, she told him it was time for him to return to the colony. The night before he was to return, Greer told Ione that there was no reason for him to go back. He would stay. She would never have to be alone again. Ione told him that only someone with a compelling reason should ever live in such isolation, and he no longer had a compelling reason. Greer pointed out that she no longer had a compelling reason either and needed to return with him. Ione smiled as she lovingly patted his cheek and said that nothing would give her more joy, yet there was something in her voice, a hint of melancholy, that seemed incongruous to him. The next morning, when he woke up and crossed the room to his mother's cot, he found her dead. Ione had been ill, Val told Greer, when he found the young man sitting next to his mother's body in a daze, but she didn't want anyone else to know, and Val, because of his great respect for Ione, had honored her request. Greer went back to the colony, withdrawn once again, preferring to spend his time in the garden with the plants and the cats, until a year later when he met Clara.

"What good would it have done to tell Keitha about that?" Greer asked in anger.

"Why wouldn't you want your daughter to know about her grandmother?" George asked. "That amazing, courageous woman, my friend." His voice choked with emotion but he continued as a tear ran down his cheek. "Keitha should know about what Ione did, about the sacrifice she made for you, for all of us. She lived virtually alone in a small cavern because it tore her apart that she could influence other people, plant an idea—"

"Do you think I would risk the same thing happening to Keitha?" Greer barked.

"You can't seriously be afraid that your ability is lying dormant somewhere in Keitha."

"I have lived with the fear that she inherited this scourge from me since the day she was born."

"I know that. Just like I know that you justify your decision not to train Keitha in deep meditation because of your fear that some latent gene will be triggered, but enough is enough."

"I *will not* risk my daughter's sanity," Greer roared.

"You did not go insane, Ione did not go insane."

"I'm the one who woke up with my mother's screams tearing through our room. I'm the one who saw the wild look in her eyes as she fought for control. I'm the one who saw how close she came." Greer fiercely hit his own chest each time he said "I'm."

"You were a boy, you don't remember everything," George stated bluntly.

"What does that mean?"

"Ione was a very strong woman, and so is Keitha. If something were awakened in Keitha, you could help her through it."

"No."

"You can't continue to say no."

"No," Greer roared, causing Slate to leap onto the floor and arch her back.

"I'm afraid that the choice is no longer yours," George said evenly. "The plants are dying."

"I know the sweet plant is dying, and I'm sorry but—"

"More than just the sweet plant."

Greer studied his old friend carefully. "How many?"

"Too many."

"How can that be?"

"As with everything, some plants show signs of decline sooner than others. There have been early indications in other plants for several years now."

"Why didn't you say something before?"

"What good would that have done?" George asked, using Greer's own words. "Keitha didn't need any more pressure."

"I could have helped you."

"Keitha was a higher priority for you."

"You should have told me. Together we might have come up with something you haven't thought of on your own."

"Well, I'm telling you now, but I'm also telling you that if you want to help me, you have to help Keitha and Catherine. You can help them find the event that the Machiavellians changed and stop it from happening."

Greer looked at George uneasily. They never talked about the Machiavellians. Clara had gone to George to ask for his help in convincing Greer to use his ability to protect the colony from the Machiavellians. What Clara could not have anticipated was that, as a result, Greer's suggestion did not work on George. Fortunately, Val, who was one of the healers that helped Terran after he arrived at the colony, was able to protect George until he died, and by then George was able to protect himself.

"Even if Keitha and Catherine are able to find the event, there is no guaranteeing that it will change what is happening to the plants. There's no guaranteeing that it will change anything for us," Greer stated.

"They tampered with the past. They took something out, or changed something in the original sequence of events causing a divergence, creating a new sequence. You have to help your daughter restore the original sequence because the one thing I know about this world is that we are running out of time. I'm not asking for a guarantee. I'm just asking for a chance."

CHAPTER 24

C atherine gazed out her north facing window in the corner of her office, behind her desk. The street appeared barren of any sign of expected March weather. There should have been snow—after all, March has always been the state's heaviest snow month on record. March came in like a lamb, and thanks to another dry winter in Denver, the weather forecasters promised it would go out like a lamb as well. She stared at the evergreens, and at the scattered dead needles covering the ground beneath them. The leafless, skeletal trees waited patiently to put out their spring finery of green leaves and pink blossoms. The sidewalk just below her window, which had seen little to no sun throughout the winter, had a layer of crust that ran along the street-side edge like piped icing. Except instead of sugar, butter, and cream, this macabre confection was comprised of the icy remnants of the paltry snowfalls from the beginning of the week stirred with auto exhaust, magnesium chloride de-icer, and the general layer of crud that had built up on the street and in the gutter. The entire visage looked gritty and bleak, matching Catherine's mood.

"Hello, Catherine."

She turned away from the window. "Ford," she replied curtly.

"You're angry."

"Can't imagine why," she said, folding her arms in front of her.

"Henry warned me that you would be."

"Wasn't that nice of him."

"Are you going to let me explain?"

"What's to explain? The man I married is talking to a friend of mine about me without my knowledge."

"Henry and I ran into each other in D.C., and we had drinks. We talked about philosophy and the condition of humankind."

She arched an eyebrow. "Really? The condition of humankind?"

"Henry looked exhausted, Catherine. I thought it was because of the political roadblocks that we're all up against, but after we talked about all of that for a while, Henry just came out and asked me what I thought the human mind was capable of. I was surprised, to say the least. I thought perhaps you had confided in him about what I shared with you concerning my son."

"I would never do that," she said indignantly.

"Yes, that became obvious the more Henry and I talked. I sincerely apologize for believing you would ever divulge something so private."

"And yet, you and Henry talked about me."

"No. We talked about cognitive ability and awareness. Henry was fascinated. He shared with me some of his own ideas, which I found equally fascinating."

"Oh for God's sake, Ford," she said, tightening her lips, "just because you ignored the five hundred pound gorilla in the room doesn't mean it wasn't there."

"We did not talk about you, just about concepts and possibilities."

Catherine shook her head and closed her eyes, her lips tightening in obvious consternation.

"You probably think that is a fine line of distinction."

Catherine opened one eye. "Probably? Come on, Ford, you know you're splitting hairs."

"Henry needed someone to talk to, Catherine. The discussion was much more important than the gorilla in the room," Ford stated bluntly, causing her other eye to pop open.

"Henry should have talked to me."

"I'm sure he tried, just as I did, and found, just as I did, that you weren't ready."

Catherine's eyes narrowed. "That isn't fair. You and Henry aren't the ones . . . What I mean to say is that I know what you went through when your son died made you consider possibilities, but there are some *things* that are way outside of even those possibilities."

"The possibilities that I've been considering, in recent years, go far beyond my own experience."

Catherine leaned her head to one side. "Care to elaborate?"

"I have found that we, the human race as a whole, considerably underestimate the ability of the mind; our concept of reality is far too restrictive."

"Well, that's a mouthful, and it tells me nothing."

"Well, Catherine, I believe that we cannot have a truly meaningful discussion unless you are willing to tell me what has been happening to you."

"Yet you had a meaningful discussion with Henry."

"I had an interesting discussion with Henry. Anything more would have meant talking about what has been happening to you, and neither of us wanted to do that."

Catherine closed her eyes again and shook her head slowly. She let out a long sigh as she tilted her head back and rubbed her face. Then she slowly dropped her head and stared at Ford. "You're going to think I'm nuts."

"I promise you, I will not."

Catherine sat down and pointed to the chair on the opposite side of her desk. "You better sit down too. This is not a short story."

Catherine began chronicling her dreams for Ford. She repeated verbatim the story of Rebecca and Oscar, and when she relayed the information about her research into the storm that destroyed Rebecca's village, her voice grew so wispy that Ford had to lean toward her to hear. Her voice returned to normal, even hinted at a little levity, as she told him about how Addy got her back to the plateau, but then became very serious as she repeated the story of the archivists and relayed the last encounter with Keitha. When Catherine finished, Ford, who hadn't spoken the entire time, remained silent and contemplative, and the longer he didn't speak the more anxious Catherine became. She began compulsively rearranging papers on her desk to keep herself from leaping up and running out of the office, out of the building.

"For God's sake, Ford," Catherine implored when she couldn't take it anymore, "say something! Say anything!"

"I apologize, but what you have told me deserves unhurried contemplation. Could you please give me another moment or two?" he asked in a voice so reassuring that Catherine sat back in her chair and tried not to fidget as she waited.

"Addy is always on the plateau with you?" he finally asked.

"Yes," Catherine said and waited for more questions, but Ford lapsed back into silence.

After what felt like an eternity to Catherine, he said, "Extraordinary." Catherine sat very still.

"So even when you refused to go with Addy, you believe she was communicating with Keitha's dog, Murphy?"

"Yes."

"I see."

Catherine felt completely exposed, but she tried to quell her apprehension and wait for him to ask her another question until her anxiety got the better of her.

"Ford!" she shouted in exasperation.

"Catherine!" he lightheartedly mimicked her cry before adding, "A little patience, please, I beseech you."

Catherine grinned. How could she deny a man who said "beseech?" She turned to her computer, opened up a document, and tried to read. As her nerves continued to torment her, she began drumming her fingers on the top of the desk.

"It's hard for me to concentrate when you're fidgeting like that," Ford remarked.

She swiveled in her chair to face him. "I can't take it, all right, I can't. Just tell me what you're thinking."

Ford nodded. "I understand. First of all, let me say that I think it's amazing that you and Keitha have been able to talk to each other, at all."

"Yeah, I think someone saying they're from the future pretty much puts it in the amazing column, or the you've-lost-your-mind column."

"I definitely would not put it in the latter," Ford stated unequivocally.

"So you think she really could be from the future?" Catherine asked hesitantly.

"I think it's entirely possible."

"No shit," Catherine blurted out. "Sorry, Ford, I just didn't expect you to . . ." Catherine let the thought trail away.

"You didn't expect me to what? Have an open mind? Envision that sort of paradigm? What?"

"I didn't expect you to believe it was real," Catherine stated candidly.

"Yet you told me about it anyway; that was very brave of you."

"Not really. Henry told me I should talk to you. I guess I was hoping you would be able to rationally explain what was happening, like someone explaining a magic trick."

"This isn't a magic trick, Catherine, and I believe Keitha is trying to explain what is happening to you."

"No she isn't. She kept showing me all those different species, which has done nothing but complicate my life, by the way, and now she keeps telling me stories, which I then have to interpret. She hasn't told me anything straight out," Catherine noted irritably.

"As I said, it's amazing the two of you have been able to communicate at all."

"Why do you keep saying that?"

"Because I keep envisioning Alexander the Great and Genghis Khan discussing war strategies. Calm might prevail for a little while, but then mayhem would ensue."

"Not funny. Why would you compare us to two male conquerors that lived fifteen hundred years apart?"

"Did you know that Aristotle taught Alexander and that Genghis Khan, despite the Western world labeling him a barbarian, believed in religious tolerance and equality amongst his warriors?" Ford asked.

"So?"

"Each man was brilliant in his own way. I would also venture to say that they were unconventional and forward-thinking, but if they found themselves in the same room, at the same time, instead of talking to each other rationally and learning from each other, they would probably . . ." He waited for Catherine to finish his thought.

"Draw swords because they couldn't figure out how the hell the other one got there in the first place? After all, no matter how brilliant and forward-thinking they might have been, the fifteen hundred year difference might have been a bit hard to comprehend," she responded adroitly.

"It might indeed, but let's say they did understand, or at least one of them did: I believe their fervent natures would still have overridden everything else before a rational discussion could've occurred, and instead mayhem would have ensued."

"Very clever, Ford, but there has been no mayhem."

"Not in the draw-the-sword kind of way; however, by your own account of events, your meetings have certainly been rife with turmoil. You and Keitha must get past your distrust of each other if you want to make any real progress."

"She hasn't given me any concrete reason to trust her. No matter how much you think it might be possible, I need some evidence that she is who she says she is."

"I think Keitha is trying to provide you with as much evidence as she can, maybe even a little more."

"No, no, no," Catherine said wagging her finger. "According to her the honey bee was a mistake, and the Endangered Species Act was pure coincidence, nothing more."

"You can't dismiss those things so readily," Ford insisted.

"I haven't dismissed anything. She is dismissing them," Catherine noted. "And what do you mean she distrusts me?" she demanded but didn't wait for him to answer. "She's the one who contacted me, remember. If she didn't trust me she shouldn't have gotten me involved."

"It doesn't sound like Keitha chose you: you share a genetic bond with her," Ford noted, and before Catherine could protest he said, "You know there have been anecdotal stories about how identical twins sense what the other is feeling or how even if they are separated at birth they grow up with the same predispositions."

"So what?" Catherine asserted. "Identical twins share the exact same DNA; it isn't the same as people who only have a drop or two in common."

"The interesting thing," Ford continued without acknowledging her comment, "is that, based on the type of clinical trials that have been conducted for extrasensory or psychic perception, identical twins don't appear to have more perception than non-twins. However, among all of the people who have reported some type of perceptive incident in their lives, it is often connected to another family member. The key appears to be common DNA, not how much there is in common, which would support Rebecca's purebred spaniel and mutt analogy."

Catherine frowned but didn't respond.

"In addition to the genetic bond," Ford proceeded carefully, "Keitha reached you because you were the one that responded to her message."

"I did no such thing," Catherine said vehemently.

"I believe you did, otherwise you wouldn't be standing on the plateau talking to her."

"Well I didn't mean to," Catherine said in agitation, throwing her hands up in the air. "I'm not the one she should be talking to. She should be talking to someone like Rebecca," Catherine said, lowering her voice. "She should be talking to my grandmother Molly. I don't think Molly ever doubted that it was her dead father that told her to open the box that contained the money that she used to come to America."

"That doesn't mean Molly would understand Keitha better than you."

"I think the fact that Molly didn't doubt herself would have given her a leg up," Catherine said and then added, "My grandmother thought that we civilized people lost a great deal when we started to distance ourselves from the natural world."

"She talked to you about that?"

"God no, my mother didn't even want her telling us the family ghost story, but Molly always managed. The rest I learned from reading Molly's journal. Well, it wasn't just her journal: it was started by Molly's great-uncle Daniel, who gave it to Molly's father, who gave it to Molly's mother, who gave it to Molly."

"Your mother didn't want Molly to tell you her story?" Ford asked, puzzled. "I thought Molly was your father's mother?"

"She was, and don't get me wrong, my mother and Molly loved each other. Molly gave my mother the journal to add in her own family history, but when it came to talking about ghosts . . . well, my mom would shut down. She even told us kids that Molly's story was just a product of the superstitious way she was raised."

"I had no idea," he said sadly. "That must have made what happened when your sister died even more difficult for you."

"Yeah, well," she shrugged. "Let's just say I wasn't surprised when I heard my parents talking about a psychiatrist."

"Why was your mother so adamant?"

"That would be because of her father, my grandfather, Martin. I remember when I was five, Molly and Martin got into it at Christmas dinner because Molly started telling the story about when she left Ireland. Martin cut her off before she could get very far and told her to stop filling our heads with her crap. Molly said just because *he* had chosen to turn his back on his heritage didn't mean *she* would. It went downhill from there. After that, whenever we had a family dinner, my mom used to put them at opposite ends of the table. Martin died two years later, without ever saying another word to Molly."

"That's pretty extreme."

Catherine knitted her brow. "Yeah, it was, and I didn't find out for a long time why he was so scared."

"He was scared? Why?"

Catherine's eyes looked distant.

"What is it, Catherine?" Ford prompted.

She focused her attention back on him and said, "My mother told me a story about my great-grandmother Shi`Ma, one that I believe was at the core of Martin's fear."

Ford watched Catherine's eyes wander away from his face again. She looked over his shoulder as if there was something or someone at the entrance to her office. He fought the urge to turn around and look, because he knew there was nothing there; she was just deep in thought. Catherine's eyes drifted back to Ford's as she began to tell him about her mother Anna's vivid recollection.

"My grandparents, Martin and Maria, were living in Colorado at the time of my grandmother's death. My mother, Anna, was a young, innocent girl at that time and only knew a little about her grandmother, Shi`Ma, who lived in Mexico. Maria always promised Anna that when she was older, and would be able to understand, they would sit down one night and Maria would tell her all about her amazing grandmother. Anna could hardly wait, and when she turned ten, she told her mother she was ready. Maria stared deep into her daughter's eyes and agreed, but before they were able to have their night of stories, Maria fell sick.

A telegram arrived only hours after Maria's death from Shi`Ma. As Martin read the telegram his hands shook, his normally pale, freckled face was blotchy from crying, but turned sickly gray as he finished reading the telegram. Two days later, after Maria's burial, my grandfather and my mother were on their way to Mexico. All Martin told Anna was that they were going to visit her grandmother Shi`Ma.

Catherine paused, waiting for Ford to indicate that she could go on, and with a nod from him, Catherine continued.

Shi`Ma stepped out of her front door to greet them when they finally arrived at her house in Mexico. Anna watched her grandmother with great anticipation. Shi`Ma's hair was snow white and she walked with a distinct limp, but her black eyes were as penetrating as they had been the day that she had given Martin permission to marry Maria. Martin and Shi`Ma greeted each other warily. They had not seen each other since that day. Maria's father had refused to see his daughter and forbade Shi`Ma to see her on the occasions when the couple had visited Martin's grandfather, Jorge. When Jorge died and Maria's parents did not attend the funeral, Martin and Maria never went back to Mexico.

Shi`Ma mesmerized Anna the first night with tales of the Lipan Apache and of her mother, Maria, when she was a little girl. Anna knew they were some of the same stories her mother had intended to tell her and fought to keep her eyes open as long as she could, but finally she succumbed to sheer exhaustion. She awoke in a small room with daylight streaming in through a small window perched high up on the wall that faced the bed Anna was lying on. Shaking off the residual strands of sleep that were still cocooning her, she heard voices raised in anger. Anna got up from the bed and carefully walked down the hallway until she was just outside the kitchen. She immediately recognized her father Martin's voice and was sure that the older female voice had to be her grandmother Shi`Ma's. She leaned against the wall to hear them better, and only then did she realize that they were arguing in Spanish, a language that Anna did not think her father could speak. She listened intently and learned that Shi`Ma had sent the telegram that had disturbed Martin so much.

Anna heard Martin repeat the two lines from the telegram: I know my daughter Maria is dead; please bring her back to Mexico. He insisted that

Shi`Ma tell him how she knew. Shi`Ma just as vehemently kept reiterating that she had seen Maria at the exact moment of her death, and in that moment Maria asked her to have Martin bring her body back to Mexico to be buried beside her father. Shi`Ma said it was Maria's final act of forgiveness.

Martin was beyond outraged. He told Shi`Ma that he had traveled down to Mexico with Anna out of respect for her, but he would not allow some old woman's superstitious story of a vision force him into burying Maria next to the man who had disowned her, and who had disrespected Martin's grandfather. Shi`Ma, in a controlled yet formidable voice, told him that it was because of a vision that she had allowed her daughter to marry Martin in the first place. She had defied her husband because she couldn't deny Maria the kind of love and happiness that Shi`Ma had never had in her own marriage, even though she knew that Maria would have to endure the terrible pain of losing children before her great joy at finally giving birth to a daughter. Shi`Ma began to recite the precise dates of each of Maria's miscarriages and the date and time when Maria went into labor with Anna.

Suddenly there was a sharp whack that sounded like someone hitting wood, which caused Anna to jump and squeal in surprise. She held her breath, thinking that the two adults surely must have heard her, but instead of footsteps she heard her father scream at her grandmother. Martin accused Shi`Ma of using information that his grandfather Jorge shared with her to frighten him into agreeing to the burial. A terrible silence followed the outburst and Anna held her breath, afraid of what she couldn't see happening in the kitchen. Then she heard Shi`Ma call Martin a fool in a voice so low and angry that it sounded to Anna as though her grandmother was snarling. Shi`Ma said it was Martin who dishonored his grandfather Jorge and his other ancestors because he was too afraid to accept the truth when he heard it. Anna shivered and rubbed the goose bumps on her arms just as Martin stormed out of the kitchen and saw her hunkered down against the wall in the hall. Martin picked Anna up, carried her back into the small bedroom, packed her bag and then his, and left the house and Mexico forever.

"I never heard that story until the last time my mother was in the hospital. She knew she was dying," Catherine's voice caught even though it had been almost seventeen years. She cleared her throat. "She wanted me to know, she wanted me to write it down some day."

Ford nodded now that he knew Catherine's father, Daniel, had left her Molly's journal. "Have you written it down?"

"Not yet." Catherine saw the look that passed across Ford's face and added, "I will." She nodded, more to herself than Ford, as if making a promise. "After my mother died I was reading the journal and the last entry she made was the story about her grandmother Shi`Ma and her mother Maria the night before Maria and Martin left Mexico to get married. My mother wrote it all down, even Shi`Ma's vision." Catherine stared at Ford with moist eyes, but her voice was steady. "The date on the entry was the day after my mother was admitted to the hospital. Her handwriting was really shaky. I don't think she had the energy to commit the other story to paper. That's why she told me."

"Don't you think Anna told you because she knew you needed to know?"

Catherine shrugged.

"Did your grandmother or your mother ever see anything?"

Catherine's eyebrow went up. She knew what Ford was asking. "I don't know if my grandmother Maria ever had any dreams or anything. My mother never mentioned anything, but she was only ten when Maria died. As far as my mother . . ." Catherine paused for a moment. "I think if Anna ever saw anything she would have told me that night in the hospital; after all, she told me about the cemetery."

"The cemetery?"

"My mother told me that before they left Mexico, her father took her to the cemetery. They visited several graves, including Martin's grandfather Jorge's, which was when she saw the date of his death and remembered all the dates that Shi`Ma had recited to Martin."

"And?"

"Jorge died before Maria had her first miscarriage."

"So Martin had to have known that Jorge couldn't have told Shi`Ma any of the dates."

"Yes."

"Did Anna say anything to him?"

"She tried, but he looked so appalled that she never brought it up again."

"Why in the world didn't she say something to you when your sister died?" Catherine looked a little disconcerted and Ford realized how thoughtless his question was. "Catherine," he began regretfully, but she stopped him.

"It's a valid question, Ford. I can tell you what my mother told me when I asked her the same thing that night in her hospital room. She was Martin's daughter, and more than anything my mother wanted him to love her and be proud of her, and she knew that meant believing what he believed and not believing her grandmother Shi`Ma. So she just forgot about what happened in Mexico, and when I started roaming around and having weird dreams after my sister died, her reaction was that I had to be suffering from grief and mental stress."

"I'm sorry, Catherine, but she must have known you weren't."

"Ah, Ford, we may not understand everything the mind is capable of, but we certainly know that people can very effectively block out memories."

"Until they come flooding back," Ford said. "That must have been so hard for you. If she had just believed Shi`Ma, your life could've been so much easier."

"My mother was dying, Ford," Catherine said evenly. "I thought the drugs were making her imagine the story because she wanted to make me feel better about what happened when my sister died."

"My God, Catherine, you didn't believe her? Even though you knew Molly's story?"

"I didn't believe Molly's story either. I just thought I had a very eccentric but wonderful grandmother," she said sadly.

"You must have logically thought, what with two of your ancestors—"

"There was no logic, Ford. I was too far removed from Molly and Shi`Ma, too *civilized*. Keitha should have contacted one of them. Molly and Shi`Ma accepted what they experienced, just like Rebecca. They were strong, amazing women, they didn't turn away, they understood. I'm too mired in how I was raised, in what is and is not plausible in our society."

"They were your ancestors, Catherine, one from your mother's family and one from your father's. Start listening to that part of you and less to society." Ford studied her intently before stating in a voice resonating with certainty, "You are the one Keitha is meant to contact; now you just need to find out why."

CHAPTER 25

"**Y**ou should stay here until I have an opportunity to talk to her first."

Greer was crouched on the ground staring at the porous black-tinged areas, seemingly oblivious to what Keitha had just said to him.

"Father?"

Greer stared up at his daughter, stunned. "How is this possible?"

"I told you. Catherine did this."

"It's remarkable. Your description was very accurate, but to see it . . . it's just remarkable." He kept staring as he spoke. "George said biological soil crust—or, technically, cryptogamic soil crust—was a living cover made up of a complex blend of cyanobacteria, green algae, lichens, mosses, micro fungi, and other bacteria." Greer stood and looked around wide-eyed. "All of it, really, just remarkable."

"Father," Keitha placed her hand on his shoulder and spoke to him as if he were a child, "you have to stay here until I send Murphy back to get you, and then you need to follow him up to the plateau. Father, are you listening?"

"I understand, Keitha. Follow Murphy when he comes back for me." Greer started to walk down the sketchy path.

"Hold it."

He stopped.

"Don't go exploring. I have no idea how far this goes," she waved her hand at the indistinct trail, "or what else might be down there, and I can't have you getting lost or distracted. I need you to stay here and stay focused."

Greer came back toward her. "Of course, you're right. I wouldn't want to inadvertently step on any of the biological soil crust. George said walking on it was enough to create an adverse impact. I'll just sit here and wait." He picked out a rock that was about the size of a small stool.

"You realize that it isn't actual biological soil crust," Keitha said, wondering if the sight of everything had made Greer forget that it was all a construct.

"It doesn't matter, we should treat it as though it were," he said, tilting his head to one side. "A simple act of respect, don't you think?"

"Yes, I do, Father," Keitha said, walking over to him.

He had always been an extraordinarily thoughtful man, and watching him struggle over the past months, knowing it was her safety that was causing his distress, had been heartbreaking for Keitha and Clara. That neither of them could alleviate his concerns, no matter how many times they tried to tell him that Keitha could take care of herself, had left them feeling useless. Keitha had thought about coming back to the plateau on her own but, from the moment she voiced the idea of Greer coming with her, she knew it was more than a suggestion: it was essential. Yet all she and Clara could do was wait and hope that somehow Greer would find the resolve to come with her.

"I can't tell you how much I appreciate what you've done. I know how hard it was for you," Keitha said, hugging her father.

"I think you and Murphy deserve all of the credit for getting me here," Greer replied, gently patting her on the back before releasing her from the embrace.

"That isn't what I meant." Keitha stared into his eyes.

"I know what you meant," he replied quietly, shifting his gaze away from her.

The same day Greer had so abruptly left his and Clara's room after Keitha suggested that he accompany her to talk to Catherine, he reappeared. He sat Keitha down and told her all about her grandmother Ione and the fear he had harbored from the day she was born. Greer's anxiety was so palpable that, when he finished, Keitha squeezed his hands comfortingly, but explicitly told him that he needed to have more confidence in himself, and if not, then he certainly needed to have more confidence in her. It was clear to Keitha that Ione had given Greer a great gift when she taught him how to control his ability, and she told him it was about time that he passed that knowledge onto her.

Greer agreed and patiently began teaching Keitha, who was a talented, yet somewhat erratic, student. However, Keitha did not have to master all of the training in order for her to succeed in taking Greer with her to the plateau. Unfortunately Greer, who was the crucial participant, could not keep his mind focused, and without focus, he could not achieve a deep trance or guide Keitha into a deep trance, and without a deep trance, Keitha would never be able to hold his consciousness once he separated from his physical state.

Greer told George that he didn't think he could stop the panic, which came from his fear of harming Keitha and was interfering with his ability to meditate. George told Greer that Val had once seen a quote by a man named Ambrose Redmoon about courage, and although Val thought the word courage had been highly misused throughout time, he thought the idea that "courage was not the absence of fear, but rather the judgment that something else is more important than fear" was insightful. It took Greer several more months, but he was finally able to detach himself from the fear that had been plaguing him and calm his mind.

Keitha addressed Murphy. "We better get going." After taking only a few steps, she turned back to Greer, and in a reassuring tone said, "This shouldn't take too long."

"I'm not going anywhere."

Keitha nodded. She just needed to hear him say it.

Keitha and Murphy saw Catherine and Addy as they crested the top of the path. Keitha breathed a sigh of relief as Murphy ran ahead to greet Addy.

"What the hell is your problem?" Catherine asked, as she folded her arms across her chest and glared at Keitha as though she were a disruptive child.

"My problem?"

"Do you know how long it has been since the last time both of you graced us with your presence?"

"It couldn't be helped," Keitha said simply, even though she had worried about this very thing constantly during Greer's lengthy struggle.

"Does time even go by the same for you?"

"Of course it does."

"Really, so what was so bloody important that you've been gone for *six months*? Six fucking months!"

"Why do you say bloody? You're not English," Keitha remarked.

"I know I'm not English," Catherine snapped. "What the hell does that have to do with anything?"

"I was just curious," Keitha said.

"You know what I'm curious about?" Catherine asked, trying to temper the irritation she felt about showing up for months on end without a sign of Keitha or any of the species. She had ranted to Henry and Ford about how inconsiderate the woman was, but they both encouraged her to continue trying. "What is it that you need me to do for you?" Catherine demanded. "I want to know right now."

Keitha looked over at Murphy and Addy happily sniffing each other. "Can't you be more like Addy? She isn't mad at Murphy."

"She isn't mad at Murphy because he's been here," Catherine said, confused.

Keitha attempted to hide her surprise.

"You didn't know," Catherine remarked, surprised but gratified. "He's the reason we kept coming back. I'd say he deserves a great big huge treat when you get back to wherever you come from."

"I thought we've established where we come from," Keitha said.

"I established, you just told stories," Catherine corrected.

"Jeez," Keitha said in exasperation. "If you want to get picky, then I should point out that saying great, big, and huge is just redundant."

"I do not need a grammar lesson from someone who can't even write."

"How many times do I need to tell you that I can write?" Keitha protested. "You are the most irritating woman."

"Take a good look in the mirror, lady."

"Stop calling me *lady*!"

"So this really is how you two interact." Greer's voice startled both women, but it was Catherine who gasped. Her eyes opened so wide that she could have been mistaken for a blue-eyed relative of the red-eyed tree frog.

"Father, I asked you to wait until I sent Murphy to get you," Keitha said, disturbed by his sudden appearance.

"He did, and so did Addy." Greer pointed down at the dogs that bounded up to his side. The two women stared; neither had noticed the dogs leaving the plateau.

Catherine continued to stare at Greer, stunned. "He's your father?" she asked Keitha, her voice matching her face.

"Yes," Keitha answered. "I was hoping to have a chance to tell you that he was with me before sending Murphy to get him."

"I'm Greer," he said, introducing himself.

Catherine didn't respond.

Greer looked at Keitha, who shrugged her shoulders to indicate she had no idea what was bothering Catherine so much.

"I'm sorry, it must be quite disturbing having me show up this way," Greer said sincerely.

Catherine seemed frozen.

"I can leave," Greer offered.

"What are you doing here?" Catherine rasped.

Greer regarded Catherine unwaveringly. "Keitha thought I might be able to help."

"Help? Help with what?"

"Help talk to you."

Catherine pondered his response before hesitantly asking, "Then you can answer my question?"

"What question is that?"

"What do you need me to do for you?"

"We're not sure," he said simply.

Catherine blinked. "I'm sorry, did you say you're not sure?"

"Yes," Greer said louder.

"She can hear you, Father. She just can't believe what you said."

"Oh, I didn't pick up the nuance," Greer stated. "I'll try to pay better attention," he said to Catherine.

Catherine raised an eyebrow and looked at him skeptically, but when she realized he was serious she muttered, "Thank you." Her eyebrows knitted together and she demanded, "How the hell can you not be sure?"

"It's complicated," Greer began.

"I'd say that's the understatement of one of our centuries. So let's just cut to the chase, shall we."

Greer looked completely perplexed.

"Something happened in your time that shouldn't have," Keitha said bluntly.

"Keitha," Greer said, startled.

"She wants to know, Father."

"You need to be more tactful," Greer said and turned back to Catherine, who was glaring at the two of them.

"I suppose the next thing you're going to tell me is that you need me to keep whatever happened from happening," Catherine said indignantly.

"I know it might be difficult for you to believe us," Greer said.

"Ya think?" Catherine responded.

Greer looked at Keitha, puzzled.

"She doesn't believe us," Keitha clarified.

"It's true, Catherine," he said earnestly before asking Keitha, "Have you told her how we know something happened?" Keitha shook her head and Greer added, "I think she needs to know."

"I doubt if she wants to listen to another story from me."

"I should tell it. After all, I was there, you weren't." Greer turned once more to Catherine.

Catherine wanted to scream at the man because his presence was so disconcerting; at the same time, she was curious. Her curiosity proved to be the stronger urge. "Fine, tell me."

"Would you like to sit?" Greer asked.

"No, I'll stand."

Keitha listened as her father artfully told Catherine about how Clara felt the shift in their world but could not remember the event; how an echo of the memory was triggered in Clara; and how Clara was able to recall enough to conclude that the Machiavellians had successfully changed something. Clara still did not know what, but she was convinced that the event the Machiavellians changed happened in Catherine's time. Greer did not include how he helped Clara recover what little she had been able to remember of the shift she felt, and he did not mention the shift that Terran felt. Greer finished and waited for Catherine's reaction. An eerie stillness fell over the plateau.

Catherine hooked a finger around Addy's collar and took a careful step away from Greer and Keitha.

"Don't you have any questions?" Greer asked hopefully.

"I wouldn't even know where to start," Catherine replied in an unsteady voice as she took another step back.

"Start anywhere you'd like," he said soothingly, trying to assuage Catherine's obvious agitation even though he also felt anxious.

Catherine's heart was racing, and the pressure in her head was causing a terrible throbbing in her ears. Addy began fidgeting at her side.

"It's all right, girl," Catherine and Greer said at the same time.

The sound of their two tight voices caused Addy to jerk her head back and forth, and she slipped out of her collar.

Catherine tensed.

"Don't scare her," she pleaded in a gravelly whisper as Addy began to turn away.

"Addy," Catherine called out, but her panic made her voice squeak, causing Addy's ears to flatten against her head.

"Please, don't," Catherine's voice was barely audible as she watched in horror as Greer knelt down, tilted his head to one side, held out his hand, and softly spoke Addy's name. Catherine knew she had to make him stop what he was doing before he spooked Addy into running. But just as a small croak emerged from her throat, Addy turned toward Greer. Catherine froze as Addy took several steps toward him, and then several more. Addy ignored Greer's proffered hand, opting instead to go directly up to his mouth to sniff his breath, and then she began to wave her tail back and forth at half-mast. Greer reached up and rubbed Addy's neck with comforting, sure strokes before getting to his feet.

The conflicting sensations of angst and astonishment coursed through Catherine, rendering her speechless. Addy, carrying herself with an air of dignity, trotted back to Catherine, who dropped to her knees enfolding the dog in her arms.

"You scared the shit out of me," Catherine managed to say, her muscles beginning to relax. She got to her feet and adroitly slipped the collar back on Addy's neck.

"Thank you," Catherine said gratefully, meeting Greer's gaze.

"Addy's a very good dog," Greer noted.

Catherine nodded.

"She wouldn't have left you. Addy just didn't know why we were both so . . . agitated, which, of course, made her nervous."

Catherine placed a hand on Addy's head. "Look, I appreciate what you did, but that doesn't mean you can start talking to me like we're suddenly friends."

"I didn't think it would make us friends," Greer stated. "I would just like a chance to talk to you."

Catherine carefully scrutinized the man as she began stroking Addy.

"May I ask you a question?" Greer inquired.

Catherine slowly nodded her head.

"What is that?" He pointed at Addy.

Catherine glanced down. "It's her collar."

"What is it for?"

Catherine looked over at Murphy, registering for the first time that he didn't have one, so she tried to explain. "You attach a leash . . ." Greer looked puzzled. "It's like a rope, you can take a dog for a walk, you attach the . . . rope here," she fingered the steel ring and felt the tags jangle against her skin, "and the dogs identification tags and rabies . . . do you know what that is?"

"Of course."

"I'm never sure what you people know or don't know," Catherine muttered before continuing. "The tags let other people know who the dog is and prove you've had your dog vaccinated."

"I don't understand? Doesn't everyone know who the dogs are and that they're well taken care of?" Greer said, concerned.

Keitha placed a hand on Greer's shoulder and shook her head. "Now is not the time."

Greer saw the look in his daughter's eyes and nodded his understanding before addressing Catherine, "I'm sorry if my questions are inappropriate."

"Are all of the dogs where you . . . when you . . . are they all wanted?"

"Yes, they are."

Keitha squeezed Greer's shoulder. As he twisted his head to look at her, he didn't see Catherine reach up and swipe at the corner of her eye.

"So," Catherine cleared her throat, causing Greer and Keitha to turn their attention to her in unison. "I guess I can give you a little more of my time," she said, rubbing Addy gently. "I owe you that much." Then she looked pointedly at Greer and said, "So these other people from your time interfered with something in my time, which changed your world, but you don't know how." She was trying hard to keep her voice from sounding incredulous.

"The Machiavellians, yes," Greer concurred.

"I assume that isn't what they are actually called."

"Was I not clear?" Greer inquired seriously. "We do not know who these people are, but we do know that they exist in our time. If we knew who they were it would make it much easier to proceed because we would know exactly who we were dealing with."

"Because then you could talk to them?" Catherine asked.

"I doubt they would listen to us," Greer said.

"But you don't know that they wouldn't."

"Yes we do," Keitha interrupted. "They have a very clear agenda. They want power and they have no qualms about doing anything they need to in order to obtain it."

"Yeah, believe it or not, calling them Machiavellians kind of gets that point across," Catherine noted. "Although it makes you wonder what Machiavelli himself would have thought."

"Why?"

"Because . . . you do understand that the term, and connotation, came about because of Machiavelli's *The Prince*, which was only one of his writings, and of course people debate what he actually intended."

"My mother gave them the name," Keitha explained simply.

"Oh, well, she's kind of literal at times, isn't she?"

"She can be."

"Okay," Catherine said, bobbing her head lightly, and when she realized Keitha was waiting for her to continue, she said, "I've got nothing else."

"Do you understand why we need your assistance?" Keitha asked.

"Not really. It doesn't sound to me like what the Machiavellians altered gave them the power you say they're salivating at the mouth to get, so why are you so adamant about stopping them?" Catherine asked.

"What do you mean 'why?'" Keitha demanded.

"What's your motivation?" Catherine retorted, raising an eyebrow.

"I appreciate why you want to understand our motives," Greer interjected, "and you are correct that the Machiavellians did not fully achieve what they were after, but they won't give up."

"What do you mean fully?"

"Just because they didn't achieve their ultimate goal doesn't mean they didn't accomplish something. They were able to cause a shift."

"But you don't even know what changed in your world. Maybe it wasn't significant, maybe your world is basically the same, so further effort wouldn't be worth it to them."

"All roads lead to Rome," Greer stated.

Catherine looked baffled.

"It doesn't matter which road you take, you'll still end up in Rome."

"Exactly," Catherine concurred.

"It's possible, we don't know, but it's irrelevant because the Machiavellians will try again."

"What makes you so sure?" Catherine questioned.

"There is another person, in our time, Terran, who has heard them. They are formulating another plan."

"Well, that's another thing. You say Clara felt this shift because she was pregnant with her," she pointed at Keitha, "and got some sort of a power surge—"

"An interesting way to put it," Greer commented appreciatively.

"Yeah, well, anyway," Catherine mumbled self-consciously and then pointed to Keitha again. "She has to be what now? Forty?"

"I'm thirty-two," Keitha corrected.

"Fine, thirty-two," Catherine said. "My point is, if the Machiavellians thought whatever they did was worthwhile, why would they wait thirty years to try again? It doesn't make any sense."

Keitha and Greer exchanged a concerned glance.

"What?" Catherine asked Greer. "What is it? Why are you looking at each other like that?" Her eyes shifted back and forth from one to the other. "Holy shit! They have! No they can't have," she said changing her mind. "Have they?"

"It's very complicated," Greer replied.

"Answer the question, have they or haven't they?" Catherine said severely. "Yes or no."

"It isn't—" Keitha began.

"Yes," Greer interjected.

"Father!"

"Holy shit," Catherine said quietly. "How many times?"

"Only one other," Greer replied.

"Are you sure?"

"As sure as we can be."

"How sure is that?"

"Terran also felt a shift, but he couldn't retain the memory of our original time," Greer said.

"Geez, you people can't remember shit."

Keitha bristled, but Greer calmly explained, "Terran has the ability. Unfortunately, although he saw both timelines, at the time he wasn't trained to the point of being able to retain both. Now he can."

"In case there's another *shift*."

"Yes," Greer replied.

"How many people in your time can communicate like this, anyway?" Catherine asked abruptly. "I mean, there was Oscar, and now there are the Machiavellians and you people. Are there hundreds, thousands? Because if each one changed something . . . it would be chaos." Her head began to throb. "Is it chaos?"

"Not all of the Machiavellians, or us people," Greer winced at his syntax, "can communicate like this. There are various abilities and various degrees of skill within those abilities; some people don't have a heightened ability at all," he paused, realizing he was beginning to ramble. "Only a handful of people have been able to achieve the type of communication we are having."

Catherine raised her eyebrow. "That you know of," she challenged.

"Terran would be able to sense if there were others."

"Really? Another ability of his?"

Greer nodded."Terran can sense perceptives in our time."

"Perceptives?"

"Clara thought most of the terms from your time, like psychic or clairvoyant, were too limiting, or not entirely accurate. That's why she began to use perceptive to describe an awareness or heightened sense of something more."

"Something more? What does that mean?"

"More means more." Greer ran his hand through his close-cropped white hair. "This is more difficult than I realized," he said to Keitha apologetically as his forehead creased in thought. "Copernicus, Curie, Pasteur, Einstein," Greer listed names he was sure Catherine would recognize, "they all envisioned more of something."

"They were geniuses."

"So were a lot of other people."

"So your point is that they had something *more*, something that heightened their awareness."

"Yes, a perceptive trait."

"Like a genetic trait?" Catherine asked cautiously.

"It is a genetic trait. It's why Oscar could communicate with Rebecca, why Keitha can—"

"Yeah I get it," Catherine cut him off roughly.

"Is something wrong?"

"You mean aside from the fact that I'm stuck in a science fiction cliché?"

"I can assure you the genetic—"

Catherine waved a hand at Greer. "I've heard about all I can stand, and I can assure you of one thing. Showing up looking like my father just to reinforce your contention that there is this genetic link between you people and me was not a wise decision."

Greer stared at Catherine blankly. "What?"

"I don't know how you did it, but you certainly have my father's hazel eyes, right down to the flecks of gold," Catherine said disapprovingly. Keitha and Greer turned to each other in alarm.

"Oh, please, don't give me the stunned expressions."

"I . . . we had no idea," Keitha maintained.

"We, indeed, did not," Greer concurred. "However, I can assure you these are my eyes. Nothing has been done to modify them."

"You expect me to believe you?"

"All I can tell you," Greer stated calmly, although he did not feel calm, "is that there may be more of a genetic link between you and Keitha than we realized." His eyes widened. "That would mean that the perceptive trait that you and Keitha share was passed down from both your mother and father, at least as far back as Shi`Ma and Molly."

"What do you know about Shi`Ma and Molly?" Catherine demanded, suddenly feeling very vulnerable.

Greer turned to Keitha, and after a silent exchange she replied, "A little, based on what was written in the journal I found."

Catherine's face puckered as though she had just eaten a lemon. "What journal?"

"The one that was handed down to Molly and then to your mother."

"How dare you read that!"

"Why shouldn't I?" Keitha asked.

"It's personal and it isn't yours," Catherine insisted.

"It's history and it was in our records," Keitha countered.

Catherine flung her arms up into the air and brought them down on the side of her legs so forcefully there was a resounding smack.

"I thought Molly's writings were very enlightened," Keitha stated appreciatively.

"Molly was an unusual woman," Catherine said with admiration.

"Obviously so was Shi`Ma. They were both perceptives, you must realize that."

"They certainly were thought-provoking women. You know, Molly never doubted that the voice she heard was her father's, and Shi`Ma knew her daughter Maria spoke to her after she died."

"I'm sorry?" Keitha asked confused. "Your grandmother Maria spoke to Shi`Ma?"

"That's what Shi`Ma told my grandfather Martin when—" Catherine stopped. "Wait a minute, why do you think Shi`Ma was a perceptive?"

"Because of what she told Maria about seeing her married to Martin."

"Interesting, yes, but the other story is more compelling," Catherine said, eyeing both of them.

Keitha and Greer exchanged another look before Keitha said, "I haven't read that one. It must be further along in the journal."

"Uh, huh," Catherine responded. There was something about the look that flashed between the other two that made Catherine vaguely uneasy.

"You believe the stories about your ancestors, don't you?" Greer asked, trying to guide the conversation away from the journal.

"I don't know what to believe," she replied, her dual meaning obvious.

"I think you do," he maintained.

"Greer," Keitha shook her head, "you're not helping."

"Catherine knows what she perceives, Keitha, she just has to admit it," Greer stated firmly.

Catherine glared at Greer but he stood his ground. She whirled around, and with Addy by her side she headed toward the area where Keitha, Murphy, and Greer had crested onto the plateau.

Keitha opened her mouth to protest, but Greer laid a hand on her arm and shook his head. "She didn't leave. Perhaps she just needs some time to think. We should wait and see."

"I hope you're right," Keitha said uneasily. They watched as Catherine and Addy disappeared over the edge. "What in the world possessed you to confront her like that? I thought you were supposed to be the calm rational one."

"I was calm and rational," he said, looking down at his daughter. "I'm afraid the time has come for her to . . . what was that phrase you said they used?" Greer mused. "Stop sitting on . . ."

"The fence."

CATHERINE HAD NEVER VENTURED off the tabletop of the plateau, and yet, as they made their way down the nebulous path, the terrain seemed strangely familiar. She told Addy not to move as she cautiously inched her way to the edge and peered over. The drop-off, although still precarious, was not as sheer as the one off the other side of the plateau: there was a rock formation that provided a swirling ledge some hundred feet below where she stood. It looked as though water had crashed against the side of the plateau, and just as the wave broke, and the intense energy weakened, the water was suddenly petrified into rock. She could literally see wave-like patterns in the pink hues.

Catherine backed carefully away and went over to where Addy was waiting patiently.

"I don't know what to think, little girl," Catherine said as she sat down on a squat rock and tried to get control of all the thoughts that were swirling around in her head. Addy stood looking up the path. "Give me a minute, all right?" Addy settled down on the ground, put her head between her feet, and watched Catherine.

Catherine was concentrating so intently that when Addy leapt to her feet Catherine squeaked in surprise right before she heard the rasping sound of footsteps approaching.

"Are you trying to give me a heart attack?" Catherine complained when Greer finally came into sight.

"Why would I want to do that?" Greer asked as he knelt down to greet Addy.

"Not literally," she said as she recalled an almost identical exchange with Keitha. "You really are her father, aren't you?"

Greer sat back on his heels, his hand still on Addy's neck. "You doubted that?"

"I'd say it's safe to assume that I have doubts about a lot of things the two of you have said."

"Why?"

"Why?" Catherine repeated, astonished by the question. "You can't be serious. This whole thing is beyond implausible, it's . . . it's, I don't know what it is."

"Astounding?" Greer proffered, standing up and slowly turning around. He stopped and stared at Catherine, his eyes filled with wonder, and said, "Yes, truly astounding."

"Why would this astound you?" Catherine inquired. "I mean, you're the ones that constructed this mélange."

"Keitha did, and you."

"Don't start with that shit."

"Keitha said you didn't want to admit that you had anything to do with any of the mélange. Is it really that much of a mix?"

"All of the species that she kept adding definitely didn't belong in this ecosystem."

"Ah yes, but that wasn't their purpose."

"Yeah, so she said. Their purpose was to pique my curiosity and get me to return. They're all gone in your time, aren't they?"

The question took Greer by surprise. "I can't talk to you about my time."

"Why?"

"Why?" he asked, flustered. "It would be imprudent."

"Well, geez, imprudent, that explains it; at least there's no fear of a temporal paradox."

"You're being sarcastic."

"Ya think?" Catherine tilted her head to the side.

"No wonder you and Keitha have had such a difficult time communicating with each other."

"What does that mean?" Catherine asked testily.

"I understand that time here can run out rather abruptly, and I told Keitha that I needed an opportunity to talk to you, privately," Greer said, redirecting the conversation without answering Catherine's question.

"About what?" Catherine asked guardedly.

"I realize how difficult it is for you to accept everything we have told you."

"Really?" Catherine sounded doubtful.

"I spent most of my life discounting one of my own abilities, but I never completely denied it, as you are."

"I don't have an ability."

"You wouldn't be here if you didn't, but I think you know that. You're an intelligent woman, Catherine; refusing to believe something in the face of supporting evidence is beneath you."

"You're not evidence, she isn't evidence, none of this is evidence!"

"Than what are we? What is all this?"

"I don't have to answer that."

"If we are not who we say we are, then it is an imperative question you need to answer."

Catherine leapt up angrily. Addy protectively moved to her side. "Just leave me alone."

"I wish we could, believe me; I wish we did not need to involve you; I wish there were more time; but we need your help, now. Please," Greer implored.

Alarms began going off in Catherine's head, but she couldn't move. It was as though she was riveted to the spot. "I can't help you," she rasped, her throat dry, "I'm no one. Don't you people understand that?"

"You are somehow connected to what the Machiavellians changed, and I can help you find the event."

"What the hell are you talking about?" Catherine yelled.

"Keitha was able to bring me here by each of us reaching a deep meditative state where I was able to link my mind with Keitha's."

"That isn't—" Catherine's mouth dropped open in shock.

"The event the Machiavellians altered is somewhere in your mind. I can help you find it, and the interference with your time can be prevented."

Catherine was so stunned she staggered forward. Greer caught her but she wrenched herself away from him and vehemently started shaking her head.

"You are completely out of your—fucking mind!" Catherine flailed her arms and hit Henry just as he was reaching to shut off the alarm clock. The sudden jolt startled him and, as he whipped his head toward her, he almost fell out of bed.

"What the hell, Catherine!" he exclaimed before seeing her ashen face. "Are you all right?"

She stared at him, her eyes huge orbs of absolute panic. As electric shocks of fear raced through Henry, he reached out to her. Catherine felt cold. Henry knew Catherine wasn't registering where she was. He looked helplessly over at Addy, who was standing next to the bed. The dog laid her head on top of Catherine's hand, and Catherine reached out with her other hand and stroked Addy's head, but her eyes remained glazed.

"Catherine," Henry said in a reassuring tone meant to keep a wild, frightened creature from bolting.

She stared at him again and Henry saw a hint of recognition.

"Catherine," he said in the same comforting voice, "can you tell me what happened?"

"I . . . he . . ." she trailed away.

"He? Do you mean Murphy?"

Catherine shook her head in frustration.

"Another he?" Henry tried to keep the surprise out of his voice.

Catherine nodded. "Her . . . her father," she said, struggling with each word.

"Keitha's father?" Henry was too stunned to keep his voice even.

Catherine nodded again. "He . . . they . . ." Unable to articulate what had occurred, she looked at Henry in desperation.

"Maybe we should go upstairs. I'll put on some coffee, you can let Addy out and maybe then you'll be able to tell me?" he offered, thinking that if Catherine engaged in a normal routine she would snap out of this dazed state.

Catherine nodded at him like a puppet, and yet he wasn't completely sure she had understood him until she got out of bed and headed over to the doorway.

"Catherine?"

She turned.

"You're still naked."

She looked down at her own body, perplexed. Henry grabbed her t-shirt and shorts—the September mornings were still warm enough for light clothing—but then he remembered how cold she felt and found a sweatshirt for her instead. Catherine put them on like an automaton.

As they sat at the kitchen table Catherine finally told Henry what had happened. When she finished Henry remained utterly still, as though all of his muscles had seized from the tension in his body.

"What are you going to do?" Henry finally asked.

"Were you listening to me?" she replied.

"I was listening intently to every word."

"They think I'm involved somehow. It makes no sense. Why the hell would I be involved? I'm no one."

"You're someone to them," he said quietly.

"God, Henry, I'm so scared," she said, her voice catching. "What the hell am I going to do?"

"I don't know," he replied, feeling helpless. "I honestly don't know."

Tears began to stream down Catherine's face. Henry rose and wrapped his arms around her, and Addy put her wet nose against Catherine's cheek, making her laugh.

"All right," Catherine said as she sniffled and used the sleeve of her sweatshirt to dry the tears. "Crying isn't going to help. I need to think this through logically."

Henry squeezed her shoulders. A plan, Catherine always did better with a plan.

"I'll talk to Ford," she said. "I have a distinct feeling that he knows more than what he's told me."

CHAPTER 26

Most of the leaves were off the trees Catherine noticed as she glanced out her office window, but with the temperature slated to reach the sixties it felt like October instead of the week before Thanksgiving. Thanksgiving, she was so exhausted that the mere thought of the preparations for the holiday made her want to bury her head and pretend that it was January already.

She swiveled her chair around so she was facing her computer screen. The email Ford sent her early in the morning glared back at her. She wondered why good news, like the bill gutting the Endangered Species Act somehow languishing in the Senate without coming up for a vote and Pombo's re-election defeat, always seemed to be countered by devastating news.

The first line of the email blazed at her from the screen: 'Catherine, migratory beekeepers in the United States have started to report that they're experiencing heavy losses in their colonies.' Ford went on to list what the beekeepers were specifically noting. A complete absence of adult bees in the affected hives with little or no sign of dead bees in the hive or at the hive entrances; several frames with healthy, capped brood with low levels of parasitic mites, indicating that colonies were relatively strong shortly before the loss of adult bees; food reserves that were not robbed, despite active colonies in the same area, suggesting avoidance of the dead colony by other bees; minimal evidence of wax moth or small hive beetle damage; and a laying queen often present with a small cluster of newly emerged attendants.

The response? Well, of course, a group needed to be formed to look into the possible causes. Ford's sources expected that the Department of Agriculture would end up taking the lead.

Possible causes. Catherine rolled her eyes, *Here we go again.*

"Good evening, Catherine."

She slowly raised her head from the document on her desk that she had been perusing.

"My God, Catherine, you look horrible," Ford exclaimed with uncharacteristic rashness.

"Good to see you too, Ford."

"I apologize, that was rude of me," he said, but the haggard look on her face and the deep circles under her eyes did nothing to alleviate his first impression.

"I wouldn't worry about it, I know how I look."

"Why? What happened?" he asked with profound concern.

"Are they looking at pesticide use?"

"I'm sorry?" Ford was not following her.

"The honey bees. Are they looking at whether or not the bee colonies were exposed to neonicotinoids? It has to be a first step: they can look at the research of the French and Germans and other countries and compare it to what is happening here. They don't have to start from scratch."

"My sources tell me the National Academy of Science is finalizing the findings of a two-year study about critical problems facing beekeepers, including invasive parasitic mites that caused catastrophic losses during the winters of 1995 to 1996 and 2000 to 2001."

"That was in the paper Hal sent me, back when all this started," she said.

Ford was fairly certain that "when all this started" was not in reference to the honey bee issue but rather Catherine's experiences on the plateau, but he continued as though they were talking about the bees. "The National Academy has also found that insecticides used in crop protection have been associated with bee mortality."

"Then they need to make that a top priority for further research."

"So far the official party line amongst the government agencies—not the National Academy, but others—is that there is currently no recognizable underlying cause for CCD."

"CCD?"

"Colony Collapse Disorder, what people are starting to call it."

"Well isn't that just great. It has a name, but no recognizable underlying cause," she stated mordantly. "So there may be synergistic issues involved, but that doesn't mean," Catherine paused. "Wait, is anyone proposing that the U.S. institute a ban, *at least* a temporary ban on specific neonicotinoids, until the underlying cause or causes are found?"

"They want to cast a wide net to develop a science-based picture of what factors may result in CCD."

"You have got to be kidding me!" Catherine couldn't contain herself. "It's the global warming . . . climate change shell game. Keep the answer moving, put it under one shell and then another. Get the shills to guess where the answer is, then move it around some more, make it look good, and all the while the ones controlling the game have palmed the real answer or answers."

"We've seen a lot of setbacks these last six years, but your acting like this is the final blow."

"How do you know it isn't? How do you know that this isn't the thing that makes it all collapse? How ironic would that be." She looked grim and then, without warning, she demanded, "Where have you been, Ford?"

"You know where I've been."

"Yes, I know. Meetings, conferences, but you haven't been here since August. I needed to talk to you."

"I called you every week. You said there was nothing new."

"You think I would talk about this over the phone?" Catherine cautioned, as though he was being completely naïve.

Ford worried about her apparent paranoia but then considered the ability of the government to eavesdrop on citizens since the institution of the Patriot Act. He could just imagine what a phone conversation about the plateau might sound like.

"You're right, the topic is far too unusual."

"Yeah, unusual, I'm sure that's how it would be termed."

"What happened, Catherine?" he asked again, but this time he wasn't going to let her get sidetracked. "Did you see Keitha and Murphy?"

Ever since the two of them talked in March, Ford had made it a point to stop in Denver every couple of weeks to see if there was any news. Although

Addy and Catherine consistently showed up on the plateau. Keitha was absent. Murphy showed up alone. By the beginning of June Catherine was starting to get annoyed, by July she was livid, and by August she was feigning indifference. It was obvious that they had solved whatever problem they thought they needed her to help with. Ford and Henry encouraged her to keep trying, but they both knew that if Keitha didn't show up soon Catherine really would quit trying.

Catherine reiterated, in its entirety, what transpired on the plateau in September. Several times she became so agitated that Ford had to wait while she paced the room, like a caged animal, before she was able to continue.

"My," Ford said when Catherine finished.

"My?" Catherine prodded.

"I'd like to hear your thoughts, Catherine. You were the one that was there." He had confidence in her capacity to assess unprecedented situations.

"For God's sake, Ford! I need your help here."

"I need yours."

Catherine ran a hand over her face, shaking her head as she did. Then she stared at him with penetrating eyes. Ford didn't flinch.

"My grandmother Molly used to tell me stories about what happened to her grandfather and great-uncle during the famine. She said it was important to understand that history happened to real people, that the decisions and choices we made impacted real people. I loved listening to her; she was such a good storyteller, I felt like I was almost there."

Ford was sure she had a point, so he remained silent.

"I think Keitha and her father are also very good storytellers. They want me to empathize with their people, believe that they are living with the impact of something we have done . . . or will do, even though they won't tell me what it is."

"Yet?"

"Yet," Catherine said in a guarded tone. "I can't stop worrying about whether I'm just being manipulated. What if Keitha and her people are the ones that want to change something, and these Machiavellian people they told me about are just a ruse? I could actually be the person who causes the change."

"A valid concern."

"So you agree with me?"

"Catherine, it is a valid concern, and you wouldn't be you unless you considered it. Now you have to ask yourself if it's a reasonable concern."

"None of this is reasonable, Ford."

"I understand, but you need to try and look at this objectively. Evaluate everything that has happened, and try to concentrate on your impression of these people. How do they make you feel, what do you sense from them?"

"You want me to decide based on my gut reaction to them?" she asked, aghast.

"I want you to base it on your perception of them," Ford corrected her.

Catherine leaned back in her chair. "God, Ford, don't use their term to make a point."

"I'm not. You have a fine insight into the character of people, Catherine. You just need to use it."

"This is not like hiring someone, Ford."

"No, there's a lot more at stake than that."

She leaned forward. "According to them."

Ford waited her out.

"I honestly don't know, all right. Each time I think about what makes me want to trust them, like Murphy and Addy, and the way Addy reacted to Greer, and the fact that Keitha is a pain in the ass. What?" Catherine asked, flustered by Ford's expression.

"Why is that a reason to trust them?" Ford asked, baffled.

"Because, if they were trying to manipulate me, they would have made Keitha pretend to be more sympathetic." Catherine furrowed her brow, "But then again, maybe they knew I would be wary of someone too understanding and so they told her to be insufferable."

"Catherine, isn't that a little convoluted?"

"No, think about it," she stressed. "If these Machiavellians will do anything to get the power they want, reverse psychology would be child's play."

"I think you're over thinking it."

"I don't think I can over think this."

Ford decided to change the focus of the conversation. "They obviously think you have the capacity to help them, that somehow you're in the right place at the right time."

"Please, Ford, don't raise the 'butterfly effect' scenario with me."

"What?"

"You know, Lorenz's paper, *"Predictability: Does the Flap of a Butterfly's Wings in Brazil Set Off a Tornado in Texas,"* she quoted, expecting him to understand. He didn't.

"I know the paper, Catherine. Lorenz was referring to seemingly small changes in meteorological modeling inputs that created large changes in the predicted outcome of the modeling. A rounded number changed whole weather predictions. Lack of sensitivity in data input could greatly affect what scientists thought was predictable. I just don't understand how that applies to your situation?"

"You know, if the butterfly doesn't . . . never mind. The point is, according to Greer, they have no idea what was changed, so there is no right place, or right time: it is total chaos."

"I think you're wrong, Catherine."

"Why?" she asked bluntly. "Tell me why."

Ford scrutinized her closely.

"Would you please stop staring at me like that," Catherine entreated tensely.

"Are you sure you want me to answer you?" he asked judiciously.

"Yes," she responded decisively, even though the weight of his words had increased her anxiety.

Ford nodded. "Let's talk about the chaos first. As you know a chaotic system appears to be random, but it is actually made up of cause and effect. Then that effect becomes the cause that creates the next effect and on and on until you have a defined event. So think about a sequence of events like the links in a chain. The first link in the chain is the initial condition, whatever that might be, and it occurs at a specific point in time. The next link in the chain is whatever the effect of that initial condition is and occurs at another specific point in time. If that effect becomes causative, another link is added, and on and on, until the final effect or outcome is reached, at which point you have a defined event with a sequence of precise cause-and-effect links that occurred at specific points in time. Now, I'll grant you my analogy is simplistic. However, within human time, and retrospectively, discrete events can be culled out of what appears to be chaos. Historians love to piece together everything that led up to a historic event, showing us how seemingly disparate pieces actually fit together."

"I understand your point, but Greer and Keitha are talking about an alteration to the historic chain of events. Either some completely new link was inserted, or an existing one was modified or removed, creating a different chain. The modified chain is the only one they know, so there is no way to back track to find the original event, the one that Keitha and her people want to leave in place, because it doesn't exist anymore for them. It would be tantamount to a historian who is living in our time suddenly knowing that something isn't quite right and then discovering that something in the mid-1800s was altered. Unbeknownst to them there was an original timeline where Stephen Douglas was elected president, not Abraham Lincoln. Tell me, Ford, how would that historian find the incident in history that was altered when all of our historical records, and our history, are based on Lincoln winning?"

"They could find the exact incident if they had a trail to follow."

"Are you listening to me? The trail's gone, Ford."

"Hansel and Gretel found their way home through a dense, unknown area of forest."

"A fairy tale? Seriously, you're going to use a fairy tale to make a point?"

"In the fairy tale Hansel and Gretel knew they were being led deep into the forest, an area they were completely unfamiliar with, and they wanted to be able to make their way back home, so they made their own trail. Keitha and her people need to find an event, and they're trying to find the trail that was left for them to follow."

"And yet, just as in 'Hansel and Gretel,' the birds have eaten the crumbs, so there is no trail left to follow," Catherine countered.

"They're looking for pebbles, not crumbs."

"What?"

"Have you never actually read the Brothers Grimm fairy tale?"

"I've heard it repeated enough times," Catherine replied. "I think I know the story."

"This is why Keitha's people take such care to authenticate events, instead of relying on hearsay."

Catherine scowled at him and stated matter-of-factly, "Hansel and Gretel, the children of a poor woodcutter, left a trail of bread crumbs to follow home and the birds ate all of them so there was nothing left to follow. That's the story."

"That was what happened the second time they were taken into the woods. The first time, Hansel put white pebbles in his pockets, which shone in the moonlight, so he and his sister were able to follow them home."

"I didn't know that part," Catherine said, embarrassed, but then added, "It doesn't matter, though, because what we are dealing with is the bread crumbs that were eaten. They may as well never have been there in the first place because they are completely gone. Nothing left to follow, wandering in the woods."

"Not if the DNA you have in common with Keitha acts like the pebbles and the perceptive genes make the pebbles shine. What if there is an illuminated trail that Keitha is following, and this trail is why Clara is convinced that," he paused to recall the correct term, "the shift happened in our time?"

Catherine stared at him, stunned.

"Have you ever heard of the 'delay-and-antedating' hypothesis or paradox?" Ford continued.

"No?" Her natural inquisitiveness trumped the turmoil that was beginning to churn her stomach.

"Benjamin Libet, a neurophysiologist and Professor of Physiology at the University of California in San Francisco, was involved in research into neuronal activity and sensation thresholds back in the 1970s. Libet's data suggested that we retrospectively 'antedate' the beginning of a sensation to the moment of the primary neuronal response."

"Meaning?"

"He noted during his experiments that there was a delay of about five hundred milliseconds between the first appearance of conscious will—monitored through electrical brain activity, to, say, move a hand—and the actual physical act of moving the hand. The conclusion, after numerous experiments, was that physical events eliciting awareness take place after a person becomes conscious of the intent to carry out the behavior and there is an automatic, subjective referral of the conscious experience backwards in time to the point when the person became aware of the intent, the 'time marker.' Hence, retrospective antedating."

Catherine began to ponder aloud as she thought through the concept. "So the brain is aware before the muscles react." She wiggled her fingers absently. "Response time. Our brains send the electrical stimulus to the appropriate part of the body, and our reaction time is dependent upon a variety of factors, the obvious being alcohol, drugs and age." She stared at Ford. "What you're saying is that when we do react, in our minds we somehow believe that it was at the same instant that we became consciously aware of the need to react even though there was a lag time, albeit extremely small."

"Libet further hypothesized that a specific mechanism within the brain is responsible for the projection of these events both out in space and back in time."

Catherine opened her mouth but closed it again and waited for Ford to finish, even though she was now certain of where he was going.

"If you are somehow involved in the initial condition of the event that changed Keitha's time, your brain could contain the primary neuronal response, the time marker. I believe it is that time marker that Greer wants to help you access before the actual physical event happens. Then perhaps it can be prevented."

"How long have you been thinking about this?" she asked, her voice trembling slightly.

"Since it was raised by one of the people I spoke about before. It has been a topic of discussion for several years."

"A topic for your discussions on the concepts of reality and the ability of the mind?"

"Yes."

"Oh for God's sake, Ford," she said, her face clenched in distress. "Don't you think you should have brought this up before now?"

Ford shook his head. "There was no reason to, based on what you had been experiencing on the plateau. The situation did not warrant upsetting you by bringing up a theory that didn't have any relevance, but the circumstances have obviously changed."

"Obviously," Catherine said, burying her head in her hands before staring at him with somber eyes. "This is just too surreal, Ford. I just don't see how any of it is possible, not with me."

"I can only imagine how surreal it must be for you. Perhaps if you look at it from the perspective of what happens in our everyday life. I would venture to say that almost everyone has stopped themselves from doing something that seemed inevitable at the time. Hesitate for an instant, and you avoid knocking over a glass, or stepping on a nail, or—"

"I get it, Ford, but in just as many instances we knock over the glass, or the nail pierces our foot. Besides, this is much more complicated."

"And yet, not. They—Keitha, Greer, Clara, all of the people in their time—need you to stop the glass from being knocked over."

"The people you've been talking with, how have they handled this antedating thing?"

"You mean in terms of what is happening to you?"

"What else would I mean?" she asked.

"Catherine, even though these people have experienced a great deal, none of them has had your experience. It's the difference between playing baseball in the neighborhood field and playing for the Rockies." Ford liked baseball as much as he liked the symphony.

"So what am I supposed to do? Just let Greer . . ." she couldn't bring herself to finish the sentence.

"You know there is evidence that many other people were thinking along scientific lines of inquiry long before Copernicus and Galileo."

"What?" Catherine knitted her brow in confusion.

"Even so, it took that conflagration of thought, that salient point in time that people point to and say, yes, that was the beginning of the scientific revolution. That was when there were enough people collectively starting to question the validity of long-held beliefs, but it took even longer for the vast majority to accept the new ideas that those scientists were holding forth."

"What are you talking about?"

"You're on the edge of a different frontier, Catherine, and I'm afraid it will take a long time before what you're involved in reaches the salient moment when another paradigm shift occurs and opens the minds of humanity even further."

"You're saying I'm on my own?" Catherine said despondently.

"No, never," Ford stated definitively, "but you are the only one that can decide if you trust Keitha and Greer."

"My gut."

"Your perception."

"And if I'm wrong?" Catherine asked, feeling her stomach twist with fear. "What then?"

CHAPTER 27

Catherine found herself staring out of the windshield for what felt like the hundredth time. She didn't even bother to look over at the passenger seat or into the back seat, she knew Henry and Connor would be there and would then be gone. Catherine gave the dream a couple of seconds and then glanced to her right and saw the expanse of land covered with waving grass, dotted with sage, and scattered with tall juniper trees. The antelope bounded over the ridge. She glanced left, the same exact landscape, and in the far distance, the mountains rose up against the sparkling indigo sky. She knew where she was, always knew where she was, and yet she couldn't stop the chill from passing through her as she turned her head forward and saw the dark clouds gathering. Some nights this was the point at which she woke herself up, but then there were other nights, nights like tonight.

She was suddenly standing, staring down at the gray pavement under her feet, no car in sight. The sun was so low that it barely winked above the peak of the mountains, and ominous black clouds had bled together and smeared across the perfect sky. She looked back down at the pavement and saw the familiar broken white line of the highway, and then her eyes drifted to her right and she saw the thick solid white stripe that ran along the edge of the pavement and the earthen shoulder that gave way to grass and sagebrush. When she turned back to look across the two lanes closest to her, she saw that the daylight had inexplicably turned to night and rain was pelting down on her.

Catherine felt the car, as she always did, a split second before she heard the horn. She had ceased screaming at the sensation of the car passing so close to her and therefore no longer woke up at this point.

Another set of headlights quickly bore down on her. The car was moving much slower than the first. She was able to get her feet to move and ran for the shoulder of the road. With one foot still on the highway, she stopped and spun back around. It was time to get this over with, to know with certainty what in her heart she already knew. Catherine tried to wipe the rain away from her face so she could see into the deep, thick night. She watched as the second vehicle, which was continuing to decelerate, passed her. Her heart began beating fast, too fast. She held both hands over her chest and pressed in an irrational attempt to force her heart to slow down.

Catherine thrashed her arms wildly, as though swimming for the surface of a body of water. She gasped for air, which made her cough uncontrollably. As she fought to stop the mounting, hacking spasm, she could hear Henry frantically repeating her name, his hand on her shoulder. She threw off the covers and struggled out of the bed, doubling over until the coughing subsided.

Henry was at her side but didn't touch her. Addy was pacing at the end of the bed. Catherine looked at them both through watery eyes and tried to speak but only a squeaky sound came forth.

"For God's sake, Catherine," Henry said in a strained voice.

Catherine shook her head as she grabbed his arm. He felt her fingers digging into his flesh. He waited anxiously, watching her fight for control, feeling completely helpless.

She could make out Henry's face in the muted glow from some outside light. He looked alarmed. She put her hand on her chest—her heart was racing—and when she pulled her hand away, it was covered in sweat.

"I'll get you a towel." Henry disappeared into the bathroom.

Catherine could feel the chill sinking into her, but she didn't move. Addy came over to her, and she managed to stroke the dog's neck with a shaky hand.

Henry re-emerged with a towel and handed it to Catherine, watching as she wiped herself down. He noticed that her entire body began to quiver.

Henry grabbed a t-shirt off the floor, where Catherine had tossed it in the night when she got too warm to wear it under the covers, and handed it to her.

"Thanks," she said, slipping it over her head before she sat on the bed.

"Were you back on the plateau?" he asked, his voice strained. He had been deeply worried about her ever since the last experience she had, when the man named Greer had asked her to let him access her mind. Access, such an innocuous word, and yet it had terrified him.

She shook her head.

"The highway?"

She nodded.

"Was it the same?"

She blinked.

"Catherine," Henry said, sitting down on the bed next to her. "Was it the same?"

"I saw who was driving the second car."

"Who?"

Catherine shifted on the bed to face him. "Me."

"You?" Henry asked in surprise.

"It was when I drove up to Montana after my dad had the heart attack."

"You're sure?"

"Believe me, Henry, it isn't something I'll forget."

"All this time you've been dreaming about that incident?"

"I think I've been dreaming about it for a long time," Catherine said quietly.

Henry took one of her hands. "Why? Do you have any idea?"

"I think they've always wanted me to know who they are."

"I'm not sure I'm following you," Henry said.

"I'm not sure I'm following me either," Catherine said, before squeezing his hand. "There's only one way for me to find out what is going on. I need to let the dream finish."

KEITHA SHOOK HER HEAD without turning to the three people who were huddled so close behind her she could hear their every breath. Clara, Greer, and Terran let out a collective heave of disappointment. The latest in a long inventory of searches, which Keitha had executed on various files within the massive record data memory, had been unable to find any thread of the story about Shi`Ma and Martin after Catherine's grandmother Maria had died.

"I'm telling you, it's just not there." Keitha spun around.

"Have you looked through *all* of the sealed files?" Greer asked.

Keitha cocked her head and glanced at Terran out of the corner of her eye.

"This search went through the last of them," Terran confirmed.

"Are you sure?"

"Greer," Keitha said, exasperated, "I told you after we talked to Catherine that there was no entry in the journal that corresponded to her story."

"That you knew of. We had to be absolutely sure. The story could have been filed incorrectly, or it could have been written down somewhere besides the journal."

"We used a great deal of time and energy so that you could be sure."

"It isn't as though Catherine has been back to the plateau," Clara noted.

"No, Mother, she hasn't."

"We needed to know," Greer stated.

"Because you think that no record means something must have prevented Catherine from writing the story down," Keitha asserted. "Well, just because we confirmed there is no record does not confirm that she is the key to what happened. The explanation could be the simplest one; she just never got around to it."

CATHERINE WATCHED AS THE SECOND VEHICLE, which was continuing to decelerate, passed her and pulled over to the side of the road. The headlights brightened the shoulder of the road in front of the car, but she was staring into the murky verge. She sensed them before she could distinguish their silhouettes from the pervasive darkness of the night. Catherine walked off the edge of the highway and waded into the morass of people and animals, and then she was standing beside her own bed.

Henry, propped up on one elbow staring at her in anticipation, saw her eyelids flutter.

"Well?" he asked, managing to sound calm.

"They were there." Catherine's voice sounded strange and disjointed, which made Henry cringe. "Keitha, her father, Murphy," Catherine continued, "and so many others: women, men, children, animals," her voice faltered. "They were all dying."

Henry scooted across the bed to her side and reached out to take her hand. She stared down into his eyes. "I could feel them dying," Catherine said, her voice racked with emotion. But it was the horrified look in her eyes that made Henry shudder.

KEITHA COULD FEEL A MOIST SENSATION against her cheek. She opened her eyes and tilted her head to the left. Murphy was standing beside her. Keitha stared directly into his watchful eyes.

"She knows," Keitha rasped. "We need to get Greer."

CATHERINE STOOD ON THE PLATEAU'S EDGE and looked down. The canyon floor seemed farther away. She could still see the cut where the water flowed, but it looked like a mere opalescent ribbon instead of the broad blue swath meandering along the base of the red and pink mesas. She scratched Addy behind her ears.

"It's all dying," she said, her voice shaking. She felt Addy's nose on her hand and looked down into the dog's luminous brown eyes just as the crunch of footsteps broke the silence. Catherine and Addy turned around.

"Thank you for coming back," Greer said.

"Where is Keitha?" Catherine turned from side-to-side. Murphy and Addy were running around playing tag, but she didn't see Keitha.

"I asked her to give us a little time to talk," Greer replied evenly.

"Hmm," Catherine nodded her head and then asked, "Why didn't you just tell me?"

Greer didn't question why she thought he knew what she was talking about. It was because of Keitha that he did, and so he just responded, "It was something you had to witness for yourself. It was the only way you would believe it."

"Witnesses are observers. I *felt* all of you."

"You perceived what was happening to us, you empathized, but it wasn't happening to you."

Catherine mulled his comment over. "You're right," she said and then added, "I'm sorry."

"Why?"

"Because of what you're going through," Catherine said.

Greer looked puzzled for a moment. "What you felt is not happening yet. That was a point in the future. A possible future."

"How could I—" Catherine stopped abruptly. The images had moved to the forefront of her mind, and she realized that the Keitha and Greer that she saw by the side of the highway were much older, and the dog that she thought was Murphy wasn't Murphy at all. "I wasn't paying close enough attention," she admitted.

"That happens," Greer said.

Catherine observed Greer closely. "What happened to not telling me about the future?" she asked.

"I didn't tell you. It was something you saw."

"I saw the future?" Catherine scoffed.

"Rebecca saw Oscar," Greer noted. "For some people the connection is fluid."

"Your daughter doesn't strike me as the kind of person who would be open to allowing me to see her life."

"Not now, perhaps, but under extreme circumstances . . ." Greer trailed away.

"I just don't understand that," Catherine said vehemently. "Why would the Machiavellians change something that would cause the extinction of the human race? Where's the power in that?"

"Not the entire human race," Greer stated matter-of-factly.

Catherine's eyebrows shot up. "How do you know that?"

"Clara, Keitha's mother, has known for a while, but she didn't want to worry anyone else if there was nothing that could be done." Greer stared into Catherine's eyes for an instant but then looked away.

"Why? What purpose does it serve?"

"They don't want us interfering with their plans."

"They know who you are?" Catherine said, startled.

"Not who we are, but they found out enough. We didn't think they had. Clara and Sylvia thought that they had put up defenses in time, but the Machiavellians must have sensed something, someone. Just as Sylvia sensed them but didn't know precisely who they were."

"If they want to stop you then why did I see so many people—men, women, *children*, and *animals*?"

"I believe in your time it was called collateral damage."

"Oh my God!" Catherine tried to keep the shrillness out of her voice. "They would kill all . . . just to stop you?"

"I think they took advantage of an opportunity to change something in your time that they somehow knew would adversely impact us."

"Yeah, annihilation would tend to be an adverse impact," Catherine remarked, stunned by how calm Greer was.

"I doubt they even thought about the ultimate outcome, like so many throughout human history who have coveted power."

"How bad are things for you? Right now I mean."

"I can't discuss that with you."

"Yeah, yeah," she said looking around some more. "Well, I don't think you'd be here asking for my help if things were good."

Greer's bearing betrayed nothing.

"Yeah, that's what I thought," Catherine acknowledged and then said, "You know, I spoke with a friend of mine just a little while ago, and he enlightened me about a theory of the unconscious build-up that occurs in the brain before a physical action takes place. I presume, actually it was Ford's supposition, that you hope that my brain contains information about what happened, what the Machiavellians changed. You want to help me access the primary neuronal response associated with that event, in the further hope that the lag time between the build-up and the actual action will give me the opportunity to make sure the change doesn't take place." Greer was so quiet that Catherine wasn't sure if she was explaining the concept clearly enough. She continued anyway, "For example, let's say the electrical build-up resulted in the physical action of me ringing a bell. We determine that I'm not supposed to ring the bell, then I need to see myself ringing the bell during the primary neuronal response, which will give me time to stop before I actually physically ring the bell."

"In simplified terms, yes," Greer said.

"That's simplified?" Catherine asked in amazement, shaking her hand at Greer when it looked like he was about to respond. "Please, don't give me the un-simplified version."

Greer remained silent.

"The problem I see," Catherine asserted, "is that we're talking about a lag time of maybe five hundred milliseconds. Half a second to stop an event from happening—it just isn't enough time."

"The lag time you're referring to was noted during experiments that were conducted in the 1970s, 80s . . ." Greer moved his hand in a circle, indicating on and on.

"So?"

"We're outside of those parameters."

"That's putting it mildly, and that just compounds the time problem," Catherine said analytically. "Because I don't think we're talking about stopping a bell from being rung."

"We don't know what we are talking about preventing, but you should know that this place, this plateau, is where past, present, and futures meet. Linear time has no meaning here."

Catherine grimaced.

"Are you all right?" Keitha asked as she approached the two of them.

"No, I'm not," Catherine said wearily. She tried to find the rock she normally sat on, and when she couldn't, she just sank onto the ground and held her head in her hands. She couldn't get the images from the edge of the highway out of her mind. Murphy and Addy, in a protective move, came over and flanked Catherine on both sides.

Greer and Keitha waited, knowing there was nothing else they could do.

Without taking her head out of her hands Catherine inquired, "You said what I saw happening to all of you was a possible future?"

Keitha stared at her father in surprise, but he held up a finger so she would not question him. "Yes," he answered Catherine.

Catherine peered up at them through her fingers. "So if we prevent the change the Machiavellians caused, that future won't happen?"

Greer was so gratified to hear Catherine say we, he didn't respond immediately. "We don't know, but we hope it will help," Keitha answered for them both.

"What if we make it worse?" Catherine asked.

"How much worse could it possibly be?" Keitha countered.

"Let's get this over with," Catherine said unemotionally as she straightened herself without getting up. When Keitha and Greer didn't move, Catherine yelled, "Now!"

Greer was the first to understand that she was agreeing to his plan. He composed himself and sat next to her on the ground. Addy and Murphy shifted slightly to make room for him, but they did not back away.

He gazed steadily into her eyes. "Are you positive you want to do this?"

Hell no, she thought to herself, but there was so much concern and compassion in his voice and in his eyes that Catherine suddenly felt very sure. She reached out and touched his hand. He covered it with his other hand.

"I'm going to help you reach a deep meditative state, and then I will help you access the part of your brain where this build-up is occurring," Greer said, as though he was talking her through a recipe.

Catherine nodded, but her nerves and muscles felt liquid, like when she dreamt about being stuck on an elevator that would suddenly start to free-fall down the shaft.

Greer took her other hand in his and, staring into her wide, anxious eyes said, "You have to trust me."

CATHERINE WAS STANDING IN HER OWN BACKYARD when the screen door opened and Henry stuck his head out.

"Are you two going to get in here? It's December, not July."

Catherine looked around. "Talk to your dog," she replied.

"Addy. Addy," Henry began calling. The dog came trotting out from around the Austrian Pine tree that sat in the corner of the yard by the fence. "There you are, girl." He held the door open as Addy adroitly leapt over the two steps, pirouetted at the last moment, and landed in the entry facing Henry.

"Show off," he said smiling. Addy wagged her tail. "Catherine," he yelled into the night, "are you coming in, or are you planning to stand out there all night and freeze?"

Catherine ran over to the house and stood at the rear entry, rubbing her arms to get rid of the cold. She could hear the sounds of voices mixing in animated conversations as she made her way into the hall that led to the kitchen. Wafting, mingling scents of food, wine, and beer washed over her.

"How long does it take a dog to shit in the backyard?"

Catherine looked at the person who made the remark and cursed Henry under her breath for inviting their jackass of a neighbor.

"Doesn't matter as long as the dog is as good as Addy," Tobias said, giving Richard a cold, hard smile before leading Catherine away.

"Asshole," Tobias muttered to her. Catherine guffawed so hard she snorted as he negotiated between the people congregated by the kitchen and emerged into the living room.

"Catherine, there you are," Bernie announced. Her name was actually Bernice, one of those names that tended to summon images of an elderly person. The name certainly didn't fit the willowy, graceful woman standing next to the couch. Catherine had once remarked that she would have made a great ballet dancer. Bernie smiled a melancholy smile when she heard this because, as Catherine found out, it was an unfulfilled dream of hers to audition for the Dance Theatre of Harlem. Bernie handed a glass of ruby red wine to Catherine. She then held up her own glass and they clinked the two together and drank.

"Sorry, that took longer than I expected," Catherine said, just as she heard the doorbell ring.

Catherine turned and saw that Henry was already at the front door. He smiled warmly at the couple who entered, took their coats, and escorted them into the house before disappearing into the kitchen where the cold beverages were. When Henry reappeared, he made his way over to Bernie and Catherine.

Henry wrapped his arm around Catherine's waist and whispered into her ear, "You need to eat something."

"I've eaten," Catherine replied, not actually sure if she had.

"You haven't," he insisted. "You can't have wine if you don't eat."

"This," Catherine raised her glass, "is the first sip I've had."

"Good, now go get some food."

"Fine, Mother," she said, trying to mimic an insolent adolescent as she twirled around and walked over to the dining room table.

Catherine picked up a plate and began perusing the various items that they had put out for their guests. It was an eclectic assortment: guacamole, salsa, an antipasto platter, a Greek platter with olives and dolmades, a cheese and meat platter with rolls to make sandwiches, chili in one Crockpot, stew in another, and desserts, several desserts. After all, it was the holidays. She thought it was odd that nothing looked appetizing to her. She glanced over at Henry and saw him eyeing her empty plate, so she picked up some cheese and salami, and after she ate them, she realized she was ravenous. She scanned the table more intently until she spotted the platter containing an assortment of cookies, but not one white chocolate macadamia cookie was left. She grinned. They were her favorites, and Henry always insisted on stashing a few away for her in the pantry.

She turned and walked toward the kitchen, gave Henry a smile and thumbs up sign, and then proceeded down the hallway that led to the back door and to their full-sized pantry. It was a throwback to the days when their house was built, when a pantry was a pantry, not a glorified closet, and Catherine had refused to give it up during the remodel. She opened the door and went in, then carefully closed the door behind her. If you were going to indulge in a secret stash of food, you hardly wanted the guests watching you. She made her way over to the shelves at the back of the room and retrieved the small tin of cookies.

Hugging her prize to her chest, Catherine looked around and saw the stepstool in a corner. She sat down, opened the top of the tin, and ate one of the cookies. It tasted so good that she reached in, snagged another, and began wolfing it down until something lodged in her throat. She tried to cough but nothing happened, not even a sound. She got up off the stool and tried to cough again, but again nothing happened. The obstruction was not budging at all. She pounded on her chest, her distress mounting, and staggered toward the door. She grabbed the knob and twisted, bursting into the hall. Someone seized her around her waist, lifting her up as though she weighed nothing. Suddenly she felt pressure bearing down on her gut, and a projectile spewed out of her mouth as she began gasping for air. Catherine stared down, through blurry eyes, at Tobias' hands, which were holding firmly onto her. She could hear Addy barking and Henry yelling her name . . . but then her head began to ache . . . something was very wrong.

Catherine looked down, her hand was on a doorknob, and she couldn't catch her breath. She was still in the pantry but the door wasn't opening! Catherine instinctively pushed as hard as she could and the door moved slightly before thudding closed again. Terror gripped her as she bent over and futilely tried once again to cough out the object lodged in her throat. She began to feel lightheaded. In desperation she reached her finger down her throat thinking if she could just make herself throw up. She began to lose consciousness.

CATHERINE'S HEAD SNAPPED UP and she grabbed at her throat, gasping for air. "Help me, help me," she screamed, but scooted back on her butt just as Greer, Keitha, and the two dogs all moved in to help her. "Don't come near me!" she shrilled, in a complete reversal.

Greer and Keitha stopped, but the dogs would not be dissuaded. They leaned their respective noses into her face, but Catherine didn't appear to recognize them as she scooted back even further and the dogs froze in their tracks, ears at high alert.

After a few moments, Greer very softly inquired, "Catherine?"

Greer had expected it to take numerous attempts and much practice before Catherine would be able to reach the deep trance necessary for him to enter her mind and guide her, but she had completely amazed him. He had never seen anyone adapt so quickly to instructions and enter a meditative state so flawlessly, as though she was already proficient, merely waiting for his guidance and his mind to complete the inward journey. However, Catherine had surfaced far too abruptly and Greer was deeply concerned with her present state because her body was rigid and her eyes glassy and distant, but not blank.

"Catherine," he said again, still soft but firm. She had to comprehend where she was and who they were. He carefully started to approach her, but she stared at him with wild eyes. Greer stopped, and Catherine's eyes grew distant once again. He had to get through to her.

"Catherine," Greer raised his voice in a command. She turned her head and stared into his eyes without any sign of recognition. He signaled Addy and Murphy and they flattened themselves against the ground and crawled up to Catherine until they were lying next to her, touching her. She blinked. Only then did Greer move forward.

He knelt in front of Catherine and carefully reached out to take one of her hands. "Keitha?" He turned anxiously toward her.

She soundlessly came up to him. "What can I do?" she asked in a quiet but strained voice.

"She's so cold," Greer said. "Take her other hand and start rubbing."

Keitha knelt next to Murphy, picked up Catherine's hand, and almost dropped it as the cold jolted through her. "Is she in shock?" Keitha asked, clinching her teeth to keep them from chattering as the surface of her skin prickled.

"Just keep rubbing," Greer directed.

"Why didn't you bring her out slowly?" Keitha whispered, the initial chill dissipating from her body.

"I didn't help her come out of it at all."

"I don't understand, you were the one guiding her, leading her," Keitha insisted. "You had the control."

Greer shook his head. "I helped her find the primary neuronal response, and then I could see what she was seeing, hearing . . . everything." He stared at Keitha. "It must be very similar to what you and your mother have experienced with Catherine. It's like watching one of Lily's plays: you see Catherine's life unfolding in front of you but you're not part of it; you're a member of the audience, you can't affect the story," he said, sounding both impressed and uneasy.

"Except, that's what we're doing here—we need to affect the story," Keitha said, agitated. "Are you saying we can't?"

"No, we can't, not literally, but we can help Catherine."

Catherine's head was moving from side to side as if she were following the conversation between Greer and Keitha, but her eyes still did not fix upon anything.

"I didn't want to resort to this, but I don't think there is any other choice," Greer said gravely, dropping Catherine's hand and raising one of his own.

"If you slap me I'll kick you in your balls," Catherine said in a thin, slightly slurred voice.

"Catherine," Greer asked, "can you hear me?"

"Yes."

"Can you focus your eyes?"

"I am focusing my eyes."

"You're not," Greer said, watching them drift. "You have to concentrate." He looked at Keitha. "We need something that will anchor her here."

"Like what?"

"Something that will resonate with her. A sound, a smell."

Keitha suddenly threw her head back and started to howl. Addy and Murphy tilted their heads, listened for a moment, and then, within a second of each other, joined in.

Catherine stared at Keitha, then Murphy, and finally her eyes came to rest on Addy, the glassy look beginning to fade. She reached out toward the dog and her entire body began to quiver.

"Help me up," Catherine managed to say.

Greer and Keitha got Catherine to her feet, but when she tried to take a step forward, her legs gave way. Greer caught her under her arms.

"Shit," Catherine said quietly.

"I think you better sit down," Greer suggested.

She shook her head. "No, I need to be on my feet."

Greer nodded but kept a supportive arm around her waist as she tried, once again, to walk. Catherine wobbled at first, and Greer felt her entire body quiver, but she quickly improved.

"You can let go of me now," she said, moving away from him.

"Do you remember what happened?" he asked.

Catherine's shoulders slumped. Greer was afraid she was about to fall again, but instead she turned to face them.

"How sure are you that it was . . . I mean, are you positive that was what the Machiavellians changed?" Catherine asked in a strained voice.

"Aren't you? Considering what you witnessed?" Greer asked.

"Witnessed?" she inquired blankly and then began to laugh uncontrollably until she saw the look of absolute dread on both Greer and Keitha's face and somehow got hold of herself. "I was the victim, you were the witness."

"You are correct," Greer agreed.

"I thought you were supposed to pull me back if it got too squirrelly for me, *and* I explained to you what squirrelly meant. So how could you not think that was a textbook instance?" she asked in disbelief.

"I'm very sorry, Catherine. If I could have brought you out of it—" Greer stopped. "I would have," he said with understanding.

"Yeah," Catherine agreed, "that was the point."

"I would have, but I shouldn't have, and you must have known that because you kept me from being able to."

"Me? How the hell did I stop you?"

"I don't know. Survival instinct maybe, because if you didn't go through both versions of the events we wouldn't know exactly what happened when the Machiavellians interfered. We needed to see it all so we can prevent you from . . ."

Catherine held up a trembling hand, "Don't."

"Would one of you please tell me what happened?" Keitha asked.

Greer nodded at Catherine, who hesitated but then began to relay everything that happened, as though she was giving testimony in court. She focused on every detail, including a description of what a pantry was and the layout of her house. She began pacing and rubbing her hands together, as though the cold chill had come back. When she got to the two divergent incidents that took place from the moment she tried to get out of the pantry door, her voice became unsteady.

". . . the last thing I remember . . . I couldn't breathe and I . . . I'm pretty sure I started to pass out and . . . then I was here."

"The amount of detail that you've retained is remarkable," Greer stated.

"Someone in *my* house, someone *I invited* into my home was trying to kill me off in the pantry!" Catherine's face flushed.

"That has to be very disconcerting for you," Greer said sincerely.

"No kidding," she said sharply. "I just don't understand. Why me? I'm no one."

"Your death would have an impact on the people around you," Keitha noted. "Ford is involved in so many critical undertakings, and then there is Henry."

"Leave them out of this," Catherine said protectively.

"I thought you wanted to understand why. I'm just trying to help you evaluate the possibilities," Keitha said.

"At this juncture I don't think we need to know the why," Greer interjected. "We just need to stop it from happening."

Catherine flinched.

"When is this celebration going to take place?" Greer asked.

"Tomorrow, December 16th," Catherine replied hollowly. "We'll just have to cancel it."

"You can't," Greer and Keitha said simultaneously.

"Oh, just watch me. I can get it done."

"You can't," Greer stated emphatically. "You have to stop the interference."

"Stop calling it that! It isn't some abstract interference. It's my life we're talking about, and guess what? If there is no party then I can't get trapped in the pantry. If I don't get trapped, I don't die!"

Greer shook his head. "I thought you understood. We needed to find the event that was changed and prevent that change, and only that change. You have no idea what would happen if you cancelled your celebration. It would impact too many lives," Greer said, trying to reason with Catherine.

"So what? They stay home or go to dinner. It wouldn't be anything significant," Catherine argued.

"You don't know that," Greer insisted. "Do you?"

Catherine stubbornly refused to answer.

"You can't cancel the party," he reiterated.

"Are you ordering me?" she demanded.

"I'm asking you to look at the situation rationally, not emotionally."

Catherine looked as though she was about to bite his head off, but instead she threw her hands in the air and stomped over to where Addy and Murphy had hunkered down and knelt between them, wrapping her arms around their powerful necks. The two dogs leaned into her, and as she sat back on her heels, they laid their heads on her lap. When she rose, Addy and Murphy looked up at her expectantly. She stroked their heads and Greer thought he saw an imperceptible nod of Catherine's head before she strode back over.

"So, someone I know is the one that the Machiavellians from your time are using to . . ." Catherine made a slicing motion across her neck.

She looked so desolate that Greer, for a brief moment, thought about calling a halt to everything just so Catherine could continue to live her life without that knowledge, but as soon as the thought crossed his mind, he knew it was ridiculous. If they didn't stop the interference, Catherine would have no life left to live.

"All we know is that it is someone in your house. That doesn't mean it's someone you know," Greer offered.

"Sure, an acquaintance, that makes it so much better," Catherine quipped edgily, hitting herself on top of her head. "The solution is obvious. I just won't go into the pantry."

Greer frowned.

"What now?" Catherine protested.

"You have to keep everything the same as the first time, before the interference."

She glared at him. "Fine, I just won't eat any of the cookies. I can go into the pantry and wait. Henry will come looking for me and then maybe he'll see who's standing at the door." Her eyes widened. "That's it. Henry will see . . . stop looking at me like that," Catherine demanded.

"I'm sorry, but it won't work. The event has to remain the same up to the point where you can't get out the door," Greer said.

"You don't know that," Catherine said ardently. "You can't, you've never even tried this before. So don't make it sound like you know."

"We only have one chance. It has to remain the same up to that very moment when events diverge," he said, just as determined as she was.

"You can't expect me to just go into that pantry, eat a cookie, and let myself choke!"

"I expect you not to choke."

"Great, glad to hear it, because that's certainly my goal." Catherine was beginning to feel giddy, the kind of giddy that can occur because of physical or mental fatigue. She tried to pull herself together and think rationally. "I cannot force myself to go into the pantry knowing that I might not . . ." She didn't finish.

"Even if you went in, you couldn't possibly eat the cookie so that you purposely get it lodged in your throat. An accident is one thing but to intentionally . . . no, that just isn't possible," Greer stated.

"I appreciate that. So where does this leave us?"

"Greer can help you," Keitha said.

"No offense," she looked at Greer, "but your help means I end up on my own, and then we're right back to the same problem. What if I can't make myself go into the pantry?"

"Greer can help you so you don't remember what you saw, and then you'll enter the pantry as you did originally," Keitha said, as if it was the most natural thing in the world.

Catherine saw Greer tense, which made her so uneasy she felt the skin on top of her head crawl. "How?" she squeaked.

"It's similar to hypnosis, only more advanced," Keitha said while watching Greer.

"Great," Catherine said, making the word sound like a scourge. "So tell me this, if I let you wipe out the memory so that I'm not aware of the danger, how can I possibly intercede and prevent it from happening? Explain that to me?"

"The first time, you said someone named Tobias performed the Heimlich maneuver on you," Keitha noted, pausing when she saw Catherine's expression. "Why are you looking at me like that?"

"I'm just surprised that you knew what it was."

"Don't be ridiculous, everyone knows what the Heimlich maneuver is."

"Well, Tobias won't be able to help me because the door won't open. I'll be stuck in the pantry."

"What difference does that make . . . oh," Keitha said with sudden realization. "You don't know how to perform the Heimlich, do you?"

"No," Catherine admitted, her face flushed with embarrassment.

"How can you not?" Keitha asked. "It's basic first response."

"I just haven't gotten around to it," Catherine replied defensively.

"We'll teach you," Greer stated, giving Keitha a warning glance.

"Let's back up for a minute," Catherine said. "If I save myself, won't that, in and of itself, be a change? What about Tobias, won't that impact him?"

Greer studied her for a moment. "I can't say with complete certainty, but I believe the means by which you live are inconsequential to the outcome. As with Rebecca, she didn't die the same way, but she still died. We need you to live."

"Again, we're in absolute agreement about that. So you'll be teaching me how to punch myself in the gut?"

"There's an alternative," Greer said. "We need to get started, though; there isn't much time."

"Before you do, I have a question about this memory removal."

Keitha looked at Greer uncertainly.

Greer returned Keitha's look but his voice was kind when he replied to Catherine, "What do you want to know?"

"You can remove *a memory*, leaving everything else just as it is?"

"Yes."

"You can be that precise?"

"I'm very skilled."

Catherine nodded but looked dubious.

"He is," Keitha said earnestly. "Greer can remove a little, he can remove a lot. He can actually make it so you don't remember us at all after this is over. How would that be? We go back to our lives, you go back to yours, never knowing we were ever here."

"You could make me forget everything?" Catherine asked Greer in a mixture of dread and awe, ignoring the fact that Keitha had just issued her a challenge.

"Yes," Greer said. "If that's what you want me to do."

"Tempting," she said, looking at Keitha. "I'd have to think about it, and right now there isn't time. Just remove the one memory." Catherine held up her index finger.

"To be on the safe side I think it should be everything from this particular meeting."

"Meeting?" Catherine questioned but then said, "Yeah, well, what else are you going to call it?"

"Do you agree?" Greer asked.

Catherine pondered for a moment before nodding her head.

Greer motioned for her to sit down on the ground, and signaled to Addy and Murphy, who came over to lay down next to her, one on each side. Greer took her hands in his, and Catherine gripped them so tight he flinched.

Greer craned his neck around, "Keitha, could you give us a bit more privacy. This is going to be more difficult than last time, and I need Catherine's undivided attention."

Keitha nodded and walked away.

"This is real, right?" Catherine asked, still clutching his hands. "If I hadn't returned here, I'd be dead tomorrow night."

Greer could see the pleading in Catherine's eyes, that and her fear. He dropped his head. "It's real," he replied solemnly.

Catherine nodded. She tried to talk but all that came out of her mouth were gulps of air and a gurgling sound in her throat, tears welling up in her eyes. Catherine let go of him so she could lift one of her hands to shield her eyes. Greer watched helplessly as she fought to remain in control.

"Get a grip," Catherine whispered harshly to herself. After a few more minutes, she lowered her hand and addressed Greer. "Will you see it happening? You know," Catherine tapped her head, "like you did before."

"No, I saw the imprint that was already in your mind. What will happen isn't there yet."

"So if I can't stop . . . I'll die alone."

Greer felt his heart catch. "This will work, Catherine," he said with conviction. "Keitha, Murphy, and I will stay right here." He was hoping the idea would offer her some immediate comfort, even though she wouldn't remember. "Keitha will know the minute you succeed."

"Right," Catherine said, almost managing to keep the tremor out of her voice. "One thing before we get started, I don't want to forget everything, ever," she stated resolutely. "Henry knows everything I've gone through, and I won't leave him all by himself with that kind of knowledge. Besides, it doesn't sound like these Machiavellians are going to give up, so we may still need each other's help, and I'll be damned if I'm starting this all over again."

CATHERINE WOKE UP FEELING VERY PEACEFUL. She rolled over to find Henry gone and immediately looked over at Addy's bed, which of course was also empty. The smell of coffee was wafting down from upstairs and she gradually forced herself to get out of the nice warm bed. There was still a lot to do before the party. She put her sweats on and mounted the stairs.

Henry was in the kitchen cutting up onions and jalapenos for his guacamole.

"Hey sleepy head," he greeted her.

"Sorry about that."

"Don't be." He put the knife down and came over to her. "I'm just glad you're getting some decent sleep for once." He hugged her and then kissed her warmly on the lips.

"Yeah, how weird is that?" she asked, frowning. "I mean, considering everything that I've had on my mind lately."

"Please, don't overanalyze it. Just be thankful for the respite."

"But—"

"No buts. Get a cup of coffee . . . we have a lot of work to do."

HENRY WRAPPED HIS ARM AROUND CATHERINE'S WAIST and whispered into her ear. "You need to eat something."

"I've eaten," Catherine replied, not actually sure if she had.

"You haven't," he insisted. "You can't have wine if you don't eat."

"This," Catherine raised her glass, "is the first sip I've had."

"Good, now go get some food."

"Fine, Mother," she said, trying to mimic an insolent adolescent as she twirled around and walked over to the dining room table.

Catherine held a plate and perused the spread they had put out on the dining room table for their guests. She nibbled on some cheese and salami and then began searching the table in earnest until she spotted the plate that contained the cookies. None of the white chocolate macadamia cookies were left. She grinned. They were her favorites, and Henry always insisted on stashing a few away for her in the pantry.

Catherine gave Henry a smile and a thumbs up sign before walking down the hall to the pantry. She closed the pantry door quietly behind her. She finished off the first cookie and, finding herself suddenly ravenous, started wolfing down a second one when something lodged in her throat. She tried to cough, but nothing happened. She got up and tried harder, but to no avail. She thumped on her chest as she made her way to the door and twisted the knob. She leaned into it as hard as she could but the door barely moved before snapping back closed. What the hell? She began to panic just as her eyes came to rest on the stool. It was actually a step stool with a metal arch rising up from the back. Catherine stumbled over to it, leaned her upper abdomen into the metal arch and pushed—nothing happened. She took a step up so her abdomen was hovering slightly over the metal bar, and just as she started to feel lightheaded, she let herself drop against it. Something flew out of her mouth and hit the floor. She gasped for air and started to cough violently. When the coughing spasm subsided, Catherine sat down on the second step of the stool and started trembling. She brushed the tears of relief from her cheeks with a shaky hand, grateful that she had learned that variation of the Heimlich maneuver from . . . Catherine furrowed her brow. She couldn't remember who had taught her.

As the adrenalin in her system began to dissipate, she stood and looked down at the glob that was plastered against the floor. She knelt down, out of morbid curiosity and not any compunction to be neat, and picked it up. There were two macadamia nuts held together by the glue of the masticated cookie. The nuts looked whole.

"This is what you get for not chewing your food," Catherine rasped, whipping around when she heard the door to the pantry open.

"How long does it take to eat four cookies?" Henry quipped as he entered the room.

She closed her fingers around the gooey mass in her hand. There was no reason to worry Henry in the middle of the party.

"Sorry," her voice sounded scratchy, "have I been in here long?"

"Not that long." His eyebrows knit together. "Are you all right? You sound kind of hoarse."

"Uh huh," she murmured through closed lips, nodding her head vigorously.

As they exited the pantry, Henry grabbed Catherine's hand, luckily the one without the glob, and whispered in her ear, "Zach's here."

"You're kidding," Catherine rasped in surprise.

"He looks pretty gloomy. We should try to cheer him up."

"You go, I need to get some water."

"Yeah, you do," Henry kissed her on the head. "You sound like Betty Davis."

"Very funny." She tried to swat his arm but he was already out of reach.

Catherine waited until Henry started down the hall before surreptitiously looking around the doorway to see if she could determine exactly why it had not opened.

"Lose something?" Zach asked, startling her.

"No, I was just—" she began and then looked back down the hall. "Henry just went to find you," she said, perplexed.

"Huh, I was getting myself a beer. Guess we missed each other."

"I thought you couldn't make it?"

"What I said was that I would come if my dinner meeting finished early."

"I guess I misunderstood," she said, continuing to survey the area around the door.

"Are you all right? You seem a little distracted, and your voice sounds strange. Are you coming down with something?" Zach backed up a step.

Catherine felt the glob that she was still clutching in her hand. "I'm not coming down with anything," she said irritably. "I just need some water. If you'll excuse me."

She walked away from him into the kitchen. Zach followed her to the entrance of the kitchen, watching as she walked over to the sink and washed her hands. As she turned away from the sink, Hal was looming behind her.

"Shit, Hal." She backed up and hit the edge of the sink. "Sneak up on people much?" She started rubbing her hip.

"I've been here almost a half hour," he said uncomfortably, and she saw the flush in his cheeks.

"A half hour? Really?" She hadn't noticed him before she went to get the cookies, the thought of which made her involuntarily reach for her throat.

"You sound gravelly. Are you coming down with something?"

"No," she snapped. "I just need a glass of water." She turned back to the sink, opened the cabinet to her right and extracted a glass. She ran the water for a couple of seconds before filling the glass.

As she drank, Hal chastised her. "You should really have cold water in your refrigerator so you don't have to run the water."

"Desperate times, Hal," she replied.

"What?" he asked, agitated.

"I have water in the fridge, I just needed to clear my throat," she stated, wondering why Hal was acting more nervous than the situation called for, at least this situation. Then again Hal, like a number of their guests, was socially awkward, which made him edgy. "Come on, let's go 'mingle,' as they say." She took him by the arm and led him into the dining room where she spotted a biologist that she had worked with when she was employed by the State of Colorado. Once she had the two of them settled into a conversation about field methodologies for collecting benthic samples, she discretely extricated herself and went over to where Henry was having a lively debate with Zach.

"Excuse me, gentlemen," she said, turning to Henry. "Have you seen Addy?"

He looked around, perplexed. "I know I saw her just a little while ago."

As if on cue, the front door banged open and Addy came bounding across the room to Catherine, almost knocking her off her feet. Catherine knelt down and hugged the dog.

"Where have you been?" Catherine asked, sitting back on her heels as Tobias came up to them.

"She needed to go out," Tobias answered, sounding slightly out of breath. "So I took her out for a walk."

"You did? I guess I didn't see you, but thanks for taking her out. You know you could have just taken her out back."

"I thought about it, but there were a bunch of people standing in the hallway, right by the kitchen," Tobias replied. It seemed easier to just grab the leash by the front door and head out."

"In the hallway by the kitchen," Catherine repeated, her skin tingling. "How far down the hallway were they?"

"I don't know. Like I said, I didn't even try to go that way," Tobias said, puzzled by the tone of her voice. "Is it important?"

"No, no, of course not," Catherine said as she stood up. "So did Addy enjoy her walk?"

Tobias frowned. "Yeah, well, I wanted to talk to you about it."

"Why? What happened?" Catherine asked, her heart rate increasing.

"Well, the walk started out good, but when we got over to that little park, Addy suddenly just froze, her hackles rose and her ears went straight up." He pointed at the ceiling.

"Something must have startled her," Henry said casually. "An animal or a noise."

"Maybe," Tobias said in a measured voice. "I don't know what it was. All I can tell you is that she flattened her ears against her head and just started running back here. I don't know about you, but I sure can't keep up with a greyhound. I started yelling for her to stop but it was like she didn't hear me. She was pulling so hard I was afraid I was going to lose my grip or that I was going to lose my balance and go down, but I knew I couldn't let her get away from me, because I'd never catch up to her." He lowered his voice. "I did the only thing I could think of." He paused. "I tackled her. I didn't hurt her," he added quickly. "Kind of stunned her for a minute, but I didn't hurt her."

"No, of course you didn't hurt her," Catherine said, when she found her voice, feeling a little stunned herself. "Look at her, she's fine." She placed her hand on Tobias' muscular arm. "Thank you," she said. "If she had gotten away from you . . . there's just no telling what could have happened."

Tobias nodded, but he looked worried. "All I can tell you, Catherine, is that whatever scared Addy must have been really bad, because when I had my hands around her chest, her heart was pounding like it was about to explode, and she was trembling."

Catherine felt an icy prickle on the back of her neck. She sank back down on her knees and stared into Addy's eyes as she cradled the dog's head gently in her hands.

Henry watched the silent, yet intense, exchange between Catherine and Addy and became alarmed. He knelt down and whispered in Catherine's ear, "What's going on?"

CHAPTER 28

K eitha and Greer quickly got up from their prone positions on the floor of the cavernous reservoir area when the connection with Catherine severed, which was at the exact moment the glob of cookie flew out of her throat. Murphy began nudging each of them, at the base of their backs, with his nose. As their minds began to clear, they saw Clara kneeling next to Terran, who was on the floor writhing in agony.

Greer struggled to get his feet under him. He became so lightheaded that he had to crawl over to them. He grabbed Terran's head in his hands.

"Look at me, look at me," Greer said forcefully.

Terran's mind was swarming with the images from the two timeframes, and despite Clara's training, he was being overwhelmed. Through the pandemonium, he heard Greer's powerful voice and was compelled to try to pry his eyes open, but it felt as though someone had glued them shut.

"Terran!" Greer thundered, causing Terran's eyes to pop open.

Greer was able to calm Terran's mind so that the younger man was able to gain control and stabilize the fragmented images, but afterward Terran looked ragged. Keitha and Greer looked only slightly better as they sipped some water. Murphy looked no worse for the wear as he lapped at a dish of water. Greer was of the opinion that they all needed some rest, but Clara wanted to know what had happened to cause them to remain in a deep trance for almost twenty-four hours. Terran also insisted that he needed to know what had transpired. They were so adamant that Greer acquiesced and relayed both what had happened on the plateau and that Catherine had succeeded in preventing her own death.

"Clara was right: Catherine was the key to the shift she felt," Terran said admiringly. "Reaching her was not random."

"Terran, you're not making any sense," Clara asserted. "I've never sensed a shift. You sensed the shift." Clara's tone softened and she spoke to Terran as though he had temporary amnesia and just needed a little prompting. "Remember? You felt a shift right when I was trying to help you get here, back when Keitha was fifteen. The shift that you didn't think changed much but proved to the Machiavellians that it was possible for them to reach someone in the past. The shift that caused the ally of the Machiavellians to go insane . . . remember?" she repeated hopefully.

"I'm sorry," Terran said looking distressed.

"I know," Clara said soothingly. "I think Greer is just confusing you with his story, that's all." Clara gave Greer a severe look.

Greer stared back in definite confusion.

"No, no," Terran began explaining to Clara before stopping himself. He wasn't thinking straight. Of course Clara wouldn't remember what happened as a result of Catherine dying in the pantry because she didn't die. The altered timeline, as far as Clara knew, never happened. So why did Greer and Keitha remember what happened on the plateau? He'd have to set that question aside. Right now, there was a more pressing question.

"What do you remember about why you were on the plateau?" Terran asked Keitha.

"What do you mean?" Keitha asked.

"Keitha, please, just answer the question," Terran pressed.

"I . . . the plateau is a neutral location. Clara suggested it so that I could connect with Catherine, because Clara believes that Catherine may be a key to tracking what the Machiavellians are going to try to change," Keitha replied, also wondering if Terran was unwell, but for a different reason.

"*Try* to change? That isn't what Terran said," Greer asked, looking perplexed. "Keitha, Catherine's—"

Terran loudly cleared his throat, causing Greer to stop mid-word. "Sorry, something felt stuck." He managed to catch Greer's eye long enough that the older man knew something was not right.

"What were you saying, Father?" Keitha asked urgently.

"Nothing. I'm so exhausted, Keitha, I don't know what I'm saying," Greer said, turning away and walking over to the area where he and Keitha had been lying. There were two pads on the ground. Greer bent down and began rolling one of them up.

"Father," Keitha called over to him, but Clara took her arm and shook her head.

"Let's head up. We can all talk about this when everyone feels rested."

"But—"

"It isn't going to do any of us any good trying to sort everything out now," Clara said, staring at her daughter until Keitha relinquished.

"You three head up," Terran said as Murphy rose from his sentry position by the rock bench. "I'll help Greer get everything else." He handed Keitha one of the two mobile lanterns that had been illuminating a portion of the cavern.

Keitha reached out and grasped the handle. She regarded Terran uncomfortably. "We will talk about all of this."

"Yes, I know."

Keitha shook her head discontentedly but walked over to Clara and Murphy, who were waiting by the entrance.

Terran rolled the other pad and collected several water containers before facing Greer.

"What is going on?" Greer asked.

"How much do you remember?" Terran asked.

"About what? About the plateau? About Clara sensing a shift that *was* Catherine dying? How about the fact that my daughter doesn't seem to remember? That Clara definitely doesn't?" Greer remarked.

"That sort of answers my question," Terran replied.

"Terran?" Greer asked, ill at ease.

"I didn't think any of you would be able to remember the altered timeline if you succeeded in stopping the change from occurring, which you obviously did because Catherine didn't die in the pantry," Terran explained.

"So why can Keitha and I remember the plateau, yet Keitha can't remember Clara sensing the shift or Catherine saving herself?" Greer questioned.

"I'm not absolutely sure. My best guess about your first question is that it's because of the plateau, which isn't completely a part of any one timeline. As for the second, I'd say it has something to do with the fact that your mind was linked with Catherine's, and you were witnessing two possible realities for her life."

"Those are pretty specific guesses," Greer said.

"What do you remember about your mother?" Terran probed, wondering if Greer had seen any of the dual images swirling through his own mind when Greer helped him gain control.

"I'm not following you," Greer said.

"How did your mother die?" he asked Greer awkwardly.

"What does that . . ." Greer started then stopped. An understanding showed in his face. "Her heart finally gave out. Val and the other healers tried everything they could, but . . . no matter. She was grateful that she had seen me grow into adulthood . . . had enough time to pass on all her knowledge, and that of her ancestors . . . to watch me surpass her abilities."

"What do you remember about Daniel?"

"My father? My father's alive," Greer said in confusion.

In the alternate timeline, not only had Ione been unable to control her ability until she went into self-imposed exile, she had lost all control when she was in labor with Greer. It was a very difficult labor, and Daniel was right by her side, insisting that she focus on him, and in her agony, she ended up ripping away Daniel's memory of her and his son. Ione was afraid that she would kill him if she tried to restore the memory, because she had already caused his heart severe damage, so she lived on her own with their son, and with her guilt. Not in this timeline, though. In this timeline, Daniel's heart was strong.

Greer was watching Terran closely. "Why was Catherine so important that the Machiavellians wanted her dead? Is it her work on the environment, or is it because she was one of our founders?"

"I don't know." Terran concentrated before saying, "I mean even at eighty-six, Catherine was a force when it came to the construct of the colonies. Without her there was a delay before this colony was established . . . the other colonies were delayed even more." Terran rubbed his temples, the effort to recall both timelines causing mounting pressure. "The founders ran out of time . . . they were rushed, the people struggled to establish . . . to get everything working properly." Terran cried out and held his head in his hands.

Greer rushed to his side. "Never mind, never mind," he said.

Terran raised his head. Greer tried not to recoil at the sight of his blood shot eyes. "No, we need to understand," Terran said, his voice weak. "I think Catherine's being a founder is important, but her ability, her perceptive ability, is what the Machiavellians are really worried about."

"She has barely begun to acknowledge her ability. How can she possibly be a threat to them?"

"The Machiavellians are still planning something, Greer. Catherine is the nexus. She always has been."

"Will Catherine be able to remember everything that happened on the plateau?" Greer asked.

"Yes, it is all part of her continuous timeline." Terran's face clouded over. "Except for the memories you extracted."

Greer shook his head. "I only extracted what happened in the pantry, and that someone in her time was being used by the Machiavellians, who wanted her dead. I had to, otherwise she could never have gone back into the pantry. She agreed, but only on the condition that she would get those memories back. Catherine said she had to find out who, in her time, wanted her dead and why. I gave Catherine what was once called a post-hypnotic suggestion. Catherine had to provide me with a trigger, something that would definitely happen or be said but at the same time was unique and would cause the memory to come back."

"What did she pick?"

"Henry wishing her a 'Happy New Year,' which she said was ironic since 2007 was likely to be anything but."

CHAPTER 29

Catherine reached out to feel the north-facing window in her office. When she removed her hand its imprint remained, but the cold quickly devoured the warmed spot. All of 2006 had been so dry, and yet just in time for Christmas, blizzard conditions were engulfing the metro area. Catherine couldn't help being enthralled by how picturesque the glistening layer of white looked, a pristine covering that hid the tarnished bare bones of the parched winter city. As Catherine watched the snow beat against the window, she saw a car slide, bounce off the curb, and barely miss another vehicle as the driver overcorrected. She grimaced as her own near miss in the pantry pushed its way into her mind. She was sick of replaying what happened, and yet she couldn't seem to put it to rest.

That night, when Henry asked her what was going on, she experienced an unsettling sensation, as though there was something critical that she was forgetting. Catherine somehow managed to smile at him and shrug. She could tell he wasn't buying her "I don't know" expression, but what the hell was she supposed to say? Well, gee, Henry I was choking on a damn cookie and I think Addy somehow knew it, even though she wasn't in the house. Which was exactly what she did tell him after the last of the guests had left and they were sitting on the couch looking at the scattered plates and glasses, which neither wanted to pick up. She tried to make light of it, saying she could just imagine the obituary caption, "Death by Cookie," which was when Henry angrily told her to *never, ever* joke about dying again. Then he hugged her so hard that she struggled catching her breath, which was when Catherine decided that Henry did not need to hear the part about the door not opening. Besides, she rationalized to herself, she probably wasn't remembering that part clearly anyway, what with the lack of oxygen and all.

A knocking sound made her whip around, and she saw Tobias standing in her doorway.

He stared over her shoulder. "Some storm."

Catherine automatically turned to look in the same direction and saw that the window was rapidly becoming obscured by the snow that was slamming into it. "Yeah, the storm," she absently noted.

"Catherine, are you all right?"

"Yeah, yeah, of course," she said as she registered that Tobias had his coat on. "Leaving?"

"Yes," he drew the word out as though he was speaking to a child. "Didn't you see Zach's email? He told everyone to shut down and go home an hour ago."

"So why are you still here?"

"I had to do a major backup of the databases, just in case I can't get back in here until after Christmas. What's your excuse? No wait, that's right, you didn't even see the email or notice that people were leaving." He stared at her closely, and when she didn't respond he said, "You've been sort of preoccupied this week. Anything you want to talk about?"

"There's nothing to talk about," she replied, trying to sound nonchalant.

"Uh huh," he said, unconvinced. "Come on, I'll give you a lift home."

"I can walk."

"In that," Tobias said, pointing at the window.

"I'd rather be walking than driving. I'll get there faster."

"I don't know, Catherine. It's coming down really hard."

"All the more reason for you to get out of here now." When he made no move to leave she insisted, "Go! I don't want you getting stuck because of me."

Tobias nodded reluctantly. "Just shut down and get out of here, please."

"I promise." She held three fingers together in the air and then waved him off before sitting down at her desk.

He pulled on his gloves and started to leave but then paused. "You're sure there's nothing you want to talk about? Maybe something that happened at the party?"

"What makes you say that?" Catherine asked, taken off guard.

Tobias pulled his gloves off and came all the way into her office. "How about the way Addy acted?" He lifted an eyebrow and waited.

"It was just all the excitement."

"She was scared, Catherine, I mean really scared."

Catherine's face looked weird. "I guess she thought I was in trouble."

"Were you?" Tobias asked, concerned.

"Nothing life-threatening," her voice quivered.

He stared at her in alarm.

"Seriously, I don't know why I'm so edgy. Must be the storm."

Tobias continued to watch her.

"Good thing you were able to get hold of Addy when she tried to bolt," Catherine said, starting to feel uncomfortable.

"She would have just gone home, that's where she was headed."

"She could have gotten hit by a car if you hadn't stopped her," Catherine said gratefully.

"Yeah, and I don't even think she really had to go out that bad."

"I thought you said she did," Catherine said, surprised.

"No, I took her out because Hal said she was fidgeting and it was bothering him."

"Hal told you that?" For some reason this made Catherine uneasy.

"You know how he can be at parties. Any little thing can bug him, and Addy wouldn't let him take her out so I thought I'd keep Hal from pestering you or Henry," Tobias clarified. He didn't like the strained look on Catherine's face. "Am I missing something?"

"No, no," Catherine tried to sound cheery. "Get going before you have to spend Christmas with us."

"As if that would be a bad thing," he said smiling.

Catherine got up and came around her desk. She hugged Tobias, and he gently hugged her back. "Merry Christmas."

"You too," Tobias said as he walked out of her office.

Catherine sat back down and typed in her password to unlock the computer. She had two emails. One was Zach's. She opened the other. There were more reports of severe declines in honey bee colonies. Catherine thought about the tiny little creature that had landed on her toe—how long ago?

"Why haven't you gone home yet," a voice demanded.

Catherine snapped her head up as her chair pitched backward. "Goddamn it, Zach!"

"Why are you still here?"

"I'm going. I was just reading an email," she replied.

"About?"

"I'm shutting down right now," Catherine said, ignoring his question as she clicked the mouse a couple of times to power down the computer, stood up, and retrieved her coat from the back of her chair.

"Do you need a ride home?" Zach asked.

"No, I'll walk."

"Are you sure? The wind is really blowing and you know it's pretty easy to get yourself turned around in a blizzard. I wouldn't want you to get lost on your way home."

"It's not like I'm heading into unchartered territory. I think I'm more than capable of finding my way home."

"All right," Zach said, pulling on his hat. "Just get out of here," he called back over his shoulder as he headed to the front door.

The phone on her desk rang shrilly, causing Catherine to jump.

She snatched up the receiver, "Hello?"

"Catherine," Henry's voice was tense, "why are you still at work, and why aren't you answering your cell phone?"

"It didn't ring," she said, digging it out of her pack and staring at the display.

"Catherine?"

"Crap, it's dead."

"Why," Henry emphasized each word, "are you still at work?"

"I'm leaving right now. I'll be home soon." She hung up before he could argue with her, threw on her coat, and headed for the door. She pulled the front door closed and stepped into the fury of the blizzard. She tugged her gloves on, pulled her hood up, and ducked her head to avoid the direct sting of the sideways-blowing snow. The stairs that led down to the street looked more like a snow slide than individually distinguishable steps. Zach's prints, however, were still visible, although rapidly filling in. She carefully followed his tracks and then set off in the direction of her house.

Catherine's legs were beginning to feel like Jell-O after slogging through six blocks of knee-deep snow, regretting her obstinate refusal of each offer for a ride home. Physical exhaustion on top of mental exhaustion was not what she needed—or maybe it was. Maybe she could finally get a good night's sleep, something that had been eluding her since the party, and not because of almost choking. She kept jerking awake just when she felt like she was about to remember something—something she was sure was important—and it was driving her crazy.

Catherine stared at the traffic light coated with a veil of snow, which gave the normally garish red an eerie, gauzy quality, and waited for it to turn green. As she looked down the normally congested one-way street, wondering why she was waiting to cross, since there wasn't a car in sight, she saw two figures approaching on the opposite side of the street.

Henry was so bundled up against the snow that she might not have recognized him immediately. But there was no missing the prancing four-legged creature at his side, resplendent in her purple coat and red booties. Catherine waved wildly as she crossed the street.

"You shouldn't have come out in this," she said unconvincingly, pulling down her scarf and revealing a broad grin.

Henry pulled his muffler down, revealing an equally large grin. "Addy insisted. You know how much she loves romping in the snow."

Catherine looked down at the obviously delighted dog. "It's almost over her haunches."

Henry threw his hands wide, keeping a firm hold on Addy's leash. "She doesn't care, and neither do I."

Catherine laughed, and the anxiety began to ebb out of her body. Whatever it was that she was trying so hard to remember would either come to her or not. And if it didn't? She felt a prickling sensation run down her back and shivered.

"Come on, before we freeze," Henry said.

Catherine rubbed the top of Addy's head before looping her arm through Henry's and guided them all home.

Author Notes

The environmental information/incidents contained in the book highlight actual issues that we are facing today. These issues are very complex and for the sake of the story only specific aspects were included. I by no means want to infer that the information is all inclusive. There is, however, no Global Resources Research Institute. That group is purely from my imagination, although I hold out hope.

There are several specific sources I cited in the book that the reader can review.

2004 IUCN Red List of Threatened Species^{TM}, A Global Species Assessment Edited by Jonathan E. M. Baillie, Craig Hilton-Taylor, and Simon N. Stuart Authors: Jonathan E. M. Baillie, Leon A. Bennun, Thomas M. Brooks, Stuart H. M. Butchart, Janice S. Chanson, Zoe Cokeliss, Craig Hilton-Taylor, Michael Hoffmann, Georgina M. Mace, Sue A. Mainka, Caroline M. Pollock, Ana S. L. Rodrigues, Alison J. Stattersfield, and Simon N. Stuart

International Union for Conservation of Nature and Natural Resources can be found online at *www.iucnredlist.org/*

Mark Townsend (2005, June 19) New US move to spoil climate accord. *The Observer found online at http://www.guardian.co.uk/science/2005/ jun/19/greenpolitics.environment1*

U.S. Fish and Wildlife Service Endangered Species Program can be found online at *www.fws.gov/endangered/*

United Nations Framework Convention on Climate Change can be found online at *//unfccc.int*

Additional issues contained in the book were based on my review and compilation of multiple documents/reports. There is much more that the reader can learn about:

The London Dumping Convention (renamed The London Convention)

The Yablokov Report

The Basil Convention

The Kyoto Protocol

The Endangered Species Act

Benjamin Libet (1916–2007)—My explanation of his hypotheses, experiments and results are from the perspective of a non-neuroscientist.

Finally, the Honey Bees continue to be in crisis. Colony Collapse Disorder has not gone away. Thankfully, there are still organizations and individuals that have not let the issue fade away.

Applause from Readers

"The first message of the book is that our actions today shape what the world will look like in very real terms in the future. This is painted very nicely by the author by helping us to anchor that future around Keitha and the rest of her colony rather than letting us rest in the complacency of feeling that as long as it happens in the future and not to us it doesn't really matter. The second message is that the power of our minds and our consciousness has the capacity to change our understanding of our world and our experience of it, should we choose to invest in harnessing our own innate abilities. Given this particular time in the state of our collective consciousness in our world, I think The Plateau is a timely and thought-provoking book."
—Christine Andrew, Enlightening Radio/CoSozo Radio

"I would say it's a book about bridges: it bridges time and place, it bridges genres, and it bridges action and consequence. I'd say it's a book that encourages us to revise our understanding of time and to reconsider our connection to the past and future. I'd say, 'You should read it!'"
—Danny Long, Associate Professor at Colorado University, Boulder

"An interesting concept from a potentially interesting perspective."
—Teresa Untiedt, Writer

"It has a great concept which could create a greater influence as a movie. The scenes make powerful images, especially the plateau ones. I found it to be a great example of what the future could be if we continue to fail the environment. The story portrays some great ideas and provides believable examples that are fun to experience."
—Kim Luyckx

"The mind is a powerful thing, and it is awe-inspiring. Henry Ford said, 'The human mind is a channel through which things-to-be are coming into the realm of things-that-are.' There are so many things that the mind is capable of. As a certified hypnotist, I truly get the power of the mind. What mess will we leave behind that they need to clean up? Ronald Reagan said, "Freedom is never more than one generation away from extinction. We didn't pass it to our children in the bloodstream. It must be fought for, protected, and handed on for them to do the same."

—Melissa Lincoln, Certified Hypnotherapist

"The book's message is kind of exactly where we are right now here on planet earth. The planet has been misused by people and corporations and governments for many decades. It has been polluted out of ignorance and greed. No one really sees the bigger picture or wants to stop their preferred way of life long enough to notice (the 'not-my-problem' disease), and with global warming added to the mix, it is causing the endangerment of so many species that the planet is in danger of mass extinction of life, including humans. The author also shows how well she did her research about toxic dumping and endangered species. She knows her subject well and shares a lot of important information that isn't well known."

—Teresa Espaniola, Artist, gARTbage

"Several things stood out for me in this book. First, it incorporates the idea of time's fluidity: how one might be able to travel between timelines or establish a place where people of different times could meet and even contribute to what that place looked like. This is a new idea for me: a meeting place for timelines. Second is the idea that sometime in the future, people will not be able to write or will look upon writing as archaic and something to disdain. This notion saddens me. I also like the idea that we can visit other times in our dreams and that our dreams can hold important information that we should act on when we're awake. Though the author uses these things as vehicles to carry the message about the importance of environmental responsibility, they were of more interest to me than the message itself."

—Barbra Espey, Greeting Card Designer

About the Author

Maureen distinctly remembers the day she realized that she was no longer writing a short story. She hit insert page break, typed Chapter Two, and then went back to type Chapter One. With unwavering encouragement from Dave and the supportive presence of her adopted, greyhound dog, Kilty, Chapter Two was followed by Chapter Three and Four and so on, until Maureen knew she was writing her first novel.

Most authors are voracious readers, as is Ms. Dudley. Growing up in Montana, she read books as though she would wake up one morning to find they had all disappeared. Before she reached junior high school, Maureen began scribbling her own short stories on pieces of paper, the backs of school notebooks, and sometimes just in her head. But after high school, she set aside her writing interests and focused on college.

Ms. Dudley received her Bachelor of Science in Environmental Engineering from Montana College of Mineral Science and Technology. After moving to Colorado, Maureen's career as an Environmental Engineer began with the State of Colorado. After more than two decades of working for state and then local governments, Maureen decided it was time for a change. She discovered that working in solitude suited her. With first Kilty and now Charley (pictured) at her side, Ms. Dudley has transitioned into her next career—writing.

The Plateau—voices of the earth, is Ms. Dudley's debut novel and the first book in a three-book series about our efforts to protect and preserve our natural environments; and how what we ultimately do, as either good or bad stewards of our planet, affects the next seven generations.

END OF BOOK ONE

The Story Will Continue In

voices of the future

BOOK TWO OF THE PLATEAU